THE DNR
TRILOGY

THE DNR TRILOGY

VOLUME 3: CLINICAL JUSTICE

DON W. HILL, M.D.

ARCHWAY
PUBLISHING

Archway Publishing books may be ordered through booksellers or by contacting:

Archway Publishing
1663 Liberty Drive
Bloomington, IN 47403
www.archwaypublishing.com
1 (888) 242-5904

This is a work of fiction. All of the characters, names, incidents,
organizations, and dialogue in this novel are either the products
of the author's imagination or are used fictitiously.

KJV: Taken from the King James Bible

ISBN: 978-1-4808-6730-7 (sc)
ISBN: 978-1-4808-6728-4 (hc)
ISBN: 978-1-4808-6729-1 (e)

Library of Congress Control Number: 2018936479

Print information available on the last page.

Archway Publishing rev. date: 03/07/2019

To Family

Brother Bill: Go forth and plunder Mother Gaia. I want you to suck as much hydrocarbon fuel out of the earth as you possibly can. Don't forget to put the pedal to the metal, as you need to crank out carbon dioxide and other alleged greenhouse gases into the atmosphere until our own sun is blotted out from the sky. In the end, it would seem that Homo sapiens are ultimately doomed as a species anyhow. If we're all going down the tube, we might as well take the rest of the planet with us! Long live horsepower, torque, and the American V–8 engine! Someday I need to line up my 1968 Shelby against your 1970 Challenger, and we need to go at it mano a mano, or perhaps hermano a hermano.

Bryan: You were only ten years old on that summer evening back in 1995 when we were hiking on the Roosevelt Trail among the redwood trees at Prairie Creek. It was your keen eye that first detected the irrefutable evidence that there are indeed big things in the forest that go bump in the night. To be honest, though, I would have been happy to have lived my entire life without having that epiphany. The times you and I went camping when you were young remain some of my most pleasant memories. Those trips brought an absentee father and his son close together. After that event, though, you and I never wanted to spend any more time camping out in the forest. For that, I am truly sorry.

S. Carol: Thank you for taking this long, strange trip with me. You can render an eyewitness testimony to the surreal events that actually occurred. We witnessed birth, life, death, good, evil, damnation, redemption, salvation, and a few miracles along the way. You let me take a step over the edge, but I will always be grateful that you kept me from falling too deep into the quagmire.

To the Computer Guru

Rachel Able: As I am a self-avowed primitive Paleolithic technophobe generally overwhelmed by most human tools any more complex than a simple fork or spoon, your skill in information technology must be acknowledged. After all, in my thirty-year career as a physician, I was never able to master the successful transfer of even one measly telephone call. As a case in point, all of my attempts at that relatively simple endeavor invariably resulted in any given telephone call being transferred to the planet Mars.

Therefore, your help was essential during the preparation of this manuscript. At times, when computer glitches occurred, my eyes would gaze upon the heavens in fearful supposition that an electromagnetic pulse had been rendered upon our country from a rogue enemy state. On more than one occasion, I was vexed with the paranoid ideation that our civilization had been pushed to the brink of a new Stone Age. When these troublesome technological oddities occurred, reams of this novel simply disappeared into some mysterious electronic ether. With a few calm clicks of the keyboard, you were by and large able to recover missing material as if by magic. In doing so, you readily defused overt violent, reactionary behavior and prevented me from taking a large sixteen-pound sledgehammer and reducing thousands of dollars' worth of expensive computer hardware into mere scrap metal. Thanks, Rachel!

CONTENTS

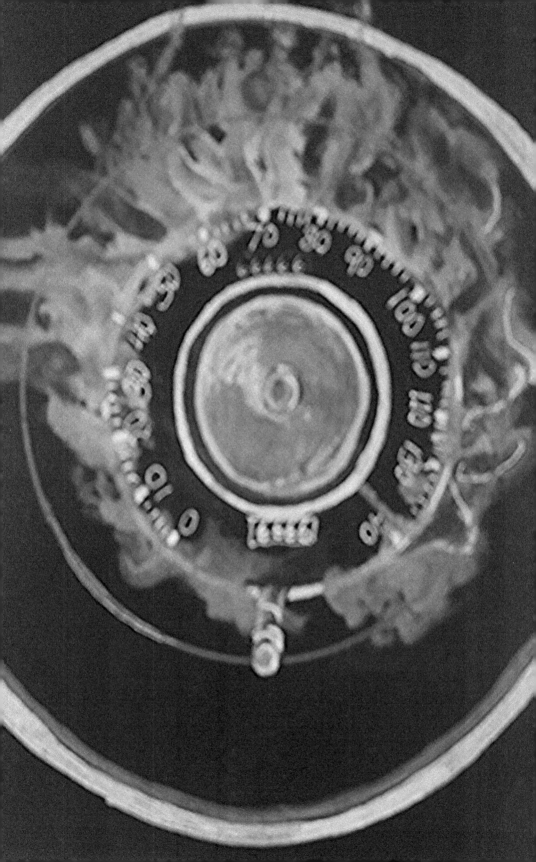

1

LA MORDITA

It had been months since a riot inadvertently orchestrated by the overtly offensive and sophomoric shenanigans of J. D. Brewster occurred in the hospital cafeteria. The medical student, who was perhaps little more than a catalyst for chaos, had unwittingly foiled the diabolical machinations of an Iranian terrorist cell that had received direct orders from the Islamic Revolutionary Guard Corp.

The vice president of the United States at the time, George H. W. Bush, was the former director of the CIA. That fact was offensive to the theocracy now ruling the nation that had arisen out of the ashes of the ancient Persian Empire. Specifically, the ayatollah blamed the prior support from America's own CIA for keeping the hated former shah, Mohammad Reza Pahlavi, in power for the better part of thirty-eight years in the country of Iran. In the past, Iran had been an ally to the United States, but sadly, that was no longer the case. The Iranians were also livid that their former shah had received extensive medical care at the hands of the Texas Medical Center's world-renowned surgeon Dr. Michael DeBakey from the Baylor College of Medicine.

Now that the shah had been deposed, what better way was there for the angry Iranians to plunge a sharp dagger into the loins of the Great Satan than to execute a successful terrorist attack upon the largest community located on the Gulf Coast of the United States? The terrorists rightly believed that the Houston Ship Channel would be an easy target. A few well-placed incendiary and explosive devices strategically planted among the oil repositories at the port would easily create an inferno the likes of which had never been seen north of a place called hades. It was a perfect plan. After all, Houston was not only the energy capital of the United States but also the adopted home of George H. W. Bush.

The cafeteria fiasco was triggered when Brewster rudely plopped a pound of raw bacon upon the breakfast table of the Iranian conspirators. Brewster did the despicable deed not because he was certain to any degree that the foreign nationals were plotting some malicious act of espionage against the United States but specifically because the men happened to be, well, foreigners.

While Brewster was receiving a vicious beatdown from the members of the Iranian cell during the cafeteria riot, which forever would be remembered as the Big Bacon Brawl, the authorities arrived just in time to apprehend the would-be terrorists and spare J. D. Brewster from serious injury or perhaps even death. Sadly, the event did not have a happy fairy-tale ending, as two of the terrorists eventually escaped from jail, and they were now at large in the Houston community. Unable to return to Iran, as they were now on the lam, they had only one available course of action to try to save face. The only thing left for the two men was to undertake a pure and simple act of retribution rendered upon Brewster. After all, he was the man who had foiled their well-engineered plot to unleash havoc upon the Houston Ship Channel.

After snooping about the administrative offices at the medical school, J. D. Brewster had become distraught upon learning about the extensive amount of money being purposefully wasted on meaningless pseudoscientific clinical trials. A former member of the MD and PhD dual-training program, Brewster had come to the painful conclusion that he had squandered an entire year of his life on no fewer than two different experimental studies investigating hepatitis infections.

As both of Brewster's research programs had come to ignominious dead ends, it was indeed a bitter pill for Brewster to swallow that he would likely never be able to rejoin the PhD program. As he stopped into the men's washroom on the top floor of the medical school to splash some cool water upon his face, he had to accept the fact that he had to keep his nose to the grindstone and complete his clinical clerkship rotations in order to graduate with an MD degree by the summer of 1982. Unfortunately, it did not appear to be in the tarot cards that Brewster would ever become a research scientist, as he had originally hoped when he had entered the Gulf Coast College of Medicine four years earlier, back in 1977.

When the medical student reached toward the paper towel dispenser in the restroom, he noticed the images of two looming figures in the mirror. The men standing directly behind Brewster were none other than the notorious Iranian terrorists who had recently escaped from jail. They had brazenly returned to the medical school campus to exact their revenge upon the combative medical student.

At first, Brewster did not recognize the two vicious adversaries, although they both looked vaguely familiar to the student, as the Iranians were still sporting their original signature look of bald beans and bushy beards.

"Hold your water," Brewster said. "I'll be out of here in just a moment, and then you bad boys can piss in this bathroom sink for all that I care."

By the time Brewster realized who the two men were, it was too late. Brewster was grabbed from behind and dragged over to the toilet stall. Without saying a word, the two men tried to drive Brewster's head down into the toilet bowl.

"Help!" Brewster screamed. "Let go of me, you camel fuckers!" Those were the last words Brewster uttered before his face was slammed against the porcelain rim of the toilet, causing the teeth of his mandible to be driven clean through his lower lip. As bright red blood poured out of his mouth, Brewster's face was forcefully submerged into the toilet water.

While the remnants of the Iranian terrorist cell were attempting to drown J. D. Brewster in a commode, the mysterious and ethereal float nurse from the temp pool, Sister Buena, already had Brewster's colleague Ben Fielder in tow, in addition to the corrections officer, Arby Fuller. The three were running toward the elevator, when they passed Harper from the maintenance department, who was wheeling a large tool chest down the hallway. "Harper!" Sister Buena said. "Grab a claw hammer for yourself and a big wrench for Fielder, who's with me here. Come with us. Now!"

"What's going on?" Harper asked as he grabbed the tools out of the rolling chest as instructed.

"It's Brewster," the float nurse answered. "He's in trouble. Hurry! This time, we're all on a tight schedule!"

Before Brewster lost consciousness, one of the assailants pulled the student's head out of the toilet water. As Brewster gasped to take a breath of air, the other terrorist proceeded to jam a wad of raw bacon into the student's mouth and then clamp his orifice shut with a strip of duct tape before forcing Brewster's head back into the toilet bowl.

After Sister Buena and her hastily assembled rescue team made their exit from the elevator lift on the top floor of the medical school, the four individuals sprinted toward the restroom where Brewster was being viciously assaulted. Just then, a cry rang out from the overhead speaker system throughout the medical school to alert the security personnel that a violent altercation was taking place on campus. "Code gray! Men's washroom, sixth floor. Code gray! Men's washroom, sixth floor."

With his baton, Arby Fuller was the first to strike when the Samaritans burst into the washroom. It was a devastating blow upon the back of the head of the nearest assassin. The first Iranian terrorist crumpled to the ground while Harper and Fielder wailed away at the other henchman with the wrench and claw hammer until he was also effectively neutralized.

Brewster, now extricated from the toilet, pulled the duct tape from his mouth and expectorated the raw bacon that had obstructed his upper airway. The terrified student, still coughing and sputtering, managed to ask, "How in hell did you people find me?"

"It was the float nurse from the temp pool who recruited us to join this merry ensemble. Hey, Brew, we just saved your sorry ass!" Fielder beamed.

Blood continued to gush forth from Brewster's lacerated lower lip as he looked about the washroom and saw neither hide nor hair of the mysterious nurse in question. When the hastily assembled rescue team realized the larger of the two assailants was still breathing, Brewster calmly walked over and placed his foot against the anterior aspect of the injured man's neck in an unsuccessful attempt to apply enough pressure to crush the Iranian's larynx. All the while, Arby Fuller shouted encouragement at Brewster to commit an act of homicide that was to be executed within the realm of the occult clinical justice system of the Gulf Coast College of Medicine. "Do it, Brew! Kill him!"

Harper managed to pull Brewster away from the scene of the crime. "Get him out of here!" Harper told Ben Fielder as he physically forced Brewster into the hallway. "Take Brewster down to the emergency room, and make sure his busted lip gets some attention."

Just then, the medical school's security service arrived. Drafting into the washroom was also the ambush reporter Antonia Alabaster from the Your Witness News television crew, who appeared ostensibly out of thin air to file an exclusive report for the Channel Four evening news.

"Are you okay, Brew?" Fielder asked as he walked Brewster down to the emergency room to get his lip sutured.

"I should say not," Brewster answered. "Two thugs just tried to drown me in shit water. That's the first time in my life anybody has ever tried to kill me!" Little did Brewster know, that would not be the only time somebody would try to kill him. In fact, as it would turn out, the violent event that had just occurred would not even be the only time somebody would try to extinguish the life of J. D. before the onset of summer!

"What happened up there today?" Fielder asked.

"Nothing," Brewster replied. "I assure you. Not a damned thing happened in there today."

⊸⊸⊸

Harrison Reed had been the head of the medical school's research program until he had a violent altercation with Moritz the Mouse from the Mexican Marauders motorcycle club. Upon Harrison Reed's unexpected resignation from the Gulf Coast College of Medicine, the person slated to assume the mantle of research director at the organization was the research scientist from West Texas known as Uncle Hank Holcombe. As the battleship USS Holcombe was officially decommissioned and in dry dock because of a case of terminal, malignant T-cell lymphoma, the administration announced that Dr. Denny Sassman would become the interim director of research at the university.

Dr. Bruce Beathard was incensed by the decision, as he felt he would have been a more appropriate candidate for the post than Dr. Sassman. After all, Sassman had received his medical degree from a less-than-prestigious osteopathic school of medicine in El Paso, Texas, while Beathard had been awarded his medical degree at an allopathic school from the Corpus Christi College of Medicine.

"Well, Denny, you look pretty smug right about now," Beathard said.

"Why are you busting my chops about all of this?" Sassman asked. "After all, if the tables were turned and administration had assigned you to be the head of the research department, I would have certainly supported their decision. In fact, I'd actually be happy for you."

"What a load of priggish pig shit!" Beathard responded.

"Let's just try to be cordial to one another and work together," Dr. Sassman said as he extended his hand toward Dr. Beathard.

Dr. Beathard sneered as he simply turned and walked away. "Why don't you pop open a cold one, Denny? After all, isn't that what you do best?"

Beathard would make it a mission to undermine Dr. Sassman by any means necessary in order for the chair to be passed over to somebody who held a laudatory MD degree and not, as Beathard thought, somebody who had been awarded an inferior DO degree from a laughably inferior institution of higher learning.

Upon the departure of Bruce Beathard, Dr. Sassman pulled open the minirefrigerator in his office and pulled out a six-pack. He rapidly slammed down one cold beer after another until his agitation subsided.

Unbeknownst to Dr. Sassman, his political adversary, Bruce Beathard, was also an alcoholic. Somehow, Dr. Beathard had maintained sobriety for years, and he was quite sanctimonious about that particular matter. He despised the evidence that Sassman inexplicably functioned at a high level despite the fact—or perhaps because of the fact—that he consumed a minimum of a six-pack of beer on a daily basis without any obvious untoward physiological consequences to date.

Although ulterior motives were involved, Dr. Beathard made another visit to Dr. Sassman's office later that same day. On the second visitation that afternoon, Dr. Beathard made an effort to appear to be at least superficially pleasant. "Say, Denny, do you still go out to East Texas from time to time and set up motion-triggered field cameras to look for the elusive Bigfoot?"

"I do indeed!"

"Let me know when you're planning on making your next trip and exactly where you'll be going. Maybe I'd like to come along with you next time you head out into the swamp."

"Well, Bruce," Sassman replied, "I already made my yearly trip with Rip Ford at the beginning of this month."

"Did you catch anything besides mosquito bites?" Beathard asked.

"Unfortunately, no," Sassman answered. "To be honest with you, despite my best efforts, I haven't caught any additional photographic evidence of this yet-to-be-recognized beast since 1966."

"You actually still believe it's out there, don't you?" Beathard asked.

"I do indeed."

"Maybe you just don't know where to look."

"No, that's not the case," Sassman answered.

"Maybe you just don't know when to look."

"I don't exactly know when I'll be going back out into the jungle, but I have an unsubstantiated theory that the Sasquatch is a migratory primate that only passes through East Texas in the springtime."

Beathard was clearly disappointed with that answer, as now he would have to bide his time in his clandestine quest to take over the directorship of the research program. "I'm sorry to hear that you've already gone on your pilgrimage this year. Please be so kind as to let me know when you're going back out into the thicket in the future."

"Wow, Bruce, I would've never guessed you had any interest in this subject matter. I find that refreshing!" Sassman said. "It would be my pleasure to bring you out into the forest someday."

"Oh, I'm definitely interested," Dr. Beathard responded. "In fact, instead of you bringing me out to the swamp, let it be my treat. I actually look forward to taking you out one day. In fact, the sooner the better, in my opinion. When I do, I'll make sure we're so deep in the woods that we'll be off the radar."

"Great!" Sassman replied. "I know it will end up being good for you."

"Definitely," Beathard replied with a sly grin. "You have no idea what a life-changing experience this will turn out to be for me."

———

J. D. Brewster had previously made a great effort to get his friend Ben Fielder into the front door of Uncle John's upstairs garage apartment in North University Place, which was located at a close proximity to the Texas Medical Center. Sadly, no good deed went unpunished, and Brewster's benevolent gesture was about to backfire.

Fielder and his girlfriend, Missy Brownwood, were in a celebratory mood after the sudden and unexpected departure of the evil Dr. Harry Reed from the Gulf Coast College of Medicine. After all, Harrison Reed was a sexual predator, and he had previously attempted to rape Missy Brownwood in the employee parking lot.

For all intents and purposes, it had appeared Dr. Reed was going to get away with the foul deed, until Ben Fielder had the wherewithal to hire Moritz the Mouse from the Mexican Marauders motorcycle club to pay a visit to Dr. Reed and rectify the problem once and for all.

The landlord of the garage apartment, Uncle John, enjoyed peace and quiet. In fact, by the restrictions of the rental contract, John demanded peace and quiet. Disregarding their own personal safety by boldly playing rock-'n'-roll music in Uncle John's garage apartment, the couple brazenly invited hostile retribution from the cranky old man, who not only wielded a twelve-gauge Winchester pump but also had in his possession hundreds of rounds of magnum-buckshot ammunition.

Missy's favorite song was "Piece of My Heart," as recorded by Big Brother and the Holding Company, featuring the late Janice Joplin on lead vocals. When Fielder had given his girlfriend the 1968 album Cheap Thrills as a gift, Missy insisted the track "Piece of My Heart" get immediately queued up and the volume on the turntable stereo get jacked up to an ear-shattering ninety decibels. Sadly, all hell was about to break loose when Uncle John heard the psychedelic blues recording blast out from the garage apartment's stereo speakers.

To actualize unfettered access to the upstairs garage apartment, Uncle John pulled his crappy 1966 Dodge Dart out onto the driveway, and then he took possession of the twelve-gauge shotgun that had been safely nestled away in the trunk of the car. John reentered the garage and attempted to guesstimate the location where the happy couple joyfully danced across the apartment floor.

When the lyrics "Aw, now, take it!" erupted from the stereo speakers, the floorboards beside Missy and Ben violently exploded. Initially, Missy and her boyfriend failed to grasp what was happening to them.

As the lyrics "Aw, now, break it!" followed in sequence, another blast from Uncle John's shotgun punctured an additional gaping wound in the floor of the garage apartment. Missy and Ben were able to peer through the large hole in the apartment floor. To their horror, they saw Uncle John ejecting a spent magnum casing out of the shotgun and then taking aim to shoot at the couple yet again.

When the lyrics "Aw, now, Mama!" spilled out of the stereo speakers, the third volley of buckshot that ruptured through the apartment floor finally disintegrated the stereo turntable, sending Missy and Ben flying out the back window of the second-story garage apartment and into the alleyway as if they were mere yard darts.

Unscathed, Ben and Missy simply abandoned all of their personal possessions and went off to find a new place to live. Wisely, in an act of self-preservation, Fielder never returned to the scene of the crime to confront Uncle John about the attempted murder the old man had undertaken.

Ben, however, would have more than just a few harsh words to say to the nephew of Uncle John. In fact, J. D. Brewster got an earful of crude expletives from his medical school colleague.

"What in hell is the matter with your uncle?" Fielder asked. "The old bastard tried to kill us!"

"Now, it was probably just some kind of misunderstanding," Brewster said.

"Misunderstanding my ass!" Fielder exclaimed. "I pulled a drive-by past the apartment on the following day, and the son of a bitch had collected all of my personal belongings and was unloading everything I owned in a yard sale."

"Wow," Brewster replied. "I'm sorry about all of that."

"Being sorry isn't going to get my shit back," Fielder said. "You owe me. You owe me big-time."

"I wish I could help you out," Brewster said, "but money is a little tight for me right about now."

After an unsettling visit from Moritz the Mouse, Brewster had to fork over several hundred dollars to Ben Fielder and Missy Brownwood to pay for new wardrobes and a stereo system.

As best as Brewster could tell, however, the whole unpleasant incident was essentially normal behavior for Uncle John—nothing more and nothing less. He did make an effort to have Feral Cheryl appropriate Uncle John's shotgun, but the endeavor was in vain, as none of John's relatives knew exactly where the irascible old bastard kept the shotgun hidden.

At some point in the future, Uncle John's twelve-gauge shotgun would no doubt again reappear to propagate havoc and further mayhem. Brewster was entering his last year of medical school, and he had to make certain he got to the finish line without any further trauma or drama. As he had already been kicked out of the PhD program, he had to be sure there were no other missteps along the way. It appeared that one of the major potential risks lurking in the shadows that could possibly derail his medical school training was another violent outburst from Uncle John. Brewster could ill afford to let that happen.

—⊸⊱〰⊰⊷—

Cleophus McDonald (a.k.a. Big Nig) and his junior partner in violence, Darryl Hewritt (a.k.a. Smeg Nog), had been surfing an unrelenting wave of crime throughout the greater Houston area in the central corridor between the North Loop and the southern extent of the West Loop freeway of the 610 belt since 1968. Smeg was still in possession of the car keys to the bronze 1970 Olds Cutlass that he and Big Nig had tried to carjack from the now dearly departed med-surg charge nurse Irene Segulla.

The attempted theft of the Cutlass during the previous year had gone sideways, and Irene Segulla had subsequently died as a consequence of the extensive facial injuries she had received during the vicious assault and physical beating she had incurred in the northern employee parking lot of the Texas Medical Center, immediately adjacent to Hermann Park.

Now that Irene's estate was finally out of probate and the Cutlass had a fresh new battery, Stella Link, Irene's niece, began to proudly drive about in her late aunt's cherished low-mileage chariot. Stella was approaching her midthirties, and although she happened to be the estranged girlfriend of the much younger medical student J. D. Brewster, she cheerfully continued to work as the secretary for the psychiatry department at the Gulf Coast College of Medicine.

Seeing the bronze Cutlass once again in the employee parking lot at the medical center was a dream come true for Smeg Nog. "Baby, baby, baby," Smeg said as he gently rubbed his hand across the hood of the Oldsmobile. "Why don't you come home with me?"

As all of the top-shelf vehicles he and his partner in crime had ever stolen in the past eventually had made their way to the chop shop, where they were all thoroughly disassembled and sold as parts, Smeg Nog was condemned to drive about in an old lime-green AMC Gremlin that was little more than a rolling turd held together with duct tape and baling wire.

Before he stole Stella's ride, it might have been wise if the car thief had peeled the Houston Oilers decal off of the back bumper. Alas, Nog decided to keep the telltale sports logo in place. When he slipped the key into the ignition of the beautiful bronze Oldsmobile, the car fired right up, and Smeg Nog sped away. He would have to be on the lookout for a similar vehicle around town, as he had to boost somebody else's license plates to help stay under the radar of Johnny Law. Although Nog loved the color bronze, he knew he would have to also change the color of the stolen Cutlass. Otherwise, Smeg knew he would likely get pinched for grand theft auto sooner rather than later.

If he shot the car with a shiny black coat and then gave the color-matched steel wheels the same detailed treatment, there was no way his partner, Big Nig, would realize Smeg Nog had violated the primary rule of the chop shop: don't keep inventory for your own personal use. After all, that was the fastest way any car thief would eventually get thrown behind bars. Smeg simply planned to lie to his partner and tell Big Nig that the Cutlass was a legitimate purchase from the used-car lot of Art Grindle and his dog, Storm. Smeg Nog failed to realize, however, that the obnoxious television celebrity and used-car salesman had moved to Orlando, Florida, long ago, departing from Houston back in the late 1960s.

The rolling stop that the car thief made on Cambridge Street caught the eye of Officer Faulkland of the Houston Police Department, who was heading north on Fannin Street in a patrol car. As Smeg Nog was extraordinarily cordial to the police officer, the thug received only a written warning and not a formal citation. At the time Nog was pulled over, it was only midmorning, and Stella Link had not yet realized her car had been stolen.

As no car-theft report had yet been filed with the police department, nothing seemed out of the ordinary to Officer Faulkland when he viewed the title, registration, and paperwork. Smeg Nog simply told the police officer that the car belonged to his girlfriend, and he'd dropped her off at work at the Gulf Coast Hospital. Smeg Nog at least had been smart enough to look at the title and registration when he had first stolen the car, and he was readily able to tell the police officer the name of the person on the documents.

No sooner had Smeg Nog pulled away and disappeared into traffic than the police officer's radio belatedly announced an alert that there was a warrant out for the arrest of Darryl Hewritt (a.k.a. Smeg Nog), the individual who'd received the traffic warning from Officer Faulkland mere moments before. The police officer was informed that Darryl was an at-large individual who was the prime suspect in the felony assault and attempted murder of an African American medical student named Willy Mammon.

Apparently, the medical student had been attacked with a lead pipe at an automatic teller machine. The suspect was likely armed and dangerous, as he might have also been involved in other violent crimes, including assault, murder, and carjacking. The suspect likely had an accomplice, but the identity of his associate was unknown at that time.

Unfortunately, the alert came too late, as Smeg Nog and his stolen car had seemingly disappeared into thin air. Officer Faulkland rightly berated himself for not being patient for just a few more moments before allowing Darryl Hewritt to simply drive away and vanish. The patrol officer would certainly be reprimanded for his impatient shortcoming. Nog had somehow dodged a bullet, and he knew it.

—————

When Smeg returned to the chop shop, he was troubled by the deference and respect the white policeman, Officer Faulkland, had bestowed on him. It was something he had never expected or previously experienced.

"Hey, Nig, I met Casper the friendly copper today. Dig this: although he was an oinker, he seemed like a nice person nonetheless. He was all, like, polite to me and shit. Didn't see that comin' or nuthin'. That was a strange experience, I tell you!"

Big Nig proceeded to chastise his junior partner. "Don't lose your hate for the crackers. Stay focused, damn you."

The young ward was dismayed when he replied, "I don't know about all of that. It sounds like being a full-time racist may turn out to be hard work."

"Of course it's hard work, you dumbass!" his older mentor replied. "Let me lay something out for you: it's much easier to garnish animosity against an entire ethnic group than it is against individuals."

"So it would seem," Smeg said.

"Look, Smeg," Big said, "I've certainly known and have also befriended other people from different ethnic groups and other races. If the truth be told, these people I would describe as different all turned out to be, well, like regular people, I suppose. It's so much easier to wield a brutal hammer of personal disdain toward larger aggregations of human beings than against individuals, who you might discover are not that much different from you after all. Buck up, fuckup. As for now, it's time for you to push your feelings of pacifism to the back burner and turn your hate switch back over to the 'on' position."

———————

Upon receiving a visitation request from Professor Denny Sassman, Brewster paid a call to his former research adviser at his office in the basement laboratory.

"Well, Brewster," Denny said, "I'm sorry you weren't able to make a trip with Rip Ford and me a few weeks ago when we went back out into the swamps to look for Bigfoot. It certainly would have been a hoot if you'd come along on the trip."

"I'm not so sure about all of that," Brewster said. "After all, the last time I took a ride with you and Ford out to the Fertile Myrtle wellhead, you pissed on me. In fact, I still have bad dreams about that whole ordeal. Yes, it was certainly a bad time to be had by all. That's for sure. That's for dang sure."

"Now, listen, grasshopper," Dr. Sassman said defensively. "You should try to let bygone events be bygone. After all, does the Good Book not say that we should turn the other cheek?"

"I think that biblical reference addressed the prospects of being slapped in the face and not being pissed upon!" Brewster laughed. "What's on your mind, Denny?"

Dr. Sassman stood up from his desk and walked over to the light switch rheostat on the wall to illuminate his dingy office. "As you know, we still have six big boys incarcerated in the lockdown primate kennel. Ever since Reagan got elected, a ridiculous amount of money is now pouring into this university for us to perform all kinds of bullshit experimental studies at the request of the federal government, among other well-financed agencies. Personally, I believe it would be smart for you to wrap up this current year of clerkship rotations and resurrect your PhD aspirations starting in July of this year. I believe if you are smart, you could still be on track to nail down a PhD degree with one additional year of research at this juncture."

"My last stab at clinical research turned out to be disastrous," Brewster said. "I didn't even clear leather. Shot my own pecker off at the hilt!"

"Chill," Sassman said. "You can do a follow-up year of electives after that and still be in the slingshot to get out of here by the spring of 1983."

At that point, Brewster was modestly intrigued. "Okay, I'll bite. What do you have in mind for a quick and dirty experimental protocol that might be able to get me back on track in the dual-training program?"

"I hope you find this project I'm going to tell you about intellectually stimulating," Sassman said.

"Well," Brewster said, "whatever you have that's moving up to the front burner will need to get me to the finish line in time for me to nail down both the MD and also a PhD degree within the next two years. Come hell or high water, I've decided that I'm going to blow this Popsicle stand no matter what. In retrospect, I think Uncle Hank was right when he told me it was time for me to get on with my life."

Denny Sassman smiled while he opened his filing cabinet and pulled out a query that had been sent to the university from, of all agencies, the Colombian Army.

"Check this out, Brewster," Professor Sassman said. "We've received a foreign grant offer of one hundred seventy-five thousand dollars if we can write up a viable protocol to study why chimpanzees in captivity throw their own fecal matter at human beings."

"You can't be serious."

"Dead serious," Sassman replied. "Is this common simian behavior random, or perhaps this is some abstract form of interspecies communication wherein the higher primates are attempting to convey a complex set of grievances to Homo sapiens that can't otherwise be expressed?"

"I pick what's behind door number two."

"You're right. It has to be number two, if you catch my gist," Sassman said with a laugh. "How does one go about proving that hypothesis? As you know, chimpanzees lack vocal cords and are unable to speak, although they clearly understand dozens of human words. This foreign military service is up to its ass in alligators trying to fight the illegal drug trade. They're curious to see if chimpanzees could, if they are indeed able to throw shit, be trained to throw hand grenades."

"Simian soldiers?" Brewster asked. "Frankly, I've heard enough."

"Hang on," Sassman said. "After all, a weaponized primate might have been a pretty handy tool if we'd had one in Vietnam. This is not a new concept. After all, Joseph Stalin tried to cross-breed chimpanzees with human beings back in the 1930s in an attempt to create a supersoldier, but human beings and chimps did not share enough gamete compatibility to create viable offspring that could survive past the third trimester."

"Are you implying that these cross-species reproductive experiments made it through the first two trimesters? I think I'm going blind in my left eye!" Brewster said. "Tell me this, Denny: Did Stalin's experiments include in vitro or, God forbid, in vivo fertilization events?"

When Sassman failed to answer and just stared at Brewster with a big grin, J. D. was stunned.

"Man, oh man, that's some seriously sick, slimy, Slavic shit! Next time I see my classmate Russian Bear, I'm going to have to unload a rash of scat upon him about this alleged Russian bestiality," Brewster said. "My old rock-and-roll bandmate from DNR, Dr. Wilt Bryan, once thought I was going to become the new love monkey at the Gulf Coast College of Medicine back in July of last year. Who knew that expression would somehow take on a whole new and different meaning?"

Dr. Sassman simply shook his head and chuckled.

"I already have a pretty good idea as to why chimps hurl shit at us," Brewster said. "They're simply pissed off because we're tearing down the rain forest with bulldozers. It's self-evident that human beings are hell-bent on exterminating every form of life that may swim, crawl, walk, or fly."

"I've long felt that way," Sassman said, "but is that really the case?"

"This is true wherever the myriad of species in God's animal kingdom may find their particular habitat. Our efforts to degrade all finite, carbon-based biological entities with whom we share the world are boundless."

"If you're right, who really cares?" Sassman asked. "I told you a long time ago that we're on the top of the pyramid. Nothing downstream to us really matters. Natural selection, I tell you."

"You're wrong, Denny!" Brewster exclaimed. "Without biodiversity, Homo sapiens are doomed. This codependence applies to all living things, irrespective if they may be found in, on, or above the surface of this doomed planet."

"We're a bit more cynical today than usual," Sassman said. "Are we not?"

"I'm just getting warmed up," Brewster said. "Someday in the distant future, when the ecosystem on our blighted orb completely collapses, the earth will simply become another meaningless, cold, dark, and lifeless speck in a meaningless, cold, dark, and lifeless universe. As I have said before, it's simply my conviction that God has backed the wrong primate, and our simian cousins have already come to that same inescapable and depressing conclusion."

"Is that so?" Dr. Sassman asked. "How magnificently maudlin of you. Stay focused. We're talking about primates here, not the world's entire ecosystem. It would seem to me that you're attempting to make an anthropomorphic analogy here."

"Don't you get it?" Brewster asked. "I'm absolutely doing just that by design! Just ask any of our hirsute friends we've incarcerated down in the lockdown kennel. Regarding this grim, fatalistic, catastrophic extinction-level certainty, it's my exalted hypothesis that the great primates will never let us live that down. That's why chimpanzees hurl shit at us! Nothing more and nothing less."

"Wow," Denny said. "You're indeed a bona fide Texan."

"After that brilliant dissertation that was chock-full of loquacious bullshit up one side and down the other," Brewster said, "I now firmly believe that I'm fully ready to defend my PhD thesis. Denny, I implore you to just hand me my diploma right now. If you'd be so kind to do just that, I'll gladly get out of your hair and merrily go about my own business."

Denny Sassman shrugged and emitted a big yawn. "So are you interested in the project or not?"

"Absolutely!" the jaded medical student enthusiastically replied. "It sounds as if a meaningless project such as this will be just my cup of bullshit."

Brewster tried to suppress the humiliating realization that his soon-to-be-resurrected career in research had degraded from the previous lofty work of doing legitimate investigation into the subtypes of infectious hepatitis that had afflicted humankind. Brewster was now suddenly about to dive headfirst straight downward into the stink-hole of monkey shit, purple or otherwise.

"Here's the setup," Dr. Sassman said. "You have to be on board and start this project on Monday, July 6, of this year. The project has to be completed by December 31, 1981. Right now, I know Bookman and his research members are working on what will likely turn out to be a dead-end project. They are trying to discover if GRID is a lifestyle disease. As soon as their federal grant money runs out, they no doubt will be destined to move forward to find out if GRID is indeed an infectious disease, as most of us believe to be the case."

"What happens at the end of December?" Brewster asked.

"The timeline for Bookman's current project also wraps up at the end of this year. After that, Bookman and his crew will be ready to tap into the grant funded by the Gays without Borders political action group. For obvious reasons, it's imperative that these GWB nitwits are able to secure a scientifically verifiable confirmation that GRID is actually an infectious disease and not a homosexual lifestyle issue. Bookman's team will then start their inoculation experiments on the great apes. The chimps are going to be the first primates that will get the proverbial axe. So between now and then, you and I will have a total of about six months to try to coax these angry beasts into heaving everything from shit to Shinola."

—⚙—

Before Brewster's departure from Dr. Sassman's office, a petite woman in her early twenties arrived, and she introduced herself as the temporary secretary who would be helping out while Dr. Sassman's usual assistant was taking time off for her wedding and honeymoon vacation. As the young woman looked around Dr. Sassman's office, she noticed the few Civil War artifacts that were proudly displayed.

"These things are like—I dunno—wicked old or something! I see that there are items in here from the American Civil War," the young woman said. "Did you fight in the Civil War, Dr. Sassman?"

Brewster and Sassman looked at each other and then started to laugh. Denny leaned back in his chair and asked, "Young lady, exactly when was the American Civil War?"

"Well, it was in the sixties, was it not?" the temporary secretary replied.

"Yes, you're correct," Brewster said, "but it was in the 1860s!"

"I'm sorry, but I get confused sometimes," the young woman said. "What was the war that was on TV awhile back that everybody got upset about?"

Dr. Sassman was at first incredulous, but he soon realized the young woman was on the level.

"Are you serious?" Denny asked. "Do you mean the Vietnam War?"

"Yes, that's it!" the temporary secretary replied. "I remember now that the American Civil War and also the Vietnam War were both fought between the North and the South, but I often get those two wars all mixed up with each other. From what you're saying, I guess they occurred at different times in history."

"Please tell me something that I am just dying to know about you," Brewster said. "Are you from a foreign country?"

"I'm from Boston, Massachusetts," the young secretary replied, "and I'm thrilled to have the opportunity to bring a little bit of culture down here to you unsophisticated southerners."

Incensed, Dr. Sassman glared at the woman and said, "I'm sorry, but the position for a temporary secretary has already been filled. Let me show you out."

Upon her expeditious departure, Brewster wanted an honest opinion from his research adviser. "Should we track her down, drag her out to the sluice of gradeaux, and then feed her to your alligators, Popeye and Bluto?"

Dr. Sassman thought for moment before he replied. "No, I don't think so. If I fed my boys something that stupid, it would just give them a serious case of indigestion. I want you to do me a favor, however; if these are the types of people who are going to eventually inherit our country, I want to make sure it's duly noted somewhere that I have a DNR code status. Entiendes?"

Brewster smiled as he replied, "You're coming in loud and clear, mi amigo."

On the last Friday in April, medical student Victoria Campos grabbed J. D. Brewster by his hand and pulled him into a dirty utility room on the med-surg unit to conduct a private conversation with the man who had become the object of her affections.

"I see now that you have been dating a fat, old, hippie, dinosaur loser chick who must be ten years older than you are," Victoria said, obviously jealous of Brewster's relationship with Stella Link. "She even wears plastic flowers in her hair. How lame is that? Oh my God, are you kidding me?"

"Now, hang on there," Brewster said. "I'll have you know—"

"There's a rumor going around that you two had some sort of fight about something, and you kicked her to the curb," Victoria said. "Strong work, hombre! Missy Brownwood told me she doesn't think you two will ever get back together again. If that's indeed the case, give me a call sometime. I know that you speak Spanish, but I'm certain there are still a lot of things I can teach you."

With that, Victoria leaned into Brewster and kissed him with passion. Brewster gently pushed his amorous colleague away as he slipped out of the dirty utility room. Upon his departure, he turned his head back toward Victoria Campos and said, "Missy Brownwood talks too much."

As the calendar rolled over into the month of May, Brewster and Russian Bear were about to start another mandatory clerkship, which happened to be the family practice rotation. Years later, at the end of Brewster's career in medicine, the term family practice specialist would become rather archaic terminology. In modern times, it became more commonplace to refer to a family practice specialist as a family medicine specialist. What possible difference could that make? The change in nomenclature was intended specifically to improve the image of these physicians who were essentially jacks-of-all-trades.

Family practice residency programs began to appear in the 1960s, but it was not until 1969 that family practice was formally recognized as an accredited specialty program in and of itself. The modern family medicine specialists evolved from the old general practitioners who began to disappear decades ago. A general practitioner had four years of medical school and one year of a general medical internship. Afterward, he or she would hang out a shingle and go to work, generally inviting all comers to walk through the clinic's front doors.

As the practice of medicine became more complex, it was clear that the general practitioner had become passé. In contrast to the now-extinct generalist, when a family medicine specialist completed a prolonged residency training program, he or she immediately became better equipped in providing health care for a population that ranged from the pediatric patient all the way through geriatric individuals.

Family medicine, by design, was a cradle-to-grave health-care specialty. As one might imagine, it was rather difficult to function effectively as a family medicine specialist. Essentially, a doctor who pursued that endeavor had to know everything about everything— and also about every damned thing in between. That was, without a doubt, one tall order.

Brewster and Russian Bear were about to undertake a one-month externship at the East Valley Family Care Clinic in Harlingen, Texas, a large medical facility that generally provided health care to the indigent Hispanic population residing in the area. The East Valley Family Care Clinic invited students in training from both the Gulf Coast College of Medicine and the nearby Corpus Christi

College of Medicine, which happened to be Dr. Bruce Beathard's alma mater.

Bear had some trepidation about leaving his wife, Larisa, behind in Houston, but Brewster was looking forward to his pilgrimage to the Rio Grande Valley. Brewster needed to step away from his relationship with Stella Link and reevaluate what she had really meant to him. He didn't have a ready answer to that question, and perhaps he never would.

Brewster and Bear would be sharing a four-bedroom condominium that had been owned by the clinic with two other students from the Corpus Christi College of Medicine. The only house rule that all of the previous visiting students had routinely violated was that the condominium had to be vacuumed, dusted, and left in a clean and pristine condition at the end of each one-month clinical rotation.

During the three-year pilot project of the clinic's affiliation with both medical schools, the condominium had never been cleaned on even one prior occasion. Dishes were left perpetually piled up in the kitchen sink, although the dishwasher was allegedly in perfect operating condition. Sadly, it appeared nobody had ever bothered to actually run the damned thing.

Somebody had previously left a head of cabbage in the refrigerator, and it had decomposed into a layer of slimy black gradeaux in the crisper. Fortunately, there was just enough room in the befouled, toxic crisper to accommodate one medium-sized Granny Smith apple. The medical students would invariably play a round-robin game of paper, rocks, and scissors to determine who would be the lucky individual to lay claim to the four square inches of clean space in the crisper for the duration of the one-month rotation.

The condominium had been Balkanized, as the angry cockroaches who had eschewed free trade, peace, religious freedom, and capitalism had engaged in a political separatist movement. The filthy, disease-laden arthropods had taken over the laundry room, and by a treaty ratified in Tehran, vertebrate life-forms were no longer allowed to enter that section of the condominium.

In an aggressive geopolitical act of fascist hegemony, the cockroaches were engaged in clandestine, nefarious, and subversive activities to probe the resolve of the transient human occupants who had foolishly embraced a policy of leading from behind when it came to suppressing the insect infestation. This myopic, effete liberal ideology only amounted to, at best, containment of the insect population but not their eradication. The multiple empty cans of bug spray piled up outside of the laundry room door provided an irrefutable silent testimony that the ongoing cold war along the demilitarized zone could explode into overt open warfare between the vermin and the medical students at any time and without warning.

⎯⎯⎯⎯

It should be noted that for unclear reasons, no female student from either medical school had ever opted to reside at the condominium, even though the students could stay there during their rotation free of charge. It was a curious circumstance, and it was inexplicable. Neither of the medical schools had ever found any evidence of sexism or misogynistic bigotry as the reason no female medical students had ever wanted to stay at that condominium. It was odd indeed. During that year, the Gulf Coast College of Medicine received a $200,000 federal grant to determine if young males and females in their twenties had different tolerances to domestic filth and insect infestation. The study was no doubt another proud example of American tax dollars hard at work.

⎯⎯⎯⎯

Brewster and Bear drove down to the condominium in the 1968 hot rod Mustang, and the students moved in on Sunday, May 3, to set up shop before the rotation officially started on the following Monday. Brewster traveled light with two pairs of slacks, five pairs of socks, and five casual pullover shirts. Hopefully, the student would be able to find a nearby Laundromat in Harlingen to help keep his minimalistic wardrobe pleasantly fragrant.

That was necessary since the laundry room in the condominium was on the other side of the demilitarized zone, which was occupied by hostile insects. Brewster had arrogantly thought that since he was going down to the South Valley, he would probably be the best-dressed man in a hundred square miles. Forgetting to pack any underwear, Brewster soon learned that going commando was not a particularly pleasant ordeal, as he continuously chafed the crown of his tallywhacker on the inside zipper of his trousers.

Perhaps it would have been easier if J. D. had just gone down to a local establishment that peddled sundry goods and purchased at least one new pair of underwear, but that would not be the case. Although Brewster was an admixture of Italian and English ancestry, his colleagues in medical school had perceived him to be tighter than the bark on a tree and therefore more likely to be of Scottish descent. Nonetheless, the student made the best of the uncomfortable situation by jamming his pecker into the neck of one of his socks and then securing the makeshift apparel with some cellophane tape.

—◦◦◦—

While Brewster and Russian Bear started their externship in the Rio Grande Valley, two hardened criminals at the Sharpstown Correctional Facility took a male correctional officer hostage and used him as leverage to demand a transfer to a different facility, as they found the food and exercise equipment in the

Houston prison to be subjectively substandard. The news details were initially vague, but Brewster was surprised to learn that the prison warden, Jana Neopoliticia, acquiesced to the demands of the two prisoners.

Neopoliticia was definitely not originally from Texas. Even by the early 1980s, Brewster noted a palpable change in the political winds of his beloved city as the oil boom drew in newcomers from all over the country.

In any event, the two inmates were promptly transferred to an alternative correctional facility without retribution. That was strange but perhaps not too surprising, as the hard-core liberal Warden Neopoliticia strongly believed that criminals broke the law because of societal woes and not because of personal character flaws. There was no such thing, apparently, as personal responsibility. Brewster briefly wondered if his friend Arby Fuller might have somehow been mixed up with the trouble that had occurred on the prison yard, but the disclosure of such details would obviously have to wait until Brewster had returned to Houston after the completion of his family medicine rotation in the South Valley.

—◁◁◁|ᴘ|▷▷▷—

The attending physician on the family practice rotation, Dr. Bob Brickman, assigned each of the four students participating in the clerkship rotation a specific examination room that would be his or her home base for the duration of the month.

Brewster would soon encounter a robust and muscular beachcomber who called himself Dude. The patient presented to the family practice clinic for the management of second-degree sunburn he had sustained on his back and shoulders while playing down at Padre Island. Usually, Dude was smart enough to wear sunscreen, but on that occasion, he had left it in his car when he went out surf fishing.

As Brewster attended to the man's blistered skin, he asked, "How often do you get a chance to go out fishing?"

"Oh, I get to fish every day," Dude replied.

Brewster added a follow-up question that seemed logical enough: "Is this your line of work?"

The patient scoffed at such a silly question. "No way, Doc. I'm on permanent disability, and I draw social security. Can't you tell?"

That was an odd statement, as the patient was built like a brick shithouse. Other than his sunburn, he showed no obvious physical maladies. Brewster was curious and pressed on. "No, I could have never guessed you were physically disabled by just looking at you. What is your long-term medical problem? Perhaps the doctors at this clinic may be able to help you in some way, shape, or form."

"I'm not deemed to be gainfully employable because I have issues with a very poor short-term memory," the patient replied. "I smoke marijuana every day, and I really enjoy it; however, it makes me goofy. Because of that, I can't hold a steady job, and I'm now disabled. All I do now is fish and swim in the ocean during the day, and then I get stoned at night. My disability pension is really good, because I can easily purchase high-quality purple monkey shit! What I don't use myself, I sell on the side, and I'm able to put a few more Hamiltons into my pocket. As I also get food stamps and assisted housing benefits, I figure I'm set for life."

Brewster suppressed the strong compulsion he felt to use his bare hand to viciously slap the ruptured blisters on the patient's back. A rare moment of civility overcame the student, and Brewster was able, with great difficulty, to comport himself in a professional manner.

"You know, there are drug rehabilitation programs available to you," Brewster said. "To be frank, from what little I know about substance abuse medicine, it's far easier to discontinue the recreational use of cannabinoids compared to either alcohol or tobacco."

The patient raised his eyebrows and stared at the medical student with suspicion. "So if I quit smoking marijuana, does that mean my brain might function better?"

When Brewster answered in the affirmative, the patient became visibly upset.

"No way, man!" Dude exclaimed. "There's no way in hell I'm going to do that. If my brain starts to work better, I'll have to come off of long-term disability. If that were to happen, that means I would be forced to go out and get a job to provide for myself. There's not a dog's chance that I'll ever get weaned from the government teat! My life is perfect right now just as it is. Is America a great country or what?" American tax dollars hard at work.

As Brewster was stewing with aggressive and violent thoughts toward the beachcomber, it was probably a good thing that particular patient never came back to the clinic for a second visit.

Russian Bear encountered an obese, Spanish-speaking middle-aged female who came into the clinic to be evaluated for a several-week history of progressive right-upper-quadrant abdominal pain exacerbated by the intake of food. Unfortunately, Russian Bear could not make heads or tails of what the woman was trying to convey to him. He realized by her facial expressions that she must have been in pain, but otherwise, he had no clear idea what was really going on.

Although Russian Bear previously had been on an exchange professorship with the Cuban medical school in Havana, he had only given lectures in the basic sciences through the courtesy of an interpreter. While he was stationed in Cuba, he was not actually involved in direct patient care. Therefore, Bear knew little of the Spanish language. If he had known it, he would have been able to readily ascertain that the patient was suffering from acute cholecystitis and would need a surgical laparotomy to have her gallbladder surgically removed.

As the entire cadre of translators were busy dealing with other patients, Russian Bear stuck his head outside of his assigned examination stall to query if there was anybody else available who could help provide translation services.

One of the medical students from the Corpus Christi College of Medicine stepped forward to claim he could help provide translation assistance to sort out what the patient's problem might be. Russian Bear instructed his interscholastic colleague to simply translate the questions he asked of the patient.

"Madam, I can tell you are in pain," Bear said. "Please tell me where you hurt." Bear then turned to the medical student who claimed to have multilinguistic communication skills. "Please translate to this woman what I just said."

The student from Corpus Christi walked up to the patient, who was sitting on the examination table, and got within an inch of the patient's left ear. He then shouted out as loudly as he could in the English language, "Madam, I can tell you are in pain! Please tell me where you hurt!"

The unfortunate patient recoiled as if her left eardrum had just shattered. As she bolted out of the clinic, it appeared she had both of her arms extended high over her head, as if making a reach-for-the-sky gesture during a Wild West stagecoach holdup from an old movie.

"Well, I guess she wasn't that sick after all if she didn't even want to answer a few basic questions," the student from Corpus Christi said.

Bear forcefully took the so-called translator aside and proceeded to chastise him for what was likely the most idiotic thing the Russian had ever seen in his entire life. After all, the woman wasn't deaf; she just couldn't speak English.

Russian Bear was embarrassed that his motherland had been

afraid of the Americans for the last thirty-five years or so. If the basic American was that stupid, his former homeland probably never had anything to be afraid of to begin with.

———◦◦◦———

Dr. Brickman informed the students that if they wanted to earn extra credit and perhaps garnish a grade of honors, they could volunteer on the weekends to work at a nearby clinic in Mexico. Brewster wanted to make honors in family practice, as he had failed to do so on any of his prior clerkship rotations. Nonetheless, he had misgivings about going down to Mexico to do volunteer work.

"A medical facility in Playa Caliente was established by a charitable medical service called Doctors across the Rio Bravo. The town of Playa Caliente is located in Estado Tamaulipas," Dr. Brickman said. "To get there, follow Mexico Highway 101 south out of Matamoros. About eighty miles or so north of the Tropic of Cancer, Highway 101 intersects with Mexico Highway Spur 5. Follow this spur east toward the Gulf of Mexico as it heads through the Castillo Marshlands and crosses the Laguna Madre over to the barrier island, where you can find El Mezquital. The medical clinic in Playa Caliente is just east of there."

"Who's our contact?" Brewster asked.

"The physician who runs the clinic is a friend of mine—Dr. Luna," Brickman said. "The people who live there are warm and gracious. They'll take you in like you're family; put you up in a local home; and then feed you homemade tamales, enchiladas, and margaritas until you slip into a diabetic coma. You'll get so fat they'll have to haul you away with a small crane! Oh my God, it will be a beautiful experience for the both of you."

"Well, I don't know about Brewster," Bear said, "but sign me up."

"You'll work as a volunteer at the clinic all day on Saturday, have a day off on Sunday to play on the beach, and then be back here to work at our clinic in Los Estados Unidos the following Monday," Dr. Brickman said. "If you want to do this, you'll need to drive down on Friday afternoon after our clinic closes here. All you'll need to get into Mexico are your driver's license and the visa form you'll have to fill out before you cross the border. They won't ask for a passport or anything like that. Tell me, Brew—are you up for this type of challenge?"

Although Brewster was initially reluctant to sign up for a volunteer clinic in Mexico, Russian Bear was enthusiastic about the possibility of experiencing a new adventure.

⎯⎯⎯⎯

When the family practice clinic in Harlingen closed for the weekend on Friday, May 8, Brewster and Russian Bear jumped into the Mustang and crossed the border into Mexico. Within a few hours, they reached the clinic at Playa Caliente, where Dr. Luna and his niece, America, who was also a physician, greeted them.

America was a young woman in her early thirties who had an ear, nose, and throat specialty clinic in Matamoros, but she also did volunteer clinical work once a month at the Doctors across the Rio Bravo facility in Playa Caliente. The two students were treated to a wonderful meal at a local hacienda, and then they were offered quarters at the modest home of the local constable.

"Sadly," the constable said, "we're finally starting to run into problems with organized crime in our little village of Playa Caliente."

"What kind of problems are you having?" Brewster asked.

"The local drug cartel, the Calle Vampiro, are starting to make inroads on this previously isolated barrier island."

"Is there anything we should be worried about?" Bear asked.

"Well, it's more than just the drug trade," the constable said. "I'm proud of my new police cruiser, but it's the only prowl car in the region. My previous lightning-fast Dodge Polara, which had a four-hundred-forty-cubic-inch Magnum engine, was apparently stolen by members of the cartel."

"To what end?" Brewster asked.

"The cartel are using the old police cruiser to shake down tourists and local citizens alike. The federales have been called in, but they seem to be incapable—or unwilling—to help out in controlling the growing crime in the area," the constable said. "Nonetheless, I believe Playa Caliente is still a reasonably safe place for the students to come do volunteer work. I personally hope you boys plan to stay for a minivacation and play on the beach before you return to Tejas."

The following Saturday was an extraordinarily busy day at the Doctors across the Rio Bravo clinic. Word had gotten out to the surrounding area that two physicians were paying a visit. Also, two medical students from Los Estados Unidos would be working at the clinic that particular day. By seven o'clock in the morning, there was already a long line of 118 people willing to wait patiently to be seen by a bona fide health-care provider.

Pharmaceutical companies cheerfully provided free basic medication for Doctors across the Rio Bravo to supply their multiple charitable clinics in Mexico. Sadly, however, things were about to change. As Brewster and Russian Bear would soon attest, Mexico was a corrupt country: 90 percent of the gross national product was controlled by only 10 percent of the population. Essentially, there was no middle class to speak of in the 1980s. There were many in Mexico on the take. That culturally acceptable form of graft was called la mordita, or, translated into English, "the bite."

Once the local Mexican administrators learned that the charitable organization Doctors across the Rio Bravo was bringing free samples of medication across the border to be dispensed in the free clinic at Playa Caliente, they had to put a quick stop to that.

A local edict was issued specifically ordering that all medications to be dispensed at the charitable clinic had to be bought from a specific pharmacy in Matamoros. Of course, that particular pharmacy happened to be owned by the cousin of the uncle of the brother-in-law of the godfather of a lieutenant who served with the Calle Vampiro cartel. There it was—the bite.

In Mexico, the bite was as pervasive as it was inescapable. There was something screwed up about a country that inflicted the bite on the very people who were coming down across the border to try to do charitable work. As no good deed went unpunished, perhaps it was to be expected.

⫷⫸

That night, the two Mexican doctors and the two American medical students were the toast of the town. The locals got together and prepared fish tacos to be served with cerveza fria. As fresh sour cream was a rare commodity, the tacos were served with salsa fresca and homemade mayonnaise. It was nonetheless a spectacular feast.

America was a beautiful woman with dark eyes; bronze skin; and long, coarse black hair. She immediately took a liking to Russian Bear, and he too felt there was chemistry between them. America asked Brewster in Spanish if he knew anything about the marital status of his Russian friend. As Bear spoke no Spanish, she boldly asked the question right in front of Brewster's medical school colleague.

Brewster subsequently informed America that Russian Bear was happily married to a strong Russian woman who was no doubt capable of ruthless acts of violence. The young woman said wistfully, "Que lastima. All the good men are taken."

She gave Russian Bear a soft peck on the cheek and then told him, "Buenas noches, mi amor perdido!"

Before departing for the evening, America turned to Brewster and said, "J. D., you and your Russian friend did good work here today. I hope you realize that you're here for a greater purpose. The volunteers who work at this clinic do indeed make a difference, and I certainly believe it will help engender a mutual appreciation between the Anglo and Latino people in this hemisphere. I'm so glad you're here."

For a brief moment, the pervasive cynicism that had eroded Brewster's faith in humanity regressed. He originally had agreed to come down to Mexico to work in the volunteer clinic at Playa Caliente simply to ensure he would get an honors grade in the family practice rotation. Now he realized that perhaps America was right. Maybe Brewster was indeed making some kind of difference to help make the world a better place.

———

Upon returning to Harlingen on the following Monday, Brewster was assigned to evaluate a patient who had presented to the clinic with symptoms of troublesome dyspepsia. The patient was a middle-aged woman who stated that she experienced symptoms of nausea and vomiting whenever her husband returned from work, and she'd come to the clinic hoping to pick up a prescription for some type of antinausea drug that might be able to help her with her problem.

The woman's spouse was a long-distance truck driver, and she only had an opportunity to see him about once a week, but that was turning out to be about once a week too often. Apparently, her husband was busy hauling illicit produce out of Mexico and directly into the US street market. It was a two-way economic venture, as he also shipped so-called manufactured goods—semiautomatic weapons—back into Mexico.

Whenever her husband came home from a long-distance haul, the first thing he demanded was a hum job. He would drop his trousers right in the foyer of their home and demand that his unfortunate wife immediately service him as the first order of business to ensure domestic tranquility.

The patient complained that her husband's plumbing smelled

like Limburger cheese, and she would invariably gag and then vomit whenever she attempted to satisfy his wanton desires with an act of fellatio. To make matters worse, whenever she gagged and vomited on her husband's pecker, that would anger her spouse, and he would retaliate by striking her violently.

Brewster had a capital idea: Instead of his dispensing a prescription for antinausea medication, why did she not simply wash her husband's plumbing with soap and water when he got home? She could incorporate the act into sexual foreplay. The woman had no idea how to successfully prosecute such prescribed hygienic measures, as she was not accustomed to bathing herself, much less knowing how to correctly apply soap and water to her husband's malodorous reproductive genitalia.

Stunned and embarrassed by such a bizarre answer, J. D. didn't want to take the matter any further, so he tried unsuccessfully to defer that duty upon one of his other colleagues. Needless to say, upon hearing his request for assistance in such a delicate matter, the other three medical students on the family practice rotation roundly laughed in Brewster's face. Russian Bear, on the other hand, rudely informed Brewster to perform an autologous act of sexual reproduction that any man on the face of planet Earth would have been incapable of actually performing upon himself.

Brewster was finally forced to discuss the case with the attending physician, and Dr. Brickman recommended that the patient go to the local supermarket to buy a banana, two apricots, and a gentle lemon-flavored liquid dish detergent. The patient was then instructed to immediately return to the clinic with her purchased items, and the student, Brewster, would cheerfully teach her what to do next.

Brewster protested that teaching a stupid woman how to wash an abusive man's stinky genitalia was outside of his wheelhouse, but Dr. Brickman angrily responded. "Brewster, are you a man?"

"I believe so," the student answered.

"Brewster," Dr. Brickman asked, "have you ever put your pecker someplace where it should not have been?"

"I believe so," the student answered.

"Brewster, when your pecker got filthy with grunge and gradeaux," Dr. Brickman said, "I suspect you weren't just going to let it rot right down to the curlicues. Tell me—were you smart enough to wash your own pecker with soap and water?"

"I believe so," the student answered.

"Brewster, you need to go in there and teach that stupid woman how to wash an abusive man's stinky genitalia," Brickman said. "Got it? Do it now!"

The following week, Brewster was gratified to learn that he had become a bona fide successful marital counselor, as the patient returned to report that she no longer developed nausea and vomiting when she performed fellatio upon her husband.

She was also happy to confide that since she'd started to apply soap and water to her own vulvar and perianal area, her happy husband no longer gagged and vomited when he went spelunking. One could only hope the loving couple lived happily ever after.

———

J. D. Brewster and Russian Bear continued to make their charitable weekend pilgrimage to the Doctors across the Rio Bravo facility in Playa Caliente. Originally, America was only going to make one visit to the clinic per month, but when she found out that Russian Bear was going down every weekend, she made a point of trying to see him there. Unrequited love was a sad thing to behold.

When the afternoon session ended on May 29 at the East Valley Family Care Clinic in Harlingen, Brewster and Russian Bear had officially completed their family practice rotation, and they were proud to learn they had both received honors in the clerkship. Determined to finish on a strong note, Brewster and Bear decided to drive down into Mexico to say goodbye to the villagers of Playa Caliente, who had become cherished family members to the two students.

After the yellow Mustang pulled off of Highway 101 onto Spur 5 to head toward the coast, a large Dodge Polara patrol vehicle pulled up behind them and flashed its red and blue lights, indicating it wanted the two students to pull over to the side of the road.

Initially, Brewster and Russian Bear failed to remember the story the Playa Caliente constable had told them earlier in the month about a Dodge Polara police car being stolen by the Calle Vampiro drug cartel and used to terrorize people in the vicinity.

By the time Brewster realized he had been duped, it was too late. The bandito driving the cruiser was tapping a .38 revolver against the outside of the door of the prowler and motioning for Brewster to exit the Mustang. There was now no doubt in the mind of either student that this was indeed the stolen police car in question, and the men in the vehicle were likely members of the Calle Vampiro drug cartel.

"Keep the engine running, and leave your car door open when you make your exit," Russian Bear said. "Pop the trunk. I need to get in there."

"What are you up to?"

"I'm afraid we're going to have to fight our way out of this situation," Bear whispered.

Without hesitation, Brewster jumped out of the car and walked back toward the two men sitting in the stolen patrol car, who were dressed as Mexican police officers. Brewster was quick to note that their uniforms were frayed and filthy, and their pants did not match their shirts.

While Brewster was observing the men, Russian Bear rummaged through the trunk of the Mustang as if looking for misplaced identification papers. Years later, when Brewster looked back on the incident, he believed the words that had come out of his mouth must have been divinely inspired, because he had no recollection of what he told the two banditos poorly disguised as police officers when they pulled over his Mustang.

When Brewster reached the driver's side of the patrol car, one of the men asked him where he and his friend were headed. Brewster replied that his colleague was engaged to be married to a woman named America, who happened to be the niece of Dr. Luna, a prominent physician in Tamaulipas. Brewster said Playa Caliente was hosting a prenuptial celebration for his friend, and they were running late. Brewster added that the constable from Playa Caliente would be sending out a patrol car to escort the two men and their Mustang into town, and Brewster wondered aloud if the big Polara was the patrol car the two medical students were expecting.

At that point, not knowing that Brewster was fluent in Spanish, the two banditos began to speak among themselves in their native language. The driver turned to his partner in crime and said, "Do you recognize this type of Mustang? This happens to be a 1968 California Special. I want to take it away from these two gringos. Just think how many muchachas I'd have wrapped around my finger if I drove around in a car like that! Do you think this asshole is telling us the truth?"

"I don't know, but if he is, the constable might be right down the road just east of us," the other bandito replied. "If he is lying, though, let's just shoot both of them now and be done with it. After all, you've got the gun, and it'll be your job to do the deed if we're heading down this path."

It took extraordinary courage for Brewster to remain calm when he heard that the two banditos were plotting to kill him and Russian Bear to steal the Mustang.

"I have an idea," the driver of the stolen patrol car said to his partner in crime. "Why don't I go out and talk to the other gringo to see if he tells the same story? If his story doesn't match what this guy just told us, I'll pull out my pistol and put bullets in both of their heads right now. I'll do it right here on the spot. If the tall man standing behind the trunk of the Mustang tells me the same story, we should just wait for them until they leave Playa Caliente. When they head back to the United States, we can just ambush them at that time. We'll just leave them out on the prairie and let the coyotes eat them."

The driver then turned to Brewster and said in English, "Senor, I am going over to your car to talk to your friend to see what he can tell me about your trip down here to Mexico."

Before the driver of the stolen patrol vehicle opened the car door, Brewster spun about and called out to Russian Bear. When Bear turned to look at Brewster, J. D. quickly ran the thumb of his right hand across his throat, but he made certain the two banditos did not see the secret signal he conveyed to his colleague. Russian Bear then turned back toward the car and pretended to still be looking for something important in the trunk of Brewster's Mustang.

"I'll be with you in a moment, Officer," Bear said. "I know that my identification papers are in this trunk somewhere."

The bandito held his pistol in his right hand when he approached Russian Bear. "Senor, could you please tell me what has brought you and your friend down here to Mexico? Do you have any identification papers?"

"I have what you're looking for right here," Bear replied. "Take a look at this!"

With that, Russian Bear wheeled sharply and smashed the bandito across the bridge of his nose with a tire iron. As the would-be assailant crumpled to the ground with blood gushing out of his face, Brewster sprinted back to the Mustang.

The other bandito, fortunately, was unarmed. Nonetheless, he jumped out of the patrol car and ran toward his fallen partner in crime to assess the situation. Brewster and Russian Bear jumped back into the Mustang, and Brewster disengaged the clutch, jammed the transmission into gear, and then spun a hard U-turn to get back onto Mexican Highway 101 in an attempt to head back north to the United States as fast as possible.

Brewster and Russian Bear were in deep shit, and their lives were clearly in peril. If any other cartel members were heading toward them from the north, there was no way they would be able to escape with their lives. As they pulled past the patrol car, the bandito who previously had been sitting in the passenger seat quickly ascertained that his comrade in crime, who had collapsed upon the ground in a bloody pulp, was permanently out of commission. Once the remaining bandito realized his partner was unresponsive, he grabbed the .38 revolver and ran back to the stolen patrol car to give pursuit.

When the big Dodge appeared to be making ground on Brewster's Mustang, Russian Bear said, "What in hell is wrong with this car of yours? Drive! I thought this was supposed to be a hot rod! Why is that bastard behind you now gaining on us?"

Brewster didn't answer Bear's question, as he was too busy driving. The ultratall 2.47 rear-end gear in Brewster's California Special made his car extraordinarily sluggish off the starting line and even slower to accelerate to its potential top-end speed. Nonetheless, Brewster hoped that in the end, he would be able to outpace the big Dodge, even if the stolen patrol car had a legendary 440 Magnum engine under its hood. Brewster also knew that he probably had a hundred more ponies under the bonnet of his trusty steed.

Although Brewster had hit a speed of 128 miles per hour, the big patrol car, which had a numerically taller 3.54 Dana rear-end gear, was a faster sprinter in a flying mile run. Ultimately, however, the Polara's rear gear would limit the vehicle's top end speed.

The big Dodge finally caught up to the Mustang and tried to pull up parallel to Brewster on the driver's side of his car. The driver of the Polara pulled out his pistol and tried to draw a bead through the patrol car's open passenger window on the two men escaping in the Mustang.

When shots rang out from the patrol car, the driver's-side rear-quarter window of the Mustang was blown out. "Drive! Drive! Drive!" Russian Bear screamed in fear.

He repeated those words over and over again, and the tempo of the repetition became faster and faster as both cars continued to accelerate. Finally, both cars were up to 138 miles per hour, and it appeared the Dodge Polara was going to try to force Brewster's Mustang off the highway.

As Brewster had a customized rack-and-pinion steering system pirated from a modern Mustang II and also an aftermarket independent rear-suspension setup, his Mustang was nimble enough to weave away from his assailant without losing control of the car every time the big Dodge tried to slam into the left flank of Brewster's Mustang. By then, the patrol car had hit its top end, but Brewster's Mustang had much longer legs, and it was starting to finally pull away from the bandito. At 160 miles per hour, Brewster's nemesis started to rapidly disappear in the rearview mirror.

About ten miles outside of Matamoros, Brewster and Russian Bear blasted past a legitimate Mexican Federale patrol car, but by that time, the two terrified men were not about to stop for jack or for shit, in whatever combination those two words could possibly appear together within the context of a sentence. By then, all of Brewster's cynicism and lack of faith in humanity had returned at wide-open throttle to vex him yet again.

Even when they had successfully crossed the border into Texas and were well on their way back to Houston, Russian Bear's eyes were fixed wide open. For hours, it appeared as if he were completely incapable of blinking while he continued the relentless chant: "Drive! Drive! Drive!"

2

JUNETEENTH

Russian Bear was able to wrestle a ten-foot-long section of rebar through the chain-link fence at a nearby construction site, and he dragged the unwieldy steel rod over toward Brewster's parked car. Bear proceeded to slip the end of the metal rod through the blown-out driver's-side rear-quarter window. He nursed the lead entry tip of the rebar rod toward the dashboard on the passenger's side of the car.

When that primary stage of Bear's elaborate demonstration had been accomplished, Russian Bear said, "This is a close approximation of where the bullet entered the car."

He walked over to the passenger-side door, opened up the car, and then slipped the leading tip of the rebar all of the way through the bullet hole that had penetrated the passenger-side-roof A pillar before it exited the exterior sheet metal of Brewster's Mustang. Bear had undertaken the endeavor to evaluate the trajectory of the bullet that had penetrated the interior of Brewster's hot rod.

Upon completing the secondary stage of the demonstration, Bear said, "This is the exact location of where the bullet made its exit from the car."

He lifted his arms triumphantly while he simultaneously raised his face up toward the sky, as if he were enjoying the bright sunshine that beamed down upon him.

Bear looked over to J. D. Brewster with disappointment, as his colleague appeared to be unimpressed with the forensic analysis of the bullet holes his vehicle had sustained. Brewster was nonchalantly puffing on a cigar while he stood at the front of the Mustang with his arms defiantly folded, and his feet were poised at an apparently confrontational shoulder's width.

"After all of this," Russian Bear said, "you still have nothing to say?"

To emphasize his last point, Bear engaged in the final dramatic stage of the demonstration by sitting back down in the front passenger seat of the Mustang. "This is exactly how close the bullet came to blowing my brains out," Bear said. "Pay attention, Brew!"

It was then explicitly clear that the bullet, as tracked by the steel rebar, had come within only a few centimeters of striking the back of Bear's head. He found one other incidental bullet hole in the left rear quarter panel of the Mustang, but as he could find no exit wound, the fate of that other projectile remained unknown.

Somewhere along the way, Russian Bear had apparently become engrossed in the Good Book that some fellow named Gideon had left behind on the neurosurgery unit several months before. He proceeded to rebuke J. D. Brewster with a quote from Mark 8:18:

"Do you have eyes but fail to see, and ears but fail to hear? And don't you remember?"

"Yes, I remember," Brewster said as he shook his head in disagreement at Bear's reference to scripture. "I remember that my 1968 California Special superfast supercar just saved my ass."

"I think this is a sign," Bear said. "I believe I have a specific calling to go back to the village of Playa Caliente someday to continue doing charitable work down there. I hope you realize that you're here on this planet for a greater purpose. Sadly, J. D., it would appear to me that you're a man who's so cynical that you're lost. Maybe someday you'll come full circle to face the Truth."

Stunned by Russian Bear's apparent new spiritual awakening,

Brewster replied, "Look here, Bear; whether this was a calling as you now claim, or not, you'd be an absolute idiot to go back down to Playa Caliente ever again. That's especially the case if the Calle Vampiro drug cartel is setting up shop in the neighborhood, as the local constable previously told us."

"What are you afraid of?"

"As if you need to ask," Brewster replied. "It should be quite clear to anybody with even one functional neuron between his ears that this would be one shit-fire way for you to get yourself killed, okay? As for me, I'll tell you right now: I'm sure as shit not about to step foot in Mexico ever again. Those bastards down there had one crack at me before, and I'll never afford them another opportunity to finish me off once and for all."

"Listen to your heart."

"Sorry," Brewster said, "but I am listening to my brain, which you seem to be lacking right about now. You'd be well advised to consider the same. I'm going to call Brickman to give him a heads-up about what happened to us in Mexico. He needs to shitcan the Doctors across the Rio Bravo project before one of our people ends up getting whacked down there."

"You just don't get it, do you?" Russian Bear said. "Something happened down in Mexico that was much bigger than either of us. You and I were about to be murdered down there, but somehow, we survived. I believe it was the hand of providence that saved our lives."

"Miracles do happen, but you never know who has been chosen to be the witness," Brewster softly replied. "I guess I just wasn't supposed to see this one."

―⦅⦆―

By the time J. D. Brewster arrived at the Vinyl Lounge, medical student Parker Coxswain was already wiping the forehead of Woolly

Mammoth with a cool cloth after the big man collapsed upon the floor. Willy "Wooly Mammoth" Mammon was a Vietnam War vet and the only African American member of the 1978 entry class at the Gulf Coast College of Medicine.

Several months earlier, Mammoth had sustained a closed head injury when he was assaulted with a lead pipe wielded by the two vicious thugs who called themselves Big Nig and Smeg Nog at an automatic teller machine across the street from the Texas Medical Center. Willy had been critically injured with a subdural hematoma that required an emergency neurosurgical intervention to save his life. Sadly, Willy Mammon was now left with a permanent seizure disorder, and he had just suffered another grand mal event. Fortunately, Parker Coxswain had witnessed the conniption event, as he was in the Vinyl Lounge heating up a bean burrito when Willy collapsed. Parker was a so-called braniac at the Gulf Coast College of Medicine, a moniker that clearly inferred Parker was a member of the elite MD/PhD dual-training program. Fortunately, Parker had extensive clinical experience and knew what to do when the neuroelectrical connections in Willy's brain had an acute short circuit.

"Are you still a little foggy in the noodle?" Parker asked the big man. Fortunately, the wooly one had only a brief postictal period after his latest seizure event. The postictal state after a convulsion was a reference to the confusion and disorientation that could occur when patients began to recover from a major epileptic attack. Likely, it was a reflection of the neurocircuitry of the brain attempting to reboot to original factory specifications.

"Thanks, Parker," Willy said, "but this fit I just had wasn't too bad." After Willy had gathered his bearings, he realized he had lost bladder control. It was the first time that embarrassing complication ever had occurred with one of his grand mal epileptic convulsions.

"Tell me, Willy," Parker said. "Should we get you down to the emergency room to get you checked out?"

"That would be a good idea," Brewster said. "You need to pay attention to what Parker's saying."

"I think I'll be okay." Willy was able to sit up on his own accord and navigate to the large couch in front of the television. "Good God, it looks like I have pissed my pants, though."

"Nothing to be embarrassed about," Brewster said reassuringly. "What do you expect? After all, you just had a short circuit between your ears."

"What am I going to do, J. D.?" Willy asked.

"You just need to throw on some fresh duds," Brewster answered.

"You and I are supposed to be starting our mandatory rotation in psychiatry today," Willy said. "It'll certainly look bad if I show up late at the start of this clerkship."

Brewster attempted to assuage the angst of his friend. "Stay frosty, big man. I'll call Feral Cheryl and let her know what happened. My girlfriend, Stella Link, and I are barely on speaking terms at this time, but I'll have her talk to her boss, Corka Sorass, and she'll let him know we'll be late today."

"I don't want to be a burden to anybody," Willy said.

"No biggie," Brewster said. "Just remember that you owe me. Maybe you can return the favor and save my ass someday."

"Deal."

"As for now," Brewster said, "let's get you back to your apartment and get you freshened up. Parker, pop over next door to the ER and score a wheelchair."

"On it," Coxswain said. "Back in a flash, and then we can get the big man hauled out of here."

As Brewster drove his friend off campus, Willy said, "Well, Brew, it looks like you've spent some quality time on tricking out your wheels. The bullet holes definitely give this old Mustang a certain, how should I say, urban panache. I also especially like the piece of plywood you've duct-taped over the rear driver's-side quarter window. You're stylin' now, my pasty friend."

"Thanks."

"To be honest, you didn't have to go all the way down to Mexico to get your ride pimped out like this. I'm certain I know some bad boys on the east side over near Hobby who would have done this for you, and they would've given you a big-ass discount to boot!"

"I'll keep that in mind," Brewster said, "if I plan on doing any further customized bodywork on this old thing."

"It would seem to me that you and Russian Bear must have had a really good time down in Mexico," Willy said. "Would you like to fill me in?"

"Russian Bear and I danced a tango with some bad hombres near Playa Caliente, but we lived to tell about it. I'll give you the lowdown someday. I'm worried about you, Willy. How often are you having these grand mal seizure events?"

"I get them about twice a month now," Wooly Mammoth replied, "and I can't predict when a seizure is going to strike. I don't get any kind of warning, like an aura, visual changes, or anything like that. It just comes on hard and fast like I'm getting clobbered in the head with a lead pipe. Come to think of it, I did get clobbered in the head with a lead pipe!"

"What have the neurologists told you?" Brewster asked.

"The neurons that are on my case say they're quite certain they'll find the right juice that'll keep this shit under control once and for all," Willy answered with what sounded like a considerable amount of skepticism. "As for now, my one mission in life is to hunt down Darryl Hewritt. I'm going to extract a pound of flesh from that boy when I find him. Maybe two pounds, and I'm talking major internal organs here."

"Are you referring to the joker you had a private interview with at the North University Place Police Department after he tried to steal your daddy's car last year?" Brewster asked. "You should've killed the son of a bitch when you had the chance. After all, it looks like he gave you a gift that just keeps on giving."

"Yes indeed. He was the guy," Willy said. "There was another big bastard with him when I got piped in the noggin, but I have no idea who that fellow might have been, as I'd never seen him before. When they rolled up on me at the ATM, the bigger fellow said to me, 'Skew me, my man. Do you know where da white wimmins is at?' It was as if he was merely a caricature of what a black thug thinks a black thug should act like."

"Do the police know all about this?" Brewster asked.

"Don't know. Don't care," Willy answered. "I am seething with hatred for these two people. I'd kill them both with my own hands if I ever had such an opportunity."

"Be careful," his colleague said, "or else this hatred will burn you up. It'll get to the point where every other emotion you have ever had will become eroded. You need to try to get over that feeling."

"God forgive me," the obviously depressed giant replied, "but I don't know if I'll ever get over that feeling. To be honest, I don't want to get over that feeling. The administration states that I should probably go talk to somebody in the psychiatry department to help me cool off, but I don't want to cool off. I want to stay angry. Well, since I'm doing a psychiatry clerkship rotation this month, perhaps it wouldn't hurt if I sat down and had a little chat with Dr. Corka Sorass at some point in time or maybe with the clinical psychologist, Dr. Petra Clayton."

—◆—

Willy and Brewster were about to meet a peculiar menagerie of deranged individuals over the next several weeks. Willy was introduced to an unfortunate young married woman who appeared to be afflicted with an acute case of postpartum psychosis. The husband had brought his wife in to be evaluated for an acute onset of bizarre behavior, as he was fearful she was a potential risk to their newborn child.

After a successful routine vaginal delivery of her first child, the patient had immediately started to hear a voice that reportedly had been casting random insults at her. At first, the insults she thought she had heard were simple phrases, such as, "You're useless." At other times, she would hear, "You're a failure." It appeared she was starting to lose her own volition, as there were times when she would be driving about and doing chores, such as grocery shopping, when the voice would tell her, "Make a right-hand turn now, you bitch!" That would cause the patient to veer off in a completely different direction for no apparent reason.

The voice she thought she heard had become more aggressive over time. The auditory hallucination had instructed her, "Cut your wrist, you sow!" and "Burn your hand on the stove! Do it now, you harlot!"

The frightening auditory hallucinations that tormented her were not like a voice in the head. To that unfortunate patient, the voice was as crisp and clear as if somebody were speaking to her from a distance of only a few feet away. It was no wonder how, in less enlightened times, individuals afflicted with such thought disorders were believed to have been possessed by demons.

Her symptoms rapidly had progressed to where the voice was giving her instructions to commit even more serious self-inflicted injuries, including suicide. Her thought processes had become more muddled and tangential as her auditory hallucinations worsened.

Postpartum psychosis, considered a psychiatric emergency, appeared to afflict mothers at a rate of somewhere between one in five hundred and one in a thousand deliveries. Generally, schizophrenia in its classic form struck when individuals were in their twenties, which happened to be the time when women were fertile and were having offspring.

Perhaps, as Mammon wondered, postpartum psychosis was simply an unfortunate coincidence and was ultimately only a case of routine schizophrenia that occurred at the wrong time, in the wrong place, and in the wrong female patient. The temporal relationship that had been noted between that patient's acute thought disorder and the delivery of a new offspring, however, was undeniable. Most experts in the field of psychiatry readily accepted that the disorder referred to as postpartum psychosis was a unique mental health disease process that was in a different mental illness category from acute schizophrenia.

Willy had been previously instructed on how to give a proper and thorough psychiatric examination. One of the components of that type of evaluation was to interview the patient to see if he or she could fully grasp the meaning of readily understood and frequently utilized idiomatic phrases.

Willy initiated the patient's primary psychiatric evaluation. "Madam, could you tell me the meaning of the expression, 'A rolling stone gathers no moss'?"

The woman leaned toward Willy with a big smile on her face and whispered, "It means that a traveling salesman should never take a piss in the kitchen sink!"

Willy scratched his chin for a moment to ponder her non sequitur response before he proceeded to write down the perplexing answer she had conveyed. He pressed on. "Madam, could you tell me the meaning of the expression, 'People in glass houses should not throw stones'?"

The answer the woman gave indicated that the patient was capable of at least limited concrete thinking, but she seemed to lack the insight to generate the abstract response Willy had anticipated. She replied, "Because you'll cut your feet if you walk around in the house without wearing any shoes."

"I have one more question to ask you," Willy said. "Madam, could you tell me the meaning of the expression, 'There's no use in crying over spilled milk'?"

The woman suddenly became violently agitated, and she lunged at Willy and screamed in his face, "Because it has wheels!"

Willy recoiled defensively as she ran out of the examination room. To everyone she encountered in the waiting room, she screamed, "Because it has wheels!"

Two psychiatric attendants corralled the deranged woman while Dr. Sorass administered an intramuscular injection of the antipsychotic drug known as Haldol, which immediately calmed her down.

Sadly, it would be many weeks before the patient was well enough to be discharged from the psychiatric unit to rejoin her family. Upon her departure from the hospital, she fortunately had no signs or symptoms that suggested a residual psychotic state, although she would remain on antipsychotic medication for a full year. However, nobody on staff in the psychiatry department, including Corka Sorass, was willing to venture a medical opinion as to whether or not she would be at an increased lifetime risk for another case of postpartum psychosis if she ever elected to have additional children in the future.

Willy wondered if somebody could become violent and psychotic at the drop of a hat, could the same thing ever happen to him in light of the trauma he had previously experienced?

—⟨⟨⟨○⟩⟩⟩—

Although D' Shea Dalton's most recent post-XRT CT scan of her brain showed no evidence of any residual or recurrent cancer, she continued to ruminate about the prospect of facing what would likely be a terminal disease process at some time in the future.

"I'm afraid, Baby Girl," D' Shea told her twin sister. "I'm terrified that someday my cancer will come back to haunt me."

"You need to put on your smiley face," D' Nae answered.

"I just can't," her twin said. "I swear the universe is just setting me up for failure. Sooner or later, the other shoe's gonna fall."

"No!" D' Nae exclaimed. "We just need to get your head bolts tightened down once and for all."

D' Shea Dalton developed chronic situational depression, and she was being treated at the outpatient psychiatry department at the Gulf Coast College of Medicine for the problem. D' Shea eventually was completely weaned off of the dexamethasone steroid medication she had been taking, which was good news, as the drug was well known to occasionally induce untoward effects upon a patient's psyche.

The young woman was started on the antidepressant medication known as Elavil, and fortunately, that treatment proved to be beneficial. She continued to make visits to talk to a counselor at the psychiatry department every other week.

A residual troublesome issue was her alopecia totalis. The radiation therapy she had received to her brain postoperatively had left her permanently bald, which greatly diminished her self-esteem. Her twin sister, D' Nae, would tag along with D' Shea to the outpatient clinic appointments, but psychiatry department rules and regulations ensured that D' Nae was never allowed to sit in on the proceedings. Instead, she was relegated to sit in the waiting room during the one-hour counseling sessions her sister found so helpful.

Brewster smiled brightly when he picked up the clinic chart and realized he was about to sit in on D' Shea's counseling session, which would be held with clinical psychologist Dr. Petra Clayton. It long had been speculated that Brewster and the Dalton twins were half siblings, but that was unsubstantiated. If that were indeed the truth, medical ethics would have dictated that Brewster recuse himself from the counseling session. As medical ethics were oftentimes a subject matter Brewster appeared to have little if any respect for, any potential kinship with the Dalton twins did not deter him from joining the counseling session. As Brewster passed through the lobby, D' Nae recognized Brewster and jumped out of the waiting chair to run over and give him a hug.

"Brew, are you going in to see Baby Girl?" D' Nae asked. "I know she'd be thrilled to see you."

Brewster answered in the affirmative, but he was startled to note that D' Nae was now completely bald just like her twin sister. He reached out to touch the young woman's scalp, and he must have had a look of concern on his face that D' Nae immediately recognized as abject fear.

Before Brewster could even ask a question, D' Nae said, "Don't worry, Brew. I don't have a brain tumor like Baby Girl. I just wanted to give her some moral support, so I shaved my head completely bald, and now I look just like her. It's just how it is supposed to be. I need to let you know that the radiation oncology doctors state that her hair will likely never grow back, and she's very upset about that matter."

Brewster tilted the young woman's head downward, and then he gave her a tender kiss of admiration on the top of her bald scalp before going in to see her twin sister. D' Shea was already in the counseling session with Dr. Clayton, and they were waiting for Brewster to arrive.

"Brewster, I think there's a young lady in here who's been waiting for you," Dr. Clayton said. "It appears she must have previously met you when you were doing a rotation on the neurosurgery service."

"Well, here's a blast from the past," Brewster said.

"Hi, Brew! You're still cute as a bug," D' Shea said.

"I knew you were in here, D' Shea, as I saw your sister waiting for you in the lobby. I'm sorry to hear that your hair likely will not grow back at this point, but I just wanted to tell you that bald is beautiful."

"Think so?"

"If I buff you out with a little bit of carnauba car wax, I'll be able to get that noodle of yours to glow in the dark!" Brewster proclaimed.

"Tell me—do you have any residual neurological problems after your surgery and radiation treatment?"

"If being bald is beautiful," D' Shea said, "why don't you just shave your head so you can look like me and Baby Girl?"

"Maybe I'll do just that," Brewster said with a smile.

"I'm doing okay, except my memory might not be as good as it used to be, but I'm still at the U of H, and my grades are holding."

"Anything else?" Brewster asked.

"Take a look at my left arm," D'Shea said, "as it's starting to shrink up a bit. I have this problem with leftover weakness on that side, but I manage."

"I'm sure you do," Brewster said. "Explain something to me. You called your sister Baby Girl, and she calls you by the same nickname. So tell me—which one of you can claim the title of being the real McCoy?"

"Well," D' Shea replied, "I suspect my twin sister has the official title, as I'm officially eleven minutes older than she is."

After her counseling session, Brewster walked D' Shea back up to the lobby to rejoin her twin sister. D' Nae said, "Baby Girl and I have something we'd like to ask you. We want to invite you to come to Hermann Park with us on the evening of June nineteenth to attend the Juneteenth Festival. We'll bring a cooler of snacks if you promise to bring a cooler with some cold beer. There'll be old-school rhythm and blues, just the kind you like."

"Tell me if you're majority age before I agree to bring the beer," Brewster said. "I don't want to be accused of contributing to the delinquency of two minors!"

"We're close enough for government work," D' Shea said.

"Well then, that's close enough for me," Brewster replied. "Do you think it would be safe for a white boy like me to show up to the Juneteenth Festival? After all, I won't go if black folks look down upon me as if I'm invading their territory. I want to be respectful about the situation."

"Don't worry, Brew," D' Nae said. "Baby Girl and I will protect you from any angry, straight-razor totin', pistol-packin' sisters who'd want to wrestle you down to the ground and make you sweat. Come to think of it, though, that might not be a bad thing for you to experience. As they say, once you go black, you'll never go back!"

After the young women left, Brewster went off to extend the invitation to Wooly Mammoth, as perhaps he and Feral Cheryl would also like to attend. Enveloped in a foul mood as a consequence to his now chronic seizure disorder, the big man did not even look up to Brewster when he expressed that he had no interest in such festivities.

———

Brewster learned that by mid-June, Dr. Hank Holcombe had been bedridden for the better part of four weeks. The research scientist named Rip Ford explained to Brewster that Uncle Hank was ready to give up the struggle. After all, Dr. Holcombe had battled his aggressive lymphoma for a whole year with little success, and he was ready for his life to come to a swift conclusion. Dr. Clemmons had moved into Hank's house to help provide care for him during the terminal stages of his disease process.

Dr. Clemmons had contacted both Rip Ford and J. D. Brewster with the explicit invitation to come visit Dr. Holcombe, as he desperately wanted to speak to them both before he passed on. Dr. Holcombe had been heavily sedated with morphine to help control his pain and also manage the severe itching from which he suffered.

Whenever Hank was awake, the itching from the cutaneous lymphoma was agonizing. Nonetheless, if Ford and Brewster were coming for a visit, Hank implored Dr. Clemmons to take him off of the morphine so he could be at least somewhat alert upon the arrival of the two students.

When the doorbell rang at Dr. Holcombe's house, Dr. Clemmons opened the door to allow Brewster and Ford to enter. Dr. Clemmons was dressed in a bloody negligee, fishnet stockings, and high-heeled pumps. In the center of the room, Uncle Hank Holcombe was completely naked except for an old pair of boxer shorts festooned with the images of orca whales frolicking in the ocean. His arms were suspended from the ceiling by a block-and-tackle pulley system. With his skin flayed open by a vigorous scrubbing with steel-wool pads, it appeared as if Dr. Holcombe were about to be crucified. An intravenous infusion was being administered through a double-lumen Hickman catheter extruding from Hank's upper anterior chest wall.

"For the love of God, what's going on in here?" Ford asked.

"I tip my sombrero to you boys," Dr. Holcombe answered. "I don't have much time. I'm just about ready to shoot through into the blue, and I want you to follow the instructions that Regina is about to give you to help me get to the finish line in my life."

Dr. Clemmons handed Brewster a two-gallon spray-pump canister, a device typically utilized to disseminate aerosolized insecticide on a target arthropod. The canister was filled with hot water that was just below the boiling threshold.

Dr. Clemmons handed Ford a similar spray-pump canister filled with ice water. Dr. Clemmons was holding a bloody wire-bristled, long-handled brush that would have been at home cleaning a metal-racked meat smoker.

"We are going to start on his back and work our way down," Dr. Clemmons said. "Afterward, we will hit his ventral side. I'll start scrubbing away at his skin with a wire brush, and then, Brewster, you douse him with the hot water. After that, I want Ford to spray him down immediately with ice water at the site I've just stripped away."

"I don't know about all of this," Brewster said.

"Are you going to help me out here, or not?" Regina asked. "This is a brutal technique, but it will temporarily exhaust the histamine that the mast cells in his skin are secreting, and it will control his severe itching for ten or fifteen minutes before the symptoms return. By the time we're finished, Hank will be able to talk to you coherently but only briefly. Hopefully, he will tell you what mission he has for you. Tonight the three of us will be hearing Dr. Holcombe's last words."

Brewster waved his hand in front of his left eye. "I'm not up for this! Uncle Hank, are you sure this is the way you want things handled?"

"Don't worry, boys," Dr. Holcombe replied. "I've already signed off on a DNR code status. I have my own fantasy as to how I want to punch my ticket, and it's going to be tonight. A huge woman in a Viking hat with long, braided blonde hair and a battle axe needs to take me down for the ten-count. I hope she will just throw me right down on the ground and then plop her corpulent body smack-dab onto the middle of my sternum. As she crushes the life right out of me, maybe she'll sing a dramatic Wagnerian number in the mezzo-soprano range."

"That's it, baby," Regina Clemmons said. "Let it all hang out!"

"If that exceeds her vocal limitations, perhaps she will at least serenade me with Led Zeppelin's 'Stairway to Heaven,'" Dr. Holcombe said in jest. "Hopefully it will be the long version. Yeah, that's the ticket! I'll get a one-way trip into the great beyond while a fat Viking-lady angel-of-death specter is sitting upon my face. When I cash in my chips, that's how I want to make my exit."

Dr. Clemmons vigorously scrubbed away the skin on Hank's body, and Brewster quickly followed with a spray-down of the area from the pump canister of scalding-hot water. Ford immediately followed with an application of ice water.

During the entire surreal ordeal, Dr. Hank would shout out with excitement. "That's the ticket! That's the ticket! Good God Almighty, that's the ticket! Hurt me, boys and girls! For the love of Jesus, hurt me bad!"

As a pool of blood and water collected at the feet of the dying man, his heart rate skyrocketed upward, while his blood pressure fell. Dr. Holcombe said, "This is the best that I've felt in a long time." He spoke as if he were giving a subjective assessment of his clinical situation. "You know, when a match burns out, it will flicker brightly before the flame is finally extinguished. Why does a match do that? I've never been able to figure out that mystery."

"What do you want from us, Uncle Hank?" Brewster asked.

"Listen up. Well, here we are, gentlemen. I've given this a lot of thought, and I want you men to liberate the big boys we've incarcerated in the lockdown primate kennel. You should recruit Zip Talbot to help you out if you must, but there's no way Dr. Caleb or Denny Sassman will ever be on board with this idea. I don't care how you do it; just get it done. That's all I have to say. Goodbye, Rip. As for you, Brewster, I pray that someday you'll find purpose in this life. Regina, I'm ready. Put me down."

"Okay, Hank. I'll always love you," Dr. Clemmons said. Those were her final words to Hank Holcombe.

Misunderstanding what Dr. Holcombe had said, Brewster and Ford began to loosen the shackles at Dr. Holcombe's wrists. "I'll untie his right hand," Ford said. "Brew, you get his left hand freed up."

"Hold on, boys. Stop what you're doing. You don't understand," Regina said. "Hank didn't ask to be let down. He asked to be put down."

Dr. Clemmons proceeded to inject one hundred milligrams of morphine sulfate into the IV that ran into Dr. Holcombe's right subclavian vein, and fortunately, he immediately drifted off into a narcotic-induced coma before the terrible pruritus symptoms recurred.

Dr. Clemmons then took an empty sixty-cubic-centimeter syringe and started to vigorously pump air into the central-line IV access device located in the subclavian vein of Dr. Holcombe. After only two syringes of air had been administered into the vein of the beloved man who would always be remembered as Uncle Hank, he simply quit breathing. His passing through the plane of existence known as life appeared to be a peaceful event. Regina said, "It is finished."

Exhausted, the two students settled down on the couch and stared at the lifeless body of Dr. Holcombe, which was still suspended in the air by the block-and-tackle pulley system. Meanwhile, Dr. Regina Clemmons wept in anguish. It would have appeared to even a casual observer that Dr. Clemmons and Hank Holcombe had become something much more than just friends.

Ford went to the kitchen and brought back a coffee cup he had found in the dishwasher. He proceeded to fill it with ice water from the spray-pump dispenser he'd used just moments before to soothe the horrific pruritus that tortured a man being eaten alive by cancer. He handed the cup of ice water to Dr. Clemmons, who smiled in appreciation.

They sat in silence together for several minutes. Finally, Brewster asked a question in a low monotone. "What in hell happened in there?"

Brewster received a nonchalant response, as if an acquaintance were making a casual commentary about something as trivial as the weather. "Nothing," Regina said. "I assure you not a damned thing happened in there today."

—◁◁◁◁◁◁◁▷▷▷▷▷▷▷—

At the end of J. D. Brewster's career, he would think back on the time when the Gulf Coast College of Medicine was still performing unitemporal electroconvulsive therapy on patients afflicted with catatonic depression in the early 1980s. With only a few years remaining in his career, Brewster was stunned to learn that the State of California, in the year 2016, had actually decriminalized child prostitution. He thought the old electrodes should have been fired up and used in a punitive fashion to make those liberals pay for their abject stupidity. Who else could have possibly deserved such a brutal punishment via transtemporal electrocution?

After a particular horror that correctional officer Arby Fuller had seen during a prison revolt back in 1981, perhaps that particular and somewhat macabre Machiavellian medical marvel called electroconvulsive therapy should have also been utilized in such a fashion on the warden at the Sharpstown Correctional Facility. That individual was a frog-faced, bug-eyed, knuckle-dragging beast of a woman with a short-cropped man's coif. She was known as Ms. Jana Neopoliticia. Outside of the incarcerated inmates, that woman was the nastiest man Arby Fuller had ever known in his entire life.

When correctional officer Arby Fuller heard that J. D. Brewster was doing a rotation on the psychiatry service, he made an appointment to talk to a counselor regarding the trauma he had personally experienced during the prisoner uprising at the Sharpstown Correctional Facility the prior month.

Arby had unfortunately witnessed a vicious act of brutality, and the image of what he had seen was indelibly burned on the back of his retinae. At that point, he couldn't get the nightmare he had seen out of his mind. The psychiatry clinic scheduled an appointment for Mr. Fuller to meet with clinical psychologist Dr. Petra Clayton. Upon Fuller's arrival, he politely told Dr. Clayton that the only person he would be willing to talk to was J. D. Brewster.

If he wasn't afforded the opportunity to see Brewster in a counseling session alone, he threatened to immediately leave the clinic without being evaluated by anyone. When Brewster walked into the room to greet his friend, the medical student was not certain why Arby wanted to have a private counseling session with no other professionals in attendance.

"Arby, the intake nurse said you were under a lot of stress but would only talk to me and me alone," Brewster said. "What's going on with you?"

"Something really bad went down that I witnessed, Brew," Arby said, "and I can't get it out of my mind. As you may recall, there was an incident at the prison last month. Two convicts were upset with the alleged poor quality of food and worn-out exercise equipment at the Sharpstown facility, so they took one of the correctional officers as a hostage. The fellow was a friend of mine, but I won't tell you his name because he wants to keep everything private as to what happened to him. What I am about to tell you was never reported to the news service."

"Let's hear it."

"To make their point," Fuller said, "the two convicts took my friend out to the central yard, and then they butt-raped him over and over again. The Texas Rangers were called in, and they brought in two badass gunslingers toting some serious hardware. I swear the scopes on their rifles were so big that those snipers probably could have read the fine print of the Houston Post newspaper as far away as the planet Mars. Sadly, though, those cards were never played."

"Why not?"

"Beats me," Arby answered. "The whole ordeal went on for over two hours, and my friend was incessantly raped the entire time. I watched the whole thing through my pair of binoculars. As horrible as it was, I felt compelled to watch the entire thing. After all, if those animals decided to slit the throat of my pal when they were through giving him the butt ram, I wanted to make certain I'd forever remember who those perpetrators were and what they looked like. As you probably have gathered, there are things that go on in the prison that the general public doesn't really want to know about. Sometimes justice can occur when you least expect it."

Brewster had already surmised that the Gulf Coast College of Medicine had clandestine contractual arrangements with Big Tom and his sons, Nick the Shiv and Joey the Bull, from the prison. As it was occasionally necessary to harvest body parts from the most despicable human refuse one could possibly imagine, what Arby Fuller had intimated was no surprise to the medical student.

"The Texas Rangers had the two convicts in the crosshairs of their high-powered scopes the entire time," Arby said. "The warden, Jana Neopoliticia, refused to give the okay to take the bastards out, as she apparently didn't want to have any blood on her own hands. As a general operating principal, it's her personal belief that those convicts were not guilty of the crimes they committed that landed them behind bars. Instead, she believes that our corrupt country, predominantly controlled by evil white people, was the root cause of their criminal behavior."

"That's absurd."

"Oh, is that so?" Arby answered sarcastically. "The story only gets better. Mind you, the warden, the two convicts, and my good friend who got raped nonstop for two hours are all white people, so I don't know exactly how the race card would come into play in such a situation. The warden allowed the two convicts to transfer to some other prison in the state of Texas, and there were no consequences for their evil deeds. My friend who got raped was awarded a compensatory package of two million dollars from the Texas Department of Corrections as long as he'll forever keep his mouth shut."

"Hush money?"

"You've got it figured out," Arby said. "The warden made everybody who witnessed the event sign nondisclosure agreements, but she was not aware that I'd seen everything. As I'd forgotten to sign the duty roster sheet when I reported to work at the prison on that fateful day, the administration didn't realize I was in the yard when it all went down. Since I didn't sign the nondisclosure clause, I'm telling everybody I know—and even people I don't know—about how corrupt the system has become."

"Arby, you've been emotionally traumatized, and I think it would be a good idea if I talked to Dr. Corka Sorass about your case," Brewster said. "Sorass should get you on a course of oral antidepressant medication right this minute."

Arby shook his head to indicate he would not be amenable to such a course of action. "It's not worth it. My application to the police academy got turned down because I was told that I have anger-management issues. What's the point anymore, Brew? Of late, I've even given some passing thoughts about punching my own time card."

"Arby, tell me right now what you're thinking about doing," Brewster said. "Have you been contemplating suicide?"

"It's crossed my mind," Arby answered. "I've considered eating a bullet. I'd make a point of doing it on the tile floor in the bathroom after I taped heavy plastic trash bags all over the walls and ceiling. If I made a big mess of myself, I wouldn't want to make it hard for somebody else to clean up all of that the bloody shit after Arby Fuller was long gone."

Alarmed, Brewster excused himself from his interview with the correctional officer and immediately went down the hallway to find an attending. Dr. Petra Clayton and Corka Sorass were conducting other evaluations at that time, and they had given explicit instructions to the intake nurses that they were not to be disturbed.

Brewster returned to the interview room to try to convince his friend to stay just a bit longer to chat with one of the staff members in the psychiatry department. Brewster correctly believed that the best clinical course of action would be for his friend Arby to go on a formal course of oral antidepressant medication in addition to receiving psychological counseling to help alleviate his trauma as a consequence of the horror he'd witnessed when his colleague was raped by two vicious convicts.

During Brewster's absence, Arby Fuller had correctly surmised that the student was going to try to employ strong-arm tactics to intercede with emergency psychiatric intervention, and that was something the correctional officer was not willing to consider at that time. When Brewster returned to the interview room, he discovered that Arby Fuller was long gone—maybe in more ways than one.

Once Dr. Sorass had completed his counseling session, Brewster finally had the opportunity to inform the attending of his concerns that Arby Fuller was going to commit suicide. An emergency forty-eight-hour psychiatric hold was placed on Arby Fuller, and he was hospitalized at the Gulf Coast facility for intense observation and psychiatric intervention against his will.

Arby was smart, however, and knew what to say, what to do, and how to act. Upon his release from the psychiatric lockdown unit, it was deemed that the correctional officer was no threat to himself or anybody else. If only that were the case...

—◁◻◫◻▷—

The Juneteenth Festival at Hermann Park was celebrated at the Miller Outdoor Theater on Friday, June 19, 1981. When constructed in the year 1968, the large outdoor venue was purposefully assembled with rusty iron panels and beams. Although it was considered an architectural masterpiece, Brewster nonetheless thought of the outdoor theater as an excuse for a tetanus booster just waiting to happen.

The medical student met up with the Dalton twins to enjoy contemporary black music that evening. As promised, the twins brought a cooler with snacks, including a large container of potato salad, barbecued beans, and ribs, while Brewster provided a Styrofoam container with cold adult beverages, as he had previously agreed. Although surprised to see a person of Caucasian persuasion at the Juneteenth celebration, the black attendees at the music concert were gracious and readily welcomed Brewster's presence at the festivities.

"About time you switched sides!" one young man wearing a colorful knit hat shouted out to Brewster. "Dig this; it ain't about race. It's about culture!"

The Dalton twins were mildly irritated when another young woman named Margo came by to strike up a conversation with J. D. Brewster.

"To be honest," Margo said, "I have never really had an opportunity to talk to a white boy before in a face-to-face situation. Is that messed up or what? You're cute! You're cute as a bug!"

It soon became apparent to the Dalton twins that this Margo character had no intention of leaving the park without Brewster in tow.

Brewster, for his part, was never able to see the big picture. He had no clue that the young woman who was flirting with him was creating a considerable amount of friction with the Dalton girls.

"Okay, skinny legs," D' Shea said, "it's time to jump on your broomstick and fly on out of here."

"Hang on, sister," Margo said. "An eight ball like you and your twin need to back out of my weave right about now. This is a big party, and it would be rude if I didn't have an opportunity to talk to all of the guests."

"We ain't your sister," D' Nae said, "and this ain't your party."

The twins were finally able to dispatch the interloper after a steely, stark stink eye and an additional snide comment or two. Finally, Margo took a powder.

"Wow," Brewster said, "Margo was cute as a bug!"

"Enough already!" the twins said in unison.

At the end of the evening, Brewster walked the young ladies back to their car, which was parked in the large, open lot in front of the zoo. There was no resolution as to what kind of relationship existed between Brewster and the Dalton girls.

"I imagine someday the three of us can determine once and for all if we truly have some kind of kinship or not," Brewster said.

D' Nae was enthusiastic about the prospective revelation. Her twin sister, however, had doubts.

"I don't know about all of that," D' Shea said. "Personally, I think the world needs to have mysteries that forever remain mysteries."

D' Nae could not see the benefit of self-imposed ignorance. "What do you mean, Baby Girl?"

Her twin sister became philosophical and countered with her own questions. "Don't you see? Would the world be as wondrous a place if it was finally proven that a creature like the Sasquatch actually did indeed exist?"

"I don't know," D' Nae answered.

"I think not!" her twin said. "Would the world be as wondrous a place if we ever actually found the Holy Grail?"

"I don't know," D' Nae answered.

"I think not!" her twin said. "Would the world be as wondrous a place if we actually ever knew if this white boy, J. D. Brewster, was our own flesh-and-blood half-sibling?"

"If I were indeed kin to you, what of it at this point in the course of human events?" the medical student said.

"Kinship is forever, I suppose. Nonetheless, maybe there are just some things that we really don't need to know about. What matters is this: if my cancer doesn't come back, Baby Girl and I will graduate from the U of H exactly one year from now," D' Shea answered. "We're both going to expect to see you at our graduation. Please promise us here and now that you'll be able to attend the ceremony."

Brewster was honored. "I wouldn't miss it for the world."

"Well, I know exactly what I want as a graduation present from you," D' Nae said. "I want you to chauffer me and Baby Girl on a road trip to California. We've never been, and we both want to go. I want you to get a black suit, white shirt, and skinny black tie to wear on the trip. I'll buy you a chauffer's hat to wear, and I'll feed you peeled grapes from the backseat of the car! I'll skewer a grape onto the end of each of my long and manicured fingernails, and I will wave my hand luxuriantly in front of your face. You can pop off each grape into your mouth at your own leisure. Of course, I'd make sure they were seedless grapes. After all, I wouldn't want you to have to spit out grape seeds from the driver's-side window at eighty miles an hour. Does that sound hot or what? How 'bout you, Baby Girl?"

D' Shea scoffed and said, "I don't know what's going on between you two right about now, but don't forget, J. D., you just might be our kin. Don't pay attention to any of that kinky shit that Baby Girl's talking about. I have my own request for a graduation present from you, Mr. Brewster."

With that, D' Shea got on her tiptoes and whispered something into Brewster's ear before giving him a kiss on the cheek.

"I'm downstream to you!" Brewster said as he laughed out loud. "Consider it done. You just have to live long enough to graduate from college, D' Shea. If you'll do your part, I'll make a solemn oath to you right now that I'll hold up my end of the bargain."

D' Nae put her hands on her hips and proceeded to scold both Brewster and her twin. "I don't know what's going on between you two right about now, but don't forget, J. D., you just might be our kin. Don't pay attention to any of that kinky shit that Baby Girl is talking about!"

After they exchanged hugs, the medical student relinquished his Styrofoam cooler to the Dalton twins before he wandered off to find his own parked car. It was time for everybody to go home.

D' Nae pointed to Brewster's Styrofoam cooler and spoke to her twin sister. "There's not much left to this, but stick it in the trunk anyhow. There's no sense in drawing the attention of the cops when you pull out of here."

Before Hermann Park was refurbished and reconfigured, there had been at one time in the remote past a narrow, paved northbound byway that cut into the heart of the 445-acre urban retreat. The road had intersected Cambridge Street just east and north of Hermann Hospital back in the year 1981.

To make the park more pedestrian friendly, that street eventually had been rooted out many years later. The extensive landscaping subsequently engineered ensured there was no residual evidence that the road had ever existed, although any lifelong Houstonian from that time would have been able to readily attest that the street had indeed been present before Brewster graduated from medical school back in the early 1980s. To attend the Juneteenth Festival with the Dalton twins, the medical student had parked his car on that street.

Those who'd attended the Juneteenth celebration departed for home, and there was an eerie silence in the park on the late spring night as Brewster walked back to his Mustang. Brewster kept looking over his shoulder to make certain he was not being followed. If he was going to be ambushed in the same fashion that had taken down his friend Willy, he was certain the attack would come from the rear. He felt considerable relief when he saw that his car was only about ninety feet away. What was there to worry about? After all, he was only about the length of a football field away from the bright lights of the Texas Medical Center.

Brewster noticed a car parked about twenty feet in front of his own vehicle, and oddly enough, it looked like the 1970 Cutlass previously owned by Irene Segulla. Of course, after Irene had been murdered, the car had been briefly possessed by her niece, Stella Link, before it recently disappeared from the employee parking lot.

It couldn't be the same car, however, Brewster surmised, as under the mercury-vapor streetlamp, it was obvious the automobile was shiny black, and the Cutlass in question had a bronze paint scheme. Therefore, he thought, it must have been an odd coincidence.

However, as Brewster approached his Mustang, he suddenly felt that something was awry. He could clearly see that the black Cutlass parked in tandem to his car had a Houston Oilers bumper sticker in the exact location of the one on the Oldsmobile owned by Irene Segulla and subsequently possessed by Stella Link.

J. D. Brewster realized he was in a world of trouble when two black men got out of the Cutlass and started to walk toward him. He was jolted to see that the men were wearing black jackets and black mock turtlenecks and had goatees. They were dressed exactly like the two men who had murdered Irene Segulla a year ago, and one of them walked with a noticeable limp. They were already waiting for him at the trunk of the Mustang when he arrived.

Brewster immediately recognized that the slightly shorter fellow was Darryl Hewritt, but it was the first time Brewster had taken a good look at the taller accomplice, whose name was still a mystery to the medical student at that time. The taller man said, "Skew me, my man. Do you know where da white wimmins is at? We wants to put you into da trunk of dis car and take you for a li'l' ride."

As Brewster correctly anticipated that he was about to get beaten to death with a lead pipe, it was imperative for him to take the offensive. "No, I don't think so. If you bastards are planning on killing me, you're going to have to do it right here and right out in the open on this street. I want to make sure God's watching all of this right now so he'll be able to issue both of you sons of bitches a one-way ticket straight to hell."

Brewster momentarily studied the faces of both men before he turned to the lesser of the two urban thugs and said, "Well, hello, Darryl Hewritt! I'm glad you brought your scumbag friend with you tonight."

What could possibly go wrong when three individuals with racist tendencies were thrown together into a high-speed blender set on frappé? The three volatile individuals probably should have been kept a lot farther away than arm's length from each other.

The invectives the three primitive, tribal warriors were about to exchange would be as gut-wrenching as they would be epic in their incendiary magnitude.

Brewster tried to provoke his deadly adversaries in an effort to bide his time as part of an escape strategy. He turned to Big Nig and said, "Well, I have not seen this nasty yard ape since you bastards murdered Irene Segulla a year ago."

"How in the world do you know the name of my colleague?" the larger thug asked. "Look like we got us here a blue-eyed white-devil slave master who been keepin' da black man down, huh?"

During his life, Brewster had been able to readily counter any racial slurs levied upon him with loquacious insults that were equally as inflammatory.

"Wake up!" Brewster said. "My eyes are green, not blue. I was never a slave owner, and you were never slaves. Get over it. Even my great-great-grandfather who fought for the Confederacy never owned slaves. In fact, the black folks who worked for great-great-granddad actually ended up buying my family's ranch after the war."

"What of it?"

"Now, if those black folks could pull off something that meaningful and constructive only eleven years after the war ended, why don't you ignorant bastards get off your lazy asses and do something meaningful and constructive with your own lives?" Brewster asked.

"Such as?" Darryl asked.

"I have an idea. Why don't you go out and get a fucking job like everybody else? The only people holding you back are yourselves. Now, even though my great-great-grandpappy didn't own any slaves per se, I'm certain he would've made an exception for you big black bucks. Yes indeed, you're fine physical specimens that would make proper porch monkeys."

Smeg Nog was bemused that the verbose yet soon-to-be dead white man was a brave, bold, and bodacious ballbuster. Assuredly,

Nog soon would be returning the favor both figuratively and literally. "Is you a racist?" Nog asked.

"Let me think about that intellectually stimulating query for just one moment," Brewster answered, trying to stall for precious time. "If not yet, I'm certainly warming up to the idea. I suspect I'll most certainly be a racist before the night is over, though! Thank you for asking."

"Just as I figured, Casper!" Big exclaimed.

"Of course, you boys should be looking in the mirror right about now," Brewster said, and it was clear he was not about to take his foot off of the accelerator of racial insults. "You make me laugh. Calling me a racist is a bit like the pot calling the kettle black. Well, if we flip over to the obverse side of this magic coin of ethnic diversity, perhaps a more appropriately offensive idiom should be declared in this particular situation, where the pot is actually calling the kettle a Negro. Did I offend you? It was certainly my intent. Man, oh man! Was that funny or what?"

Brewster chortled out loud as if he were a man laughing in the face of certain death. Come to think of it, he was.

"Say the N-word. Say it right now, and I'll drop you. I'll do it quick, and you won't suffer very much. I'll just stand behind you and take you out with just one blow to the back of your head," Big Nig said. "Otherwise, I'm going to nail you to a cross, and I'm going to burn you alive. I'll even wear a black sheet and a pointy black hat. Well, hell's bells, honky man! I'll become a black Klansman. I'm going to start a new terrorist organization, and I'll be coming to a neighborhood near you. Before I kill you, I need you to tell me exactly how you know my partner's name."

"Oh, Darryl never told you how we met? Well, it was at the police station. Darryl was spilling his guts regarding everything he knew about you."

If Brewster had any chance to escape from his predicament, it was now or never. He turned back to Smeg Nog and continued to berate the junior partner. "Darryl, before you steal my car and light me up, there's one thing about you that I just don't recall. Maybe you can fill in the details. After all, you should at least honor the very last request of a man who's about to be murdered. I just don't remember at this time what happened when Willy Mammon took a swan dive off of that six-foot ladder at the police station. Did my friend blow out your right leg, or maybe it was your left leg?"

"You weren't there!" Smeg said. "I don't remember you."

"Well, now you just hurt my feelings," Brewster said, "because I certainly remember meeting you. However, as I don't remember which of your legs was injured, I'm just going to have to cover all of the bases."

With that, Brewster unleashed a furious blow to the groin of Smeg Nog with the toe of his shoe, causing the junior criminal partner to fall to his knees. The medical student made a mad dash for the Mustang, but the big man closed quickly. Brewster never made it. Big smashed the lead pipe across Brewster's neck, and the blow knocked him off his feet. When Brewster slammed into the ground, he felt agonizing pain radiating through his neck and down into his shoulder. *Good God!* Brewster thought. *These bastards are going to kill me!*

In desperation, Brewster rolled under the car. He grabbed on to the drive shaft and held on fast to try to prevent his assailants from pulling him out from the bottom of the vehicle. Maybe someone had heard the commotion. Maybe someone would call for the police. Maybe some condemned evil soul cast into hell could get a nice, tall glass of ice water once in a while. Maybe, but not bloody likely. Sweat stung his eyes, and pain clouded his reason. While the thugs couldn't finish him off with the lead pipe while he was still underneath the Mustang, he was trapped. It would only be a matter of time before they would extricate him from his modest shelter of temporary refuge.

"Drag him out, Apoo!" Smeg said in a weakened, raspy voice as he continued to suffer from the vicious blow he'd received to his reproductive organs.

Suddenly, Brewster was presented with a new clue to the identity of Smeg's partner: the larger assailant was apparently named Apoo. Brewster had no idea whether Apoo was a first or last name, but at that moment, it didn't really matter.

If Brewster could only hold out long enough, somebody would surely come down that street at one time or another. If so, then maybe his lethal adversaries would simply be scared away, and the medical school student would live to fight another day. Unfortunately, that would not be the case. As fate would determine, no Good Samaritan was destined to come down the road that dreadful night and successfully disperse the melee.

Finally, Smeg Nog regained his breath after the swift kick to his scrotum. He dusted himself off as he rose from the pavement to declare, "Well, Apoo, I do believe it's time to teach this white-devil slave master a lesson he'll never forget."

"It look like white boy here don't want to come out and play," Big Nig said. "Don't be coy, Casper. We ain't done with you. We ain't done with you by a long shot! Come on out, and we can play a little game of ghetto stick ball."

Try as they might, Smeg Nog and Big Nig were unable to expose Brewster's head from underneath the bottom of the car, which would have easily afforded his assailants the opportunity to crush Brewster's skull.

Smeg Nog decided to do the next best thing. He turned to his partner in crime. "Well, Snow White here just busted my balls. It's time for us to return the favor. Hey, Casper, I hope you weren't planning on having any children, because we is about to remove you from da gene pool. If there was only one white boy left on this damned planet, that would be one too many white boys altogether as far as I'm concerned."

"I'm not planning on going anywhere, asshole!" Brewster said.

"Now, that's the fighting spirit I'd expect out of a subhuman piglet like you." Smeg laughed. "As far as da white wimmins go, dat be a ho of a different color. My man here and I be rapin' in them white bitches up da ass all da live long, and if we had da chance, we be doin' it until Gabriel blows Bevo. I'd love to keep you around jus' so you could watch me be doin' yo' nasty-ass bitch mama like dat."

"You don't know my mama," Brewster said valiantly. "She totes a straight razor. If you roll up on her, she'll cut your balls off and shove them up your ass, you filthy animal. She hates Negroes—and apparently with good reason."

The medical student should not have continued to antagonize his two black adversaries. He was about to make matters a lot worse for himself.

The two assailants were able to pull Brewster's legs free from underneath the car, which exposed the medical student's pelvis. While Smeg Nog pried Brewster's legs apart, Big Nig enthusiastically reared back with the lead pipe.

"It's time to rack 'em and crack 'em!" While the two angry thugs beat Brewster mercilessly in the groin with a lead pipe, Smeg Nog gleefully enhanced the recreational interlude by singing the tune made famous by Walt Disney's Seven Dwarves: "Whistle While You Work."

Brewster had previously undergone a left orchiectomy for an undescended testicle years ago, before he was even an adolescent. That meant he was only endowed with a right testicle occupying his scrotum at the time he was receiving the beatdown.

Sadly, J. D. Brewster was fully aware of what was about to happen next. He braced himself as best as he could for the inevitable pending assault upon his already marginal reproductive capabilities, but at 11:48 p.m. on June 19, 1981, Brewster's remaining right testicle finally exploded after multiple, repeated ball-busting blows to his groin. When the medical student lost consciousness, the two assailants were finally able to completely extract their unresponsive victim out from the undercarriage of the old Mustang.

"Let's get out of here," Smeg said. "I'll take the lead in my Cutlass, and then you follow me in this asshole's Mustang."

"Let's take dis car straight to the chop shop," Big replied. "We need to thoroughly disassemble the white boy's Mustang, and then we need to thoroughly disassemble the white boy."

Smeg Nog pointed at the seriously injured and unresponsive J. D. Brewster before concluding, "There is not much left to this, but stick it in the trunk anyhow. There's no sense in drawing the attention of the cops when you pull out of here."

3

POSITIVE TAILLIGHT SIGN

When Brewster regained consciousness, he became immediately terrified when he realized he was trapped in the trunk of his own Mustang. He knew that if he could not escape from his dire predicament, his assailants would murder him as soon as they arrived at some secure and clandestine location. It was hard for Brewster to concentrate, as it felt as if his pelvis was on fire. He was wedged firmly into the car trunk, essentially immobilized in a fetal position. Brewster found he could barely maneuver from being trapped on the left side of his body. The pain in his groin was excruciating.

Most men recognized the horrific sensation of being racked. It was a rather crude reference as to what happened when a male sustained a painful blow to the groin, and the testicles sustained a jarring concussion. The pain radiated through the pelvis and into the lower abdomen. The unpleasant experience was so intense that it would invariably drop a man to his knees. If the magnitude of the blow to the testicles was high enough on the Richter scale of being racked, such an insult could even cause acute nausea and vomiting.

Anybody who ever had enjoyed watching a professional football game on television had no doubt witnessed the visage of being racked. When it occurred, it appeared as if one of the players on the field had been sniped from the end-zone cheap seats with several hot, smoking rounds emitted from the barrel of a Barrett M107A1 .50-caliber rifle.

Once racked, the injured football player would invariably roll about on the turf with bulging eyes and saliva foaming at the mouth. Without fail, the color commentator, who was most likely a retired athlete, would smirk while he proceeded to broadcast the offhand comment that the injured player in question either had his bell rung or perhaps had gotten the wind knocked out of him. Oh yeah, that was the ticket.

When a sports fan heard such an inaccurate expression being spewed over the airways during a televised football game, the viewer could rest assured that the injured player in question had just had his testicles drop-kicked through the goal posts.

The colloquial expression racked referred to what happened at the beginning of a game of pool. Billiard balls were positioned in the triangular rack on a pool table before one of the players slammed the white cue ball into the triangular assembly to figuratively and literally break the congregation of billiard balls at the start of the competition.

Well, that allegorical reference turned out to be a perfect description of what Brewster had experienced, but unlike with simply getting racked, the pain Brewster was forced to endure was unrelenting. Somehow, the injured student had to stay focused on how he could extricate himself from the trunk of the car despite his physical anguish. Unfortunately for Brewster, that would turn out to be a tall order, as the only testicle he possessed had been traumatically pulverized in the assault he had sustained from the two vicious thugs who'd kidnapped him.

Having only limited motion in his free right arm, Brewster was nonetheless able to find the small tool kit he kept in the trunk of the Mustang. With great difficulty, he was able to unlatch the lid of the toolbox, and he immediately found a medium-sized pair of vise grips that he would need to aid in his escape.

Brewster's old Mustang hadn't originally left the factory with a cable-actuated trunk-release mechanism that a driver or passenger could operate with a lever from the interior cabin of the vehicle. Brewster had easily installed an aftermarket one as a convenience feature, and it was a simple device to operate. The floor-mounted lever that would open the trunk was affixed to the floorboard adjacent to the window-side seat rail. The lever would place tension on the release cable that ran underneath the floorboard carpet all the way into the trunk of the car. The distal end of the cable was affixed to the lock mechanism of the trunk.

All Brewster had to do was use the vise grips to grab the end of the trunk-release cable and then pull it firmly in a lateral direction. Doing so would pop open the trunk, but unfortunately, the task at hand was easier said than done. On multiple occasions, Brewster tried to affix the vise grips to the end of the cable, but as he only had one free hand, he had great difficulty in adjusting the proximity knob that controlled the amount of force required to make the vise grips bite and lock into position.

After failing several times, Brewster began to weep in frustration, as he believed his life was about to come to a violent end. He cried out, "God, please get me out of here!"

As he was being unwillingly ferried about town, his next attempt to pull the trunk-release cable was finally successful. The lock popped open. Brewster used his right arm to keep the lid of the trunk in a down position, as he had to wait until the car came to a stoplight to bail out and make his escape by running out into the traffic directly behind his Mustang.

Big Nig, who had commandeered Brewster's Mustang, was

trailing Smeg Nog, who was driving the lead Oldsmobile Cutlass. Big heard the trunk lock pop open, but fortunately, he misinterpreted the noise as Brewster simply thrashing about in the back of the vehicle.

"I hope you had a nice nap, white boy," Big said. "I know it must be a bit cozy back there, but don't worry. In about another ten minutes, all of your worries will be over."

Brewster felt the Mustang roll to a gentle stop, and he noted what must have been cross traffic coming through at an unidentified intersection. He loved his car and always would, but it was time to say goodbye once and for all to not only his hot rod but also the hoodlums who had taken him hostage.

Brewster threw the trunk lid wide open and jumped out just as the light turned green. Big Nig realized Brewster had escaped out of the trunk of the car, but by that time, the thug had already entered the intersection and was committed to proceed. Big Nig said, "Damn! White boy got away! He got away, and now he knows my name!"

He stood on the car horn to try to get the attention of Smeg Nog in the lead vehicle, but it was too late, as their would-be victim had just escaped their clutches. Brewster hobbled over to the driver's-side window of the car that had briskly stopped directly behind the Mustang, and he saw that the driver was an elderly black woman with flawless white hair.

"Please! You have to help me!" Brewster said. "The man in that car ahead of you kidnapped me, and I've just escaped! I have been seriously injured. Please. You have to help me!"

Without a word, the woman hit the automatic passenger-side door lock on her sedan and allowed Brewster to enter her vehicle. She boldly made a sharp U-turn right in the middle of the intersection in front of oncoming traffic, and then she sped away to take Brewster back to the Texas Medical Center.

Although Brewster was doubled over in pain, he suddenly

became aware that the woman who had rescued him was none other than the floating nurse from the temp pool. When his long-term memory banks were finally somehow rebooted, Brewster was able to recall that the woman driving him back toward the Texas Medical Center was none other than Sister Buena!

Brewster was awestruck when he remembered that it was Sister Buena who had come over to his house the day his father passed away. When Brewster was being tortured at the child-care center when he was but a mere lad, it was Sister Buena who'd rescued him from the wrath of the evil Grinch beast, Mrs. Arlington. He also remembered that it was Sister Buena who had interceded when he and his brother, Bill, had been put into an oven when their deranged mother attempted to gas them both to death.

"Oh my God, you're Sister Buena!" Brewster said with a trembling voice. "I remember your name. How did you get here? How could this possibly be? I was only a small child when, when–"

Sister Buena looked impassively at J. D. Brewster and replied, "Well, well, well, if it's not Mr. J. D. Brewster. Yes, I have known you all of your life, and I'm somewhat surprised you don't know what I am by now. I thought you were brighter than that."

"How did you possibly find me? Brewster asked. "How did you know I was in trouble?"

"Well, you're the one who asked for help when you were trapped in the trunk of the car," Sister Buena replied as she pulled into the emergency room entrance of the hospital. "We're here now. I believe you're strong enough to get out of the car and make your way through the emergency room doors. I wish I could stay with you, but I have to go now. I'm on a very tight schedule."

No sooner had Brewster made his exit from the vehicle than Sister Buena pulled back onto Cambridge Street and disappeared into the northbound traffic on Fannin.

—◈—

Brewster never made it to the registration desk, as he stumbled and fell upon the floor of the waiting-area lobby in the emergency room. Medical staff loaded Brewster onto a gurney and took him back to an emergency room stall after he explained to the registrar what had happened to him.

After a wallet biopsy confirmed his identification and insurance status, J. D. overheard the triage nurse explain the details of his circumstances to the on-call emergency room resident physician, Dr. Paul "Pooty" Shorts.

"We have one of our own here!" the triage nurse exclaimed. "Medical student J. D. Brewster was assaulted at Hermann Park while attending the Juneteenth celebration, and he sustained significant injuries to his groin and perineum. We don't know exactly how he got back over here from the park, because at this time, he can barely walk. Apparently, he's here as a consequence of a positive taillight sign, as best as anybody can tell."

—━━━━━━

The nurse was referring to an all-too-common event that occurred at the emergency room: a critically ill or injured patient would get dropped off in front of the emergency room entrance, and the vehicle that had conveyed the patient to the hospital would simply speed off into the dark night without as much as a fare-thee-well.

Positive taillight sign was also an appropriate expression to utilize when an obtunded individual was dumped in the lobby without any obvious available friends or family members in the vicinity who could readily explain the nature of the patient's illness or injury.

Should not somebody remain behind in those kinds of situations to at least offer the patient emotional or physical support? Perhaps such expectations were unrealistic in this modern epoch, although a coherent medical history as to what illness might have befallen the patient in question was obviously imperative.

Needless to say, positive taillight sign was a derisive term that reflected emergency room staff's frustrations regarding the all-too-frequent lack of a critical corroborating history about the patient's underlying medical problems, medications, surgical history, transgenerational family medical issues, drug allergies, use of alcohol or tobacco, drug use (illicit or otherwise), and the like.

A positive taillight sign, sadly, often meant the emergency room staff were about to embark into the realm of veterinarian medicine, when they had to render medical aid to a critically ill individual incapable of any meaningful or coherent verbal communication.

The emergency room resident physician addressed the triage nurse about the patient recumbent upon the gurney in front of him. "Wait just one minute. I know Brewster. Are you telling me that this idiot went to Hermann Park tonight?"

"Apparently so," the nurse answered.

"He's, well, a white man," Shorts said.

"Obviously," the nurse said.

"You're telling me he went to the Juneteenth celebration?"

"Asked and answered," the nurse said in exasperation.

"What a dumbass. Juneteenth is for black people and black people only. If somebody beat the holy shit out of him at the Juneteenth celebration, he's got nobody to blame but himself. Jesus, what was he thinking?" Dr. Shorts said.

"Attention, Kmart shoppers!" Brewster cried out. "I'm J. D. Brewster. Come talk to me, damn it! I speak English, you know!"

"Beats the shit out of me," the nurse answered Pooty Shorts while completely ignoring the medical student.

"Did he not expect that something like this could happen to him if he went to Hermann Park tonight? If you ask me, he got what he deserved," Dr. Shorts said.

"I agree," the triage nurse replied, "but just because he's a flaming moron doesn't mean we don't have to take care of him. Even an idiot like Brewster deserves at least some modicum of medical care, albeit the least we could possibly muster on his behalf would be all that he really deserves."

Although Brewster was alert and communicative at that moment, his colleagues continued to openly debase him as if he wasn't even present.

"Hello?" Brewster said. "I'm right here. I'm not dead, you know!"

J. D. was merely a peon who didn't deserve to be graced by the divine radiance of the emergency room staff. As Dr. Shorts and the nurse continued harshly critique the medical student and openly laugh at him for foolishly attending the Juneteenth celebration, Brewster quickly accepted the likelihood that much-needed emergent medical attention might not be forthcoming anytime soon. Why should he expect anything less? It was apparently nothing more than Brewster's appointed time to be bombed from high altitude with atomized and aerosolized shit.

When the radiology technicians finally came down to transport Brewster away for a scrotal ultrasound and a CT scan of his abdomen and pelvis, the medical student had been waiting in the emergency room stall for more than two hours. The radiologist informed Brewster that he had a fracture involving his pubic ramus bone, and his right testicle had been ruptured. Of course, no left testicle was identified, as it had been surgically extracted years before.

Of great concern, the imaging studies confirmed that Brewster's scrotum was filling up with blood. Sadly, in all likelihood, Brewster would require an emergency orchiectomy to remove what little remained of his exploded and now completely useless right testicle.

After he was transported back to the emergency room stall,

Brewster's pain had not abated in the least. J. D. wondered why nobody in the emergency room had even offered him any analgesics, despite the student's repeated yet futile requests for such a merciful and compassionate intervention.

Despite the fact that he would periodically cry out in agony, no medical student, intern, resident, or attending even bothered to look upon Brewster after he returned from his round-trip to the radiology department.

By the fourth hour of his emergency room visit, Brewster's scrotum was the size of a large cantaloupe. All of the usual skin folds in the region had been stretched out as flat as a flapjack, and the epidermis of the scrotal sac was rendered as thin as a sheet of cellophane.

When his scrotum had taken on a bluish hue and it was clear his own colleagues in the emergency room had abandoned him, Brewster crawled off of his gurney and went to the red crash cart parked in the hallway. Nobody bothered to stop him or even ask him what was going on when he broke the seal of the crash cart and started to pull out its contents.

The medical student palmed the supplies he needed and casually discarded the rest of the sterile—and most assuredly expensive—other extraneous medical equipment and medications upon the floor. At that point, he didn't give a shit about anything—or anybody, for that matter. Brewster found a number-ten scalpel blade but no handle. He found Betadine swabs, a vial of 2 percent local lidocaine anesthetic, several five-cubic-centimeter syringes, and a twenty-five-gauge needle to help him with the surgical procedure he was about to perform upon himself. He would have preferred a smaller twenty-seven-gauge needle to ram into his ball sack, but Brewster had to make the best of the situation.

Brewster washed down his swollen scrotal sac with three consecutive Betadine-impregnated cotton-tipped swabs and then injected the midline scrotal raphe with the local lidocaine anesthetic. The raphe was the midline demarcation that separated the right and left hemispheres of the scrotal sack.

The medical student was surprised he couldn't even feel the sharp stab of the hypodermic needle when he injected the lidocaine anesthetic into the skin. Brewster didn't realize the intrascrotal hemorrhage he had suffered had caused the skin of the scrotum to get pulled taut enough to induce a local and regional autoanesthetization. As it turned out, Brewster likely could have made a surgical incision on his own scrotum without using any anesthesia at all.

Brewster subsequently inserted the number-ten blade into the scrotal raphe and proceeded to make a long midline incision, which essentially was the technique that an upscale steakhouse chef would employ to butterfly an eight-ounce medium-rare filet mignon. Upon making the incision, the pressure was relieved, and a copious amount of serosanguineous fluid gushed out from the open wound as if a dam had been breached. Oddly, as that occurred, Brewster recalled the oft-recited scripture from John 19:34.

The relief Brewster felt was immediate, but it was time to get somebody's attention. After all, should he not get admitted to the urology service for further appropriate management? Brewster was wearing a hospital gown that was open in the back. As blood and fluids continued to ooze out of his scrotal vault, Brewster popped off the gurney and started to walk about the emergency room as if he were Diogenes the Cynic in search of the elusive honest man. Brewster left behind a splattered trail of bloody fluid and tissue fragments, which were the terminal, residual elements of his ruptured gonad.

Realizing that his life would never be the same and that he would never be the proud progenitor of any biological offspring, Brewster recalled the ancient conversation Diogenes had had with Alexander the Great. From his self-imposed exile, while living in a barrel, Diogenes had exclaimed to the Macedonian conqueror, "What you have taken away, you can never give back!"

Those words further fueled Brewster's downward spiral into the realm of an all-consuming hostile, sadistic sociopathy. He wandered into the empty break room and made certain that his bloody scrotal contents somehow managed to get smeared across the front locker door of the triage nurse and also the on-call emergency room resident physician, Pooty Shorts. After all, as long as he was taking a pleasure cruise about the neighborhood, he might as well start marking his territory.

On June 19, 1981, without the endowment of any remaining functional reproductive gonads, Brewster came to embrace the fact that he had been thoroughly transformed into a dark, angry, prejudicial, mean, and nasty son of a bitch.

From then on, he would levy unmitigated grief and retribution upon anybody who pissed him off. While strolling about on his mission to draw attention to his personal, painful, problematic predicament, Brewster gleefully sang the song made famous by Walt Disney's Seven Dwarves: "Whistle While You Work."

—◁▥◁◦▥▷—

What happened to the proverbial squeaky wheel? Contingent upon the circumstances as to who, what, where, or when, the squeaky wheel might get either option A, the grease, or option B, the street.

It was clear to anybody who witnessed the trail of blood and fluid on the emergency room floor that J. D. Brewster had been transfigured into the squeaky wheel incarnate. Fortunately for J. D. Brewster, he would get option A. Bypassing the emergency room staff, the radiologist who had reviewed the medical student's devastating imaging studies notified the senior urology fellow, Dr. I. P. Stream, and his attending, Dr. Freewater, about the catastrophic injury J. D. Brewster had sustained to his reproductive armamentarium.

Dr. Stream pulled back the curtain on the emergency room stall and said, "Hello, love monkey! It's been awhile, but I am sorry to see you under these circumstances. I'll complete my residency training by the end of this month. I always hoped I'd have an opportunity to visit with you again but not under a situation as dire as this. Dr. Freewater and I reviewed your imaging studies with the radiology service. It looks like somebody wanted to hurt you."

"I believe they succeeded in their endeavors," Brewster said.

"Your right testicle has been run through a wood chipper at high speed," Stream said. "It looks like there's essentially nothing left of it. I assume you must have had left testicular cancer in the past. There is no evidence of a left gonad hiding anywhere in your ball sack."

"Right off the bat, I'd like to personally thank you for your professional and compassionate demeanor," Brewster said sarcastically. "However, your clinical assessment regarding my past medical history is not quite correct. In my youth, I was afflicted with cryptorchidism, and I underwent a preadolescent reparative orchidopexy. Unfortunately, it appeared intraoperatively that my left testicle was blighted, so they simply yanked it out of me. That was many, many years ago."

Dr. Freewater arrived and shook Brewster's hand before saying, "Let's take a look at the damage that's been done." While Dr. Freewater visually inspected Brewster's perineum, he said, "That's a pretty ragged incision along the raphe. Tell me—which one of these emergency room knuckle heads butchered you like this?"

"I'm sorry you don't appreciate my fledgling surgical skills," Brewster replied, "but I did this to myself. After I'd been down here for a total of four hours without anybody even seeing me except for the radiologist who originally read my imaging studies, my scrotum was as large as a volleyball. To be honest, I thought I did a pretty good job in evacuating my own ball sack."

"Good God," Freewater said. "You actually drained yourself?"

"I did the deed," Brewster answered. "I'm looking forward to also performing an appendectomy on myself someday, or maybe a frontal lobotomy. All kidding aside, I was in agony, and I simply took matters into my own hands. The pressure has been relieved, but I'm still in a great deal of pain."

"When was the last time you had anything to eat or drink?" Stream asked.

"As we're already coming up on six o'clock in the morning," Brewster answered, "I can assure you I've not consumed anything for at least the last nine hours. The only thing that's keeping me upright at this time is the IV fluid that's been dripping into me after my arrival. Not only did I have to evacuate the contents of my own scrotum, but I even had to change out my own bags of lactated Ringer's solution. I shit you not! I think they just forgot about my sorry ass back here."

"That's pathetic," Freewater said, "but things are about to change right about now. Stream and I are going to do our level best to get you tuned up, and the sooner the better. I'm going to file an incident report about the negligence that has occurred here this night regarding your care—or, should I say, lack thereof—but in all likelihood, the hospital administration will probably only shitcan the complaint. After all, you're just a medical student."

"Thanks," Brewster replied. "I resemble that remark."

"I want you to knock out his H and P and then get it dictated on the stat line," Freewater told Dr. Stream. "Find out who's on-call for anesthesia. Since Ron Chelsea passed away, that schedule has been all screwed up."

He then turned to J. D. Brewster and said, "I'm sorry about what happened to you, Brew, but I don't think I'll need to belabor what the long-term consequences will mean to you now that both of your testicles are gone. That just sucks for you in a major-league way, but remember, life is not fair. I'm getting out of here now to stoke up the fires for OR suite number two, and I'll see you upstairs before the anesthesiologist blows nighty-night gas up your schnoz. I promise we'll take good care of you, buddy boy."

Before Brewster was transported out of the emergency room for his belated surgery, I. P. Stream said, "Say, Brewster, let me ask you something, and this is a serious question. Right now, your intrascrotal domain has been compromised. We can't put prosthetic testicles in you at this time, but perhaps you'd want some in the future. What do you think?"

Brewster thought Dr. Stream's concern about the ultimate contents of the scrotum was but a trivial matter. Nonetheless, J. D. paused for a moment before he offered a genuine reply.

"Let me give you a serious answer to your serious question," Brewster said. "Yes, I'll opt for prosthetic testicles as long as you can assure me they will be made out of brass and will be the size of baseballs."

"Nice!" Stream replied.

"I must insist that each prosthetic gonad get personally signed by Roger McGuinn, who was the front man for the Byrds, before you suture these big brass 'nads back up into my empty scrotum. I want them to clang together when I walk, and I would certainly appreciate an audible melodic resonance that will meet or exceed the tonality achieved by the bells of Rhymney. I hope I'm not asking for too much here, but do you think you can pull that off for me, sport?"

"Okay, smart-ass," I. P. Stream said with a smile. "Now, I've never been to Wales, but let's see what I can do for you. I've one last delicate issue to talk to you about. Before we take you into surgery, we're obligated to ask you if you would want us to initiate complete resuscitative efforts or would prefer a DNR code status if things go south during your operation."

"I still have a lot of mayhem to commit before I cash in my chips," Brewster replied emphatically. "I want a full-court press. Now, if my heart and lungs quit working altogether and you bozos do a slow code or maybe even pop open a can of Mr. Pibb while I'm being transferred to the eternal care unit, I'm going to come back to haunt your ass! Entiendes?"

"I do indeed."

"All kidding aside, I need to tell you something. You and Dr. Freewater have to patch me up as best as you can. There are two men out there walking around in the city of Houston who did this to me, and if it is the last thing I ever do, I'll make them pay for this. After I accomplish this task, I'm certain I'll be going straight to hell. I'll not only expect it, but I'll deserve it, I tell you. To be frank, Dr. Stream, I'm actually okay with all of that."

The resident physician gave Brewster a military salute. "You're coming in loud and clear, mi amigo."

⊷⊶

When Brewster awakened postoperatively, he immediately discovered that a large Foley catheter had been jammed into his edematous penis. The inflated Foley balloon was lodged snugly in his bladder, and it caused a sensation that he needed to urinate. He forced his bladder to contract, but it had no bearing on the discomfort that the indwelling Foley catheter induced.

"Nurse!" Brewster cried out. "I have a burning sensation in my urethral meatus at the tip of my penis. It's killing me!" Brewster was annoyed when he realized that his nurse happened to be none other than Ben Fielder's girlfriend, Missy Brownwood. It was not that Brewster disliked Missy, but she was a notorious gossipmonger.

"Quit whining," Missy said. "The Foley cath stays in for now."

Another annoying issue was the surgical drain tube that had been purposefully left in his scrotum. The drain tube had been placed intraoperatively to help evacuate the postsurgical blood and fluid that otherwise would have assuredly continued to accumulate.

"What in hell is this drain tube poking through my ball sack?" Brewster rudely asked.

"It's a Penrose," Missy answered. "Quit playing with it, or I will tie your hands down to the bed rails."

Just then, correctional officer Arby Fuller and the research scientist, Zip Talbot, entered the room and began to serenade the medical student with a song they sang to the tune of "Primrose Lane," originally recorded by Jerry Wallace back in 1959. "Penrose drain! Life's a holiday when a Penrose drain—just a holiday when a Penrose drain—is in you!"

Brewster howled with laughter but realized it was the first time he had seen the correctional officer since Arby's visit to the psychiatry department, when Arby had professed suicidal ideations.

"How are you, Arby? I've been worried about you."

"I'm good, Brew," Arby answered. "I want to let you know that I've taken up a hobby that has helped defuse a lot of my aggression."

"What might that be?" Brewster asked.

"Hunting!" Arby exclaimed. "I feel really good when I can blast the holy fuck out of some unwitting, innocent, and innocuous lower vertebrate life-form into smithereens! I'm feeling so calm and serene right about now, that I'm thinking about becoming a Buddhist monk!"

"Wow!" Brewster exclaimed. "I'm really glad you found something to do that's so productive and fulfilling. Obviously, killing other living beings for pure pleasure offers incalculable ecological benefits to the world at large. Well done!"

Brewster then turned his attention to Zip Talbot. "Hey, Talbot, tell me something: I've always wondered how you got your nickname, Zip. Is that supposed to pay homage somehow to our established postal zoning system?"

"Hardly," Talbot answered. "It's an onomatopoeia."

"How so?"

"As you know," Talbot explained, "I burn through girlfriends like a box of matches. Zip is the sound that all the ladies hear when I'm pulling up my trousers and beating a hasty path for the front door!"

"That makes sense," Brewster replied. "By the way, what's your real first name and that one might actually find on your birth certificate?"

"Zipper."

"What?!"

Later that day, Brewster's next visitor was none other than Dr. Denny Sassman, whose mannerisms were cordial yet oddly businesslike. After they exchanged superficial pleasantries, Denny seemed somewhat cool and aloof. Denny was renowned for being a boisterous individual, and his current atypical reserved demeanor was not lost on Brewster.

"Professor," Brewster said, "I've known you for quite some time, and I can tell something's on your mind. Tell me what's going on."

"Look, Brewster," Sassman said, "everybody in the research department feels terrible about what happened to you, but difficult decisions had to be made. It's quite clear that you're out of commission, and you'll not be able to tackle the Angry Simian Fecal-Projectile Study in the near future. It's a time-sensitive project, and it was absolutely mandatory for you to jump into it immediately after your psychiatry rotation finished. Your unfortunate circumstance has forced my hand to select another braniac to carry the mantle."

"Denny," Brewster pleaded, "don't boot me off the study."

"Too late," Sassman said. "As of this moment, we've now ended your enrollment in the dual-training program. This administrative decision is final."

Brewster should not have been surprised, because after all, it was a well-established fact that the Gulf Coast College of Medicine didn't tolerate any signs of weakness. Having an empty ball sack was most assuredly a sign of weakness. "I'm guessing I can fill in the blanks right about now," Brewster said.

"I'm sure you can," Dr. Sassman said. "Don't worry about a thing, though, because if you stay on track, you'll still be able to walk away with your MD degree by June, '82. Well, that's about it. I hope you have a speedy recovery."

As the research adviser beat a hasty retreat toward the door, Brewster went apeshit when he realized he was no longer going to be the point man to study ape shit.

"That's about it? Is that what you just said?" Brewster asked as he raised his voice. "I can do this study, and you know it. I want back in. Damnation! You can't do this to me, Dr. Sassman!"

Without looking at the medical student, Denny Sassman issued a firm reply before he departed. "Yes, I most certainly can do this. Do you remember the movie Shane? What did the character played by Alan Ladd do at the very end of the movie? Well, there you are. I'm sorry, Brewster, but it's now time for you to change horses and ride off into the sunset. Deal with it."

Brewster vividly recalled the faces of the two men who had viciously assaulted him. As it turned out, they had stripped away from him a lot more than just his right testicle. With seething hatred, Brewster realized the words of Diogenes the Cynic were now more appropriate than ever before: "What you have taken away, you can never give back." From then on, revenge would be the only thing that motivated J. D. Brewster.

⎯⎯⎯⎯

"I'm truly sorry that white boy got away," Big said as he looked underneath the hood of Brewster's '68 California Special Mustang, "but we're looking at a mighty 428 engine over here. Makes it all worthwhile, I suppose. Let's strip this baby, and then we'll torch the shell."

"Seems a shame to take it all down like that," Nog said.

"You know the rules," Big said. "The only reason I keep your ass around here is because you can turn a wrench with the best of them."

"Comes natural," Nog said.

"How so?"

"Pops was a crew chief tank mechanic during the war. His team could swap out a Continental engine and tranny on an M18 Hellcat faster than you could piss on an oleander bush in the backyard."

"Is that so?" Big asked. "That explains why you had a hankerin' for that World War II Walther P38."

"I guess."

"Put it out of your mind," Big said. "Just a white man's war over white man's hatred. Old Adolf sure got pissed at those heebie-jeebies, though. Frankly, that was beautiful."

"Pops told me there was a rumor going around during the war that Hitler had Jew blood in him," Nog said. "That's why he also hated himself so much. 'Splains a lot, if you ask me."

"Not our problem," Big replied.

"Maybe it is," Nog said. "I've been thinkin' 'bout what Casper said before we busted him up at Hermann Park. He was never a slave holder. We were never slaves. I just don't think I can hate like you do any more."

"Well, just listen to you," Big said. "Did you have one of those come-to-Jesus moments? I've seen that scar on your arm. Did you forget that it was done to you by da' white man?"

"I got cut up by *a* white man," Nog said, "not by *all* white man." You never told me why you hate the Caspers so much. I have an even better question: Why do you hate yourself so much?"

"Don't know what you're talkin' about, man," Big said.

"Is that so?" Nog asked. "I ran into a fellow the other day at the freight docks. His name was Jarvis McDonald. Any kin to you?"

"My cuz," Big said. "What did y'all talk about?"

"The weather, politics, how long Big Earl can tote the mail for the Houston Oilers before he's little more than a broken-down, crippled old black man with a bad back—you know, the usual."

"Bullshit," Big said. "What did y'all talk about?"

"I learned that your daddy was a white man and a bad one to boot," Nog said. "Is that why you hate white people as bad as you do?"

"Shut up, Darryl!"

"It all makes sense to me now if you indeed inherited cracker blood from some nasty, badass white daddy who spawned you. Fact is, you've got cracker blood coursing through your nappy veins right now!" Nog said. "Gotta' be why you be hatin' on your own self as bad as you do."

"I'm not going to tell you again," Big said. "Shut up, Darryl! If you ever mention that again, I'm going to end our partnership on the spot. If that happens, I promise you it won't turn out to be a corporate dissolution that'll have a particularly happy ending."

———

Three days postoperatively, detectives Watt and Culp paid Brewster a bedside visit. Detective Culp was the first to speak. "The last time we interviewed you was when Irene Segulla was murdered. We want to tell you that we've found your stolen Mustang, and it's a good-news, bad-news scenario."

"That so?" Brewster asked.

"Before Watt and I get into all of that, we need to ask you about the men who assaulted you at the Juneteenth celebration at Hermann Park. Speak up. We're all ears."

"I can tell you a lot," Brewster said. "I recognized one of the individuals to be a man named Darryl Hewritt."

"Well, well, well," Watt said. "Why am I not surprised?"

"There's more," Brewster said. "I was able to learn that the name of his accomplice was Apoo. I don't know if that was a first name or last name, nor am I actually certain as to how that name is correctly spelled. In any event, I can testify that these were the two same men I saw a year ago in the employee parking lot just before Mrs. Irene Segulla was assaulted."

"How can you be so sure at this time?" Detective Culp asked.

"I know without a doubt," Brewster said. "These guys were wearing the same type of black jackets, black mock turtlenecks, black berets, and also fake goatees that I saw them wear a year ago. Everything in the universe seems to be connected somehow."

"You've given us a very solid lead," Watt said. "We don't know who this Apoo character might be, as nobody with that name rings any bells. Nonetheless, I can assure you he'll be on our radar soon enough. This is an ongoing investigation, and I shouldn't tell you this, but we've been hunting for Darryl Hewritt now for quite some time."

"Why has he not been arrested as of yet?" Brewster asked.

"Somehow, he slipped away recently after being stopped for a routine traffic violation. Be of good cheer, Brewster; I have a suspicion that Hewritt and his friend Apoo will be getting a visit from the Houston Police Department very soon. We'll stay in touch with you and let you know when this investigation wraps up. Get well soon."

With that, the two detectives stood up and walked toward the hospital room door to depart, but there was clearly unfinished business to attend to as far as Brewster was concerned.

"Wait just a minute there, Deputy Dog!" Brewster called out.

"Hey, pal," Culp said, "do we look like cartoon refugees from the Terrytoons Studio?"

"Sorry," Brewster said sheepishly. "You said you had information about my Mustang. Don't leave me flapping here in the breeze, gentlemen. Give me the lowdown."

"The good news is that we have found your car," Detective Watt replied without looking back.

"The bad news is that it was completely stripped, doused with gasoline, and then incinerated," Detective Culp added. "I don't know what you said to those guys, but you must have really pissed them off. If you hadn't somehow escaped from the back trunk of that Mustang the other night, it's highly likely we would have found your cremated remains inside the unibody skeleton of that hot rod of yours. In all likelihood, you would have still been very much alive when they lit you up. I shit you not."

These bastards are going to pay, Brewster thought. *I wonder how long it would take to skin a human being while he's still breathing. Should I go for a human rug in front of my fireplace or perhaps a matching set of lampshades? Decisions, decisions.*

—————

On the fifth day of his hospitalization, the endocrinology service was called in for a clinical consultation. A formal recommendation was submitted that it was time for the castrated medical student to get started on replacement testosterone injections.

"The testosterone injections will help prevent premature male osteoporosis and loss of muscle mass," the specialist explained. "It will certainly improve your energy level, and hopefully, it will help maintain a normal libido. There are things I just can't predict, however. Over time, we might have a better handle as to the long-term risks and benefits of replacement male hormone treatment. It's undetermined as of this time as to whether or not replacement male testosterone therapy will increase your future risk for prostate cancer or coronary artery disease."

"I don't give a shit about any of that," Brewster replied. "Actually, I do hope I get premature coronary artery disease. That way, I won't live as long."

"Don't be rude," the endocrinologist said. "What's the matter with you? Do you have suicidal ideations?"

"Not at this time in my life," Brewster answered, "but I won't deny that I have homicidal ideations."

"Snap out of it. Despite these shortcomings about not having a full understanding of all the potential problems that may happen down the road, it's my recommendation for you to proceed with testosterone shots starting today," the endocrinologist explained. "I'll venture it'll make you feel better…"

Brewster received his first replacement testosterone injection while he was still hospitalized, but the medical student would soon embark on a potentially injurious course of action after he was discharged to home. J. D. foolishly embraced the philosophy "too much is just enough," and postdischarge, he would eventually receive a double dose of replacement testosterone injections on a monthly basis by visiting both the outpatient internal medicine clinic and the outpatient endocrinology center. He had no qualms about this act of malpractice, and he certainly had no regrets. The replacement testosterone made him feel good. It made him feel strong. It made him feel, well–*aggressive.*

As a consequence of the fact that a patient's medical records were not necessarily shared between one specialty department and another, Brewster deviously initiated a double-dipping treatment plan, which was only possible because neither the internal medicine clinic nor the endocrinology center had any idea he was receiving testosterone injections at both outpatient facilities at the same time.

Within short order, Brewster's colleagues and family members noted that the medical student was starting to pop up with a new outbreak of postadolescent facial acne on the anterior aspect of his neck. In addition, the fuse on the already irascible J. D. Brewster was now even more closely cropped to the powder keg. Of course, Brewster already had had problems with anger-management issues long before he ever received his first dose of replacement testosterone injections.

⊸⊸⊸

By the time Ben Fielder stuck his head into Brewster's hospital room on the med-surg unit, he had thoughtfully put the whole situation together. "It would appear that the two jokers who busted you up were the very same ones who took down the Mammoth and killed Mrs. Segulla last year. Do the police have it figured out who these guys are?"

Brewster replied in the affirmative. "Yes, but they just can't seem to find the perpetrators."

"What are your plans now?"

"If the criminal justice system cannot deal with these guys," Brewster said, "I will. I can tell you right now that these guys ruined my life. I'm seething with hatred. I'd kill both of them with my own hands if I ever had such an opportunity."

"Be careful, or else hatred will burn you up," Ben said. "It will get to the point where every other emotion you've ever had will become eroded. You need to try to get over that feeling."

"God forgive me," the obviously depressed medical student replied, "but I don't know if I'll ever get over that feeling. To be honest, I don't want to get over that feeling. The administration states that I should probably go talk to somebody in the psychiatry department to help me cool off, but I don't want to cool off."

"Why not?" Fielder asked.

"I want to stay angry."

"No, you don't!" Fielder challenged.

"Maybe you're right," Brewster conceded. Since I'm technically still doing a psychiatry clerkship rotation this month, perhaps it wouldn't hurt if I sat down and had a little chat with Dr. Corka Sorass at some point in time or with the clinical psychologist Dr. Petra Clayton."

—◦◦◦◦◦◦—

Subsequent visits from a stream of well-wishers over the course of Brewster's two-week hospitalization stay did little to improve the medical student's foul disposition. Brother Bill brought J. D. a Newton's cradle kinetic rack pendulum-ball play set. Five silver ball bearings were vertically suspended by strings from an overhead rack assembly and then aligned to touch each other. When one of the balls was pulled out and away from its fellow matching rack mates and then allowed to collide back with the other balls in a pendulum fashion by the force of gravity, the ball at the distal end of the alignment would swing away from its stable mates, almost as if by magic. Wow! How thoughtful.

—◦◦◦◦◦◦—

Months before, at the now defunct Buck Wong Oriental Buffet, Cousin Antonia had accused Brewster of acting like the character Captain Queeg from the old motion picture, The Caine Mutiny. On this visit, Antonia brought her brother, Ray, along for the ride, as Brewster had not seen him for quite some time. True to her word, Cousin Antonia brought two large brass ball bearings for Brewster to gently fondle in an effort to help keep his mind off of his current medical malady. Wow! How thoughtful.

—◦◦◦◦◦◦—

Feral Cheryl and Missy Brownwood made a point of changing out Brewster's wound dressings twice a day and monitoring the infectious cellulitis that had developed in his scrotum. In addition, a

minor proximal suture-line dehiscence complication occurred that
would be allowed to heal up by secondary intent. Nonetheless, the
shallow, open scrotal wound would require the young ladies to apply
frequent applications of antibiotic ointment. Brewster was terribly
embarrassed to have any woman, nurse or otherwise, visually inspect
the shattered remnants of his now-expired reproductive life. As far
as Brewster was concerned, perhaps the germicidal applications
were scheduled a bit too frequently. Wow! How thoughtful.

—⊸⊸⊸⊸⊸—

Borscht was a classic Eastern European soup, obviously favored
by Russians. Though it was generally a concoction containing
red beets, there were quite a few varieties of the staple, including
borscht made from red cabbage. There was also a green subspecies
of the meal that might contain sorrel. Usually a vegetarian soup that
might contain other items, including onions, carrots, potatoes, and
the like, borscht could be served as either a hot or cold dish.

Invariably, Russians enjoyed a large dollop of smetana (sour
cream) in the middle of the bowl of soup. Occasionally, even meat or
marrow might be added to borscht, but there was only one unifying
thematic element that ran the gamut throughout the derivations of
that particular Slavic treat: it all tasted like shit.

Russian Bear and Larisa made a point of bringing Brewster a big
bowl of fortified borscht to help expedite his recovery. They were
eager to learn of their friend's approval, but Brewster responded
with only a weak smile when he was asked if he enjoyed the taste.
Brewster believed that only a whole bottle of Tabasco sauce added to
the admixture of unidentifiable meats and vegetables would make
the borscht at least marginally palatable.

Brewster thought it was no wonder that Von Paulus and the
German Sixth Army had been annihilated at the Battle of Stalingrad,
as the poor Russian bastards who had fought back the Nazis must

have been coerced into eating that kind of crap. Brewster thought that if he had been forced to choke down that wretched swill at gun point, it would have put him in the mood to bear arms, too.

Brewster encountered a large, fibro-fatty, rubbery meatball in the borscht. Before he bit into it, the unidentified, irregular ovoid lump of flesh had a peculiar, rancid odor. Even more disturbing than the strikingly offensive flavor was the unpleasant texture the meatball displayed: it was like rubber.

When Brewster queried Larisa as to the exact nature of the heterogeneous, amorphous, malignant mass of quivering flesh he struggled to gnaw on with gut-wrenching difficulty, she cheerfully replied, "We added heavily aged pig testicles to the borscht to make you more feral and more virile!"

"Holy shit!" Brewster exclaimed. "You added what to this soup?"

"Eat it up," Larisa said. "It will make a puny man like you strong like a bull. Robust, hirsute, unibrowed Almasty females with receding foreheads and primitive sagittal crests on their skulls will no doubt be drawn to you the very way that dung beetles are compelled to ingest the fecal droppings from a dyspeptic pachyderm!"

"You added what to this soup?"

"These Almasty she-beasts dwell in the caves of the Caucasus Mountains, and they have long, sharp, vampire-like incisors. These creatures could make you cry like a little schoolgirl. It would be good for you, no?"

Wow! How thoughtful.

⟞⟝⟞⟝

Primed to discuss at length the brutal assault Brewster had endured at the hands of Darryl Hewritt and his accomplice, Wooly Mammoth pumped Brewster for as many details concerning the event as possible. After conferring with the big man, Willy said, "You might be a pasty white boy, but I have to hand it to you. Man, you've got balls! I have a present for you. I want you to put this on the bumper of whatever car you own whenever you get around to replacing the old Mustang. It will tell everybody in the entire world that you're one nasty bastard who shouldn't be messed with."

Brewster opened the box Willy had given him and discovered a giant pair of red rubber testicles, the kind that ranchers and cowboys often affixed to the bumper-hitch receivers on their pickup trucks. Wow! How thoughtful.

―――――

The Dalton twins learned from Willy's father that Brewster had been seriously injured and was in the hospital. Upon their arrival for a visit, D' Shea said, "A white boy like you would have to be an absolute idiot to go over to the Juneteenth celebration. Isn't that right, Baby Girl?"

"No doubt about that," her twin replied.

As the twins saddled on either side of Brewster on the hospital bed, D' Shea said, "Being the progressive and sensitive African American women that we are, we brought you a treat that we just learned that all you white boys like to eat. We have a box of deep-fried Rocky Mountain oysters that we picked up from that place over on South Main called Taco Hell. They're really spicy!"

"We want you to eat them while they're still hot," D' Nae added.

The twins had brought a plastic fork, and they took turns feeding Brewster the rubbery, spicy, deep-fried bovine testicles. Wow! How thoughtful.

―――――

Brewster's mother, Helliarma, and Uncle John paid J. D. a visit at the hospital prior to his scheduled discharge, as Uncle John apparently had a specific present for the medical student.

"You know, the worst thing in the world is when a physician puts a cold stethoscope upon the chest of a patient," John said. "Well, I have a present to give you that will make your patients flip head over heels with ecstasy!"

Uncle John subsequently handed Brewster a small leather pouch with purse strings. "I want you to wrap this tiny leather pouch around the bell head of your stethoscope. That way, it'll keep it toasty warm."

"My goodness!" Brewster exclaimed, genuinely impressed. Brewster was honored that his cranky old uncle had been so generous. Brewster erroneously believed it was a magnanimous gesture, the likes of which he had never seen from Uncle John at any time in the past. "This is truly a very nice present, Uncle John. Where did you buy such a gift? I've never seen anything like this ever before."

"Although you're the least favorite of all my kin," Uncle John replied, "this is nonetheless a personalized, customized, and unique special offering. I made this leather pouch, and then I tanned it myself. I ran over an ally cat with my old Dodge Dart, and I squashed it like a pancake. It was all very sad. I didn't want the carcass to go to waste, so I decided to cut off its ball sack, and then I turned it into a tiny purse so it will keep your stethoscope warm. I'm glad you like it! If you want to be an angel investor and kick in a little bit of seed money, I think we're looking at a cottage industry that has unlimited upside potential. I'll shoot over an investment prospectus to you as soon as you get discharged."

Brewster was appalled. "For shit's sake, Uncle John, are you telling me that you harvested the scrotal sack from a dead animal to make me this tiny purse? That's disgusting! How in hell could you possibly do something like that?"

"I don't exactly remember," Uncle John replied, "but as you know, there are a lot of ways to skin a cat."

Wow! How thoughtful.

On the evening of July 4, 1981, Brewster finally was given medical clearance to be discharged to home after the prolonged course of antibiotic therapy was finally completed and the surgical staples and drains had all been successfully removed. Before Brewster made his departure from the hospital, he had one additional unexpected visitor. A large obese woman with plastic daisies in her hair emerged out of the darkness and bravely approached the forlorn young man. She reached out to hand the medical student a plastic flower she had taken out of her unkempt mane. As she did so, she said, "Hello, J. D. I believe you already know who I am. My name is Stella Link. I think it's time you and I get to know each other a bit better. We should find a quiet place somewhere to have a nice little chat."

4

FREQUENT FLYER

To Stella, Brewster appeared as handsome as ever. However, she had no illusions that Brewster was anything more than a callous cad. Although she was well aware that her blood pressure, diabetes, and cholesterol problems were again out of control, Stella had sacrificed herself to recapture Brewster's affection.

She had done so despite the ultimate untoward outcome her self-imposed neglect would have on her overall health and longevity. In doing so, Stella again felt run-down, with a poor energy level, and was again afflicted with polyuria and polydipsia from the hyperglycemia associated with untreated adult-onset type II diabetes mellitus. She was nonetheless determined to put up with the troublesome symptoms, as J. D. Brewster, for unclear reasons, meant that much to her.

"Stella, you look fantastic," Brewster said. "I'm truly happy to see you again. Honestly, I've missed you very much."

"I love you, Brew," Stella replied. "I've been miserable since we broke up. I want you back in my life."

"Stella, there is something I need to tell you," Brewster said with trepidation, "and it may have bearing as to whether or not you'd want to rekindle any kind of romantic relationship with me."

"What's wrong?"

"After the injury I sustained," Brewster said, "I'm now sterile, and I'll never be able to sire any children."

"Do you think that matters to me?"

"Frankly," Brewster answered, "I just don't know. You and I never talked about this matter, but I know that you're now in your midthirties. Theoretically, your window of fertility may be closing within the next few years or even sooner."

"You don't know that to be a certainty."

"I suppose not," Brewster said, "but I'm indeed certain of this: if you and I delve into a long-term relationship, you may become embittered with me if I'm unable to render progeny on your behalf. You need to think long and hard about this matter before you and I start seeing each other once again."

It was, surprisingly, the most unselfish and altruistic revelation Brewster had ever made to the woman who inexplicably continued to care for him deeply.

What Brewster revealed when he bared his soul was not a surprise to Stella. As the secretary for the department of psychiatry, she had ready access to patient records under the guise of attending chart reviews for clinical consultations. The medical records department would always avail copies of both inpatient and outpatient records to the psychiatry department without any questions asked. Stella Link had immediately discovered the true nature of J. D. Brewster's serious injuries within only a day of his hospitalization.

What she had initiated was a standard departmental operating procedure. After all, Brewster was completing his one-month mandatory clerkship on the psychiatry service, and Stella easily made the claim that Dr. Corka Sorass had requested an update as to what serious traumatic malady had befallen his medical student.

Stella had long kept her own medical problems a secret from her boyfriend, because she was always afraid he would look upon her as an inferior female specimen. Would Brewster have actually rejected Stella if she'd revealed her medical complications to him? Perhaps she had underestimated the man she loved. Then again, perhaps not. In any event, she was not going to take any chances.

As a consequence of her diabetes, age, and morbid obesity, Stella had other medical problems that she had kept a secret from Brewster. Stella battled polycystic ovarian disease with menstrual irregularity, and sadly, that was a direct consequence of her other comorbid conditions. In layman's terms, she was barren.

When Stella had learned that Brewster's injuries had rendered him sterile, she actually felt a sense of relief. Her own fertility issue was one less physical flaw that she would ever have to discuss with Brewster. If the subject of childbearing, or lack thereof, ever became an issue in their relationship, Stella could cleverly make sure the onus of infertility was on Brewster's shoulders and not hers. As oft touted, all matters were equitable regarding the respective realms of Venus and Mars.

Upon finding a quiet place somewhere to have a nice little chat, Stella intimated to Brewster that his sterility had no bearing on how she felt about him, and she professed assurances that her love for him was unconditional. Acutely aphonic because he was incapable of true mutual reciprocation, Brewster could only impassively look into Stella's eyes. He had never been loved like that before, and truth be told, he would never be loved like that ever again.

Sadly, he failed to fully realize what Stella Link meant to him. Stella would have made Brewster a far better human being had they been destined to become lifelong partners. Brewster was unable to conceptualize the vast benefits of a relationship cultured by companionship and contentment that might have been bestowed upon him. In the famed lyrics once sung by the late, great Otis Redding, "You don't miss your water, you don't miss your water, and you don't miss your water until the well runs dry..."

"Dry run or not," Brewster said, "if this works, we'll draw up a formalized plan for when we can liberate the great apes from their incarceration once and for all."

"How do you plan on getting back into the lockdown primate kennel?" Ford asked. "I thought Denny yanked your lab access when you got kicked out of the dual-training program."

"Idiots in the admin never asked me to return my key to the office," Brewster said.

"Did you get the helium balloon?"

"Picked it up at the Hermann Park Zoo just this morning," Brewster answered. "It's really cute; it's technically a balloon within a balloon. The outer balloon is completely transparent, but the inner balloon is an opaque, latex head of a mouse."

"Mickey?"

"Presumably so," Brewster answered. "Therefore, I'd be quite surprised if there weren't any serious copyright violations going on here. In any event, I've got the damned thing stuffed in my locker."

"Let me eyeball it," Ford said.

As Brewster handed the balloon over to Ford, the research scientist appeared to be pleased. "This will work," Rip said. "Give me until five minutes after the hour. That should allow me enough time to set up shop outside of the locked electronics closet where the security agent keeps an eye on the video monitors. At five after nine, float the balloon in front of the ceiling-mounted security camera, and then get the hell out of there. We'll see exactly how long it takes for the security monitor to note that the view of the lockdown kennel has been obscured by the balloon."

"Wait one moment," Brewster said. "I've spied on that guy once before. Either he has adult onset diabetes mellitus that's under poor control, or perhaps he has benign prostatic hypertrophy with lower urinary-tract obstructive symptomatology."

"What makes you think so?"

"Simple," Brewster said. "Dude needs to take a piss about every hour or so."

"Good point," Ford said. "It'll just make my job a little tougher—that's all. Whenever he leaves the monitor room, I'll have to tail him to see if's he's making a pit stop to hit the head or if he's planning on walking down to the lab to see what's awry with the security camera. Ready to rock?"

"Let's roll!"

At exactly 9:05 a.m., Brewster strategically released the helium balloon in front of the lens of the security camera in the lockdown kennel. As they'd preplanned, Brewster's intention was to leave the primate enclosure immediately. As he walked briskly toward the double-locked egress, Brewster suddenly realized he was in serious trouble. He heard the voice of Dr. Caleb, who was about to enter the primate kennel from the main animal lab. With no recourse except to hide, Brewster lunged into the under-sink cabinet and pulled the doors shut as he held his breath.

Brewster's sudden movements startled the two caged chimpanzees, and they screamed at the top of their lungs with marked anxiety.

"Shut up, you goddamned trogs!" Dr. Caleb said in futility as he entered the unit.

Hot on the heels of Dr. Caleb were two other medical school security guards who also entered the primate kennel. "I got a call on my walkie-talkie from the video monitor room that something was obstructing the security video camera down here," one of the security agents explained. Well, as Bart and I were right outside in the hallway at the time, we just poked our noses in here to see what in the heck was going on in here."

"Looks like a helium balloon blew in here from the little birthday party they're throwing for Zip Talbot in the breakroom," Caleb said as he looked up toward the ceiling-mounted video camera. "There's a string tied to the end of the balloon. I'd appreciate it if one of you boys just grab it and haul the damned thing down."

"Want to take a hit of helium?" the security guard named Bart asked.

"Right on!" Caleb replied.

While hidden within the under-sink cabinet, Brewster was amazed that the security guards and Dr. Caleb were sharing hits from the helium balloon and telling each other jokes in high, squeaky voices.

It was more than an hour before Rip Ford returned to the primate kennel to find that Brewster had remained hidden within the confines of the primate kennel the entire time. "My back is killing me," Brewster said. "I'm glad you got down here to spring me, as I was too afraid to stick my nose out of this cabinet."

"I'm so sorry, Brew," Rip said, "but the security agent in the electronic monitor room never left his post the entire time while I was up there spying on him."

"Tell me about it," J. D. said. "Our plan was rather idiotic to begin with, as we never guessed that the dude in the monitor room would send down a radio message to the security team that walked in on me. To make matters worse, Dr. Caleb also showed up before the security detail even arrived. My fledgling medical career would have ended on the spot if I got caught in here!"

"I swear, Brew—you must have a truck load of bravery and then some jammed into your ball sack," Rip professed. "I'm frankly amazed that you were able to keep your shit together while those guys were just a few feet away from you and breathing down your damned neck!"

"Thanks," Brewster said wistfully, "but as for me, I'd rather have a scrotum filled with testicles than bravery!"

"Are they not one in the same?"

As Brewster had squandered an entire year in the dual-training program, he was now behind schedule in completing his mandatory third-year clerkships, including pediatrics and gynecology. Realistically, he didn't have a chance to get those specific rotations salted away until late in the summer or fall of 1981. In the meantime, perhaps he could make himself useful in the emergency room. After all, he had already marked his territory with blood and serum on the long night of neglect when his right testicle was violently ruptured.

Dr. Bryan and Dr. Frank Barber both gave Brewster the thumbs-up to start a rotation in the emergency room on an elective basis, starting on Monday, July 6. Both attending physicians felt obligated to allow Brewster to get shoehorned into place.

As it turned out, Dr. Freewater was dead wrong in his assessment that the incident report filled out concerning the neglect Brewster was subjected to on his tortuous long night in the emergency room would fall on deaf ears. In fact, the exact opposite occurred.

Unbeknownst to Brewster, the on-call emergency room resident physician and the triage nurse got blistered by the administration and were subjected to one week of suspension without pay. In addition, unfavorable critiques were permanently recorded in the department of human resources and also with the residency training program. Perhaps Brewster had somehow found favor in an unknown and unidentified administrative politico.

Brewster was about to embark on a rotation with several medical students he had never worked with before. One of the students, Susan Carroll, was a shy and slim young woman with straight brown hair, thin lips, and hazel eyes. The emergency room resident assigned to the team was Dr. Pooty Shorts, a man J. D. Brewster harnessed a great deal of hostility toward.

Intellectually, Brewster realized that even if medical assistance had been rendered in a more expedient fashion on the night he was assaulted, he still would have lost his right testicle and ended up being sexually sterile. In any event, Brewster still held Dr. Shorts personally responsible for a significant amount of the pain and emotional anguish that he had to endure on that fateful night.

⸺⬩⸺

Dr. Bryan thought it would be nice to play a joke on J. D. Brewster in an effort to welcome him back to work. He knew his old band member from the rock-and-roll group DNR invariably liked to play pranks on other people, practical or otherwise. Unfortunately, the joke Dr. Bryan engineered was about to horribly backfire. Brewster was instructed to see two women who had shown up to the emergency room with alleged complaints of severe migraine headaches. Curiously, Brewster discovered the patients were clad in a bikinis, fishnet stockings, and open-back pumps.

"Hi, sweety!" one of the women said. "I'm Mary Ellen Fokkengruber, and this is my sister, Bertha. We get migraine headaches from time to time, and the only thing that we've found helpful in the past that successfully alleviates our symptoms is when a stud like you gives us a vigorous breast massage!"

With that, Mary Ellen hit the play button on a boom box she had brought into the exam stall with her. Suddenly, the David Rose Orchestra's 1962 instrumental hit song "The Stripper" blared out over the speakers for all to hear. Brewster immediately realized he had been set up when he noted that the entire emergency room staff had gathered outside of the draw curtains of the emergency room stall to witness the student's reaction.

Mary Ellen and Bertha removed their bikini tops and began to gyrate around the room. Bertha pulled Brewster's face between her well-endowed silicone-impregnated breasts. What happened next, however, was shockingly unexpected. Brewster firmly pushed the young women away and, without a single word, grabbed the boom box. While the sound of a slide trombone continued to howl from the song playing on the cassette tape, Brewster swung the device like a ball and chain in an Olympic hammer throw. Brewster smashed the boom box against the wall, launching shards of plastic and metal shrapnel about the emergency room.

The young women and the emergency room staff looked on with slack-jawed amazement as Brewster simply dropped the remnant boom box handle upon the floor and then went about his business without any modulations noted upon his flat, featureless facial expression that was curiously devoid of any discernible emotions. Brewster felt his right fist clench, along with the undeniable urge to punch out his old bandmate from DNR. Fortunately, wisdom prevailed and Brewster picked up the chart from the adjacent stall to evaluate the next patient as if nothing awry had happened.

———

Susan Carroll encountered a patient in the emergency room who would ultimately require an ASAP referral to the psychiatry department for a formal intervention. While the patient was waiting in the ER lobby, the security service caught him urinating in a potted shrub in the foyer!

Susan had mistakenly believed the patient was merely histrionic. Perhaps he was acting in such a bizarre manner in a devious attempt to cut to the front of the line. After all, by acting crazy, the patient would more likely be evaluated by the medical personnel in the emergency room rather expeditiously.

Once Susan had spoken to the individual however, she quickly realized this was not the case. The patient was gay, and he had developed irrational fears about the disease known as GRID. Suffering from persecutory ideation, the terrified individual was convinced that President Ronald Reagan had introduced GRID into the gay community to essentially exterminate homosexuals and eventually create a world that was one hundred percent heterosexual.

Susan Carroll called over the emergency room resident, Dr.

Shorts, to help evaluate the patient. Procedure-oriented, Pooty Shorts had little if any interest in emergency room clientele who didn't require sutures, extirpation of foreign objects, fiberglass-cast applications, or other such direct, hands-on intervention of traumatic injuries.

Upon his arrival to the emergency room stall, Dr. Shorts informed Susan Carroll, "We don't have time for this kind of crap. This patient's a frequent flier, and we're about to give this three dollar bill the big brush-off."

"What's a frequent flier?" Susan asked. "I'm not sure of the meaning of that particular terminology."

"A frequent flier is a dirtbag who makes multiple visits to the emergency room over a short period of time," Pooty Shorts replied. "Invariably, they're either lunatics or one of the many DiSPOSe addicts who only clutter up our hallways."

"What's a DiSPOSe?" Susan asked.

"That's simply an acronym for 'drug-seeking piece of shit.' Here's a learning opportunity. I want you to see exactly how I'm going to handle this freak of nature. I'm going to shine this guy and get him the hell out of here as soon as possible so we can focus on the real problems here in the emergency room."

Dr. Shorts addressed the deranged patient with a stern countenance. "Hello, sir. My name is Dr. Paul Shorts. I understand that you've broken the secret code about the gay-related immunodeficiency syndrome. I must tell you that it's a fact that this disease is indeed a government plot to exterminate the unredeemable."

"What types of people are deemed to be, well–unredeemable?" the terrified patient asked.

"Well, all of the homo-satchels, such as you, are included. Gay people and the lesbos are obviously public enemy numero uno. In addition, troublesome Negroes and their low-life, white trash counterparts who shop at Walmart actually round out the top three groups of deplorable people that are undoubtedly on top of Uncle Sam's hit parade list of Homo sapiens who should be immediately culled from the wretched herd of humanity."

"I knew it!" the patient proclaimed, suddenly feeling validated.

"Well," Shorts added, "I must inform you that you're not the first person who's already figured out this conspiracy. It would appear that you know the truth to everything except the precise vector that's responsible for transmitting this lethal disease from person to person. I know the answer, and I want to share it with you."

"Tell me, tell me, tell me!" the patient demanded.

Pooty leaned over to whisper into the patient's ear. "It's moths!"

Dr. Shorts subsequently pulled a small glass vial out of the top of his white coat pocket and handed it to the patient. Inside the glass vial was a small, confused moth fluttering harmlessly about. As the patient shrieked, he jumped off of the emergency room gurney and subsequently fled the Texas Medical Center campus in abject horror. Although appalled, Susan was too shy to rebuke the resident, who sadistically laughed at his own handiwork.

"This is the third time this week that this little flying furry fucker has cleared out an ER bed on my behalf! I'm sorry that I ever underestimated the undeniable charm of this tiny bug," Dr. Shorts exclaimed.

Before the month of July was out, the Gulf Coast University Hospital was inundated with misguided members from the gay and black community who had heard the unsubstantiated rumors that the disease GRID was transmitted by direct physical contact with genetically modified moths that were secretly released through lethal and mysterious chem-trails that were dispersed by B–52 bombers flying high in the skies over Texas.

On one of Brewster's night-shift rotations, a well-known DiSPOSe arrived in an obtunded state. The patient was the notorious heroin addict Moxie Hightower, who was a frequent flier. Hightower would invariably arrive at the emergency room from time to time for drug-overdose management.

None of the emergency room staff members could recall Moxie ever arriving without the ubiquitous positive taillight sign. The entire emergency room staff knew the patient on a first-name basis, as Moxie would come to the hospital for a tune-up at approximately eight-week intervals. His visit was one of those occasions.

Brewster and the attending physician, Dr. Frank Barber, evaluated the patient. After the Narcan antidote used for opioid overdose situations had taken effect, Moxie Hightower had suddenly awakened.

"Moxie, Moxie, Moxie," Dr. Barber said to the patient with marked exasperation, "what are we going to do with you? Someday you're going to come in here stiff as a board, and I won't be able to raise you from the dead. Is that what you want? The members of my emergency room staff have come to the point where they now hold you in utter disregard as a fellow human being. Is that how you want to be remembered?"

"Well, as the old saying goes, if the shoe fits, wear it," Moxie sadly replied. "In my case, perhaps the old saying that applies to me should go, 'If the foo' shits, wear it.'"

The Narcan had now taken full effect, and Moxie Hightower was surprisingly lucid. He demonstrated remarkable insight into his unfortunate circumstances.

"Dr. Barber, I've failed rehabilitation so many times, I just don't deserve to live. I don't know what happened to me. I just tried heroin for fun a couple of times at the encouragement of some of my so-called friends. Just like that, I got hooked."

"That's exactly how it happens," Dr. Barber said.

"Now I just live to get a fix," Moxie said. "Nothing else matters to me anymore. I've prayed over this matter but to no avail. God must not be listening anymore. He's probably wandered off to some other part of his universe and is working on other more important projects. Why would he have any time for a failure like me? When I officially kick the bucket, I want to donate my body to this medical school, as perhaps I'll be a more valuable commodity to somebody else once I'm finally gone. Remember, Dr. Barber, I've already agreed to a DNR code status. After all, as far as I know, I'm already dead."

After Moxie Hightower signed the discharge form and was released back out onto the streets where he lived, Dr. Barber could only sadly shake his head in futile dismay. After the emergency room physician's wife had been kidnapped and likely murdered at the hands of the Calle Vampiro drug cartel back in '77, Frank Barber was a man who was lost and seemingly without a purpose for his own continued existence.

Rhetorically, he asked, "What possible difference does any of this make? Am I just keeping a finger jammed into a hole that somebody shot through my own sombrero?"

Brewster replied with lyrics from the Steppenwolf song "Rock Me" from 1969: "I don't know where we've come from. I don't know where we're going to, but if all this should have a reason, we will be the last in know. So let's just hope there is a Promised Land and hang on till then as best as you can."

<hr />

Homer Livingood was building a new home off of US Highway 59, south of Sharpstown. His neighbor in an adjacent lot behind his backyard wall had an enormous Chilean mesquite tree with a canopy that was easily forty feet in diameter. The tree was growing right along the back fence line, and it had infringed upon Homer's backyard.

The foreman for the construction company said the troublesome tree was going to interfere with the roof line of the new home being built. Contractually, the builder was not responsible for cutting back the tree canopy, and he informed Mr. Livingood that he had to take care of the offending tree branches before the roof struts could be affixed to the masonry walls that had just arisen.

Homer owned a chain saw and also a tall stepladder, so he proceeded to hire a local handyman who had left an advertisement flyer on the billboard at the entryway of the local supermarket. As it would turn out, the so-called handyman would end up stealing the chain saw and ladder and setting up his own tree-trimming service in the Gulf Coast area.

Homer surmised that if something was to be done right, he would have to do it himself. Mr. Livingood proceeded to buy a brand-new ladder, but he decided to simply rent a chain saw to quickly get the job done. It appeared the ladder he bought was significantly shorter than the one he had previously owned, but as time was of the essence, the job had to get done one way or another.

Homer successfully completed the task of pruning the invading tree branches and was about to climb down the ladder, when a complication occurred. He was unable to shut off the rented chain saw, and the goddamned thing was stuck on full, wide-open throttle. If he had simply pitched the chain saw down to the ground, the rest of his life would have been a happy ride on the gravy train.

Unfortunately, Homer Livingood panicked and tried to manipulate the runaway chain saw into the off position while he was still standing on the stepladder. Looking back on the ordeal many years later, Homer would never be able to fully account for what had gone so terribly wrong.

Prior to his undertaking the arboreal assault upon the unruly mesquite tree, Homer's wife had offered her help in supporting the base of the ladder. As Homer was a man, he foolishly refused to accept any help from the little lady. That was his first big mistake, but surely many more things would go awry on that fateful day.

Perhaps there was a partially cut tree branch that still had some residual spring load and it recoiled upon the ladder. Perhaps Homer simply lost his balance. Perhaps Homer should not have gone to the very top of the ladder, where it warned in bright red stenciled letters, "This is not a step! Do not stand here!" In any event, Homer found that he was flying over the backyard fence and was about to land on his back in his neighbor's yard.

Homer Livingood became alarmed when it appeared the flying chain saw, which was still running at wide-open throttle, was about to land on his face. As he correctly surmised that such a catastrophic accident would be a lethal event with a subsequent closed-casket wake, he extended his right arm to fend off the potentially deadly onslaught that gravity had compelled to fall upon him.

Homer was particularly fond of his right arm. He'd joyously and unselfishly shared with his right arm every meal he had ever consumed. When he was a younger man, Homer and his right arm would go out on the town and solicit trouble together. At times, when Homer confronted unwelcome solitude compromised by an autonomous libido, his right arm would lend a hand to help cheer him up.

Yes, Homer and his right arm were the best of friends, and they deeply cared for each other. Nonetheless, when push came to shove, Homer Livingood gave up his right arm faster than a scoundrel named Judas Iscariot had given up a certain itinerant rabbi to the palace guards at the big Garden of Gethsemane slumber party, circa AD 33.

After gathering his senses, Homer realized the middle finger of his right hand was now touching his right elbow. Intuitively realizing that was not the correct anatomical position for his right upper extremity, he saw that the chain saw had cut straight through the ventral aspect of his right forearm, cleaving both the right radial and ulnar bones while gnawing a life threatening rent into his right radial artery. The only things that still connected his right hand to his mangled arm were the small shreds of tendon and skin on the dorsal aspect of the upper extremity.

As the adrenal glands, snugly positioned bilaterally atop the superior poles of Homer's kidneys, squeezed down with all of their endocrinological prowess, the epinephrine pouring into the injured man's bloodstream dramatically and acutely drove up his blood pressure and heart rate to the point where his severed radial artery was blasting bright red blood across the lawn. Realizing he only had about ninety seconds or so of life left in his body, Homer at least had the wherewithal to remove his belt and use it as a tourniquet to stem the hemorrhaging. At that point, Homer was calm and collected, and he realized that although seriously injured, he would still live to fight another day.

Perhaps God had a sense of humor, as generally no stupid deed would go unpunished for long. Homer soon realized he was not out of the woods, as his neighbor's dogs, Stinky Pete and Hercules, had arrived on the scene to investigate the commotion. As the two canines were not familiar with the injured man sprawled out in their backyard, they looked upon Homer with the same enthusiasm that any child would have had for an ice cream truck that had just pulled up into the driveway.

As the canines attempted to abscond with Homer's partially amputated hand, the injured man was forced to hold on to the end of the belt being used as a tourniquet within his clenched teeth as he tried to swat away the two dogs with his free left hand.

His neighbor, at the time, was hosting a birthday party for his eight-year-old grandson. No fewer than ten children were inside the house, enjoying cake and ice cream while watching Marvin the Martian in a life-or-death battle royal with Bugs Bunny on television.

The sounds of the running chain saw; the barking dogs; and Homer's futile screams, which were only marginally muffled through the make-shift tourniquet belt clenched securely between his teeth, finally aroused the fearless neighbor into action. Once aware that something evil or dangerous was going on in the backyard, the brave neighbor sent out his eight-year-old grandson to investigate the matter and locked the sliding glass patio door behind the young boy.

When the child found a blood-splattered Homer Livingood with his back propped up against the back fence, the hapless middle-aged man was still trying to fend off Grandpa's two terriers, which no doubt were trying to eat him.

As the still-running chain saw danced about on the ground nearby, the young lad's eyes grew to the size of dinner plates. After gently swaying for a few moments like a pair of old boxer shorts airing out on a clothesline, the horrified boy turned around and ran away. At that point, Homer accepted the likelihood that his life was winding down to a rather embarrassing conclusion.

"Ah, to hell with everything. God, please forgive me for being an idiot. I might as well just let these damned dogs finish me off once and for all. I hope I taste good!" Homer declared.

Momentarily, the helicopter air ambulance service arrived, and Homer Livingood was flown away to the Gulf Coast General Hospital. After the helicopter landed on the heliport pad, Homer was carted into the emergency room, where he was met by Dr. Bryan, medical student Susan Carroll, and members from the trauma team.

Dr. Bryan calmly but swiftly issued a set of orders to those who were going to be involved with Homer's care. "Susan, hold on firmly to this man's midhumerus, and get that belt off of him. Get a proper tourniquet applied to that site. Fresh vital signs, people—I need them now. This man's looking pretty gray. He may have already lost half of his blood volume. Let's get an additional IV line, and let's make it a subclave. Get Pooty Shorts over here, and have him ram it home. Where in hell is the phlebotomist from the lab? Susan—you know how to draw blood, don't you? Grab a rainbow for a stat CBC,

PT and PTT, type and screen, and a bare-bones chem-six panel. Don't order a full SMAC; that just takes too damned long, and the lab won't run it stat anyhow. As far as the chem goes, I just need lytes, BUN, and creatinine for now. We will sort out everything else later."

When Dr. Bryan was informed that the ortho resident was on the way down, the attending said, "We'll give the bone cloners the right of first refusal. However, I'm rather certain this is out of their strike zone. Better get Dr. Printer down to the ER. Call him now, as he is never more than a stone's throw away from here anyhow."

Dr. Printer was a hand surgeon and the only subspecialist in that field at the Gulf Coast University Hospital. He was always on call 24-7. He was the proud owner of a twenty-seven-foot fishing boat that had offshore capabilities. Despite owning the boat, the physician had never taken it out on the water. Sadly, Dr. Printer hadn't had even one day off for vacation over the past three years.

Although it was not often that Dr. Printer had to be called into the hospital to attend to emergency hand injuries, from a contractual standpoint, he was always on call. That simply meant he had to be within an hour's drive from the hospital at any time, all the time. He was a prisoner—a well-paid prisoner, but a prisoner nonetheless. To say that Dr. Printer was facing burnout would have been an understatement.

Upon his arrival, Dr. Printer went straight to the emergency room stall to evaluate Homer Livingood. "So I heard you had a slow dance with a running chain saw while you were standing on top of a ladder. Mr. Livingood, you are, without a doubt, a major-league dumbass. Be that as it may, I'm here to try to reattach your hand to the rest of your arm. By the grace of God, perhaps we can salvage your limb."

That afternoon, Homer would receive the first of a total of eight operations that would be ongoing for more than a year. Within less than a month after his original operation, Homer began to experience high fevers and shaking chills that would go on night after night for several weeks on end.

Unfortunately, by the time follow-up imaging studies were obtained, his right ulnar bone had already putrefied from a raging case of osteomyelitis. As it turned out, the bone in his right arm had become infected with nasty bacteria called Enterococcus faecalis, which happened to be organisms commonly found in dog shit—what a surprise. No doubt Stinky Pete and Hercules must have been involved in some unsavory canine anilingus bonding activity before they munched on Homer's partially amputated forearm. Why would a pair of canines lick each other in the ass? Well, quite simply, because they could.

Homer would ultimately end up losing his ulnar bone and his wrist. A steel rod was employed to stabilize the right arm, and after multiple bone grafts and long-term antibiotic therapy, doctors finally declared that Homer was about as good as he would ever be. Sadly, he also lost several extensor tendons in the dorsum of his right hand as a consequence to the nasty infection he had sustained.

From then on, whenever he was cut off while driving on the freeway, he couldn't give the finger to a fellow driver. Instead, he was reduced to giving an adjacent offending motorist the "claw."

For the rest of their days, Stinky Pete and Hercules would look upon Homer through the chain-link fence at the end of their backyard with lust. After all, they had sampled the extraordinary epicurean elegance of human flesh, and it tasted good...

———

Perky and Peter Cheeks were two skilled competitive ballroom dancers. Try as they might, however, the married couple could never score better than a red-ribbon finish when performing before a panel of judges. Other dancers always walked away with the first-place trophy. On the third Saturday night in the month of July 1981, their fortunes finally changed, as they won the first-place prize for that evening's heated competition. As the couple brought home not only a small pewter trophy, but also a new set of plastic place mats festooned with brown and tan images of happy, fluttering moths, it was indeed a cause for celebration!

Perky was so pleased with her husband's flawless performance that she wanted to give him a special, sexually intimate gift that most married men were only fortunate enough to receive on their birthdays or wedding anniversaries, and that was only if they were very lucky.

It would be an extraordinarily satisfying act of lovemaking only shared on seldom occasions. Most sexually deprived married men with a pair of blue balls could have readily guessed the happy interlude that was about to occur.

After applying a liberal amount of lubrication on a glass vase complete with a complementary bouquet of faux plastic flowers, Perky shoved the vase, flowers and all, up her husband's ass.

As her husband cried out in ecstasy, it was time for Perky to add icing to the cake. To enhance the thrill her husband experienced, Perky Cheeks inserted a clear acrylic tube into her husband's rectum and subsequently prodded a small young rodent to run down the tube and enter into a dark and foul chamber replete with noxious fumes.

In parlance that would have been more at home in an upscale bar where complex, snooty cocktail beverages were crafted, Perky inserted into her husband's sigmoid colon what could have been described only as a gerbil chaser. Wow. Some guys get all the luck!

For unclear reasons, it appeared that the small rodent didn't particularly enjoy the experience of being forcefully shoved up somebody's ass end, so the small mammal made a valiant effort to bite and claw its way through the bowel wall to find its way to freedom. All the while, Mr. Cheeks was dancing about the living room in joyful agony while his wife cheerfully clapped her hands to set the rhythm.

It always seems that some embarrassing or unfortunate circumstance occurs to spoil a fun party. In the particular case of the medical student Brewster, that would invariably happen when Uncle John would indulge in an excessive amount of adult beverages and then put a lampshade upon his head before reciting the Pledge of Allegiance.

In the case of Perky Cheeks, she realized the good times had drawn to a rapid conclusion when bright red blood began to gush out of her husband's anus. Perhaps, in regards to making any direct comparison between the situations described above concerning the humiliating examples of J. D. Brewster's family member and the husband of Perky Cheeks, it was six of one and a half a dozen of the other. Go ahead; pick your poison.

Jumping out of the proverbial piss pot and into the rectum, the unfortunate rodent finally gnawed its way through the wall of the sigmoid colon, and it found brief respite in Peter's peritoneal cavity before the gerbil finally succumbed to asphyxiation. In its last angry act of retribution, the gerbil evacuated its bowels and bladder inside the free space of the peritoneal cavity before the abused tiny mammal gave up the ghost. How sad.

Peter Cheeks was suddenly in a world of trouble. Not only had a gerbil chewed through his bowel wall, causing massive bleeding from his sigmoid colon, but the creature had proceeded to shit and piss inside of the internal open space within the man's abdomen. That was not a good thing. Upon the couple's arriving at the emergency room and explaining the peculiar circumstances to Dr. Frank Barber and medical student J. D. Brewster, the on-call surgical team was immediately called down to take charge of the situation. The student and the attending were rendered speechless by the story, but they were compelled to look on as the surgical team put Mr. Cheeks onto the elevator that was to take him directly to the surgery suite. As the patient departed, Brewster said in a nonchalant manner, "Well, I guess that's something you don't see every day."

Without looking back at his student, Dr. Barber said, "I've never ceased to be amazed at the weird shit that walks through these emergency room doors. Tell me, Brewster—how are you holding up in light of, well, the bad things that happened to you?"

"I'm filled with hatred to the point where I can't even see straight," Brewster replied.

Dr. Barber uttered an unexpected response. "That's good. I suspect other well-meaning friends and family members have told you that you need to let things go."

"They have indeed," Brewster replied.

"After my wife was kidnapped and disappeared at the hands of the Calle Vampiro cartel," Barber said, "I can never let things go. What you've been told, my young ward, is a crock of shit. You must be able to harness and focus every fiber of hatred in your very being. You must hope and pray that someday you'll be able to render your own brand of clinical justice if the opportunity might ever arise at some distant point in the future. After my wife vanished, the unadulterated and uncompromising hatred that now fills my soul is sadly, the only thing I have left."

⸻

Mr. Cheeks required a colostomy, which, in layman's terms, meant he had to shit into a bag taped to his outer abdominal wall. The decomposing dead rodent, several droppings of gerbil shit, rodent fur, and a glass vase complete with plastic flowers were successfully evacuated from the patient's body. After a thorough and repeated peritoneal lavage, Mr. Cheeks would be hospitalized for several weeks, requiring antibiotics to manage his life-threatening infectious peritonitis and associated sepsis. In retrospect, Mr.

Cheeks probably would have been better off if Perky had just taken a loaded gun and simply gut-shot the poor bastard.

The pathologist would end up having a field day when he completed his report about the foreign objects that had been recovered from the patient. As a case in point, the pathology report that accurately described the vase and the plastic flowers Perky Cheeks had shoved up her husband's derriere went on for no fewer than eleven pages.

The pathologist went to great lengths to find out the particular brand name of the vase, its precise dimensions, and where the item was locally retailed. He did the same for the artificial flowers, right down to counting and thoroughly describing every plastic stem, leaf, and petal that could possibly be forensically analyzed.

When the pathologist completed his laborious catalog of kinky colonic kitsch, the doctor was kind enough to contact Perky Cheeks and her husband to see if they wanted to have the vase and plastic flowers returned to them, which they did. The pathologist then put the vase and plastic flowers into a giant ziplock bag and mailed the package back to the married couple via express delivery. Wow! How thoughtful.

⌁⌁⌁

Officer Faulkland sent a radio message to the HPD that he was trailing a 1970 Oldsmobile Cutlass that appeared to be a stolen vehicle, as it had license plates that had been previously assigned to a different car. The police cruiser maintained a separation of no less than three car lengths from the Cutlass in question, which was driven by a black suspect who appeared to be the sole occupant of the vehicle. Faulkland immediately realized the man was none other than Darryl Hewitt, an at-large career criminal who had been stopped near the medical center in the month of May. The officer had made a previous fundamental mistake by letting the suspect go before completing a background check for any outstanding arrest warrants. The police officer was not about to make the same mistake twice.

Informed by a radio transmission, Faulkland learned that the suspect was likely armed and most likely had an accomplice believed to be named Mumbo Jamar Apoo, a.k.a. Cleophus McDonald, a.k.a. the Big Nig. The officer was informed not to engage in a hot pursuit until adequate backup was available. Fortunately for the law enforcement officer, that was only minutes out. When he saw that the Oldsmobile had nestled into a nondescript warehouse near the fourth ward, the cruiser passed by the establishment as if nothing were out of the ordinary. Unbeknownst to the police officer, the small warehouse was the chop-shop operation for Smeg Nog and Big Nig. Once past the warehouse, Officer Faulkland strategically circled the block to wait for additional manpower, firepower, and the all-important emergency search warrant.

As Smeg Nog entered the chop shop, he called out to Big Nig, who was busy lowering a late-model engine and transmission assembly into a plywood crate.

"I'm telling you what, Big; I must be living a charmed life," the junior partner said. "I thought I was being followed by a Casper copper, but when I pulled into the shop, he just drove on past."

Big Nig stopped what he was doing and looked over to his accomplice and then back over to the Oldsmobile Cutlass that Nog had driven into an open bay. He looked over to his junior partner once again and asked, "What are you not telling me about this Cutlass?"

"Nothin' to say."

"You told me this was a legitimate purchase from a used-car lot," Big said. "Don't tell me now that you're riding around in a hot set of wheels."

"Well—"

"Damnation straight to hell, Darryl!" Big exclaimed. "You know the rules. We don't drive around in merchandise we've obtained on the street! That's inventory, little man, plain and simple. It all comes to this shop to get stripped and shipped."

"Straight up, Big, I boosted this car two months ago." Darryl Hewritt was compelled to make a confession. "It used to belong to that white nurse we up and whacked in the parking lot at the medical center a year ago. I wanted this car, and I just had to have it. Well, the car just mysteriously reappeared, and since I already happened to have the car keys for this beast, it was a natural, my man."

"Is that so?"

"All I had to do was change the color scheme from bronze to black and score a new set of plates from some other car," Smeg said.

Smeg's partner in crime took a peek out the door and saw a Houston Police Department cruiser parked about a block away. The jig was up, and Big knew it. Big walked over to the large wheeled tool chest and palmed a nine-millimeter automatic that he kept hidden in the top drawer. Sadly, his partner was totally unaware of what was going to happen next. In fact, it had never occurred to the junior partner that his criminal associate ever carried any hardware.

"Darryl, do you know why you have the nickname Smeg Nog?" Big asked.

"Well, I can only guess it's because I be da nig nog who like da egg nog when the fat bearded white man in the red suit be comin' down the chimney to terrorize all the little colored chillun' just befo' he up n' steals all their shit during the Kwanzaa celebration."

"Good guess, but no, that's not the right answer," Big Nig replied. "It's because you're a nasty little bastard who got da' smegma breath."

"Why you be dat way?" Smeg asked. "What's the matter with you? What's smegma anyhow?"

"It's da' dirty, stinky dick cheese dat you smell like, you dumbass!" his partner in crime replied.

"You disgust me," Nog said, "and I do mean all of you. That includes the half of you that's colored-up all proper like, and also the other half of you that got contaminated by some filthy, red neck cracker that was pimp-slappin' yo' mamma!"

"Damn it, Darryl, I told you never to bring that up again!"

"Time to rub your nose in it, half-breed!" Nog crowed. "It's getting' pretty late in the afternoon. I'll bet your nasty-ass white half would like a tasty crumpet and a spot of tea right about now. When you're slurpin' from some fine porcelain saucer, don't forget to extend your pinky finger. It'll make you all genteel, and all refined, and all sophisticated, and shit like that!"

"At this time, I'm officially dissolving our partnership."

With that, Big Nig pulled out the concealed weapon and shot his partner in the face, right underneath his left eye. When he realized he was about to be murdered, Darryl Hewritt stuck out his right hand in a defensive motion. Before the projectile struck him in the face, the bullet blew off his right thumb.

As Smeg Nog collapsed to the ground, Big grabbed a yellow hard hat and an orange safety vest from the wardrobe of disguises he kept at the chop shop. He grabbed a pickax that was on hand and ran out the back door and into the alleyway without a moment to spare. He briskly walked down a block and then purposefully emerged right in front of the police car that was still parked on the street. He cheerfully waved at the policeman as he walked right past the prowler.

It appeared to Officer Faulkland that Big was nothing more than a utility worker in the vicinity. After Big passed another block, he pulled off his disguise and jumped onto a city bus to flee the scene.

Once the search warrant and the police backup finally arrived, Officer Faulkland and his associates broke into the chop shop to find that Darryl Hewritt was critically wounded but still alive. His partner, Mumbo Jamar Apoo, was nowhere to be found.

Once the ambulance arrived, Smeg was loaded onto the

transportation gurney. The EMT staff members in attendance were quick to realize that the critically injured individual was clinging on to a bloody object that turned out to be the man's own right thumb! After the police obtained a confession and statement from Darryl Hewritt, the emergency medical technicians placed the severed thumb in a plastic bag and promptly packed it in an ice chest to be sent with the patient to the emergency room at the Gulf Coast University Hospital.

Upon his arrival at the emergency room, Darryl Hewritt was lethargic. He was greeted at the door by none other than J. D. Brewster and the emergency room resident, Dr. Shorts. Brewster couldn't believe who had just rolled into the hospital, and he promptly called Willy Mammon to come down to join the party as soon as possible. As Willy was working on an ophthalmology elective, he had the luxury of taking frequent breaks in the Vinyl Lounge just down the hall from the emergency room.

After Willy received the most gracious invitation from J. D. Brewster to attend an impromptu soiree in honor of Darryl Hewritt, Mammoth was able to make it to the emergency room in seconds flat. As the emergency room technicians transferred the patient onto a gurney in an open emergency room stall, medical student Susan Carroll arrived to lend assistance. IV fluids were already running, and tubes of blood had been obtained and sent to the laboratory for analysis. The cardiac monitor revealed that the patient's heart rate was starting to brady down, and the patient was on the threshold of going into a cardiopulmonary arrest. It was imperative that they stabilize the patient before sending him to get an emergency CT scan of his head.

"I'd better get the crash cart right now before we lose this guy," Dr. Shorts said.

Upon Willy Mammon's arrival, Darryl Hewritt suddenly realized he was in the hands of his mortal enemies.

"Did they put my thumb in that ice chest at the foot of my bed?"

Hewritt asked. "I don't want to lose it. By the way, I'm sorry for what I did to you fellows in the past."

Mammon opened up the ice chest and found the thumb wrapped in a ziplock plastic bag. "Yes, I have your thumb right here. I am going to give it to Mr. Brewster, and he's going to save it in an envelope for you. That way, you won't lose it."

The Mammoth didn't even bother to put on a pair of gloves when he pulled Darryl's thumb out of the ziplock bag and handed it to J. D. Brewster. With all of the commotion occurring during the emergency situation, none of the other medical personnel noticed when Brewster proceeded to sniff Smeg Nog's severed thumb as if it were a Cuban Churchill before he stuffed it into a trash bin!

When Brewster had done so, he popped his eyebrows up and down quickly and looked at Darryl with a big smile on his face. The only one who witnessed the crime was Smeg Nog himself, but at that point, he was becoming too weak to even muster a protest.

"By the way," Mammon said, "Mr. Brewster and I would strongly encourage you to consider accepting a DNR code status."

Susan Carroll didn't understand the meaning of what apparently had been some kind of a tasteless inside joke, as Willy Mammon and Brewster both laughed at the peculiar proclamation. Susan had no time to contemplate the significance of Willy's callous demeanor when Darryl Hewitt experienced an acute cardiopulmonary arrest.

A code blue was called, and Dr. Shorts and the code team worked furiously without success to try to resuscitate the patient. Susan Carroll helped out as best as she could, but she had no clue why both Mammon and Brewster simply stood on the sidelines as if they were zealous sports fans intently watching a game of football.

When an end to the code was finally called, Dr. Shorts pulled off his gloves, dropped them upon the face of the dead patient, and said, "I am going to wander off and dictate a death summary. As this is a murder victim, you know the drill, boys and girls. This is another stinky stiffy for the coroner."

Everyone departed the emergency room stall except for Brewster and Willy Mammon. After they had given each other a celebratory high five, Brewster said, "I want to cut off this bastard's testicles and jam them into his mouth before they haul his corpse off to the morgue."

"It is finished," Willy said in an effort to wisely restrain his colleague from mutilating the dead body. "Look, my pasty friend, don't do anything stupid. This is going to be a case for the forensic pathologist. Besides, if you defile this dead body, you're nothing more than a sadistic barbarian."

"Well, as the old saying goes, if the shoe fits, wear it. In my case," Brewster added, "perhaps the old saying that applies to me should go, 'If the foo' shits, wear it.'"

⸺⸺

Antonia Alabaster and the Your Witness News team arrived and asked for a statement, but the attending physician, Dr. Bryan, was not inclined to talk to the media. As Dr. Shorts was off in the medical record section, dictating a death summary, he was not available to step up to the plate to issue a statement either. Although it was not a medical school or hospital policy to have medical students do anything in such a capacity, Dr. Bryan told Susan Carroll to talk to the reporters.

"Throw these jokers a bone, and then get them the hell out of here," Wilt said. "Tell the media that a man arrived to our ER via ambulance with a gunshot wound to his face. Fill them in that sadly, our resuscitative efforts were unsuccessful."

"Anything else?"

"One other thing," Wilt said. "Don't give them any more information other than that. Don't tell them the name of the patient. This whole ordeal should not last more than a minute or so. Now, listen, Susan: the reporter, Antonia Alabaster, is Brewster's cousin, so I don't want J. D. talking to the television crew at all. Brewster is one verbose son of a bitch, and he doesn't know when to shut up! After what Brewster went through last month, he's become a loose cannon."

Susan Carroll followed the instructions given to her, and the television news crew left the emergency room with a compelling but incomplete story. After all, as the saying went, "If it bleeds, it leads."

After morning report on the following day, Dr. Shorts asked the medical students to stay behind for a discussion before the emergency room shift began for the day. Expecting a rare didactic session, Susan Carroll and the other students were surprised at the blistering verbal assault rendered by Dr. Shorts.

"Susan, what in hell is the matter with you?" Pooty Shorts asked. "I'm the resident, and I'm the one who's supposed to be talking to the media if they want to interview somebody. I missed a chance to be on TV because of you. I don't give a shit that Dr. Bryan instructed you to talk to those people. That was my job, and you ruined it for me. I wanted to be on TV, and now I might not ever have another chance. Don't you ever do it again!"

"I'm sorry, Paul," Susan said as she started to cry.

Brewster snapped. He grabbed Pooty Shorts by his necktie and physically dragged him out of the conference room. He proceeded to whisper something into the right ear of Dr. Shorts that no doubt was some type of threat. J. D. kicked Pooty in the shorts and chased him down the hallway before he returned to his other colleagues, who looked upon him with shock and awe. Brewster politely asked each of them to quickly leave the conference room.

When he locked the door so nobody else could enter the room, he was surprised to see that Susan Carroll was still sitting at the conference table.

"Would you like to split a jelly doughnut with me?" Susan asked. "Now, jelly doughnuts are near and dear to my heart, so I don't just go about offering them to other people in a willy-nilly fashion. I see now that you have been dating a fat, old, hippie, dinosaur loser chick who must be ten years older than you are. She even wears plastic flowers in her hair. How lame is that? Oh my God, are you kidding me?"

"Why in the world does everybody bust my chops about Stella Link?" Brewster asked. It was not a rhetorical question, but nonetheless, he didn't receive an answer from Susan Caroll. "To be frank, she's the most decent human being I've ever known."

"Well, that might be true, but there's a rumor going around that you two had some sort of fight about something, and you kicked her to the curb. Strong work, mi amigo!" Susan exclaimed. "Anyhow, I'm not sure what to think now. Missy Brownwood told me she thought you two were getting back together again. If that's not the case, give me a call sometime."

"Well," Brewster said, "Missy Brownwood talks too much."

When the security service finally arrived to break down the door to the conference room, Susan Carroll and J. D. Brewster heard angry shouts and a heavy-handed fist banging on the door from the outside hallway. They paid little heed to the commotion as Susan pushed Brewster back into his chair before she sat squarely upon his lap.

Possessing sharp incisors, Susan whispered into Brewster's ear, "I'm going to make you cry like a little schoolgirl. It would be good for you, no?"

The young woman bit Brewster's earlobe hard enough to draw blood. Although he moaned in pain, J. D. made no overt effort to thwart Susan's advances. Momentarily, Brewster and his amorous colleague were suddenly showered with shrapnel from wood splinters when the door to the conference room was finally breached with a battering ram.

5

THE RORSCHACH TEST

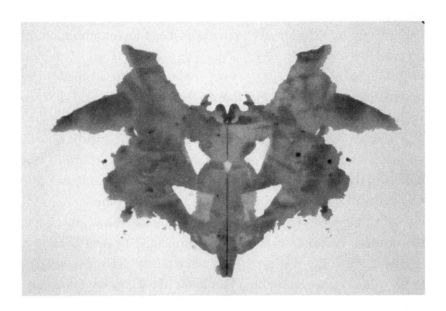

As Brewster jumped off the couch, he pointed to the slide projector image on the screen and said, "What a stupid question. Can't you see it? It's obvious. If you don't know what you're looking at, Dr. Sorass, maybe you need to get your eyes checked."

Corka Sorass leaned back in his chair and said, "Well, I do wear glasses, come to think of it. Why don't you just humor me? Just tell me what you think you see in this Rorschach inkblot."

Brewster sat back down on the psychiatrist's couch and said, "If this was a snake, it would have slithered off of the wall to bite you in the ass."

"So you think this somehow looks like a snake to you?" Dr. Sorass furrowed his brow as he looked over to Brewster. "I'm sorry, but that's absurd."

"For shit sake, pay attention! I didn't say it looked like a snake!" Brewster exclaimed. "This inkblot clearly shows two very large and very angry Negroes who are facing each other while they're beating the holy shit out of a little old lady who is lying on the ground in front of them. As you can see, they're kicking her. She's extending her arms up into the air. She's obviously pleading for mercy, but to no avail."

"Well, why would these two people beat this woman?" the psychiatrist said. "What did she do to them that would deserve such a severe punishment?"

"That's it—blame the victim," Brewster said sarcastically. "It was all her fault. Sounds like some seriously sick liberal bullshit you believe in there, Dr. Sorass. I guess in retrospect, you're correct. She was guilty of something. She was guilty of being white."

"Most people look upon this inkblot and see something happy, like a moth," Corka Sorass said as he leaned toward Brewster. "Perhaps you're afraid of moths like some people around here seem to be. Don't you see something that looks like wings on either edge of the inkblot?"

"Now that you mention it," Brewster said, "I do see what look to me to be wings—affixed to the two very large and very angry Negroes. Perhaps they're black winged demons or black bats that are straight from the bowels of hell."

The psychiatrist rarely made judgmental comments regarding anything his patients openly declared in counseling sessions; however, Dr. Sorass was about to make an exception on that particular occasion.

"Mr. Brewster, I find that your comments are quite disturbing.

You seem to have a thematic fixation on a certain specific minority racial group."

"You might be on to something, Dr. Sorass," Brewster said with a sly grin. "What do you think it means? Am I nothing more than a compulsive, agoraphobic masturbator? That might indeed be the case, because I truly believe I've been gender confused since birth. You see, sometimes I feel like I'm a man who's been trapped inside a woman's vagina."

"That's what we're here to find out," Sorass said. "I want you to take a look at the next Rorschach pattern and tell me how you interpret what you are looking at."

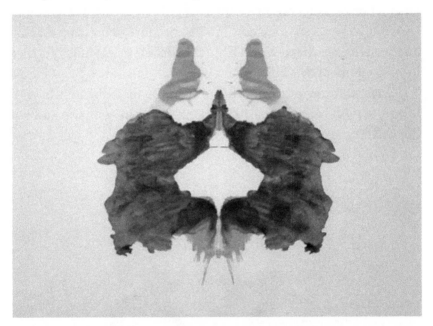

"Oh, this one's easy," Brewster responded. "What I see here are two very large and very angry Negroes who are facing each other and who are giving each other a high five after they just administered a beatdown to an old white woman after they tried to steal her car. It's obvious to anybody who has eyes in his head. Look at it, Professor! My goodness, is this a happy image or what? They have blood on their faces and their feet after they kicked a woman to death, and they have grimy shit all over their hands. It certainly would appear they really enjoyed killing that unfortunate little old white lady. It must have been a sporting event for the two bastards in this image!"

"Mr. Brewster," Sorass said, "your visions are very dark."

"Think about it," Brewster said. "Hunting for polar bears, hunting for white doves, or hunting for white women and administering lethal beatdowns in order to steal their social security checks—it's all the same to these barbarians, right? Sounds like a shit pot full of fun, if you ask me! Are all of these Rorschach inkblots going to be abstract images of black-on-white hate crimes? If so, this is going to turn out to be a very long day. I might need to go out, cop a whiz, and then fire up a hand-rolled Churchill before we get much further into any more of this bullshit."

"I can tell you're finding this to be quite tedious," Sorass said. "Okay, Mr. Brewster, please have a look at this next image, and tell me what it means to you."

Brewster took one glance at the image and said, "This one is a piece of cake, but thus far, it is the most personally offensive image I've seen today. What we have here are two very large and very angry Negroes who are facing each other while they are boosting a V-8 engine out of an old Mustang. If you must know, it's not just any V-8 engine. It happens to be a 428-cubic-inch-displacement Ford Cobra Jet that has been stroked and bored to over four hundred fifty cubic inches. With the experimental Conelec fuel-injection device, port matching, and long exhaust headers, that baby will crank out something just a little bit south of about four hundred eighty horsepower. Wow, what a thing of beauty! Just to think that an automotive engineering marvel such as this is being stolen by two very large and very angry Negroes—it's enough to make any automotive aficionado sick to his or her stomach."

Dr. Sorass said, "You keep referring to the leading-edge images as being identified as individuals of African American persuasion. How can you make such a claim from this inkblot picture you are now looking at?"

"It's quite easy," Brewster answered. "Just take a look at this image. The two guys who are stealing the engine both have an enormous reproductive appendage. Any guys who possess prodigious peckers of that capacity have to be black men. For shit's sake, those beef logs are only semitumescent, yet their peckers are still hanging down to their knees. Holy shit, Batman! However, I don't know why they appear to be wearing pointy high-heeled shoes. Maybe they're a couple of homosatchels. What do you think?"

Oddly enough, Dr. Sorass took another look at the Rorschach inkblot and nodded in agreement. "I guess I can see what you're talking about. Let's move forward." Dr. Sorass advanced the slide cassette projector, and the next image appeared on the screen. "Tell me how you interpret this next inkblot."

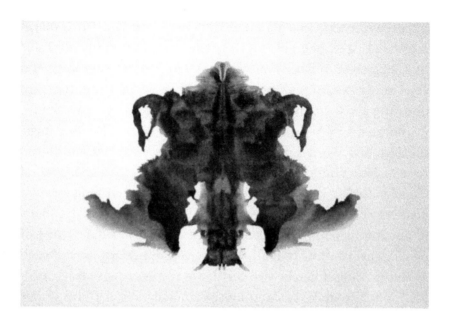

"This one's a bit tougher. Let me look at it for a moment before I come up with an answer."

Brewster studied the inkblot a bit before he conjured a response.

"Okay, I see it now," Brewster said. "At first, it was a bit tricky, but it's all come into focus. What we're looking at is an unfortunate white man who just got the shit beat out of him by two very large and very angry Negroes with a lead pipe. The victim's feet are at the bottom of the image, and his head and shoulders are toward the top of the screen. The lower realm of the inkblot readily reveals the macerated remains of what used to be the man's right testicle. As you can readily discern, his gonad just got pulverized into an amorphous mass of bloody goo. Can you see it?"

"This is supposed to be your interpretation," Sorass said, "not mine."

"Swell," Brewster replied. "Let me spell it out for you. His lifeless right testicle has just exploded, and the shrapnel is splattered as a linear vertical streak against the asphalt between the figure's two legs. I'll wager, Professor, that you have no idea what that would feel like. Well, I certainly do. Having your right testicle explode is not exactly a trip to the beach. My goodness, this image certainly brings back many happy memories. Thank you for sharing these inkblots with me. Nice job, Professor!"

Corka Sorass stroked his beard as he studied Brewster's face. "I believe I don't have to subject you to any additional Rorschach inkblot pictures. It would seem to me that you're a hard-core racist."

"Wow! Do you think so?" Brewster asked. "It never occurred to me."

"Have you felt this way all of your life?" Sorass said. "If you have, it is my opinion that it was a big mistake to allow you to enter medical school back in 1977."

"I have no problem with black people," Brewster said emphatically. "In fact, I like black people. In fact, there is a woman who works here as a nurse on the med-surg unit whom I've known since she was only eleven years old. In fact, she was raised by my uncle, and I consider her to be my cousin, and I love her as such. In fact, this woman has a relationship with a black man who may very well be one of the best, if not only, friends I have ever had in my entire life. In fact, this man is close enough as a friend that we're able to talk shit to each other over the nuances of our very own idiosyncratic, racial predilections. Should I throw out any more 'in facts' for you to chew on? So no, I don't have a problem with black people."

"What then?" Sorass asked.

"Simple as pie," Brewster said. "I do have a problem with jigs, spooks, porch monkeys, yard apes, urban thugs, black racists, and the evil parasites who are the moochers and bloodsuckers in our society. Are there white people out there who fit the bill of being evil? Sure, but I wasn't attacked by white people. Mrs. Irene Segulla wasn't attacked by white people either. I'm speaking to you from a very specific frame of reference. Forgive me for this pun, but it colors the way I look at things now. To be honest, my concern is about the victims who get preyed upon. These are the people who're actually trying to walk the straight and narrow, and that includes black and white people alike."

Sorass scoffed at Brewster's sociological critique. "So you consider yourself a victim?"

"It sounds to me as if you've not been keeping up with current events!" Brewster answered in anger. "Do you want me to drop my trousers? I've got prima facie evidence right here, Doc. Take a look. You're free to count the number of testicles currently occupying space within the constricted universe of my empty ball sack. Not only will I help you do the math, but I'll even spot you the only numerical digit in this mentally taxing mathematical equalization: it happens to be zero."

"Not so fast," Sorass said. "It would appear that you are ignorant of a term that was introduced as early as the 1960s: social justice. Do you deny that society at large owes something to a race of people who were once held as slaves against their own free will? I see that you're a man who should be knowledgeable of the past, as you have a bachelor of science degree in history. You are in fact, a published scholar in that particular academic field. The burden of slavery is uniquely a sin of southern white people, of which you're one. In my opinion, southern white people owe black people a lot. You specifically owe the black population of this country reparations and a whole—"

"What?" Brewster asked. "Take a hike, Doc."

"Don't interrupt me," Sorass said. "You've had your turn. In light of the fact that you're very well aware of what was done to blacks in the past, occasionally, we must look the other way when something bad happens, such as what you now erroneously perceive to be black-on-white racism. I don't believe that black-on-white racism can actually exist. The very words you used have indicated that you are a bona fide racist. A man like you might not have the moral fortitude to become a physician. I want to make something completely clear to you: whether or not you're allowed to continue with your medical school training here at the Gulf Coast College of Medicine is totally contingent upon my recommendations to the administration."

J. D. Brewster got up from the couch and stood in front of the chair where Dr. Sorass was sitting. The medical student loomed over the psychiatrist and said, "Wait just a minute, Professor. You're certainly not treating me like the patient. In fact, if I didn't know better, it would seem to me that you're hanging me out to dry. Am I your patient, or is the administration at the Gulf Coast College of Medicine your client? Or perhaps society at large is now your primary concern? It can't be all three of us, now, can it?"

"My primary responsibility is to—"

"Shove it!" Brewster said. "Social justice my ass! I believe in something that's far more valid, and that's personal responsibility. Look, I know you came from some shit-hole country in Eastern Europe, but you moved to New York City after the war, and you lived there for many years before you came down here to Texas. Tell me, Professor—what did you think of New York City?"

Without hesitation, Corka Sorass answered Brewster's question. "It was and still is the greatest city in the world. New York City is a very cosmopolitan and very open-minded city. It was nothing like anything I've ever encountered down here in the South. After all, there were never any slaves in New York State."

"You are wrong about that, Professor," Brewster said. "What a load of sanctimonious crap. Up until July 4, 1826, New York City had more slaves than any place in the United States outside of Charleston, South Carolina. That was only thirty-five years before the outbreak of that little fraternal squabble that began at Fort Sumter in '61. In fact, there were still a lot of slaves in New York City up until the conclusion of the American Civil War, so don't try to sell me some kind of a white, southern, horseshit, bullshit guilt trip! I can tell you right now that I'm not buying it."

"Please sit down," Sorass said. "You're invading my personal space."

"Abraham Lincoln was a major-league hypocritical dick," Brewster said as he took a seat on the psychiatrist's couch. "If he really gave a shit about the slaves, why did the Emancipation Proclamation only free the slaves in the eleven states that had withdrawn from the Union? In fact, Abraham Lincoln freed nobody! At the time, the Confederate States of America was a separate nation. Prior to the American Civil War, there was nothing in the United States Constitution that said a state, or a collection of states, could not legally and willfully withdraw from the Union if so desired. That's a fact. Lincoln's declaration to outlaw slavery in a completely different country he had no authority over was simply a straw-man proclamation. What a joke."

"What are you saying?" Dr. Sorass asked, missing Brewster's sociopolitical point. "Don't tell me that you believe the institution of slavery was appropriate."

Brewster waved off the psychiatrist's comment. "Yes, slavery was wrong. No rational human being can think otherwise, but reparations have already been paid. At the last count, more than six hundred thousand Americans died during the American Civil War over that issue. It would seem to me that reparations have been paid in blood. There was a sin of slavery, but it was not uniquely a sin among southern whites. I resent your implication that the states north of the Mason-Dixon Line were somehow, pardon the expression, lily white and clean over what Lincoln called a peculiar institution."

"What if I concede that contentious point to you?"

"As well you should," Brewster said. "If the government wants to hand over any monetary reparations, then I am going to be standing in line to collect a few dollars to put into my own pocket. I claim to you right now that I'm black and proud of it. I declare that I'm transblack. When I was a little boy, I found a black Raggedy Andy doll on the playground in my neighborhood, and I kept it. That fact in and of itself proves that I was already identifying with black people. I'll wager that as a transracial person, I'll be able to become the head of the local chapter of the NAACP if I so desire."

"So you're now a black man?"

"Just for this week," Brewster said. "Maybe next week I'll get a motorized rickshaw, move to Florida, and then declare that I'm a woman from the Philippines."

"You are a lunatic. I actually don't think it's possible for a white man—or a white woman, for that matter—to join the NAACP, much less become an administrator for that particular organization."

"I'm telling you," Brewster said. "It will happen someday just because people will declare themselves to be transblack. It's a free country, and I'm free to choose my own race. After all, don't liberals espouse that race is merely a state of mind? If so, I'm only asking for you people to practice what you preach. If the government is going to be passing out monetary reparations, count me in, soul brother! Right on!"

The psychiatrist shook his head and looked upon Brewster with dismay.

"You asked if I was a racist and if I had been one all of my life," Brewster said. "I can categorically report to you that yes, I am indeed a racist, but I only became one at 11:48 p.m. on June 19, 1981."

"How can you possibly know at what exact time you became a racist?" Dr. Sorass asked.

"That's an easy question to answer," Brewster replied. "That's the precise time when two very large and very angry Negroes beat me in the groin with a lead pipe until my only viable testicle exploded. Oh, did I mention that I am now sterile? Yes, I became sterile, and I'll never sire any children. My bloodline dies with me. I can't tell you how extraordinarily happy I am about all of that. As best as I can tell, human beings have three primary directives; we're hardwired to defecate, masturbate, and procreate. I've distilled the first two items down to a fine science, but the third item on the list will now forever escape me. Yes, there is no doubt about it; I am now sterile, and I became a racist at the exact same time. Wow! What a coincidence."

Try as he might, Corka Sorass was unable to refute the foundations for Brewster's world views. Therefore, it was time to delve into other subjects.

"I've looked at your college transcripts, and I find it curious to note that you took a science course called Extraterrestrial Life," Sorass said. "Tell me—what did you get out of that class? Do you personally believe there is other intelligent life out there in the universe?"

"Who cares? Besides that, who in hell could possibly know the answer to that question?" Brewster replied. "Whether or not the answer is yes or no, it would be an amazing revelation. On one hand, I ascribe to what's known as the Fermi paradox. If there's intelligent life out there in the universe, where is it? Surely, if there are other civilizations more advanced than ours, they should've been here by now. I'd imagine that alien visitors who may have come here already would have likely set up a few Laundromats and fast food joints to make a quick buck or two."

"Were you always the class clown?"

"Sorry," Brewster said. "I just can't help myself. If beings from outer space haven't come here to mess up our economy, then these illegal aliens are likely here to have an anchor baby to get free government services, like housing, education, and welfare checks. After that, I suspect things will quickly snowball out of control with wave migration. Sadly, I predict that every one of those scrawny, giant-headed gray illegal alien bastards will likely register as Democratic Party voters. Perish the thought."

"Try to be serious for once."

"For shit's sake," Brewster said, "every illegal alien who has entered our country has come here with that particular objective. In any event, thus far, there has been no verifiable indication that such a visitation from some other part of the galaxy has ever occurred. On the other hand, I must tell you that when I was on my psychiatry rotation with you last month, I met a patient who stated that his father worked for a mortuary service in Roswell, New Mexico, back in 1947."

"What of it?"

"He made the outrageous claim that a flying saucer crashed there in July of that year," Brewster said. "This mortuary service that employed the man's father was allegedly commissioned by the 509th Atomic Bomb group out of Roswell to provide no fewer than three small caskets in order to transport extraterrestrial biological entities to Fort Worth, Texas, on a B-29 bomber. Well, that story sounded like an industrial load of manure to my ears, but nonetheless, the universe is vast indeed. It would be somewhat hard to believe that the Creator expended such a great deal of energy to make an entire universe for creatures as unworthy as Homo sapiens."

The psychiatrist was momentarily stunned. "Wait just one moment. Are you trying to tell me that you are a deist? Have you not heard of the big bang theory?"

"Well, of course I've heard of that cosmological postulate," Brewster replied. "In fact, my classmates and I became well versed in the subject matter during my college course on extraterrestrial life. The scientist named Georges Lemaître was the first to propose that the universe was an infinitely expanding entity that could be tracked back eons ago to a singular quantum event of origin. He actually introduced that concept more than fifty years ago, so this is nothing new. I believe that most astrophysicists contend that the universe is probably twelve or thirteen billion years old. Why would I have a problem with any of that?"

"I am just trying to understand your logic, or lack thereof," the psychiatrist said. "If you're a deist, you believe that something called God created the universe. Nothing exists outside of the realm of space-time. Therefore, this so-called God of the multitudes of Walmart-shopping, unenlightened humans who inhabit this planet simply can't exist. Nor could a whimsical figment of the imagination spawned in feeble minds ever create the universe. I would surmise that someday the laws of astrophysics are likely to confirm that the universe simply created itself out of nothing at all."

"I'm sorry, Professor, but you're a flaming idiot," Brewster said. "If nothing exists outside of the realm of space-time, then any laws of physics that could possibly account for a self-initiating and self-propagating universe could not exist outside of the realm of space-time either. Did you think about that? If, by definition, God is omniscient, omnipresent, and omnipotent, then He's certainly not bound by the realm of space-time; he created the laws of physics that account for the big bang. In fact, He created space-time."

"I'm confused," Dr. Sorass said. "Before we started this session, I asked you to write down no fewer than three operative principles you hold to be true in your life. I will recite your beliefs in the order you wrote them down. Number one: 'No good deed goes unpunished.' It would seem to me that sadly, you're a very cynical young man. Number two: 'Everything in the universe is connected somehow.' Well, if you believe in the big bang theory, irrespective as to whether or not it was an act of God, I'll grant you that everything in the universe must be connected somehow. What I'm having trouble with is the following statement that you wrote down. Number three: 'God backed the wrong primate.' That self-deprecating remark indicates to me that you're an atheist or, at the very least, an agnostic. This third operative principal is incongruous with somebody who is a deist."

"No, not at all," Brewster said. "How dare you think I'm an atheist? I believe that God created the universe, but we, as human beings, are total failures who're no longer worthy of his attention anymore. Please explain something to me, Dr. Sorass. Stella Link told me long ago that you're of Hebraic persuasion and are originally from Eastern Europe. If you're Jewish, how could you be an atheist? That makes no sense to me at all. After all, are not the Jews directly responsible for the monotheistic foundation of no fewer than three of the great religions found on this planet? I, for one, am indeed grateful for that."

"From an ethnic standpoint, I am indeed Jewish," Sorass answered. "However, I'm enlightened, and that is why I'm an atheist. Religious Jews, specifically people like Dr. Yeshua Rabbi, are anathema to me. Frankly, I can't even stand being around the foolish people who live in the backwater, fly-over parts of this country. Because they're primitive and ignorant peons, it's not surprising to me that they get bitter, may cling to their guns and superstitious religions, and are generally xenophobic."

Never in his life had J. D. met an ethnic Jew who was an atheist. It was now becoming rather unsettling for Brewster to even be in the same room with Dr. Sorass. The medical student suddenly remembered the expressed reservations that his mentor, Dr. Yeshua Rabbi, had also felt about the psychiatrist.

Brewster couldn't quite put his finger on the matter, but it appeared to the medical student that Dr. Sorass was a man who must have easily reached the sixty-five-thousand-mile mark on his odometer. If that were the case, the psychiatrist certainly seemed to be in need of a front-end alignment, oil change, tire rotation, and radiator flush.

"You now know about my ethnic constitution," Dr. Sorass said. "What of yours?"

"My brother traced our parental lineage all the way back to the Mayflower," Brewster responded. "My mom, however, is Italian, and she's a first-generation American. Her mother had pale blue eyes, porcelain-white skin, and blonde hair. She was from Modena in Northern Italy. My maternal grandfather, however, was dark and swarthy, and he was from the heel on the boot of the peninsula.

I have no doubt that godless, heathen Moors paddled across the pond and contaminated the Italian gene pool. All in all, that's a good thing, though, because that's how I'll be able to claim I'm black when our country starts to hand out reparations. God bless the child who's got his own, who's got his own."

"According to Christian tradition, I surmise that this is not the first time a Jew and a Roman have ever been embroiled in a contentious verbal sparring match," Dr. Sorass said wryly.

Brewster appreciated the offhand religious and historical reference. J. D. smiled and replied, "Nor do I think it will likely be the last."

"Tell me—what kind of books do you like to read?"

"I haven't done any leisure reading in years," Brewster replied. "I only concentrate on textbooks and medical journals now. Sadly, I think that'll be my lot in life. Once I get my MD degree, or perhaps I should say *if* I get my MD degree, I'll be looking at a life of nonstop continuing medical education. The minute I stop learning, I'll become obsolete."

The psychiatrist was specifically interested in seeing if there was anything in the popular culture that had any influence on the medical student recumbent on the couch in his office.

"Okay, if you don't read books, do you at least take in movies once in a while?"

"I saw the movie Jaws awhile back," Brewster said as he shrugged. "I really enjoyed that motion picture."

"Yes," the psychiatrist responded, "but that movie came out more than half a decade ago. Have you seen anything since then?"

When Brewster answered that he had not seen a movie in many years outside of his elective college class on the subject of film appreciation, Dr. Sorass asked the medical student what his all-time favorite motion picture was.

Brewster thought for moment before he answered. "Without a doubt, I would have to say that it would be the 1957 motion picture that nailed down no fewer than seven Academy Awards, including Best Picture, Best Director, Best Actor, Best Screenplay, Best Musical Score, Best Film Editing, and Best Cinematography. At the end of the millennium, I'm certain this work of art will be recognized by the American Film Institute as one of the top-ten motion pictures of all time. Of course, I am talking about David Lean's undisputed masterpiece, The Bridge on the River Kwai."

"That's a peculiar choice, or so it would seem to me."

"Although it's true that Alec Guinness deserved the Oscar for Best Actor," Brewster said, "in my humble opinion, it was the finest work that Bill Holden ever did. He should have at least been nominated. It was a stunning performance. Needless to say, since every character in the movie, except for Dr. Clipton and the commando who was portrayed by English actor Jack Hawkins, ends up getting greased at the end of the film, it's kind of a downer. It would not exactly fall under the genre of 'warm and fuzzy' flicks, if you know what I mean. I would surmise that any man who was stupid enough to take his girlfriend to see that motion picture at the theater back in the year 1957 didn't get any nookie for a month! Nonetheless, I believe it to be the most important motion picture that's ever been made."

Dr. Sorass found Brewster's answer a bit curious. "Was it not just a war movie? If so, it would appear your tastes are a bit pedestrian."

"No, not at all," Brewster said as he wagged his index finger at the psychiatrist. "Yes, the setting was the war in the Pacific theater, but that was simply a vehicle to explore the depths of bravery, loyalty, duty, and altruism that humans may at times be capable of demonstrating to the fullest measure. More importantly, it explores humankind's desire to find meaning in life by leaving some kind of beneficial legacy, however transient, in a world perpetually torn apart by hatred and primitive tribalism."

"So I surmise that you would see yourself in the role of one of the protagonist commandos?" the psychiatrist said erroneously. "A man like you, infused with such a degree of overt hostility, would naturally gravitate to such a role."

"No, I don't think so," Brewster responded. "I actually admired the Japanese officer who oversaw the prisoner-of-war camp. The character's name was Colonel Saito, as portrayed by the great Japanese-American actor Sessue Hayakawa. In the motion picture, the colonel was duty bound to complete the Bangkok-to-Rangoon railroad, even though he must have known the planned future Japanese invasion of India was sure folly. To be frank, such a military tactic would have made as much sense as the Germans trying to invade Russia during World War II. In any event, the acting by Hayakawa was flawless, and he was nominated for Best Actor in a Supporting Role. Although the character played by Hayakawa was doomed to failure, he was duty bound to try to accomplish the task nonetheless. I found that admirable."

"Do you believe that your own life is spinning downward into what may turn out to be an ultimate failure?"

"Don't know," J. D. answered. "Hope not."

"Maybe you similarly feel that you're duty bound somehow," Sorass said. "It's not for me to say, but have you ever considered that you're simply trying for the sake of trying?"

Brewster shrugged and refused to verbally answer the professor's question. He simply circled his head about in an odd counterclockwise fashion.

"Besides an actor, Hayakawa was also a great Japanese film director, was he not?" Sorass erroneously asked. "He directed a movie years ago, the name of which I don't recall, that explored the boundaries of what human beings understand as the concept of reality and truth. After all, is there such a thing as an absolute truth, or is truth personal and purely subjective?"

"No, you're wrong on both matters," Brewster replied. "The name of the motion picture director you're referring to is none other than Akira Kurosawa, not Hayakawa. The film you're talking about was called Roshomon, from 1950."

"I stand corrected."

"As for me," Brewster said, "that movie was an artsy-fartsy load of crap. In that particular motion picture, everybody sees the same crime, but every damned witness reports something completely different! That's ridiculous. Look, I'm a simple man who tries to travel in straight lines. Truth is like the speed of light in a vacuum; it's factual and immutable."

"You're a bit of an enigma, Mr. Brewster," Dr. Sorass said. "I've been ordered to make a coherent report about you to the medical school administration, and we're going to get this done today, come hell or high water. I'm going to ascertain the truth."

"What is truth?" Brewster asked. "Do not Roman and Jew have the same truth? Are you talking about an objective truth that's factual and immutable, or are you going to generate an administrative report based on your own purely subjective truth, much like those characters who allegedly witnessed a crime at the gates of Roshomon?"

The psychiatrist became uncharacteristically angry and raised his voice. "Enough! I understand that one of your assailants has been shot and killed already, likely at the hands of the other individual who beat you with a lead pipe. Do you have any satisfaction in at least knowing that one of the perpetrators who attacked you is now dead?"

"Not in the least!" Brewster replied. "Yeah, the bastard got shot in the face all right, but I'm certainly not satisfied about it."

"What is it then?"

"Simple, Dr. Sorass," Brewster said. "I wasn't the one who pulled the trigger."

"I have one last question for you, and then we'll be finished," the psychiatrist said. "You must be honest with me. You must tell me the truth, be it Roman, Jewish, or otherwise. Based on your own perceptions of reality, you must answer this question as if truth is an absolute—factual and immutable just like the speed of light in a vacuum. If you would have a future opportunity to ever encounter this other at-large assailant who attacked you, would you try to harm him in any way?"

"What I am about to say to you is the truth that is an absolute—factual and immutable," Brewster answered without hesitation. "Not only would I kill him, but I'd also make certain he suffered horribly up until the point he quit breathing. After he was dead, I would try to disrespectfully mutilate his corpse to ensure that he would need to have a closed-casket funeral. That way, his mama wouldn't be able to look at his face before the bastard got planted into the ground."

"No!" Sorass said in shock. "What you just said indicates that you've developed homicidal psychopathic ideations."

"If the shoe fits!" Brewster said. "How well did that go over? Did you find what I said to be the highly offensive, bloodcurdling, racist invective I intended it to be? Are you incensed yet? I would certainly hope that what I just told you has made your butt pucker so badly that you just sucked the seat cushion you are sitting on halfway up into your sigmoid colon. I, for one, would readily admit that perhaps I might still have some minor residual anger-management issues I must contend with from time to time. Would you not agree?"

Unfortunately for Brewster, that was the straw that clearly broke the camel's back.

"Yes, you clearly have anger-management issues, and if you're not able to get that under control, you're going to be a danger not only to yourself but also to other people," Dr. Sorass said.

"You can take that to the bank!" The medical student cackled with a malevolent laugh.

Dr. Sorass stood up from his chair and walked toward the front door. "Mr. Brewster, you must come with me right now. We're going to administration, and I'm going to personally make my recommendations regarding the status about your future education at this institution. I insist that you be there with me while I make this presentation."

As Brewster's medical school career appeared to be coming to a premature conclusion, he followed Dr. Sorass down the stairwell toward the medical school's department of administration. The dean of the institution was about to get a surprise visit from Sorass, who was about to render a devastating blow to the medical student's future.

If Brewster had been looking for an opportunity to murder the psychiatrist, the stairwell would have been the perfect spot to commit such a crime. For Brewster, intellect prevailed, but not as a conscious choice between what was right and what was wrong. By then, Brewster had already resigned himself to the likelihood that he was about to be thrown out of medical school, and he tried to make peace with that fact.

A side door to the stairwell opened, and Sister Buena appeared, accompanied by two men wearing dark gray suits and sunglasses. As soon as she recognized Dr. Sorass, Sister Buena turned to the two men who had followed her into the stairwell and said, "Gentlemen, this is the man you're looking for!"

Once Sister Buena identified Dr. Sorass to the two strangers, she quickly departed the stairwell and disappeared down the hallway.

The two mysterious men flashed their badges to Dr. Sorass and identified themselves as special agents with the Federal Bureau of Investigation. After reading the psychiatrist his Miranda rights, they took him into custody and charged him with war crimes committed during World War II.

As the two agents pulled Sorass away from the stairwell, Brewster recognized that Dr. Rabbi was leaning against the back wall with his arms folded. For unclear reasons, Yeshua had a big smile on his face.

Upon his apprehension by federal law enforcement officers, the only thing Corka Sorass could do was stare down upon the ground while he was pulled outside and placed in a large four-door sedan to be hauled away. In short order, he would be stripped of his American citizenship and then deported, with no possible chance to return to the land of the free.

After the end of World War II, Operation Paperclip had been successful in bringing many Nazis over to United States who had special technical or scientific skills. However, the average run-of-mill Nazi collaborator who had participated in crimes against humanity was considered to be persona non grata. Dr. Corka Sorass was clearly persona non grata.

Brewster ran back to talk to the rabbi and asked, "What in hell just happened?"

"There are a lot of things that may be said about the truth," the medical student's mentor replied. "One thing I've always believed is that the truth is like cream: it will eventually rise to the top."

"That may be true," Brewster said, "but if you're standing on the banks of a pond of gradeaux, I can assure you that the scum also rises to the top."

"Corka Sorass was not from Hungary," Dr. Rabbi said. "He was actually from Poland. You're not going to believe what I'm about to tell you. Although Jewish, he was a Nazi collaborator! His father paid a great deal of money to have Corka's identification changed on the town's records from being a Jew into being a Gentile. His father only had enough money to have the identification of his son changed and not the names of his two daughters, Byda and Beeda Sorass."

"Stella previously told me that Dr. Sorass had two sisters who were lost during the war."

"Little did the old Sorass patriarch realize," Rabbi said, "Corka would commit an extreme act of betrayal. Corka sold out his family to the Nazis!"

"What?!"

"Not only his own family," Rabbi added, "but also the entire population of Jews in the vicinity who had been hiding in cellars, garages, and attics."

"I can't believe what I'm hearing!"

"Shameful, I tell you," Rabbi said. "Once these unfortunate souls were rounded up on railcars, Sorass also participated in the beatings that occurred."

"You know this how?"

"I was there, J. D.," Rabbi said. "I was an eyewitness. I remember that Sorass was a beast of a man who hit me across my back with a truncheon to force me onto a cattle car. I never forgot the face of that Sorass. I was also on the same railroad car destined to haul his two sisters, Byda and Beeda, to the gas chambers."

"Wait! His own sisters?"

"Those two beautiful young women couldn't believe their own brother ended up betraying the family. Corka also ensured that all those other people who had at one time been friends and acquaintances would face certain death."

"How could somebody like Sorass reveal the hidden locations of not only his neighbors but also his very own flesh and blood to the Nazis?" Brewster was dismayed and needed answers. "Was it for personal monetary gain?"

"There are many forms of hatred," Yeshua Rabbi replied as Brewster was compelled to cast his eyes to the floor. "Some people learn to hate others who may belong to a different race or ethnic group. Some people just learn to hate themselves. Go figure."

———

Brewster ran back to the department of psychiatry, where Stella Link was holding down the fort. Brewster was surprised to see that Stella appeared to be calm and collected.

"Do you have any idea what happened to your boss today?" Brewster asked.

"I had an idea that something was going down," Stella replied. "The FBI had been here more than once to ask me about Dr. Sorass, but they told me not to tell anybody about their visits here to the medical school. Before you got here, I already received a telephone call from Marita Midas, who's working down in patient registration. She saw that Dr. Sorass was being arrested and taken off campus. I wonder now if he was into child porn."

"No, that wasn't it," Brewster said. "It was the Rabbi who figured out that Sorass was a Nazi collaborator. Although he was Jewish, Sorass sold out his own people during World War II."

"I have no idea how somebody could do something so dreadful," Stella said, stunned by what she had just learned about her former boss.

"There are many forms of hatred," Brewster replied. "Some people learn to hate others who may belong to a different race or ethnic group. Some people just learn to hate themselves. Go figure."

"Well, before Dr. Sorass disappeared, did he give you the green light to continue with your medical school education?" Stella asked.

"No, and that's a big problem," Brewster said with obvious concern. "I'm inclined to believe that the professor thought I was a stark raving lunatic. Perhaps he's right about that. In any event, before Sorass was grabbed by the two FBI agents, I was being dragged down to administration. I'm not entirely certain, but I think he was about to drop the hammer on me."

"Don't worry, lover boy," Stella said. "It's all under control."

Stella turned to her word processor, and in a matter of seconds, she fabricated a letter addressed to the dean of the medical school. The letter indicated that Brewster was cleared, from a psychiatric standpoint, to resume his training in the clerkship rotations. She backdated the letter to the previous day and then used a rubber stamp to apply a facsimile of the signature of Dr. Sorass to the bottom of the page.

"I'm going to take this recommendation for reinstatement down to administration myself," Stella said. "While I'm gone, try to stay out of trouble for once in your life."

"I promise!"

"When I'm down there," Stella added, "I'm going to pretend that I know absolutely nothing about the mysterious disappearance of the head of the department of psychiatry. I wonder how long it will take for the medical school to replace his sorry ass."

As Stella left her desk, Brewster said three little words to his girlfriend that he had never spoken before to anybody else in his entire life: "I love you."

Although she had a huge smile on her face, she didn't turn her head to look back at Brewster when she replied, "Well, lover boy, it's about damned time!"

—⟶⟨⟩⟵—

As the month of August 1981 rolled into view, Brewster was about to prove that it was impossible for a leopard to change its spots. Just as he had done in his undergraduate work at Dick Dowling University, J. D. decided it was time to tune up his mediocre GPA by using a tried and true technique; it was again time to buff with fluff.

Brewster signed up for an elective rotation in the subspecialty of geriatric medicine. Basically, it entailed making visits and writing a few meaningless clinical notes on the charts of patients incarcerated in the off-campus elder center affiliated with the Gulf Coast General Hospital. After all, how tough could it be to hose down a handful of demented octogenarians admitted to the nursing home for custodial terminal care? With the passage of time, Brewster realized he was only becoming more callous and disconnected from other people, and frankly, he didn't care.

One of the most interesting people Brewster encountered during the geriatric clerkship elective was a man whom everybody knew as Ray "Ivory" Keynes, a volunteer who helped out at the nursing home. In essence, Ray was a middle-aged candy striper. At the time Brewster met Ray, the hospital volunteer was already fifty years old.

Ray Keynes had survived on long-term social security disability since the age of twenty-three. Ray had an alleged diagnosis of psychogenic blindness. Was it real or a fabricated affliction? In any event, it was a medical malady that Brewster had great interest in. After all, when under stress, Brewster frequently experienced the unpleasant transient sensation of the loss of vision in his left eye.

Clearly, what Ray experienced was something completely different, however. Ray apparently could actually see, but he claimed—or pretended—he was blind when the circumstances suited him. He would drive to the nursing home every Monday and Thursday, get out of his car, put on a pair of dark sunglasses, extend a blind man's cane, and then hobble into the nursing home, where he would play the piano at lunchtime to entertain the patients.

On one occasion, after a lovely rendition of Frank Sinatra's "Strangers in the Night," Brewster gave Ray a big thumbs-up from across the room. Although allegedly blind, Ray smiled, waved back at Brewster, and said, "Hey, I recognize you! You're the medical student who used to be the front man for the 1960s cover band DNR. Why don't you come down here and belt out a few tunes with me?"

Brewster replied in the affirmative, strolled down to the makeshift stage, and cranked out a baritone interpretation of "Over the Rainbow" in the key of C. A new duo was formed, albeit on rather shaky ground. With the snap of a finger, Brewster had become a sleazy lounge lizard.

On Mondays and Thursdays, Brewster and Ray "Ivory" Keynes would show up to the nursing home, wearing white tuxedo jackets they had picked up from the Salvation Army store. Their ensembles were complete with black strap-on bow ties. Although Brewster's jacket was a bit bulky, most of the patients suffered from diminished visual acuity, so his wardrobe malfunction generally went unnoticed by most.

Brewster placed a brandy snifter on top of the piano, and the patients were encouraged to generously tip the two entertainers. On more than one occasion, Ray was caught with his hand in the proverbial cookie jar, trying to abscond with all of the tip money.

Over just a few days, the medical student learned to despise Ray "Ivory" Keynes. Not only was Ray's avarice annoying, but as it turned out, the man vociferously embraced idiotic liberal convictions. Ray had conjured up something he called his own personal Keynesian theory, which professed a bizarre and evil concept that total government spending could have a positive effect on production output, inflation, and the overall economy. Despite logical discourse, Brewster failed to convince Ray otherwise. Brewster unsuccessfully argued that the opposite economic outcome would be the case if Keynes's moronic ideas ever saw the light of day.

Complicating matters was the fact that Brewster had to force his partner to cease and desist from stealing all of the contributions the patients placed in the brandy snifter. In Brewster's opinion, if one was not able to reason with an adversary, then there was nothing wrong with the tried and true technique of overt blackmail. Brewster shamelessly threatened to denounce the allegedly blind piano player as nothing more than a fraud.

In the end, Brewster turned out to be less than a paradigm of virtue in his own right. As it would turn out, the medical student was eventually able to pocket the lion's share of the tips in the brandy snifter, leaving behind Keynes as an embittered, aging sod who merely claimed he was blind.

As it turned out, Brewster's rotation on the gerontology service would be a short one. On Friday, August 14, Stella arrived at the nursing home to pick Brewster up for what was ostensibly only going to be a lunch date. Brewster was surprised to see that his suitcase was propped up on the backseat of Stella's sedan. She must have picked it up from his apartment in Bellaire. Brewster grabbed the bag and then unzipped the top of the case to discover that Stella had taken the liberty of packing his clothing and toiletry articles.

"We're going to spend a week up at my parents' farm near Waco," Stella explained. "It's high time you meet them. After that, you and I are going to spend some serious quality time together."

"Stella, I simply can't take that much time off!" Brewster protested. "I have two more weeks to go on this geriatric medicine rotation, and I'm not officially scheduled for any vacation time until the holiday season at the end of the year."

"It's all taken care of," Stella answered. "You're probably totally unaware of the fact that when the letter to the medical school administration miraculously appeared declaring that you had been granted psychiatric clearance to return to your clerkship rotations, there was also a very important second letter sent to the dean at that same time."

"There was a second letter?" Brewster asked. "What did it say?"

"Specifically, you'd been given a medical order. Ostensibly, it was from Dr. Sorass, and it was allegedly written just before he was hauled out of here by the FBI. The letter was signed with his rubber signature stamp, and it instructed you to take two weeks of mental health vacation before the end of the month of August," Stella said. "Well, lover boy, the end of August is right around the corner. As medical orders must be strictly followed, it's now time for you to take your two weeks of mental health vacation."

J. D. broke out in laughter at the clever ruse his shifty girlfriend had pulled off with the help of a word processor and a rubber-stamp facsimile of the signature of Dr. Sorass. It appeared Stella Link was indeed a kindred spirit. She was obviously a woman who could brew up her own personal brand of mischief.

"I love you," Brewster said as he shook his head in amazement at his girlfriend.

Although she had a huge smile on her face, she didn't turn her head to look at Brewster when she replied, "Well, lover boy, it's about damned time! I hope you're as excited about this trip as I am."

"We shall see," Brewster shrugged.

"Wait a minute—what's wrong now?" Stella asked as she furrowed her brow. "Talk to me, Brew. What's on your mind? With your last reply, it seems to me that you're, well—a bit pensive, I guess. I'll gladly give you a peso for your thoughts!"

"I just don't know if this is a good time for me to take a powder, Stella. That's all," Brewster said with mild apprehension.

"Why?" Stella asked as she slipped the car key into the ignition. "Time to smell the flowers, if you ask me."

"My mind is going a hundred miles an hour and I feel as if I'm coming apart at the seams." Brewster explained.

"Jesus, Mary, and Joseph!" Stella exclaimed as she proceeded to scold her boyfriend. "Chill out, lover boy. There shall be no angst, brooding, self-recrimination, confessions, introspection, or soul-searching existential quests for the meaning of life on this road trip. I'm also warning you right now that you're here-by banned to rant against a God you perceive to be in absentia. You're forbidden to levy invectives against a morally ambiguous universe or bitch about the complex vagaries deeply entrenched within the mysterious and elusive sacrosanct realm of the art and science of medicine. No, sir! Won't hear a word of it, or I'll box your ears. Rest assured that I'm much bigger than you are, so I'm fully capable of taking you out behind the wood shed and dispensing the much deserved thrashing that you've so rightly deserved for far too long."

"What?!"

"I'm doing all the driving," Stella said, "so sit back, relax, shut the fuck up, and don't give me any grief!"

While the jangly sound of the Byrds, featuring Roger McGuinn's atomic twelve-string guitar blared through the car's radio speakers, J. D. Brewster circled his head in a peculiar counterclockwise motion before he finally offered a wry smile and a resolute response of resignation. "Well, it looks like I'll be going away for a while."

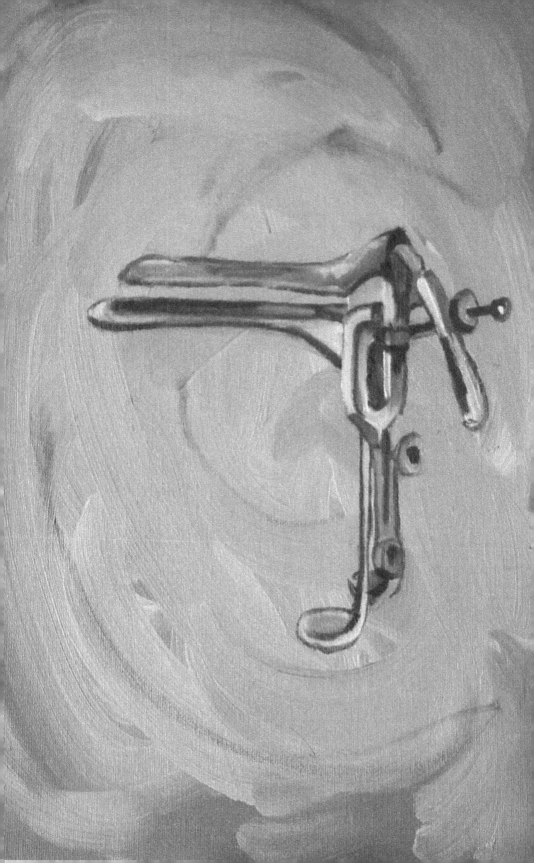

6

FEMALE PLUMBING

It was late in the afternoon by the time Stella and J. D. finally made it up to the Link family farm near Waco. Brewster was a bit nervous about meeting Stella's parents, and he wanted to make a good impression. As the depth of his affection for Stella Link had finally crossed the threshold into something akin to love, Brewster finally decided once and for all that he was going to ask Stella to join him in the state of holy matrimony.

He had no idea how he would ever be able to afford a decent engagement ring in order to make a proper marriage proposal, as he still was facing the financial burden of having to buy some type of motor vehicle to replace his Mustang that had been stolen, stripped, and torched. Since his car had disappeared in late June, he'd been either bumming a ride from Stella or making the dangerous round-trip commute between Bellaire and the Texas Medical Center on his old, beat-up bicycle that had ferried him about during his high school years.

As Stella's car rolled to a stop at the end of the road that led to the farmhouse, her mother and father were already outside, eagerly waiting to greet the couple. Stella's parents had two hounds, Rufus and Bonehead, who cheerfully howled long before Stella's car was in sight in order to alert the elderly parents that company was arriving. Stella's folks had another elderly mutt that lived on the farm, named

Damnit, but the passage of time was robbing the loyal but elderly canine of its auditory acuity.

Stella's mother, Mabel, quickly stepped forward to give her daughter a big hug and a kiss on the cheek. "Stella! You got the Cutlass back! About time, if you ask me. Please introduce me to your boyfriend!"

"Mama, I'd like you to meet J. D. Brewster," Stella said.

The medical student extended his right arm to greet Mabel with a handshake but was startled when Stella's mother brushed his hand aside to envelope the young man in a bear hug.

"Welcome to our home," she said as she issued a kiss to Brewster's cheek. "We've heard so much about you! This is my husband, Porter, but all his friends just call him Pork."

Brewster turned to greet Stella's father with a customary handshake, but Pork also embraced Brewster with a hug. "Hola, mijo. Mi casa, su casa. Let's get your bags inside!"

Mabel and Pork lived in a moderately sized four-bedroom, three-bath home that appeared to have been constructed around the mid-1950s. Needless to say, it was a ranch-style house. What else could one expect in Texas?

"I know that my daughter, somewhere along the way in life, became a hippy," Pork said to Brewster. "Maybe Mabel and I made some kind of a mistake as to how she was reared, but we're just old-fashioned country folk. I hope you'll understand our simple request that you two young people have separate bedrooms while you stay here with us."

"Now, wait just one minute, Daddy!" Stella spoke out in protest. "I'm almost thirty-four years old, and I believe I'm fully capable—"

Brewster interrupted his girlfriend by placing the index and middle fingers of his left hand across her lips. "Mr. Link, whatever accommodations you and your lovely wife have prepared for Stella and me would be most appreciated, and Stella will respectfully honor any of your house rules."

Stella glared at her boyfriend momentarily before feigning acquiescence to the circumstances. She bared her teeth at Brewster as she said, "Whatever you say, lover boy."

Impressed with the young medical student's respectful manners, Pork leaned toward his daughter's ear and whispered a specific warning: "Don't go out of your way to blow up another relationship this time, Stella. You're not going to have many more chances like this in life. This man's a keeper as far as I'm concerned."

Stella's anger subsided over the designated sleeping arrangements, and she patted her elderly father on the top of his hand and said, "Daddy, I'm glad you approve."

After Stella and Brewster had a chance to freshen up, Mabel set the dinner table with the family's finest china and silverware. Dinner was served at a quarter to seven, and it included potato salad; ranch-style beans; slices of sharp onion; home-made dill pickles; slices of soft, fresh white bread; and a slow-smoked barbecue brisket with a perfect red-rimmed smoke ring that any barbecue aficionado would have known to be a sign of perfection. What else could one expect in Texas?

"I make a point of wrapping a bit of foil around the skinny end of the slab to keep it from drying out during the slow-smoke setup," Pork said to Brewster. "Tell me—what do you think?"

When Brewster took a bite, it was as if he had died and gone to heaven. He looked up to the ceiling, raised his hands, and said, "Hallelujah!"

"I am glad you like it," Mabel said. "I'll tell you what: if you up and officially take Stella as your own and give her your last name, we'll teach you how to smoke brisket just like this!"

Stella was sipping a Mr. Pibb soda at the moment her mother embarrassed her in such a fashion, and the carbonated beverage blasted out of her nostrils and onto her dinner plate.

"Mother, will you please?" she said, still choking on the soft drink. "What in hell is the matter with you?"

Brewster gently reached out, patted his girlfriend squarely between the shoulder blades, and replied, "I'm thinking that would be a good idea, Mrs. Link. Thanks for the suggestion."

The gravity of the profound statement Brewster had just uttered was somehow lost on his girlfriend as she used a napkin to mop up the mess she had just made.

Brewster could barely get a bite of food into his mouth throughout the dinner, as Mabel and Pork inundated him with an incessant barrage of questions. The medical student was being vetted, and he knew it. Actually, Brewster was okay with all of that. He felt it was an honor for Stella's parents to ask specific and detailed questions about him and his family.

"Mrs. Link," Brewster said as he finally had an opportunity to get a word in edgewise, "I must note how much you look like your late sister, Irene Segulla. Irene and I became friends before she passed away. If it was not for her, I would have never met Stella, nor would she have ever asked me out on a date. I guess if the truth be told, I was a bit shy. It was Stella who was bold enough to make the first move in our relationship."

Mabel was quiet for a moment, and then she finally spoke in a soft voice. "I understand now that the two men who murdered my sister were the same two men who assaulted you. That's all so very strange. Stella told me that after the beating you took down in Hermann Park, you're now as sterile as a block of granite and you'll never be able to sire any children."

Brewster raised his hands defensively and glared at Stella, looking for some explanation as to why she would reveal a matter that was personal, private, and also quite embarrassing for the medical student.

"Well, it's not the end of the world, son," Mabel said wisely. "I'll tell you what: if you officially take Stella as your own and give her your last name, we'll be happy if you adopt children someday!"

Stella was sipping her Mr. Pibb soda at the moment her mother yet again embarrassed her in such a fashion, and the carbonated beverage blasted out of her nostrils and onto her dinner plate.

"Mother, will you please?" she said, still choking on the soft drink. "What in hell is the matter with you?"

Brewster gently reached out, patted his girlfriend squarely between the shoulder blades, and replied, "I'm thinking that would be a good idea, Mrs. Link. Thanks for the suggestion."

That time, the gravity of the profound statement Brewster had just uttered registered with Stella, and she fully understood its implications.

Overwhelmed with emotion, Stella threw her arms around Brewster. With tears of joy, she cast him out of his chair and squarely upon the dining room floor as if she were a linebacker who had just flattened the opposing quarterback during an all-out blitz.

If Stella behaved in such a fashion while overcome with joy, Brewster decided he would make it a point from that time forward to make certain he never, ever pissed Stella off. It was hard for Brewster to imagine what she was capable of doing if she ever got angry.

On the following morning, Brewster and Stella were awakened by Pork Link feeding his three dogs their breakfast. Apparently, the senior canine, who had proudly been the previously designated alpha male in the pack, was suffering from early dementia in addition to hearing loss.

The elderly and frail dog was unaware that the other members of his pack were eating breakfast without him. Stella's father shouted out orders to the old dog in apparent futility.

"Get over here, Damnit! Listen to me, Damnit; go eat your breakfast before Bonehead and Rufus scarf it down."

The ancient creature finally strolled over to the dog food and gave it a sniff, and then stretched out on the floor beside the bowl of kibble without eating anything.

"Damnit," Pork Link said, "I mean it!"

By then, it was too late. Rufus and Bonehead had set upon the bonus round of dog food, and they wolfed it all down. The old dog did nothing to try to stop the other pack members from stealing his food. Stella realized the old family friend was not long for the world. Brewster realized that somebody along the way had bestowed the perfect name upon the old canine.

Brewster was intent on learning how the farm operated. Later that week, Stella's father asked Brewster to give him a hand in the barn. Several cats lived in the barn, but Mabel and Pork did not consider those animals to be pets per se. The creatures were employed to keep the rodent population under control around the farm.

Endowed with an efficient skill set, the cats ensured the rodent population was, at most, negligible. Once a week, Pork or Mabel would throw out a bit of cat food to supplement the meager regular feline diet of an occasional rat or mouse. On the afternoon Brewster went out to help Mr. Link, about half a dozen cats appeared to gratefully receive leftover scraps from the dining room table in addition to a handful of dry cat kibble. Pork Link pointed at one of the animals that had lined up for a free meal. The old farmer then turned to Brewster to make an earnest observation.

"That is, without a doubt, the ugliest cat I've ever seen," Pork said. "It must have mange or ringworm or some other nasty illness that's chewing on its hide. It doesn't have any hair on its legs or tail!"

"Well, as far as I can tell," Brewster said casually, "that's not a cat at all. That animal would appear to be a marsupial. Specifically, I think it's a possum—and a big one at that."

Without saying another word, Pork Link went into the house and returned with a twelve-gauge Winchester pump shotgun.

"Eat a load of this buckshot, you Yankee varmint son of a bitch!" Pork declared.

As the shotgun blasted away at the terrified marsupial, the interloper sped off as fast as possible. Fortunately, none of the buckshot hit its mark. As Mabel and Stella rushed out of the house to see what the problem was, Brewster began to laugh, as he suddenly realized that Stella's father and his own uncle John could have been twins separated at birth.

Mabel ran back into the house, came back with a frying pan, and smacked her husband over the head with the cooking implement. "What in hell is the matter with you, you old coot? Sometimes I'm certain you're losing your mind! You're going to be sleeping on the couch again tonight. I mean it!"

Brewster and Stella just looked on in stunned silence.

Texas was a miserable place to be during the month of August. That was a fact. Although not exactly within the boundaries of hell, Texas at least shared the same zip code previously assigned to hades by the United States Postal Service.

As Pork Link had been banished to the couch, he found it difficult to fall asleep. The old ranch house didn't have central air-conditioning, and the refrigerated window units were always operating under a great strain in the late summer to try to keep the home under seventy-eight degrees Fahrenheit at night.

Mr. Link rose from the couch, stripped off his boxer shorts, and went to the kitchen, where he assumed a recumbent position on the tile floor beside the refrigerator.

"I like ceramic tile," Stella's father whispered to himself. "It's cool to the touch. On a hot day, I can lie upon it butt naked, and it'll suck the grunge right out of my congested pores."

That line of thinking was all fine and dandy as long as Pork Link's daughter, afflicted with obesity and adult-onset type II diabetes mellitus, didn't need to get up in the middle of the night to urinate and then get a glass of water to drink in an attempt to contend with her occult hyperglycemic complications.

The kitchen was pitch black when Stella popped open the refrigerator door to pour herself a cold glass of ice water. The refrigerator door subsequently smacked her sleeping father on the top of his head. As the light from inside the refrigerator illuminated her father's naked body, Stella panicked, as she thought her father must have gotten off the couch, wandered into the kitchen, and suffered a sudden-death event in the middle of the night.

Stella screamed at the top of her lungs. Her father, now roused, jumped off of the kitchen floor and banged his head upon the open refrigerator door, and then he too began to scream at the top of his lungs. The commotion awakened Brewster and Mabel, and they both ran down the hallway and into the kitchen to assess the situation.

Brewster flipped on the kitchen light, and when Mabel saw her daughter and her naked husband standing in front of each other and screaming at the top of their lungs, Mabel Link went to the cabinet where the pots and pans were stored.

"I swear to God, I'm going to give you something to scream about!" Mabel declared as she pulled out her trusty skillet. "I'm going to bash your head in!"

With that, Mabel smacked her husband upside his head with the large frying pan. Pork Link ran out of the house with his wife in hot pursuit. Brewster took another look and saw that Pork had both of his arms extended high over his head as if he were making a reach-for-the-sky gesture during a Wild West stagecoach holdup from an old movie.

Brewster turned to his girlfriend and said, "In order for me to know how alarmed I should be at this particular juncture in the space-time continuum, does your father have a DNR code status, or is he a full-court press?"

"After I saw him standing naked in front of me," Stella replied, "I'd prefer you run a Mr. Pibb code on the old codger if my mom isn't lucky enough to finish him off with that frying pan first."

While her parents chased each other on the front lawn, Stella calmly found a jug in the refrigerator and poured a cold glass of water to drink.

"Stella, are you okay?" Brewster asked.

"No, I am most assuredly not okay," his girlfriend replied. "No child should ever have the misfortune of seeing either of her parents naked. That's just not right. That image is burned in the back of my brain, and I'll never be able to get it out of my head. You know, I don't drink much alcohol, but maybe it's a good time for me to start. I have a question, and it's an important one."

"What is it, snookums?"

"Tell me the truth, J. D.—if you live long enough to become an old man like my father is now, will your scrotum someday look like a giant, gummy, wrinkled raisin that has the color of an overripe kumquat?"

"Well, hell's bells, Stella," Brewster replied, "that's what my damned scrotum looks like now!"

"Well, if that is the case," Stella said, "I'm now officially a virgin again, and I'm going to stay that way for the rest of my miserable life. If you ever get horny in the future, you're just going to have to take matters into your own hands, lover boy. For my own peace of mind, please don't tell me if you plan on using your right hand or your left hand. That would be just too much information for me to process right about now."

"While your parents are dancing a waltz on the front lawn," Brewster said, "maybe you and I can take this opportunity to have a romantic interlude."

"Oh, hell no!" Stella replied. "Right at this moment, I'm definitely not up for a batter at the plate who'll strike out looking after only three fat pitches, and then roll over to take a nap."

Brewster softly laughed to himself as he truly began to look forward to a future life of marital bliss with Stella Link.

Upon Brewster's return to Houston, it was time for J. D., Brother Bill, and Feral Cheryl to pay a visit to Uncle John, who had apparently bought an old Checker Marathon four-door sedan used as a taxi in the past. Although the vehicle had more than three hundred thousand miles on it, the old taxi had at least received scheduled maintenance along the way. That was certainly more than could be said for John's miraculous Dodge Dart.

John explained to his foster daughter and his two nephews that he needed only one vehicle and was going to give away the Dodge Dart.

"That is good news, Uncle John," J. D. said. "As you know, during this past month of June, my car was stolen. I currently don't have a vehicle, and I'm going to need to buy one. Perhaps I could have the Dodge Dart. In fact, you wouldn't have to give it to me. I'll offer you three hundred dollars for it. I believe that would be a fair price."

"No, I don't particularly like you," Uncle John replied. "I'm going to give it to the little colored girl over here. She comes to visit me more often than you do."

After being jilted the previous year, it was time for Cheryl to rub the younger Brewster's nose in it.

"Well, it would seem that nobody in this family particularly likes J. D., so I thank you for this generous gift, Uncle John. I'm happy to see that I'm your all-time favorite, as well I should be. I just want J. D. and Brother Bill to know that."

She leaned over, gave Uncle John a kiss on the cheek, and then turned to look at J. D. and Bill Brewster. She had an enormous smile on her face as she put her thumb up to her nose and wiggled her fingers. Brother Bill laughed out loud and gave Cheryl a high five. However, J. D. was clearly not amused.

After the trio had departed from John's home, Brewster approached Cheryl with a specific proposition about a capitalistic commercial venture that perhaps could be mutually beneficial to all concerned parties.

"Okay, wild child, I know very well that you don't need that old

Dodge Dart. You have a pretty decent set of wheels already. I'll make you the same offer that I made Uncle John. Let me buy it from you."

Cheryl appeared to be amenable to the suggestion. "Okay, it's yours for three hundred fifty dollars, and that's nonnegotiable."

"Oh, spare my life!" Brewster replied. "That's highway robbery!"

Nonetheless, Brewster pulled out his checkbook to consummate the deal.

"Don't forget the words of the English poet and playwright William Congreve: 'Heav'n has no Rage, like Love to Hatred turn'd, Nor Hell a Fury, like a Woman scorn'd.' I believe that was written circa the year of our Lord 1697," Feral said, and she leaned forward and gave Brewster a soft kiss on the cheek.

"The riposte from thy foil, my lady, hath wounded me mightily," Brewster said as he bowed to his cousin.

Determined to get in the last word, Cheryl replied, "As well it should!"

——◊——

"You boys should have brought me into the fold on this ape shit breakout conspiracy a long time ago," Talbot said. "I could've even helped out early on with some of the preliminary planning for this caper."

"Sorry, Zip," Brewster replied, "but Rip and I weren't so sure you'd be downstream to any of this."

"I'd guess you might be right if this didn't happen to be Uncle Hank's last request before he gave up the ghost."

"Now, don't get sidetracked like you usually do," Ford said. "Were you able to disable the security video camera in the lockdown kennel?"

"I took a small crescent, and I was able to unscrew the coaxial lead from the back of the camera."

"Time for another dry run," Brewster said. "I sedated the smaller

O-ring with fifty milligrams of Benadryl, and now it is bedtime for Bonzo. I can't be seen coming out of here until the coast is clear, so the rest is up to you two boys."

Ford and Talbot opened the orangutan cage and pulled out the smaller of the two orange-colored apes. The coconspirators gently slid the noble beast down into a wheeled trash receptacle and tightly clamped the lid down before they rolled the trash container out of the lab and into the hallway.

"The nurse from the Department of Occupational Safety and Infection Control, Mrs. Coffee, will meet us beside the roll-up door at the loading dock," Rip whispered to Talbot.

"If this dry run looks like it's going to work," Talbot said, "we're easily going to need an entire crew to help us pull this off when we're ready to give this caper the green light."

"Oh, this is going to work out all right," Ford said.

As the two men turned the corner, they were startled to see that Mrs. Coffee was being harassed by a member of the medical school's security detail. "I don't care if you came down here to give the research staff a lecture about workplace hygiene," the security agent said. "You're not credentialed to be down here at this time."

"I'm sorry," Mrs. Coffee said sheepishly, "but what should I have done? After all, I was given a specific work assignment to be here."

"I'm not going to write you up," the security guard said, "but next time you come down here, you'd better have a signed authorization slip from the admin."

When Mrs. Coffee realized Talbot and Ford were a mere twenty feet away with a precious load of living contraband safely encased in a wheeled trash container, she discreetly ran her right thumb across the anterior aspect of her neck.

"Oh, this is not going to work out all right," Ford said.

Ford and Talbot turned and hightailed it back to the primate kennel, where Brewster was patiently waiting. The medical student readily recognized the looks of terror upon the faces of his colleagues when he asked, "What's up?"

Talbot grabbed Brewster by the lapels of his white jacket and pulled him close. "Abort the mission!"

After Zip Talbot unloaded the sleeping orangutan back into its cage, he escorted Brewster and Ford discreetly out of the kennel, through the animal lab, and into the main hallway. "I need to go back into the kennel to reattach the coaxial cable to the back of the security video camera before anybody's the wiser. In the meantime, you boys had better get back to the drawing board."

———

J. D. Brewster's gynecology clerkship was about to start on Monday, August 31, 1981. Brewster was eager to roll up his sleeves and get the mandatory rotation under his belt. In the commonplace parlance of the Gulf Coast College of Medicine, urologists were oftentimes referred to as male plumbers, and their realm of expertise was male plumbing. Conversely, gynecologists were oftentimes referred to as female plumbers, and their realm of expertise was, as one would correctly surmise, female plumbing.

Brewster and another medical student, Cynthia Dates, were waiting for the third member of their party to show up in the Vinyl Lounge so they could start their rotation on the gynecology service. When Bobby Dalles finally arrived, it was time for the three students to go upstairs and get to work. Although Brewster knew both of his colleagues, he had never worked with either of them on a clinical rotation before.

"Say, Bobby," Brewster asked, "after you got arrested at Mardi Gras for trying to climb up into that tree and grab some plastic beads, do you now have a police record?"

"Damn straight, Skippy!" Dalles replied. "I was charged with public intoxication and disturbing the peace."

"At Mardi Gras?!" Brewster asked. "I'm stunned."

"Yeah, at Mardi Gras," Bobby said. "I shit you not. What was really hilarious about the whole thing was that I didn't even have any alcohol in my system at the time when I tried to climb up that stupid tree. In retrospect, perhaps I should have been as wasted as a purple monkey. Let's hope it doesn't torpedo my plans for getting into a decent future residency training program. We'll let the cards land where they may."

Unfortunately for Bobby Dalles, his rather innocuous criminal record would one day come back to bite him in butt. That one simple, stupid, sophomoric transgression would ensure that Bobby's future family practice residency training program would take place in the backwater community of Hope, Arkansas. Assuredly, nothing good could ever come out of a place like that.

The gynecology attending, Jefferson Davis Clapner, had the nasty reputation of being a sexual predator. In 1979, one of his resident physicians had walked in on Dr. Clapner while he was actively engaged in copulating with a patient who was in the stirrups and strapped in the lithotomy position, ostensibly for a full pelvic examination. Although that was a clear violation of medical ethics and the Hippocratic oath, nothing had ever come of the malfeasance, as the alleged event was considered to be consensual.

Nonetheless, the resident physician who had barged in on the distasteful intimate interlude reported that he clearly had heard what the patient said to Clapner. While cojoined with Dr. Clapner in the act of exchanging bodily fluids, the patient cried out, "The eagle has landed! Ram it home, you big bastard!"

Since that time, Dr. Clapner's secret nickname among the medical students and house staff members had been, obviously, the Eagle.

Unfortunately, the resident physician, Dr. Heloise Rodman, had an equally vile reputation. As a nasty, vindictive, politically savage, walleyed bitch on wheels, Dr. Rodman was the type of human being who would exact revenge against anybody she perceived as having ever slighted her at any time. That would be the case whether or not the insult levied upon her was real or simply imagined.

The following anecdote will readily clarify the generous and compassionate spirit that dwelled within the heart of Dr. Rodman. In the fall of 1980, the Gulf Coast College of Medicine honorably and charitably initiated a health fair for the misfortunate women in the vicinity who had been afflicted with Down's syndrome. The individuals were bused from a state-sponsored custodial institution to the Texas Medical Center, where they would receive complimentary breast and pelvic examinations.

After only an hour or so of performing gratis medical examinations on the physically and mentally challenged individuals, Dr. Rodman reportedly looked out the window of the gynecology suite and saw that there were still additional patients gathered upon the small, grassy knoll in front of the hospital entryway, awaiting medical evaluations. Heloise Rodman went ballistic at the sight.

"When are they going to get those fucking retards out of here?"

She was truly Woman of the Year material. One could only hope such an evil and soulless demon spawned in the bowels of hell would never seek a career in public office.

—

Dr. Clapner addressed the three medical students and informed them it would be a split rotation with a two-week stand on the obstetrics service and then two weeks spent on the gynecology service.

"To kick off this rotation," Clapner said, "Dr. Rodman will play a game of pimp and pone. Okay, Heloise, you're now free to take over."

As Dr. Clapner departed, Dr. Rodman looked over to Dr. Cynthia Dates and said, "Okay, Goldilocks, you're up to bat. Here is the first pitch: What's the name of the nonmalignant cyst that can frequently occur on a female patient in the labial region?"

The medical student readily replied, "It sounds like you are making a reference to a Bartholin cyst. Is that correct?"

Dr. Rodman was clearly annoyed and did not confirm that the medical student had answered the question correctly.

"I believe that was a base hit!" Cynthia boldly proclaimed.

"Okay, smart-ass, here is the second pitch," Dr. Rodman said in an attempt to retaliate with the second question. "What are at least three indications that you should proceed with a cesarean section at the time of delivery?"

Cynthia Dates thought for moment and then replied, "I think I have this. There are obviously multiple situations that could occur that would prompt an obstetrician to consider a cesarean section at the time of delivery. Some of these include breech presentation, fetal distress, a previous remote delivery via a cesarean section, and a huge baby, medically referred to as macrosomia. I believe I just named no fewer than four indications for a cesarean section. How did I do? No matter what happens with the third question, I believe I have already won this round."

Brewster and Bobby Dalles were delighted that their colleague had nailed down multiple correct answers, and they clapped politely as if they were watching a golf tournament.

"I'm not done with you yet, studette," the resident physician said. "Here's the third pitch: Of the three most common gynecological malignancies, including cancer of the cervix, cancer of the ovary, and cancer of the uterine body, which is the most prevalent?"

"That would be cancer of the uterus." Without batting an eye, Cynthia Dates answered the question with confidence. "The incidence is on the order of about forty thousand cases or more per year in the United States. Well, it would appear I just knocked a grand slam out of the ballpark, and as for you, Dr. Rodman, you just got poned!"

While Brewster and Bobby Dalles gave each other a celebratory handshake, Cynthia Dates tried to do the same to the attending, extending her right arm to shake the hand of Dr. Heloise Rodman. Unfortunately, the resident was a sore loser and didn't reciprocate the gesture of civility offered by the medical student.

The resident couldn't believe she had lost, even though, at best, she'd been just trying to coast her way to a victory. After all, she believed it was her birthright to win every time. She couldn't conceive how she had been so soundly defeated. It had to have been somebody else's fault for her to go down in flames that way. Maybe she could blame that pesky Russian Bear, who had just completed his mandatory OB-GYN rotation, for meddling in the pimp-and-pone process. That's the ticket! Blame the Russians! After all, he probably had given the right answers to Cynthia Dates before she started the rotation.

Somehow, Heloise would try to figure out some way to delegitimize the remarkable and unexpected victory her adversary had secured. As Dr. Rodman briskly turned to walk away, she barked out, "Stay the fuck away from me! Just fucking do as I say! Get to work."

In deference to Dr. Rodman's perpetually warm and cheerful disposition, the medical students and the other house staff members bestowed the ironic nickname of Evergreen upon her. However, a fresh breath of alpine air was something nobody would ever mistake Heloise Rodman for.

Cynthia Dates didn't bestow any favors upon herself when she had to perform her first pelvic examination while Dr. Rodman supervised. The patient Cynthia evaluated was being seen for a case of raging bacterial cervicitis. As a heavy, pustular, mucoid discharge was tenaciously clinging to the cervical os, the medical student used a wooden cervical spatula to harvest a sample of the infected material from the patient. The contagious, foul material had to be submitted to the laboratory for analysis. A problem arose when the medical student tried to transfer the septic pustular cervical drainage into an open petri dish.

"What seems to be wrong with Miss Pussy-Puss?" the patient asked. "To be honest with you, I've been riding some big, beefy boners lately."

Cynthia Dates attempted to offer gentle and respectful assurances to the anxious patient. "Well, as best as I can tell, you're likely afflicted with what will turn out to be a lethal case of what we refer to in the medical profession as some bad-ass twat-rot. Now, don't you worry, little sister; we should be able to clean all this infected shit out of you as soon as I'm able to wheel a fire truck in here and get you hosed out."

"Gee, thanks!" the patient said cheerfully.

"Think nothing of it," Cynthia said. " A word of advice, however: the next time you get horny and feel compelled to take a ride upon an ugly stick, why don't you at least consider getting doinked by a fellow human being and not, as it would appear, a sick-dick donkey lined up against the back wall of the glue factory?"

Without a doubt, the recommendation of restricting coital fidelity to species-specific biological entities was some of the most sound and rational advice that any member of Homo sapiens could ever have offered to another living being of his or her kind.

Try as she might, Cynthia Dates could not dislodge the thick, malodorous goo onto the collection plate. She decided to try an unconventional and previously untested technique of getting the cervical specimen securely placed on the petri plate. She slapped the edge of the spatula against the rim of the plate, thinking that momentum would safely transfer the infected wad of putrid pussy plasma directly upon the center of the specimen plate.

Once again, however, God would prove that he had a tremendous sense of humor. When Cynthia attempted to transfer the material in such a novel fashion, the thick wad of green cervical mucoid slime helicoptered across the room and landed squarely on the blouse of Heloise Rodman, right below the neckline.

When both the patient and the medical student burst out into laughter, Dr. Rodham was mortified. The resident physician put on a pair of gloves and went to the sink in the examination room to try to wash off the nasty wad of crotch snot from her clothing.

As Cynthia Dates approached the resident physician to offer some assistance, Dr. Rodman said, "Stay the fuck away from me! Just fucking do as I say! Get back to work."

Brewster had spent his first two weeks of the rotation on the obstetrics service, and it had gone without a hitch. He even had the pleasant experience of delivering several babies, but it was nonetheless a sore reminder to him that he was now infertile and would never sire any children of his own.

"You seem to be a very nice student," one pregnant patient said to Brewster when she presented for her routine checkup during her thirty-four-week gestation period.

"That's very kind of you to say," Brewster replied.

"This will be my third child," she added. "You know, it's so easy for my husband and me to have a baby. My husband must be choking at the gills with sperm. Every time I turn around, he's getting me pregnant!"

Brewster nodded, bit his lip, and then quickly left the exam room. During his OB-GYN rotation, Brewster's sterility would engender more anger and hostility over time. It was something he would never be able to come to grips with.

The other issue was that during his assignment to the obstetrics service, Brewster did not get to witness or participate in a single cesarean section procedure. All of the women who went into labor during his rotation had successful vaginal deliveries. In fact, Brewster would complete his entire medical career without ever witnessing a cesarean section, and he would always feel he had been shortchanged in regard to that aspect of his medical education.

After one successful delivery of a female infant, Brewster stood on guard at the patient's perineum, waiting for the expulsion of the afterbirth. When it came, Brewster said, "Okay, the placenta is coming out now."

"What's the placenta?" the mother asked.

"The placenta is the product of conception that helped keep your developing baby alive when she was in your uterus," Brewster explained.

Excitedly, the new mother proclaimed, "I love the sound of that word! It sounds like the name of a Mexican restaurant where they serve two-for-one margaritas during happy hour. That's the ticket! If I owned a Mexican restaurant, I'd name it La Placenta. That's what I am going to name my new baby girl."

It was a done deal. The name Placenta ended up on the child's birth certificate. Years later, Brewster would look back on that surreal event and sadly realize that some unfortunate human being was walking around on the planet with the name Placenta. How, Brewster wondered, could the mother of this unfortunate child be so shamefully stupid? Maybe someday Placenta would end up with a sibling sister named Goiter, or perhaps a baby brother named Hemorrhoid. That would have been a good thing because, after all, misery liked company.

Once Brewster slid over to the gynecology subrotation in the middle of September, things got weird in a hurry. He was requested to perform a pelvic examination on an elderly lady named Ms.

Monika, who had an apparent perineal abnormality. Brewster entered the exam room to evaluate the patient with the resident physician, Dr. Rodman. The patient had complained of raw tissue extruding from her pelvic area, so Brewster and a female medical assistant helped the ancient patient get into the stirrups for a formal pelvic examination.

What Brewster found was shocking: the patient had a rectal and vulvar prolapse. In layman's terms, the patient's vagina and rectum had turned inside out and had fallen no fewer than four inches below the pelvic floor. Brewster had never encountered anything like that and was stunned at what he saw.

"How long have your internal organs been turned inside out like this?" Brewster asked.

"I don't know," the patient replied. "I suspect it's been this way now for well over ten years. This happened to me after my husband passed away. Generally, I've been able to use either a banana or a cucumber to keep everything shoved back up inside me. Of late, that technique has not been working all that well."

"How so?"

"The other day, when I was in the supermarket," Ms. Monika said, "I ripped a big one, and a zucchini flew out of my ass. It was somewhat embarrassing, as I was standing at the checkout counter when it happened. When the clerk thought that I was trying to steal fruits and vegetables, I was subsequently subjected to a full body-cavity probe. Very sad that somebody would think I could do something like that."

"Please don't tell me that you would ever consider eating any of those items after they've been shoved up inside your body," Brewster said.

"Don't worry, young man," the patient answered. "I'll usually boil the shit out of any fruit, vegetable, bratwurst, or schnitzel that's been jammed up inside me for any more time than an hour or two before I would ever dream about eating the damned thing. Eating something like that raw? You're a silly boy now aren't you?"

The medical student had to excuse himself briefly from the exam room until he recovered the vision in his left eye. Once Brewster regained his composure and returned to the exam room, the elderly woman continued. "If you must know, it was Dr. Clapner who suggested a month ago that I start using a 52 ring Churchill cigar as a pessary. He told me just to jam a big Cuban stogie inside my twat to hold everything in place. He asked me to specifically use the famous Cohiba brand."

""I think I've heard enough," Brewster protested.

"Not by a long shot, young man!" the patient exclaimed. "On a curious note, why would he always demand that I should bring back all those cigars to him once I'd had them stuffed up inside my crusty love box? I'll have you know, I have my own ideas as to what he may have done with all of those cigars."

"I'm sure you do."

"I bet he keeps them in a humidor in his office. Between you and me, I'm certain Jefferson Davis Clapner is a sick, horny pervert. Now just if you're wondering, this nasty female resident physician standing over here who's pretending to supervise these proceedings should damned well keep that filthy, diseased, herpetic pecker of his on a short leash," the patient said as she glared at Heloise Rodman with contempt.

With great dismay, Brewster had to ask a follow-up question. "Good Lord, if this has been going on now for ten years now, why did you come in at this time to finally get this problem addressed?"

The patient gave Brewster the most obvious and coherent answer he had ever heard to any question he had ever asked anybody in his entire life: "Well, don't you think it is about time?"

Fortunately, the patient was successfully managed by elective surgical intervention. She eventually underwent a hysterectomy, and her atrophic vaginal and rectal vaults were surgically secured in their proper places within the pelvis.

—◆◆◆—

Brewster's colleague Bobby Dalles was having a similarly unpleasant experience with his own patient population he encountered on the gynecology service. Unlike Brewster, Bobby Dalles found fat women decidedly unattractive. One day a morbidly obese woman afflicted with the Pickwickian syndrome came in for an evaluation.

As Bobby Dalles was reluctant to even go into the room to interview the patient, Heloise Rodman put her nose into the air and, in an exaggerated fashion, started to sniff loudly.

"I smell a pussy!" Rodman said.

"Good God!" Bobby replied. "Are you telling me that you can smell this patient's netherworld all the way out here?"

"No, you dumbass!" Rodman answered. "I smell you. Get in there, and do your job, you pussy!"

The medical student followed the order, and he soon discovered the patient had a most annoying problem: she claimed that an unsavory rodent had taken up residence inside of her vaginal vault. In layman's terms, she had a rat up her pussy.

The medical student obviously needed clarification as to the nature of her chief complaint. After all, she actually couldn't have had a live rat up her pussy, now, could she? A frightened gerbil perhaps but certainly not a rat.

Dalles attempted to gently and politely pursue clarification regarding the patient's peculiar anomaly while refraining from causing the patient any undue alarm. "For shit's sake, what in hell are you talking about, lady? That's the craziest goddamn thing I've ever heard in my entire life!"

"Every time Chocolate Stud done draw down and be snackin' da juicy side," the patient said, "he comin' out all toe up. See?"

Bewildered, Dalles scratched his head and replied, "Absolutely. I'm getting the attending in here now. Don't move."

Dr. Clapner remembered the patient, as he had delivered her baby in the past. During the vaginal delivery of her only child to date, the patient had suffered a complication of a vaginal tear that had extended into the rectum and required surgical repair.

Upon his entry into the patient's exam room, Clapner proceeded to personally perform a vaginal evaluation with a lighted speculum on the catastrophically obese woman.

Clapner feigned sympathy when he said, "I feel your pain. I see what the problem is, and I'm going to take care of it."

The attending had found that he had accidentally left a curved suture needle behind during her last operation. Whenever the woman became sexually aroused and experienced vaginal tenting, the needle would poke through the posterior vaginal vault. That was the reason that every time the "Chocolate Stud done draw down and be snackin' on da juicy side, he comin' out all toe up."

In other words, when her sexual partner engaged in an act of vigorous cunnilingus, his tongue would get lacerated by the residual surgical needle poking through the posterior aspect of her vaginal vault.

"I found it!" Clapner exclaimed. "You do indeed have a rat up your pussy, but I'm going to take it out. Do you want to see it?"

"Lord no!" the patient said. "Just pluck it out, and cast it far from me!"

No sooner had Clapner removed the offending sharp object with a needle driver than the woman fell fast asleep. Patients afflicted with Pickwickian syndrome had morbid obesity, hypoventilation, and hypersomnolence. They were able to fall asleep anywhere, at any time, and at the drop of hat.

After the hirsute pachyderm dozed off, Clinton turned to Bobby Dalles and said, "I'd like to tap this big keg! Do you think this giant sperm whale would ever notice anything if I just dropped my trow right here and right now and then rammed it home? I bet I could unload my wad into this pathetic monster before this big, hairy, hoglodite ever woke up!"

"No offense, Dr. Clapner," Bobby said, "but you are one sick son of a bitch."

Clapner smiled as he nodded and replied, "If the foo' shits, wear it!"

———

Bring Your Child to Work Day turned out to be a catastrophe for the outpatient gynecology clinic. The office manager, Jerry Sparks, had an eleven-year-old son named Joshua, and the preadolescent boy came to the clinic that day as part of a junior high schoolwork assignment. The exercise was an attempt for students to learn exactly what their parents did for a living.

The young lad's father, Jerry, gave him a specific assignment. Once the scheduled patients had signed in on the registration log upon their arrival, it was Joshua's job to hand each patient a clipboard that held a standard review-of-system, self-assessment form. Every patient was required to complete one upon each visit to the gynecology outpatient facility.

After they had done so, the patients waited in the lobby. Joshua was also instructed to politely offer the patients a cup of coffee while they waited to see a physician. Joshua's appointed tasks appeared to be relatively straightforward, but the office manager had no idea how his son was about to be permanently traumatized on that fateful day.

Suzanne "Sweet" Craft was a bizarre patient afflicted with Munchausen syndrome. People who had that peculiar and rare psychiatric problem had been known to injure themselves in order to garnish medical attention.

Two years prior to her current clinical presentation, Mrs. Craft had been hospitalized for a septic right shoulder that had required orthopedic intervention to surgically debride the joint. Afterward, she'd subsequently required the administration of prolonged antibiotic therapy, as directed by the infectious-disease specialist.

When it was clear Mrs. Craft was well enough to be discharged from the hospital, she had jammed a pencil into her shoulder to reinfect the joint. To ensure her hospitalization would be prolonged, she had made certain to contaminate the sharp end of the pencil by first introducing it into her anal verge before stabbing herself with it. Suzanne "Sweet" Craft was not exactly the kind of person most people would've wanted for a next-door neighbor.

After the peculiar patient had signed the registration log and completed the review-of-system self-assessment assay, Mrs. Craft took her seat beside a younger man who had driven her to the clinic that day.

"Mrs. Craft, would you and your son like a cup of coffee while you are waiting to see the doctor?" Joshua Sparks asked.

"This toothless bastard here ain't my son," the patient replied. "My boy's in prison! I'm so proud of him because he up and shot himself one of them there coloreds. Yes indeed. Killed him dead. This feller here ain't my kin, I tell ya! Well, maybe he is, but I'm not rightly certain. Anyhow, he just wants to get down my panties and steal my drugs."

"What?!" the young boy asked.

"The biggest problem I have," Mrs. Craft said, "is that in the trailer park where I live, I'm surrounded by white trash. My trailer park must have, without a doubt, the lowest form of white people that a person might encounter on the face of this planet."

The toothless ridge runner who sat beside the patient loudly panted while he was actively trying to finger Mrs. Craft under her skirt right there in the lobby, in front of all of the other patients in the waiting room. Wearing a pair of coveralls without a shirt, the barefoot hillbilly just grinned and bobbed his head ever so slightly while a spittle of tobacco juice dribbled down his chin.

For unclear reasons, the patient suddenly became agitated. She jumped out of her chair, pulled down her panties to her ankles, and then hopped like a horned toad toward the registration desk to issue a demand that apparently warranted immediate attention.

"I have a medical emergency, and I need to be seen now!"

Joshua was a polite young man who had the wherewithal to say, "I'll go back and inform the doctors that you need to be seen soon. Can you tell me what is wrong?"

As it turned out, the question the young boy had asked was a big mistake. The patient replied, "I'll show you what's wrong!"

With that, Suzanne "Sweet" Craft pulled her dress up over her head and exposed her perineum to Joshua Sparks. The patient was infected with the worst case of venereal warts anybody in the clinic had ever seen. The enormous, frond-like sexually transmitted lesions were hanging from her vulva like the stalactites one might find while spelunking in a Carlsbad Cavern.

The infected vulvar fronds appeared to move on their own accord like the dangerous suckered tentacles an unfortunate scuba diver might encounter if ever attacked by an aggressive, giant Humboldt squid in the Sea of Cortez.

The patient proclaimed, "I got me some kind of cancer crawling out of my buzz box! Somebody needs to fix this goddamn mess, and I want to be treated proper, not like I am some kind of skinny pig!"

Even more remarkable than Mrs. Craft's horrible case of sexually transmitted venereal warts was the fact that somebody, or perhaps something, was actually taking the time to have sex with that wretched animal. Perhaps her sexual consort was the toothless ridge runner sitting in the lobby while he drooled a waterfall of tobacco juice down his chin. In any event, Joshua Sparks had just witnessed a nightmarish visage.

The young lad's eyes grew to the size of planetoid celestial bodies.

After vomiting on the bare feet of Suzanne Craft, the horrified boy turned around and ran away.

The loud commotion in the lobby brought forth J. D. Brewster and Cynthia Dates to see what was going on. After assessing the situation, Cynthia grabbed a wheelchair and swung it around behind Mrs. Craft. The medical student subsequently grabbed the woman by the shoulders from behind and then pulled her down into the wheelchair.

"I can tell you this, madam," Cynthia told Mrs. Craft. "You're going to be treated like neither a skinny pig nor a guinea pig, for that matter. In fact, as you're already a genuine feral javelina, you're not going to be treated here at all. Open the door, Brew!"

Brewster ran to open the front door while Cynthia rapidly wheeled the patient out of the clinic. Cynthia then harshly dumped the patient upto the hallway floor, as if Mrs. Craft were a load of contaminated refuse that the custodians needed to load up and reduce to carbon ash in the medical school's incinerator.

Brewster looked upon Cynthia Dates with astonishment. "You clearly have anger-management issues, and if you are not able to get that under control, you're going to be a danger not only to yourself but also to other people!"

"You can take that to the bank!" The medical student cackled with a malevolent laugh.

⸻◦⸻

Sadly, Joshua Sparks would never fully recover from the image registered in the occipital cortex of his preadolescent brain. Within a few years, Joshua would become a celibate, ascetic monk. He would eventually move into the swamps and forests of East Texas, where he could hide out in isolation. After all, there had always been long-standing rumors that there were people living out in the forests of East Texas who had not had contact with other human beings since the end of the Civil War.

⟨⟨⟨⟨⟩⟩⟩⟩

Big rolled into his apartment complex after he stepped off the city bus line. As he'd just made a harrowing escape from the chop shop, he only had a few minutes at most to grab his bug-out bag and disappear. The cops were coming, and as far as he knew, they were probably right around the corner. He'd successfully made use of stolen identities in the past, and this time would not be any different.

As he fled his apartment, he heard the unmistakable sound of police sirens heading in his direction. If Smeg had survived the gunshot wound to his face, his former partner was no doubt singing like a canary. Big jumped into a nondescript sedan parked underneath the apartment complex carport and then drove to the local grocery store to grab some additional provisions before he booked out of town and went underground.

"Did you bring the grocery list this time?" D' Nae asked.

"Oh, ye of little faith," D' Shea smugly replied as she waved a piece of scrap paper in front of her sister's nose. The Dalton twins had stopped at the local grocery store to pick up mothballs, a six-pack of Mr. Pibb, and a case of Top Ramen noodles, which were on sale at the price of eleven for a dollar.

D' Shea and her sister couldn't believe their eyes when they saw Big standing directly in front of them in one of the cashier lanes.

As the career criminal left the grocery store, D' Nae said, "Baby Girl, I'm on him like white on rice. Score some dimes! Go over to the pay phone, and wait for me. I just can't believe we've run into this dirtbag yet again. Wait until we tell Brother Brew!"

"I'm on it," D' Shea said. "Give me the skinny on that bad boy's set of wheels as soon as you get it all scoped out."

7

LUKE 18:16

Brewster's one-month mandatory pediatric rotation began on October 5. Although he had never been around small children to any great degree during the course of his adulthood, he nonetheless anticipated that the clerkship was likely going to be an enjoyable experience. He held that cheerful optimism despite the obvious fact that seeing small children on a daily basis would be a painful reminder of his own reproductive limitations.

At that point in his education, the medical student had not participated in any specialty or subspecialty rotation, mandatory or otherwise, that had truly captured his interest. He had only about seven months to go before he would complete his medical school education, yet he still had no idea what type of residency training he wanted to pursue after he graduated from the Gulf Coast College of Medicine.

He would have to decide soon. Perhaps if his pending clerkship in pediatric medicine turned out to be a gratifying encounter, J. D. Brewster would consider enrolling in a postgraduate residency training program in the field of child care.

Victoria Campos, who had done a previous rotation with Brewster on the nephrology team, would be joining him for the pediatric clerkship. In addition, Bobby Dalles would round out the trio on the pediatric service under the attending physician, Dr. Gerard Garble.

Although somewhat eccentric in his mannerisms, Dr. Garble had a reputation of being an extraordinarily bright physician with a heart of gold. Knowing that motor vehicle accidents were a main cause of childhood death and injury, Dr. Garble would happily purchase an infant car seat for his pediatric patients if a child's own parents did not have the financial wherewithal to acquire such a mandatory safety item of their own accord. The resident physician who would be overseeing the students during the rotation was Dr. Terry Hopland.

As the Vinyl Lounge was thoroughly depleted of nutritional sustenance at the beginning of that October, the three medical students elected to meet in the hospital cafeteria before their new rotation started. As soon as the three colleagues had taken seats, Brewster's old friend Mehdi magically appeared with a tray of complimentary coffee and three fresh, warm bear claws.

Victoria turned up her nose at the complex-carbohydrate confections and said, "I'm sorry, but that thing just has way too many calories for me to eat. You boys are welcome to have mine."

Without looking up, Bobby Dalles took a plastic fork and split the third breakfast treat down the middle. He stabbed half of the bear claw with the fork and then waved it in front of Brewster's face. J. D. proceeded to inhale the pastry right off of Bobby's fork, and he swallowed the item whole without even chewing it.

At the same time, Bobby picked up his half of the bear claw and forcefully stuffed the pastry into his mouth with his fingers. He used the middle digit of his right hand as if it were a plunger to make certain the entire item was lodged up against his hard palate. Dalles then ingested the bear claw with one gulp of black coffee. It appeared he had not even tasted his half of Victoria's bear claw.

Appalled by such a disgusting display of uncouth table manners, Victoria shook her head and looked at her two colleagues with dismay. "Philistines! Tell me—do you guys ever get doinked?"

"Only if I am well rested, have twenty dollars in cash, a pocket full of breath mints, and hold off on taking my high-blood-pressure medication for an entire week or longer," Dalles replied. "Despite all of that, you probably won't get much mileage out of me after I pop the cork. Even on a good day, I might still fall asleep while I'm getting worked over. That can be a bit embarrassing at times. Usually, the woman I've hired for an intimate encounter will never make it to the finish line."

"Too bad, so sad," Brewster said.

"Well, it's not like I could ever really give a shit one way or the other about any woman's physical or emotional needs." He turned to J. D. and asked, "How about you, Brew?"

As per usual, whenever Brewster could not offer an intelligent reply, he looked back impassively at his colleagues and made a peculiar counterclockwise circular motion with his head.

⎯⎯⎯

Estella Sisfuentes was only two weeks shy of her eighth birthday. She was in second grade and was doing well in school, although a boy named Theo, who sat beside her in Mrs. Crohn's class, was becoming a bee in her bonnet. Invariably, when Mrs. Crohn was at the chalkboard and her back was turned toward her students, Theo would make a point of reaching over and knocking Estella's three-ring binder off of her desk.

When the other students would laugh at the shenanigans, Mrs. Crohn would turn around and scold Estella for being so careless with her school papers. Frustrated, Estella explained the circumstances to her mother and father, as she needed advice on how to constructively deal with the disruptive confrontations, which were becoming more frequent.

Her mother seemed to have great wisdom about such matters and suggested that young Theo secretly liked Estella but didn't know how to tell her he wanted to be friends with her except by acting in such a silly fashion.

Her mother proposed an excellent recommendation. As Estella and Theo lived in the same neighborhood, Mrs. Sisfuentes suggested Estella ask Theo to walk her home after the school bus let the children out at the designated stop at the end of the block. Not only was that suggestion a capital concept, but it was also an idea that would end up saving Estella's life one day.

When asked if he would escort Estella home, Theo replied, "Okay, but you have to keep it a secret! If anybody knew I did this with you, they would make fun of us."

When the children arrived at Estella's house, Mrs. Sisfuentes invited Theo inside for a snack. "Theo, you're welcome at our home. Please come inside! When Estella comes home from school, she enjoys a snack of a sliced manzanita with peanut butter. Would you like some?"

Estella's mom was stunned when the young boy whispered that he liked peanut butter but had never eaten an apple before. Therefore, the lad was unable to render a cogent personal opinion regarding his likes or dislikes regarding the consumption of that common staple, although it was an item considered to be generally pervasive throughout the fruit-and-vegetable section of virtually every supermarket in North America.

"Well, I guess we'll have to change that," Mrs. Sisfuentes replied. "After today, you can proudly say that you have eaten your first apple. Estella likes sweet red apples, but today I have a special treat for you: a firm, tart green one. I just know you are going to love it."

Estella's mother sliced up a Granny Smith and applied a thick layer of peanut butter to each segment. When Theo took a bite of the after-school snack, the members of the Sisfuentes family suddenly became his friends for life. It was sad to think that such a humble gesture of hospitality was the most benevolent act of love and kindness ever bestowed upon the young boy. It was nonetheless a life-changing experience, as Theo would never be the same.

Estella took her new friend by the hand and asked, "Would you like to play a game of Chutes and Ladders?"

What a wonderful day it was for Theo. He had never played a board game before. As one might have surmised, Theo's life up until that point in time might have been best described as a suboptimal existence.

Despite the young boy's condemnation to a wretched environment where child abuse and neglect were prevalent, there was a thin silver lining that outlined the black cloud perpetually looming over Theo's head. Grace, hope, faith, and charity could still be found, even among the most dire of circumstances, but only if a righteous person who gave half a tinker's damn was willing to step up to the plate.

———•••———

Everybody knew Franco Sanchez by his nickname, Perro Grande. He raised dogs in the neighborhood, but assuredly, they were not the type destined to become household pets. After entering the United States illegally in 1978, Perro garnished modest off-the-record income from the nearby clandestine pit bull arena and also from his sale of cocaine to the nearby kids at the local high school. He was nonetheless readily able to lease a lower-middle-class home directly across the street from where Estella and her family lived. His lowrider '63 Impala was chopped and channeled, and it displayed a large translucent decal of the Lady of Guadalupe on the back window. A Mexican flag was affixed to the left-hand side of the rear bumper, and a large and overtly offensive adhesive sticker on the right-hand side of the bumper boldly declared, "Dog fighting is our culture, not our crime."

Sadly, the dogs Perro Grande trained to fight were physically abused and treated with unspeakable cruelty. Perro would enhance the natural fighting spirit in his pit bulls by allowing them to violently disassemble cats and other smaller pet dogs that he stole from his neighbors who lived in the community.

As for the brief and brutal life of Perro's pit bulls, it was always a fight-to-the-death command performance once they entered the arena. If one of Perro Grande's pit bulls was seriously injured in the arena during a dog-fighting match and it was apparent the damaged goods would no longer be able to physically compete in the future, Perro would simply destroy the canine without remorse.

Perro utilized a variety of medieval methodologies to kill an injured dog. Oftentimes, he would strap a concrete block to the dog's neck and then drown the misfortunate creature in a large basin of water. If Perro was feeling particularly cruel, he would saturate the dog with salt water and use a split electrical cord plugged into a wall socket to electrocute the tortured animal until a complete cardiopulmonary arrest occurred.

Perro found the stench of burning hair and flesh particularly intoxicating. The act of killing a dog would invariably result in an overwhelming, intense aggressive arousal in Perro Grande which only whetted his desire to witness canines maul each other to death.

Mr. and Mrs. Sisfuentes had a sneaking suspicion their neighbor from across the street was perhaps somehow a bit off beam, but they could never confirm anything. On one occasion, Estella's miniature dachshund mysteriously disappeared. The backyard fence of Estella's home had been broken down, and it was clear the animal had been stolen. Although they called the police and requested a neighborhood patrol, nothing ever came of their formal complaint.

On a Thursday afternoon in October, the air was cool, and the humidity was low. Local Houstonian nomenclature deemed that it was one of those rare, perfect so-called Colorado days that compelled Texans of all stripes to go outdoors and enjoy the onset of the fall season. Try as she might, Estella was unable to teach Theo how to skip a rope. Every time he attempted the intricate coordinated activity, he would trip himself, or the rope would end up slapping him in the shins.

"I have it figured out," Theo finally said. "Watch this!"

Theo would spin the rope over his head, and it would land a few inches in front of him at a dead stop. Then he would carefully step over the rope one foot at a time. He proclaimed, "See? I can do this! It's just in slow motion. It's your turn."

Estella took the jump rope and said, "Theo, you're so silly!" Like a dervish, she began to rapidly skip through her jump rope routine, including alternating hops from one leg to the next. Unfortunately, her gyrations made Estella look like wounded prey to the two pit pulls watching with great interest behind the chain-link fence on the property of Perro Grande across the street. Oddly, the dogs did not bark as they proceeded to scale the chain-link fence and make a beeline sprint toward the two children.

Ignoring the boy, the two pit bulls took down Estella as if she were a living meal—which was exactly what the young girl represented to the two vicious canines. Instinctively rolling up into a ball and trying to cover her head and neck region with her arms, Estella screamed in terror as one of the pit bulls reached in to grab her left leg at the ankle in an effort to extend the lower extremity at the knee while the other dog started to consume her left calf muscle.

It was a well-coordinated attack, and Estella was being eaten alive.

A yard rake with thick metal tines was leaning against the side of the house of Mr. and Mrs. Sisfuentes. Theo grabbed the rake and brought it down hard against the back of the pit bull that was consuming Estella's leg. No sooner had the first dog recoiled in pain than the other dog took its opportunity to also start eating the girl's left leg.

Once again, Theo brought down the sharp tines of the rake hard against the back of the assailant. When the stunned canine briefly retreated, its pack member rapidly moved back in to continue dining. As the same ordeal repeated over and over again, the pit bulls attacked Estella in a horrific round-robin fashion.

It was as if the two children had been condemned to hell for sins they had never committed. When Mrs. Sisfuentes heard the screams of her daughter, she ran out onto the front lawn to see what was wrong. As Theo was unable to fend off the two canines, Estella's mom began to kick the pit bulls in the ribs as hard as she possibly could. Unfortunately, her kicks had no bearing on the determined intent of the canines, which continued the onslaught. It appeared the dogs were oblivious to what Mrs. Sisfuentes was doing. There was no time to call the police. Estella would be dead by the time they had arrived.

Estella's mom had only one chance to save her daughter, and that was to see if Arturo, the next-door neighbor, was home. A proud veteran of the Korean War, Arturo possessed a .30-caliber M1 carbine. Everybody in the neighborhood knew that Arturo was not a man to be trifled with, as he always kept the loaded gun by the front door of his home. Arturo's carbine had long proven to be an effective deterrent against burglars and hooligans. She called out to Theo, "I'm going for help! Please save Estella!"

When Mrs. Sisfuentes returned with Arturo in tow, his carbine was ready for business with a thirty-round banana clip snapped into the magazine receiver. Arturo, however, had to make certain no stray slugs of lead would end up striking Estella or Theo.

"Theo, stand behind me!" Arturo leveled the muzzle of the weapon squarely into the ear of his first adversary and said, "Adios, muchacho!"

With that, he pulled the trigger. Bloody gray matter splattered all over the sidewalk. One adversary was down, but there was one yet to go. As the first pit bull fell over dead, its pack mate resumed the attack on the young girl. The dog behaved as if it were a land shark in a feeding frenzy. Fortunately for Estella, Arturo's carbine would assure that the second dog would meet a terminal fate similar to that of the first animal.

━━◦◦◦◦◦━━

Dr. Gerard Garble pulled the resident physician aside and said, "Look, Terry, take Brewster down to the emergency room with you right now. An eight-year-old girl just arrived by ambulance. She apparently was attacked by one or more canines. Frank Barber is working the case, and he's bringing in ortho and the trauma boys. I don't know the extent of the young girl's injuries, but it sounds like she's going to get hauled off to the OR pretty soon. Get down there now, knock out a pediatric H and P, and make sure it's on the chart before she goes to surgery."

When Brewster and Dr. Hopland arrived at the emergency room, they went straightaway to find Estella Sisfuentes to discover what exactly had occurred.

"Estella," Brewster said, "can you tell Dr. Hopland and me what happened to you?"

The young girl mustered a soft whimper to reply. "I don't know what I did wrong, but two dogs came up to me, and they started to eat me."

"Sweetie," Dr. Hopland said, "did you get hurt badly?"

"I think my left leg is gone," the young girl replied, "but it's okay because it doesn't hurt very much."

Prior to her arrival at the ER, the emergency medical technicians who had arrived at the Sisfuentes house via ambulance had wrapped Estella's left lower extremity in heavy gauze after extensively washing down the wound site with multiple bottles of saline fluid.

The ER attending, Dr. Frank Barber, looked at the heavy dressing and then turned to the medical student to give out instructions.

"Take it all down, Brew. Let's have a look-see at what's going on here."

After the bandage scissors cut away the gauze dressing on Estella's left leg, Brewster immediately went blind in his left eye. The gastrocnemius, soleus, peroneus longus, peroneus brevis, and tibialis anterior muscles were all gone and presumably somewhere deep in the gastrointestinal tracts of the two dead dogs. In fact, all of the musculature had been stripped away from both the tibia and fibula bones of the lower extremity, and the bones were completely bare of flesh.

"Wait! I can't see!" Brewster exclaimed. "I can't see!"

Terry Hopland turned to Brewster and said, "Go throw some cold water on your face. Come back here as soon as you pull yourself together. I swear, Brew; you need to grow a pair!"

The EMT crew had drawn a rainbow out in the field, and the tubes of blood had been sent immediately to the laboratory as soon as Estella arrived at the ER. When Brewster and Hopland had reached the emergency room, the stat lab results had just come back for the medical staff to review and evaluate.

Dr. Hopland had a curious look on his face after reviewing the laboratory results, and then he handed the lab slip over to Frank Barber to let him look at the unexpected parameters. How could that be? Estella's hemoglobin and hematocrit were normal. The patient should have died from exsanguination, but there was no clear evidence of any loss of blood. It wasn't a matter of hemoconcentration either, as the specific gravity on the urinalysis was normal, as were the serum BUN and creatinine levels.

Perhaps there was extensive crush injury from the powerful jaws of the pit bulls that had effectively clamped the ends of the arteries that supplied blood to the left lower extremity. That was it. That had to be it. There was no other logical explanation to account for the finding and to explain why the young patient had a normal pulse and blood pressure. That was the ticket. How else could such findings have been explained in an eight-year-old girl whose left leg below the knee had been eaten down to the bones by two dogs?

Dr. Barber instructed Dr. Hopland and the two nurses present to roll the patient over onto her right side so he could have a better chance to examine the posterior aspect of what had once been Estella's left lower leg. What Dr. Barber saw left him dumbfounded.

"What in hell am I looking at here? Is this the popliteal artery, or am I looking at the posterior tib?"

"Well, if my memory for basic anatomy serves me correctly," Dr. Hopland replied, "you're just distal to the patient's knee, so you must be at the proximal end of the posterior tib."

The artery was not crushed. It had simply been sheared away by the sharp teeth of the canines. The rent in the distal aspect of the artery was patent, and with his gloved hand, Dr. Barber could feel the end of the artery pulsate with each beat of the patient's heart. Blood should have been gushing out of the artery, blasting across the emergency room stall and all over the floor. The patient should have bled to death long ago. There was no scientific or rational explanation for what Dr. Barber had just witnessed with his own eyes.

Dr. Barber suddenly felt light-headed and had an unusual sensation of vertigo the likes of which he had never experienced before. It seemed he was standing sideways at the top of the back wall of the emergency room stall, looking down on the proceedings. He was having an out-of-body experience!

As the color receded from his face, Dr. Hopland asked, "Frank, are you okay?"

"No, I'm not okay," Dr. Barber replied. "In fact, I don't think I'll ever be okay again."

Just then, the orthopedic surgery service and trauma team arrived, and it was clear Estella was going to require an at-the-knee amputation of her left lower extremity. The limb could not be salvaged. As her mother and father signed the procedure permit consent form without coercion, the patient was whisked away while she bravely said, "Goodbye, leg; I'm going to miss you!"

When Dr. Barber entered the washroom in the hallway near the Vinyl Lounge, Brewster's visual acuity had returned to normal, and he was drying his face with a paper towel after emotionally composing himself. Meanwhile, Dr. Barber got down on his knees in front of one of the sinks in the washroom, as if he were a man in prayer. Without looking up, he explained to the medical student what had just occurred.

"I just saw a miracle, Brew," Dr. Barber said. "That eight-year-old little girl should have bled to death. I found the posterior tib. The artery was ripped wide open. It was completely patent, I tell you, but no blood was coming out of the sheared end of the vessel."

"No, it must have been just a proximal crush injury that prevented blood from flowing out the distal end of the lacerated artery," Brewster logically replied. "Nothing more and nothing less."

The medical student's casual reply made Frank Barber jump up in anger. The attending grabbed Brewster by the collar of his short consulting jacket and forcefully pushed him up against the back tiled wall.

"No, goddamn it, you're not listening to me!" Dr. Barber screamed, only inches from Brewster's face. "I'm telling you right here and right now that I've just witnessed an intersession of Divine providence!"

Although startled, Brewster pulled himself away from the grasp of Dr. Frank Barber and replied, "Miracles do happen, but you never know who has been chosen to be the witness. I guess I just wasn't supposed to see this one."

Estella would be fitted with a left lower-extremity titanium prosthetic leg. She would go through several of the devices until she had reached her mature height and weight. With the biological welding of her epiphyseal plates when she was about nineteen years old, it was finally assured that her full measure as an adult woman had plateaued. The subsequent prosthetic leg she would be slated to receive at that time would be one she could utilize for many years to come.

———◦———

An improvised explosive device during the Gulf War mangled Theo's right leg below the knee, which warranted an at-the-knee amputation and a permanent titanium prosthetic limb. When he and his future wife, Estella, stood together side by side, they appeared to be matching bookends. Theo and Estella would remain happily connected to each other for their remaining days.

———◦———

As for Franco Sanchez, a.k.a. Perro Grande, the career-criminal illegal alien was arrested and charged with assault with a deadly weapon in addition to cruelty to animals. Although he received legal counsel from the Hispanic supremacy group Hispanics without Borders, he was subjected to a trial with a jury of his peers. Although every jury member was Hispanic, Perro Grande was nonetheless found guilty on all charges. After his conviction and five-year prison sentence, he was subsequently thrown out of the country.

Despite that fact, Sanchez kept coming back into the United States illegally time and again. He would be arrested and convicted of no fewer than seven felonies over a three-and-a-half-decade span of time. Sanchez invariably found refuge in the sanctuary city of San

Francisco, where he was immorally protected by city officials from the long arm of the federal immigration service.

Sanchez would eventually murder a young woman named Casey Steinway, who was on vacation with her father in San Francisco. He shot the young woman in the back of the head, and sadly, she was pronounced dead at the scene.

The career criminal allegedly found a handgun and claimed he didn't know the gun was dangerous. In a court of law, he changed his story and stated that he thought the gun was a toy. Upon cross-examination, he committed perjury. He finally admitted the gun was real, but he didn't think it was loaded. Instead of being convicted of murder, Sanchez got a slap on the wrist, and he received a modest monetary fine for the minor crime of discharging a weapon in public.

How could such a thing have happened? If people like Perro Grande were bona fide examples of the criminal element that the City by the Bay was trying to recruit and protect, the feds should have cut off all funding to that shithole aggregation of politically unenlightened losers until the Golden Gate Bridge had completely oxidized and disintegrated into the Pacific Ocean. San Francisco had apparently become a morally inferior, musty sepulcher filled with the rotting, archaic bones of a bygone Victorian era.

As the wretched State of California was stupid enough to decriminalize childhood prostitution in the year 2016, one should not have been surprised that the state was stupid enough to let somebody like Franco Sanchez roam the streets and cause further mayhem.

The progressives of California might as well have given a career criminal like Franco Sanchez a driver's license and then allowed him to vote, as long as he voted for liberal candidates in perpetuity. Perro Grande would have made an excellent mayoral candidate for San Francisco. Rest assured that was indeed the very next psychopathic item on an apocalyptic political horizon. No borders, no wall, no

USA at all. In the end, that was what it was all about, was it not? Yeah, that was the ticket!

Were the citizens of America offended by the idiotic belief in a self-proclaimed sanctuary status wherein certain cities had erroneously believed that progressive local public policies superseded federal law? Well, perhaps everybody should have been, irrespective of whether a person's primary color was red, blue, or an amalgamation of the two.

⚙

Many years later, Brewster would encounter an Impala low-rider in a grocery store parking lot in Houston. A large and overtly offensive adhesive sticker applied to the right-hand side of the bumper boldly declared, "Dog fighting is our culture, not our crime."

While many people looked on and applauded, Brewster took a car jack out of his trunk and proceeded to break every window on the car and then slash its tires. Perhaps it was safe to say that J. D. Brewster would never really get over any of his anger-management issues.

⚙

At the outpatient pediatric clinic, Dr. Garble assigned Victoria Campos to see the patient in the second exam room. The medical student went in without her resident or attending for supervision, as she was far enough along in her medical school training to feel comfortable in taking a history, doing a thorough exam, and being able to formulate an initial medical opinion.

The patient was a four-year-old little boy who'd been brought in to be evaluated for extensive deep scratches he had sustained on his face, allegedly inflicted by the family pet. When Ms. Campos asked the patient's mother what kind of animal could possibly be capable of dispensing such deep wounds that would warrant sutures and a tetanus booster, the mother proudly held out a photo of the family pet from the wallet in her purse.

Victoria Campos was left speechless when she took a good look at the photograph. It revealed a small boy sitting in a bathtub filled with soapy water. Sitting beside the boy in bath was an enormous cat that appeared to be none too pleased about its predicament.

In the photographic image, the cat had extended its front paw outside the confines of the bathtub in what was clearly an initial attempt to make an escape from the unpleasant hygienic measures it was being subjected to. The animal possessed, without doubt, one of the largest feline paws Victoria had ever seen outside of the rare times when she watched reruns of the old Mutual of Omaha's Wild Kingdom television show.

"My goodness," Victoria said, "what a beautiful animal. Would you mind very much if I showed this photograph to some of my colleagues? I believe they would be most interested in seeing this picture."

"Why, by all means," the mother replied.

Victoria ran out of the room to get the attention of J. D. Brewster, who was busy evaluating another pediatric patient at the time.

"Listen, Brew," Victoria said. "I know your tiny brain is inundated with useless, esoteric bullshit that's so lame you couldn't get doinked at a cocktail party hosted by the Horny Houstonian Harlot Society even if you were the only hombre who showed up for the fiesta. Nevertheless, I need your help here. Take a look at this picture. Qué es esto? What can you tell me about ese gato grande, por favor?"

Before Brewster had even looked at the photograph, he was thoroughly impressed with the complex and multilayered aspersions Victoria had cast in his direction.

"Wow, Victoria! That was really hot! Perhaps you should hang out with me and the boys down in the Vinyl Lounge, and you can exchange vicious insults with us while we're watching the Rectal

Roberts Ministry Hour. You know, they broadcast that show right out of Hope, Arkansas."

"I would be willing to chew tobacco, fart out loud, and spit on the floor while you're watching that happy, holy, hillbilly horseshit," Victoria said. "It's a done deal as soon as you say adios to that fat, hippy, loser, dinosaur chick who wears the plastic flowers in her hair. I can't believe you got back together with her. Qué estaban pensando, mi amor? After all, there is still time for me to become your one and only mamacita caliente. No es cierto, gringo? By the way that your forehead is starting to sweat, I can tell you're getting all worked up into a hot, foamy lather. Before you wander away to go jerk off in the broom closet, tell me what's in this picture!"

Victoria and Brewster locked eyes and smiled at each other. If they had gotten just one centimeter closer to each other at that moment, they both would have likely thrown caution to the wind. *What's going on here?* Brewster thought to himself. *I'm engaged to be married, and here I am, flirting with another woman. There must be something seriously wrong with me!*

"Speak up, Brewster," Victoria said. "Sometimes I wonder if there's something seriously wrong with you!"

Brewster snatched the photograph out of his colleague's hand. He took one look and said, "Victoria, the animal in this picture happens to be a juvenile edition of a creature that has the scientific designation Felis concolor, also commonly known as the mountain lion, cougar, or North America's puma. Their life span is on the order of approximately eight to thirteen years in the wild, and a large male can grow up to, and even over, one hundred kilograms of body weight. They can easily take down, kill, and even consume a human being if—"

Brewster looked up to see that Victoria Campos was long gone. As she disappeared down the hallway, Brewster suddenly realized he must have overwhelmed her with his useless, esoteric bullshit. Unfortunately for Brewster, the broom closet adjacent to the outpatient pediatric clinic was locked up tighter than a drum at that particular time, and the forlorn student had apparently been sadly abandoned. He was left to helplessly ponder the vagaries of God's vast and mysterious universe with an empty blue ball sack.

Victoria found a telephone and asked the hospital operator to connect her to an outside line so she could call Child Protective Services for an emergency intervention. The next order of business would then be a timely telephone call to the local Houston chapter of the ASPCA, as per the instructions of the resident, Terry Hopland.

—◦◦◦◦—

By the time Bobby Dalles would complete his mandatory pediatric clerkship at the end of October 1981, he would hold only two convictions about the entire specialty of child-care medicine. First, the outpatient pediatric clinic should have kept the phone number for Child Protective Services on speed dial, and second, there should have been a mandatory federal license requirement if one ever planned to engage in the act of procreation. Both of those fundamental beliefs had come into sharp focus by the third week of October.

A young unmarried couple brought in their two-year-old son to be evaluated for an injury that allegedly had occurred while he was innocently playing in the backyard of their home. When Bobby examined the young patient, curiously, he found concentric rings on the child's buttocks. Some of the lesions were blistered, while others appeared to have a deep eschar. Uncertain what he might be looking at, Bobby asked J. D. Brewster to take a peek and render an opinion.

Brewster took a look at the situation, but as usual, he was unable to see the big picture. He said, "I'm not sure what in hell we're looking at. Could this be an example of erythema annulare? I really don't have a clue. Go grab Garble. By now in his career, he's seen everything under the sun. I bet he'll immediately recognize what this is."

When Dr. Garble walked into the room, he took one look at the toddler and then at the couple. Without saying a word to the parents, the attending motioned with his index finger for his two medical students to follow him out of the exam room.

"Follow me, boys," Dr. Garble said with a considerable degree of alarm in his voice. "I'm sad to say that I have seen this before."

Dr. Garble led the two medical students into the staff breakroom, where there was a refrigerator and a countertop electric stove with two burners. The attending unplugged one of the electric heating elements from the stove top and handed it to the two medical students.

"I am certain the culprit that caused this injury must have looked something like this. There's no doubt in my mind that this child was burned on top of an electric stove top somewhere. Nice."

As Brewster was destined never to have any children, he was livid that any parent could subject his or her child to such abuse. The medical student bent over, covering his left eye with the palm of his hand. "Snap out of it," Dr. Garble said. "We've got work to do. Listen, Brew: you call the police and then Child Protective Services. Do it in that order. Bobby, take this electric stove-top element with you, and let's go confront these two bungholes."

Dr. Garble and Bobby Dalles returned to the exam room. Bobby casually pitched the electric stove-top element onto the top of the examination table, and it landed right beside the three-year-old child. Dr. Garble stuck his hands into his pockets and asked, "Does anybody have anything to say?"

The father of the child pointed to the woman in the room and said, "She did it. The thing was crying, and it just wouldn't shut up. My girlfriend was royally pissed, and she said to the thing, 'I'm going to give you something to cry about!' That's when she put it on the stove and jacked up the juice."

"You lying son of a bitch!" the girlfriend said. "It was you who did it this time around!"

"You've done this more than once?" Bobby Dalles asked.

"Boy, you should have heard the thing scream!" the boyfriend said. "It didn't know how to get off of the stove, so it just sat there and screamed and screamed while we cooked its little ass. As I recall, we used the left front burner. Is that correct, snookums?"

"Well, of course we used the left front burner, dumbass," the baby's mother replied. "The last time we tried to teach this thing some manners, we attempted to use the right front burner, and the baby's pants melted onto the element, and it shorted out the damned burner unit. That's why we used the left side of the stove this time around. It's the only part of the oven that's currently operational anymore."

Dr. Garble looked around the exam room and saw an extension to an IV pole. He pulled the pole off the rolling stand and held it like a baseball bat. He turned toward the idiotic couple with malicious intent.

"What do you think, Bobby?" Garble asked. "Is it time for the dispensation of a little bit of clinical justice?"

The police suddenly arrived, and the parents of the child were arrested before the attending physician had an opportunity to step up to the plate and take a few well-deserved practice swings. By court decree, Child Protective Services ensured the baby would be enrolled in foster care, and the parents would never see their offspring ever again.

Dr. Garble and his wife were exasperated to learn that their fourteen-year-old son, Travis, was being suspended from high school. Travis was a freshman and initially had done well in school. For no apparent reason, he had become disruptive and combative in school, and he was failing the course of English composition. Dr. Garble and his wife had met with the English teacher the week prior to the boy's suspension to try to ascertain what kind of problem Travis was having in that class.

The teacher explained, "I don't understand your child. There are only three components to the grade that a kid gets in my class. First, there are the long tests, and your son has an outstanding ninety-six average on those exams. Second, there are the pop-quiz exams, and your son has an eighty-nine average on those particular tests. With that, your son should be making an A in English. The third and final component is where we seem to have a problem. Since the beginning of October, your son has not turned in any of the weekly composition assignments. He has a zero there, and that is what has dropped him down to a failing grade."

Travis was looking out the window of the classroom when his father said, "Tell me, Travis—why have you not turned in any of your weekly compositions? Your mother and I ask you every evening if you have any homework, and your answer is always no. How could this be?"

"Well," Travis said, "it should be quite obvious to the both of you by now that I have been lying. Frankly, there are less two decades left in this millennium, and the cold war that now exists between the Soviet Union and the United States appears to be ready to break into all-out, overt thermonuclear annihilation."

"What on earth does that have to do with your homework?" Mrs. Garble asked.

"It should be implicit," Travis replied, "that whether or not I complete a weekly English composition, it will have absolutely no bearing on my life—or anybody else's, for that matter. This will especially be the case after ninety-nine percent of all of the above-ground vertebrate life-forms become vaporized."

"Are you vying for the Nobel Peace Prize, or are you just trying to be a smart-ass?" Dr. Garble asked.

"Neither," Travis said in defense of his geopolitical ideological position. "As human beings have so miserably failed as stewards of this third rock from the sun, it seems to me that God has backed the wrong primate. So before we hand over what's left of the planet to cockroaches and other arthropods, I'm just going to enjoy the ride for now until I am violently and irrevocably reduced to subatomic components."

On the day Travis was kicked out of school, Dr. Garble went to pick up his son from the vice principal's office. The disciplinarian said, "Your son is picking fights in school. Several weeks ago, one of your son's classmates, Chevy Copa, was arrested for vandalism and destruction of public property. We can't confirm if your son was involved in any of that mischief, but the temporal relationship as to when your son's behavior started to radically change is uncanny. He refuses to work with the school counselors, so we have no choice but to suspend him from school at this time."

—◁◁◁∫∫▷▷▷—

As Brewster walked down the hallway, he noted that a solitary adolescent male figure was trying to carve his initials into the arm of a wooden chair in the outpatient pediatric clinic conference room with a small pocketknife.

"If you're going to try to leave a legacy that proclaims that for one fleeting moment, you were at one time a cognizant and sentient being that passed through this universe, you are definitely going to need a much bigger knife," Brewster told the young man.

"Maybe so," Travis said. "I guess all that I want to say is that I was here."

"After the end of World War II, when American GI servicemen were returning from battle, a ubiquitous notation began to appear all over this country. Found on subway walls and tenement halls, it was a singular mysterious proclamation: 'Kilroy was here.'"

"Who in hell was Kilroy?" The adolescent looked up to ask the medical student.

"Well, stranger, that's indeed the million-dollar question. Kilroy, as it turned out, was nobody. Kilroy, as it turned out, was everybody," Brewster replied. "As the answer to your semirhetorical question may indeed have a broad spectrum of possibilities, where exactly do you see yourself within this conundrum?"

"Hopefully somewhere in the middle," the teenager answered.

"So would most of us, I would presume," Brewster said. "You must be Travis Garble. I heard you were going to be hanging your hat over here for a while at the pediatric clinic now that you've managed to get yourself suspended from high school."

The young man looked at Brewster's name badge and said, "My cousin is Missy Brownwood, and her mother is my father's youngest sister. Missy said you used to be in the 1960s rock band DNR. She also said you have a reputation for being a troublemaker."

"I categorically reject that allegation," Brewster replied. "I'm just trying to get through life the best I can, like everybody else. It would seem, however, that I have an uncanny knack for being in the wrong place at the wrong time. Besides, Missy Brownwood talks too much."

"Well, well, well, it looks like perhaps you and I may have something in common," Travis said as he pulled on his right earlobe.

"Come take a walk with me," Brewster said. "Now, damn it, quit dicking around with our furniture before I have to come over there and slap the holy crap out of you for being a little vandal. Let's go over to Hermann Park and shoot the shit for a bit. Maybe I can figure out what exactly makes you tick."

—◆—

Brewster and Travis sat on a bench at Hermann Park for several minutes in silence. When Travis pulled out a cigarette from his top pocket and dangled it between his lips, Brewster reached over and swatted the cancer stick out of his mouth.

"I'm not going to be accused of contributing to the delinquency of a minor," Brewster said. "You can't smoke cigarettes if you're hanging out with me. That's not going to happen on my watch. I have something much better than that."

Brewster reached into the top pocket of his white consulting jacket, pulled out two fat Churchill cigars, and gave one of them to Travis.

"You're going to man up and take on one of these bad boys today. Don't inhale the smoke into your lungs. Just let it roll around in your mouth," Brewster said. "The nicotine will be absorbed through the mucous membranes of your upper aero-digestive system. As you only weigh about a buck thirty, it's going to mess you up badly. I actually suspect you're going to get as sick as a dog. You'll experience a very strong sensation of feeling light-headed, with associated severe nausea. When you blow beets, I want you to pick up a stick and sift through the chunks on the ground to make certain you didn't puke up your own testicles."

"Are you serious?" Travis asked.

"I'm on the square with you," Brewster replied. "In fact, as we speak, I personally have an empty ball sack as a case in point. I'd let you check it out, but that would just be gay. Tell me, young man— are you ready to fire up a Churchill?"

"Absolutely, but aren't cigars as bad for you as cigarettes?" Travis asked.

"No doubt about that. Less risk for lung cancer than smoking cigarettes, but there's a much higher risk for contracting cancer of the upper oropharynx," Brewster said. "With our current medical technology, if you come down with head and neck cancer, you'll end up getting a commando procedure where they'll simply cut your face off."

"What?!"

"I shit you not," Brewster said. "You'll end up becoming a social recluse, and you'll be excluded far beyond the realm of other human beings for the rest of your miserable and painful life as the cancer eats away at your mouth and throat. Without a doubt, it's one of the most horrific deaths you can possibly imagine. In fact, when you die, you may very well drown on your own blood as the cancer breeches the lining of your carotid arteries and jugular veins. Good God Almighty! Would that be a spectacular thing to be able to experience or what? Now, shall we dispense with any more of these superficially pleasant anecdotes regarding the potential pitfalls of tobacco consumption and proceed to light up this campfire?"

It was gratifying to know that Brewster was not contributing to the delinquency of a minor as the two sat on the park bench and puffed away on the cigars. Once Travis began to feel a bit dizzy from the nicotine, it was time for Brewster to probe into the nature of the young man's sudden and unexpected journey into darkness.

Brewster realized he had to be cautious. The medical student would have to ensure that any questions he asked of Travis were supportive and nurturing by intent. Nothing Brewster said could ever demonstrate a threatening or accusatory tone, which would obviously be frightening to the already spiritually challenged young man. In light of this prerequisite imperative, Brewster elected to begin his counseling session with a soft and gentle initial approach in an overt attempt to foster the well-being of the troubled adolescent.

"For fuck's sake, you're one major-league dumb shit! I'm certain your parents would be ashamed to be in the same room with you right about now. After all, I would be, and I don't even give a shit about you or whatever trivial, silly-ass problem you think you might have. What in hell is the matter with you?" Brewster asked. "Grow up. Perhaps it's a blessing that I'll never have any children, because if I had one who popped out like you, I'd likely try to strangle the nasty little bastard with his own umbilical cord. You'd better spill your guts to me right now, you sorry, slimy sack of snot. Tell me this minute why you're running around with a concrete cinder block shoved up your ass!"

Fortunately, it appeared Brewster's soft, subtle, sanguine, and supportive approach allowed Travis finally to open up and explain what was troubling him. In retrospect, Brewster might have eventually made an excellent psychiatrist or psychological counselor, as he might have been much more of a "people person" than anybody had ever realized.

"I attend the private all-boys private high school known as St. Francis over on Memorial Drive," Travis said. "I have to take a city bus to go to school, and I'll do so until I get my driver's license. There's a nice little old lady who always rides with me on the bus, and her name is Mrs. Paddington. About a month ago, this lady got on the bus and was about to put her money into the coin box, when the bus driver hit the accelerator. Mrs. Paddington fell down and slid along the aisle of the bus as her change scattered everywhere upon the floor."

"That's terrible!" Brewster said. "What did you do?"

"Chevy Copa and I rushed to help pick up her change from the floor and pay her fare," Travis said. "Chevy and I couldn't believe what the bus driver said next. He turned his head back to see what was going on and said, 'Get the money in the damned coin box, and get your ass in a seat, or I'll throw you off this bus!' Then he slammed on the brakes, and both Chevy and I fell directly on top of Mrs. Paddington. She got banged up pretty badly."

"Are you serious?" Brewster said. "It's no wonder why you have a chip on your shoulder."

"I can't make this shit up," Travis said. "After Chevy helped Mrs. Paddington find a seat, I went kind of crazy, I guess. I took out my pocketknife and carved open the cushion I had been sitting on to expose the thick foam rubber of the bus seat. I then broke out my lighter and set the bus seat on fire. It ignited almost instantaneously, and then I threw the damned thing out the window."

"Remind me to never piss you off," Brewster said.

"When the driver saw the flaming bus seat fly out the window through his rearview mirror, he hit the brakes and said, 'All you boys is a goin' ta jail!' Well, to hell with that crap!" Travis exclaimed. "I bailed out the window like an airborne ranger, and then I ran like a son of a bitch. When the police came, my friend Chevy claimed he was the one responsible for causing all the trouble. That's when he got arrested. Sadly, he got expelled from school after that. Tell me—what would you have done?"

"Okay, there are several lessons to be learned here," Brewster replied. "The first thing you should know is that no good deed goes unpunished. The second thing you should understand is that your friend Chevy was an idiot. When the cops came onto the bus to see what was going on, Chevy should have said that some other kids set the bus seat on fire and then jumped out the window and ran away. Your friend should have told the cops he had no idea who the perpetrators were, because they were all evil little black bastards, and he had never seen them before."

"Are you serious?" Travis asked. "That sounds like a terrible thing to say."

"Well, you won't get any argument from me about that fact," Brewster said, "but when all else fails, don't forget to point your finger at black folks. If something ever goes wrong in the future, even if black people had nothing to do with a particular troublesome predicament you may find yourself in, blaming the Negro will always be an easy out for you or your friends. After all, black people have long been America's scapegoats, and they somehow perpetually manage to fulfill their societal obligation concerning this matter quite nicely as far as I'm concerned."

"I can't believe you're telling me this!" Travis said.

"Wake up, junior," Brewster said. "The cops would have surely believed that cock-and-bull story about black people, I tell you. If Chevy Copa had simply told a lie like that, he would've lived happily ever after. What he did was just a simple attempt to try to save your sorry ass from the frying pan. I guess he thought you were his friend. Why anybody would want to try to befriend a skulking little bastard like you is beyond me. Sadly, what Chevy did was not a noble thing to do, believe you me! It was just plain stupid."

Young Travis looked at Brewster with astonishment at the advice the medical student had dispensed. "If you blame black people for some evil crime they haven't committed, isn't that a pure act of racism?"

Brewster was far from finished with his counseling session. "Oh yes. Absolutely. Rest assured it's top-shelf, grade-A racism. Listen, young man, if you are going to engage in any endeavor, you need to try to do it to the best of your abilities. If you are going to be a racist, be the very best racist you can possibly be."

The young ward appeared to be dismayed. "I don't know about all of that. It sounds like being a full-time racist may turn out to be hard work."

"Of course it's hard work, Travis!" the older mentor replied. "Let me spell something out for you: it is much easier to garnish animosity against an entire ethnic group than against individuals. I've certainly known and befriended other people from different ethnic groups and other races. If the truth be told, those people I would have described as different all turned out to be, well, like regular people, I suppose. It is so much easier to wield a brutal hammer of personal disdain toward larger aggregations of human beings than against individuals, who you might discover are not much different from you."

"Words of wisdom, no doubt," Travis said thoughtfully.

"The third thing you have to learn to do is try to control your anger," Brewster said. "Be careful, or else hatred will burn you up. It will get to the point that every other emotion you have ever had will become eroded. I should know because I too have anger-management issues, or so it would seem. You should not take your hatred out on inanimate objects. That's foolish and counterproductive. After all, the bus seat you set on fire had never done anything to you to warrant such an extreme and dangerous act of violence."

"What other alternative course of action should I have considered?" Travis asked.

"Simple!" Brewster said. "Instead of acting out like that on an innocent bus cushion, you should've looked for a future opportunity to exact revenge on the bastard who was driving the bus. Personally, I probably would have dry-gulched the son of a bitch with a lead pipe. That would certainly have been most gratifying, at least from my perspective."

Travis appeared to be disturbed by that particular pearl of wisdom from Brewster. "Really? I can't see myself using a lead pipe in such a fashion. That sounds like—I don't know—ghetto warfare or something like that."

"When you seek retribution," Brewster said, "you have to be a grown man about such matters. It will be necessary for you to find your own way. For example, you might personally find that my choice to use a lead pipe as a weapon in that particular situation has, shall we say, obvious urban overtones that you might find unsavory. After all, a lead pipe is indeed a primitive weapon. Therefore, you might be much more comfortable with a shiv or a ball peen hammer."

"Now you're talking!" Travis said enthusiastically.

"To my way of thinking, it'll be a real sign of maturity when you figure out exactly how you want to punish somebody," Brewster said. "You'll need to think long and hard about how you'll want to take down that bus driver. Remember, you'll also need to give great consideration as to how you'll be able to get away with the crime you're going to commit and not get caught. Whenever you take him down—and I know you eventually will—you'll need to make certain that he suffers. That must always be your primary directive."

"I feel so much better after talking to you, Mr. Brewster," Travis said gratefully. "I could never have such a helpful conversation like that with my own father."

"Well, thank you," Brewster replied. "It's good to know I have some paternal skills, although they will likely never be exercised beyond the scope of this conversation we're having today."

"Do you know something?" Travis asked. "You'd make an excellent school counselor. I wish you could offer advice like that to all of the kids who go to my school. It all makes sense to me now."

"I'll certainly make a point to avail myself to you and your classmates if I can ever help any of you boys get a leg up on life."

"You've given me a lot of very solid and helpful information, and I'll never forget what you've done for me today. I think I'm ready to get back to my studies now. I hope you'll not mind it very much if I contact you in the future if I ever need any more righteous spiritual guidance."

"Not at all, my little friend," Brewster replied. "I was just happy to help."

The leader of the black militant separatist group known as the Fraternity of the United Kinship of Urban People, also known by the simple acronym FUKUP, realized something was medically wrong with their newest member, Big Nig. Located in a compound in the forests of East Texas, every member of FUKUP had received mandatory orders to participate in martial-arts training and calisthenics. They were also expected to become proficient in the use of small-arms weaponry.

At first, Big had enthusiastically participated in those activities, but over the course of the past month, he'd been running fevers and rapidly losing weight. It had gotten to a point where it was necessary for him to rest more. When Big started to manifest large purple lesions on his face and extremities, it was clear that it was time for him to be unceremoniously cast out of the compound of radicals.

"When you came to us looking for a place of refuge, why didn't you tell us you had the GRID?" the group commander said. "You've got exactly twenty-four hours to pack up your grit and get the hell out of here. I know exactly how the federal government is trying to kill off us black folks. If I end up finding out that you brought any dangerous moths into this compound that might end up spreading the GRID to any of my other warriors, I swear to Allah I'll snuff you myself!"

"This is my new home," Big replied. "Kiss my ass, buddy; I have no plans of leaving here in twenty-four hours."

Suddenly, Big was looking down the barrel of a gun.

"Yes, I guess you're correct," the group leader said. "Now you no longer have twenty-four hours to get out of here. You're leaving this compound in five minutes."

With no place to go, Big packed up his meager belongings and proceeded to drive down a series of county roads that would eventually meander back to Interstate 10. Once on the highway, he would head westward to a small and unassuming little town located on the Gulf Coast of Texas called Houston.

8

Book of Revelations

U ncle John's next-door neighbor, Mrs. Gallo, was an elderly and frail widow. Sadly, she had never come to terms with a life that was destined to be lived in total solitude. With her full and bushy postmenopausal Mediterranean mustache, she tried to keep herself busy with gardening and charity work through her church.

At that time of the year, the Bermuda grass in Houston was already starting to turn brown, and Mrs. Gallo's shrubs were about to transition into the fall season. While she was picking up dog poop from her front lawn with a plastic grocery bag she wore over her right hand as if it were a glove, Uncle John approached her, wielding his formidable twelve-gauge shotgun.

As far as Uncle John was concerned, it was high time that the long-standing object of his raging sexual desire be taken hostage. When grabbed from behind, Mrs. Gallo screamed out, "John, what in hell do think you are doing? Let me go! Help! Somebody help!"

As Uncle John dragged Mrs. Gallo at gunpoint into his own home, it turned out that the elderly woman's voracious and passionate cries for help were not in vain. Antonia Alabaster and the Your Witness News team of ambush journalists arrived on the scene even before the police. Antonia pleaded with Uncle John to do the right thing and simply surrender, but Uncle John refused to cooperate.

"I suggest you get out of here, Antonia! You're not invited to this party."

Momentarily, the Houston city police arrived. When it became clear the authorities were dealing with a hostage situation, the Houston SWAT team eagerly appeared. It was soon apparent that the SWAT team was dealing with an infamous and crazed individual named Uncle John.

The Urban Assault Vehicle, complete with an electrically operated 7.62-millimeter, six-barrel GAU-2/A Minigun mounted in a hydraulically activated top turret, suddenly showed from the armory. As the authorities were armed with a modern Gatling gun capable of spewing out four thousand rounds of molten lead per minute, it would have appeared to even the most casual observer that Uncle John was about to have a bad day.

The commander of the SWAT team turned up the volume on the bullhorn and shouted out, "John, let Mrs. Gallo go free, and nobody'll get hurt!"

Brewster's angry uncle suddenly appeared at the front door of his home. Not only was he gripping a twelve-gauge shotgun, but he also had a rusty .38-caliber revolver with a fractured shell-ejector rod stuffed down the front of his trousers. John held Mrs. Gallo tightly in front of him as if she were a human shield.

"You coppers aren't going to take me down!" Apparently, Uncle John had been watching too many James Cagney gangster movies.

He pushed Mrs. Gallo off the front porch, blasted a round of buckshot from his weapon into the air, and then beat a hasty retreat back inside his house and slammed the door shut. Uncle John should not have done that. After all, he was in Texas. Rightfully so, Texas was like a whole other country.

The SWAT commander chuckled while he gave a direct and simple order: "Light him up!"

With lead projectiles blasting through the door and the front windows of his house, John crawled on his hands and knees to make an escape through his back door and into the alleyway behind his garage apartment. Uncle John had apparently underestimated the Houston Police Department, as he suddenly found himself surrounded by men wearing black SWAT uniforms. His only recourse was to simply give up. He threw his guns down, stretched out into a prone spread-eagle position, and surrendered.

While Uncle John was being handcuffed and rolled over into a more manageable position, he suddenly had a strange sensation that a fat woman wearing a Viking hat was sitting upon the middle of his chest, crushing the life out of him. John had a full-blown cardiopulmonary arrest before he was placed on a gurney to be loaded into the waiting ambulance. The EMTs' efforts to revive him were unsuccessful, and Uncle John was subsequently transferred directly to the celestial eternal care unit. Sadly, only a handful of his relatives would appear for his funeral.

Instead of feeling sadness upon John's demise, Brewster felt only a strange sense of relief. After all, the self-destructive medical student was hell-bent on getting through his life as fast as he could, and another hurdle had been removed from his path.

Now that John was dead and buried and Brewster had completed all of his mandatory clerkship rotations, it was time for Brewster to try to coast to the finish line. Only half a dozen or so subspecialty electives remained that he still needed to get under his belt in order to complete his medical school training by June 1982.

As he had already been unceremoniously discharged from the PhD program, there was likely no way he could ever get a dual degree now. If that were indeed the case, so be it. In a little bit more than half a year, he would take a powder. Perhaps, Brewster thought, he should just disappear much like Blomeo Colima had done when he had finished his fellowship training on the gastroenterology service.

Upon his departure from Houston, Brewster envisioned that he could employ his own empty scrotal sack as a carry-on bag to store a toothbrush, a stick of deodorant, and a clean pair of socks—time to pack lightly. Maybe Brewster could even tan the damned thing and put a little handle on it.

At a bare minimum, if Uncle John had still been alive, he should have been able to add some drawstrings to Brewster's otherwise useless ball sack, much like what he'd done on the stethoscope bell-warmer prototype the crazy old coot had crafted out of the scrotum of a dead cat.

Once done, Brewster planned to grab Stella by the hand, and then they could both leave Houston behind in the rearview mirror of life. After all, a lot of unhappy memories were starting to pile up, and J. D. thought that for the sake of his mental health and perhaps his own immortal soul, a change in venue was clearly in order. Perpetually filled with anger, Brewster realized he now had pathological homicidal ideations. If he stayed in Houston much longer, somebody might end up dead, and that somebody might end up being a man named J. D. Brewster.

Brewster had been completely wrong in his prediction that the pediatric rotation he had recently completed would be easy or enjoyable. However, he was about to embark on a rotation in the field of dermatology. What could possibly go wrong? He'd pop a few zits, slap on a little benzoyl peroxide, wash his mitts, and then call it a day, right? It'd be as easy as pie; it would just be a little more powder-puff fluff to buff the GPA.

The dermatologists were given the nickname dermatodes, which was a play on words. Nematodes and trematodes were the legitimate scientific classifications for certain types of worms. The neologistic word dermatode was a less-than-complimentary term that implied that dermatologists were, as a class of physicians, little more than invertebrate lower life-forms. As with everything in his life, Brewster would soon discover that he was also wrong about his expectations regarding the upcoming elective clerkship rotation. In fact, it would turn out that he was dead wrong.

The attending physician and director of the department of dermatology was Dr. Stiles, who was widely renowned about the Texas Medical Center for his early model convertible Corvette. Homosexuality was generally frowned upon in Texas in the early 1980s. Dr. Stiles lived with a male pathologist named Dr. Murdock. It had always been the couple's romantic plan to save up enough money to take a long-term sabbatical, hit the open road on the remnants of old Route 66, and explore America before it forever disappeared.

The dermatology resident, Dr. Lincoln Cole, was also gay, and he reportedly had vociferous, histrionic disputes with Dr. Murdock over matters of affection that the resident directed toward the dermatology department director.

Although relatively free of bodily hair except for in his loins, Dr. Cole was endowed with a thick ridge brow. For that reason, Lincoln was not surprised to learn that the medical students had given him the unflattering nickname of Missing Linc.

It appeared Dr. Murdock was not willing to share Dr. Stiles with the resident physician, much less pull train during a petroleum jelly-infused three-way slumber party. J. D. Brewster did not give a hoot in hell about any of those oddities as long as his new attending or the resident physician didn't hit on him during his one-month rotation, which was slated to start in November.

At the beginning of the rotation at the outpatient dermatology clinic, Dr. Cole assigned Brewster to look in on a new patient who was complaining of a skin lesion involving the center of his chest, directly over the proximal sternal region. Although polyester leisure suits had been out of vogue for three years, the patient Brewster evaluated was wearing one, complete with platform shoes.

"Well, sir, what brings you in to see us today?" Brewster asked the patient.

At that point, the patient took down the top two buttons of his shirt and exposed his anterior chest wall to Brewster. The patient had an enormous tumor extruding through the middle of his sternum that looked like a knobby pink hand grenade about twelve centimeters in maximum diameter. It was oozing a small amount of blood from around the edges of the tumor mass.

"Good God! How long have you had this damned thing growing out of the middle of your chest?" Brewster asked. "I'm going to get the resident physician over here to see this, as I've never encountered anything like this in the past."

"It has been going on now for about two years," the patient said, "and it's really painful! I have a sharp, stabbing pain, and I would give it a score of nine on a pain scale of one to ten."

"Two years?" Brewster asked. "What do you mean two years? If this thing was causing you that much excruciating pain, why did you wait so long to come in and have your problem evaluated?"

"Can't you see?" the patient replied as he elaborated with a casual flip of his mane. "I'm a musician!"

Well, in retrospect, that was a good explanation. Brewster thought to himself that the next time he really screwed up and was about to get dragged out onto the carpet to get reprimanded for some venial infraction he might have inadvertently committed in the course of life's events, such a line of defense would become a perfect default declaration. "Can't you see? I'm a musician."

As it would turn out, an explanation of that nature made sense for somebody who was wearing a goofy leisure suit and platform shoes, but for unclear reasons, that same response would not have the same dramatic impact in the court of public opinion on the rare occasions when Brewster would try to use such a line of reasoning during unpleasant or awkward circumstances.

The resident physician, Dr. Cole, palpated around the edges of the lesion and found that the adjacent anterior chest wall was quite soft. "I am going to get the attending physician over here to see this."

"Do you think it's a crab?" Brewster asked.

"Beats the shit out of me," Cole replied in a whisper. "If it's indeed a cancer, I've never encountered anything like this in the past."

Once the attending had arrived, Dr. Stiles was also apparently buffaloed about the lesion that afflicted the patient. A CT scan was ordered, which revealed a huge mediastinal tumor that had eroded through the sternum and anterior rib cage only to directly invade the dermis. Therefore, it was likely not a primary cutaneous malignancy but a cancer that had started underneath the skin and invaded up through it.

The resident physician had taught Brewster how to perform a punch biopsy procedure. Once Brewster had performed the biopsy on the chest-wall mass of the patient in question, the pathology report revealed that the tumor was consistent with a rare, malignant, aggressive high-grade thymoma.

The cancer had devolved out of the patient's own thymus gland, which was an intrinsic component of the immune system. Once the crab pickers showed up, it was immediately decided to present the patient to the tumor board. A recommendation was made at that patient management conference to employ multimodality treatment: surgery, radiation, and combination chemotherapy that would utilize the relatively new drug called cis-platinum.

Amazingly, the patient would eventually achieve a complete remission. Years later, once the patient hit the ten-year mark from the time of his original cancer diagnosis, a designation of "cured" would eventually be rendered. Maybe some patients had all the luck. Perhaps there was a more salient explanation. He was a musician!

———

During the following week, an agent from the Internal Revenue Service showed up to interview Dr. Stiles. It appeared the attending physician had not filed a federal tax return for several years. Erroneously believing the federal government was way too busy to keep track of everybody who owed Uncle Sam a few pesos here or there, Dr. Stiles thought it would be easy to skate along happily ever after as if nothing were wrong. Sadly, the Department of the Treasury felt quite differently about the matter, and the government placed a lien on the dermatologist's property.

Uncle Sam went as far as to confiscate his beloved old Corvette. Once the car was gone and it was clear Dr. Stiles and his boyfriend, Dr. Murdock, would likely never take a magical road trip across United States, their interpersonal relationship was suddenly over. Brewster gathered that perhaps Dr. Murdock was a rather shallow individual. If not, maybe he just really liked old Corvettes.

Murdock not only broke up with Dr. Stiles but also, surprisingly, moved in with the resident, Dr. Cole. Nobody saw that coming. Perhaps Dr. Murdock was a materialistic hussy just looking for a sugar daddy. Brewster didn't realize at that point that Dr. Stiles was going to be in a foul mood for the duration of the dermatology rotation and want to bite somebody's head off. As Brewster was not particularly adept at reading body language or interpreting facial expressions, it would be only a matter of time before he would end up pissing off the attending and paying the consequences.

———

While he was on patrol, Officer Faulkland recognized a car reportedly being driven by Mumbo Jamar Apoo barreling west on Bissonnet Street. As Apoo approached the cross section at Mandell Street, the police officer received a direct order from police headquarters over the radio that he should not engage the subject until a sufficient backup in manpower and firepower arrived on the scene.

It had often been said that patience was a virtue, but unfortunately, that was a recessive attribute that had never fully become manifest in the brief life of Officer Faulkland. To his detriment, that would sadly turn out to be a major character flaw.

When the prowler pulled over Big Nig, Officer Faulkland jumped out of the car with his service revolver already pulled from its holster. As he leveled the barrel of his weapon directly at the career criminal, Faulkland shouted, "Get out of the car now! Get your hands up where I can see them. Mumbo Jamar Apoo, you are under arrest. Get your hands up now!"

The cavalry was on its way. Both Big and the policeman could hear a blaring siren heading in their direction from an adjacent side street. Faulkland took a quick glance to see how far away the backup cruiser was at that point, but that was all the time Big needed.

The nine-millimeter projectile violently expelled out of the barrel of Big's automatic slammed into the right side of the chest of Officer Faulkland, approximately a hand's breadth lateral to the midsternal line. Critically wounded, the police officer fell down onto his left side. To make matters more dire, his service weapon was now also on the ground, and it was just out of his reach. At the age of thirty-three, Officer Faulkland quickly came to the painful realization that his life was about to be prematurely terminated.

The backup patrol car was only seconds away while Big Nig loomed in a menacing fashion over the fallen police officer. "Please," Faulkland said. "I have a wife and two kids. You don't have to do this. Please. I'm begging you!"

"Is they white?" Big Nig asked as he cocked his head to the side with a thin smile.

The fallen police officer was unable to grasp the nature of the question, as his life had already begun to ebb away. "What did you say?"

At that point, Big become angry and repeated the question. "I'm asking you about your wife and kids. Is they white? Answer the question, bitch!"

As foamy blood started to pool into the mouth and throat of the fallen policeman, he was no longer able to answer any questions asked of him.

"I needs to know," Big said. "If'n they be all white, they ain't like me!"

The backup police cruiser arrived. It slammed on its brakes to come to a screeching halt only about forty feet away from where Officer Faulkland was about to be murdered. Big realized he didn't have a moment to spare to finish off the wounded policeman.

"If I was an Injun in da old West, I'd just take your scalp right about now. Sorry, but this will have to do." Big leveled the muzzle of the weapon squarely into the ear of his first adversary and said, "Adios, muchacho!"

With that, he pulled the trigger. Bloody gray matter splattered all over the sidewalk. One adversary was down, but there was one yet to go. The only thing Big had to do was put a hot, smoking round into the backup police officer who had just arrived. Once he'd done that, there'd still be a chance to escape.

Under a hail of incoming express delivery of lead projectiles, Big managed to grab the dead policeman's service revolver. As he retreated to the front of Officer Faulkland's patrol car, he attempted to return the deadly fire with the two guns that were now in his possession.

The newly arrived police officer took cover behind the back of his patrol vehicle, and Big couldn't get off a clean shot to bring him down. No sooner had Apoo run out of ammunition then additional patrol cars started to arrive to the fiesta from all directions. Although late to the party, Big's new dance partners were armed with shotguns.

Long ago, Mumbo Jamar Apoo had made a vow that he would never allow himself to be arrested and sent to prison. When he was surrounded by the authorities, he momentarily thought that the better part of valor would be to charge toward the incoming policemen. To do so would ensure that his life came to swift conclusion. He would simply be gunned down in the street, and that would be the end of it.

If he did so, he held the fantasy that the late Mumbo Jamar Apoo would soon become a martyr in the perceived struggle against white oppression. For certain, the police officers who surrounded the career criminal were just itching for the opportunity to drop him like the rabid animal he had always been.

Sadly, in the end, Big didn't have the courage to commit suicide in a banzai frontal assault against the insurmountable blue line he was now facing.

"I'm done!" Apoo shouted out in fear. "I'm out! I'm down!"

He threw his guns down, stretched out into a prone spread-eagle position, and surrendered. Perhaps, Big Nig thought, he would live to fight another day. Unfortunately, no one involved with the apprehension of Mumbo Jamar Apoo could have ever predicted that his reign of terror was not finished yet—not by a long shot.

⚊⚊⚊⚊

On the following day, Feral Cheryl, Willy Mammon, and J. D. Brewster gathered around the television in the Vinyl Lounge to hear about the details concerning the arrest of Mumbo Jamar Apoo. The anchorman on Your Witness News stated that the arrest of the man who called himself Big Nig had ended a thirteen-year crime spree that dated all the way back to 1968. Now that he was behind bars, Apoo was singing like a canary. He was openly revealing all of the facts and figures concerning dozens of unsolved crimes that had occurred within the 610 Loop for well over a decade.

Apoo and his now-dead associate, Darryl Hewritt, had committed their first act of murder in the botched robbery of a cigar shop on South Main, when they shot the wife of the store owner and also another employee. They had also assaulted and murdered several other people during the commission of carjacks and heists that occurred at parking lots and automatic teller machines throughout the greater Houston area. It was reported that most recently, in the last year, a nurse who had worked at the Gulf Coast General Hospital, Irene Segulla, had died at the hands of the two men.

In addition, the brutal grocery store parking lot murder of a middle-aged Hispanic gentleman named Sam Aria had also been linked to the duo. Apoo claimed he'd committed those crimes as an act of warfare against social injustice, and therefore, he blamed the white man for his life of crime. The television report stated that there were more details to follow.

Brewster jumped out of the chair he was sitting in and proclaimed, "I swear to God that if Uncle John had just stayed alive long enough to hear that they arrested the person who murdered his wife, he would have been able to make peace with the universe."

"You think?" Wooly Mammoth asked.

"Yeah," Brewster said. "If so, maybe I would have been able to make peace with Uncle John. I'm just sorry he died without ever knowing that justice will soon be served. I tell you, it's just not right. Cheryl, I'll bet you're ready to celebrate the fact that the man who also killed your father is now behind bars."

Cheryl looked away from the television and started to cry. She finally looked back over to Willy and Brewster and said, "There's so much more that I have to say about what happened back in 1968.

I've been keeping this inside me for years, but I have revelations to declare."

"What's wrong, Feral?" Brewster asked.

"I love you boys, and I know that you both love me too," Cheryl said while she gasped for a breath of air. "I hope that what I'm about to tell you won't change how you feel about me."

Brewster and Mammoth looked at each other briefly without saying a word and then looked back to Cheryl. The medical students braced themselves for what they were about to learn as Cheryl rendered her revelation.

"As you both know, I was hiding in the back storeroom when my daddy and Erna were executed. For all of these years, I've been telling the big lie that I remained hidden in the back the whole time, and the two killers never knew I was even there. Well, that's not the truth. Far from it," Cheryl said.

"Get it all out!" Willy exclaimed.

"Mumbo Apoo and that other fellow found out that I was hiding back there, and they dragged me out of the storeroom," Cheryl said. "For the love of Jesus, those animals made me lie down right between Erna and my dead father when they did it to me!"

"What happened?" Willy asked.

Cheryl began to weep bitterly and said, "I closed my eyes so I couldn't see, but the pain was terrible. It was as if my insides were being torn out from me. Dear God, I was only eleven years old. I wasn't even old enough to have my first menstrual period yet!"

There was nothing else to say. The big man buried his face in his hands, and he too began to weep. While gasping for air Brewster was wildly waving his hand in front of his left eye. After several moments, Brewster's vision finally returned, although he was still emotionally shaken.

After finding that his efforts to try to console Cheryl were futile, Willy walked over to Brewster and put his big hand on his colleague's shoulder. Any verbal communication at that moment would have been superfluous. The two men simply looked at each other and nodded with pursed lips and furrowed brows. If the opportunity would ever avail itself, Brewster and Mammon would have no qualms about the dispensation of retribution through the clinical justice system. In fact, at that point in time, it became their mission in life. Brewster and Mammon were now dangerous predators.

—⦅⦆—

Brewster had long been fascinated by a specific nature film in which a pack of wolves coordinated an attack to bring down a baby moose. They came in from all sides at the same time. He had often wondered what unseen force in nature could possibly drive the wolves to know how and when to do exactly what they did. The pack split up and could not see each other in the woods. What trigger got pulled to make the canines attack like that? The same question should be asked about the nature of human beings, he thought. What kind of trigger gets pulled to make human beings instantaneously and simultaneously strike out without saying a word? Maybe there is something dark and primal in us. Maybe that's why human beings have such an affinity to be around dogs and keep them as pets, and vice versa. Maybe when it comes right down to it, humans are not much more than two-legged wolves. Maybe when it comes right down to it, Brewster was right all along. Maybe God just backed the wrong primate.

—⦅⦆—

On the following morning, when Brewster returned to the dermatology clinic, it would soon become apparent that no good deed went unpunished. Upon learning that his attending physician, Dr. Stiles, had had a falling out with his significant other, Dr.

Murdock, Brewster erroneously believed that a demonstration of compassion was in order. The medical student was also aware that Dr. Murdock and the resident dermatology physician, Dr. Cole, had become intimate. On several occasions during his dermatology rotation, Brewster witnessed Dr. Murdock and the Missing Linc leaving work together, and they appeared to be particularly chummy.

As far as Brewster's overview of life, he didn't care one way or the other about a person's sexual orientation. Nevertheless, he was aware that the attending physician was in pain, so he offered what he thought would be a harmless condolence. Sadly, most of Brewster's endeavors during his short, tumultuous, gladiatorial consignment at the Gulf Coast College of Medicine would backfire. His attempt to offer compassion would be no exception.

"I can tell by your dour demeanor that you are experiencing residual grief now that you've broken up with your significant other," Brewster said as he approached Dr. Stiles. "I just wanted to let you know that I wish you the best, sir. It's often been said that every dark cloud has a silver lining."

Brewster had uttered a fairly benign yet compassionate remark. It was a sentiment that many human beings conveyed on a daily basis throughout the world during the course of such commonplace, troubling circumstances. After all, every average human being on planet Earth likely sustained scars from the trials and tribulations of life from time to time. However, neither J. D. Brewster nor anybody else he had ever been associated with at the Gulf Coast College of Medicine could have been considered an average human being.

Dr. Stiles motioned for Brewster to come closer and said, "You are one smarmy and loquacious son of a bitch, aren't you? Did you think that was funny? Listen to me, you dumbass. How dare you try to invade my private space? Who in hell do you think you are? I bet you thought this rotation was going to be a powder-puff gig. Well, guess what? I'm Pontius Pilatus, and I'm going to refer you back to the house of Herod before you ultimately get crucified."

"I'm sorry!" Brewster said honestly. "I meant no offense."

"Too late for that," Stiles replied. "You're going to spend the rest of this powder-puff rotation with the psychotic crab pickers in the Department of Experimental Chemotherapeutics. They have a metastatic melanoma subdivision, and I know you'll just love working over there. Good luck, asshole."

"Wait a moment!" Brewster said as he suddenly realized he was going to have to do some serious work to finish out that rotation. "I never thought a rotation on the dermatology service would ever turn out to be powder-puff fluff in any way, shape, or form."

"Oh, is that so?" Dr. Stiles sneered. "That's what they all say."

—⸺⸺—

The Department of Experimental Chemotherapeutics, simply known as the EC, was a subdivision of the department of medical oncology where the extraordinarily gifted and highly motivated crab pickers developed experimental clinical trials to try to rescue terminal cancer patients from the jaws of impending death. To their credit, the crab pickers would knock out a home run from time to time. They had a reputation for being an aggregation of socially awkward longhairs, usually unkempt and in serious need of a complimentary discount coupon to attend a day spa to help them reconstitute their own marginal personal hygienic status.

Brewster would come to learn that there were two stark subdivisions of medical oncology. One subdivision attracted decent and compassionate individuals who would most likely employ a holistic approach to the management of cancer patients. The other subdivision attracted bench experimentalists and clinical researchers who should have been kept locked up in a laboratory someplace where few, if any, human-to-human interactions could occur. Truthfully, the field of medical oncology had always demanded an admixture of both types of individuals employed within that subspecialty.

The oncology fellow working in the experimental chemotherapeutics division who had been assigned to the metastatic melanoma clinical trial protocol was a bashful little man afflicted with an annoying case of facial seborrheic dermatitis. Plagued with a perpetually red and scaly nose, Dr. Axelrod was an extremely shy individual. His facial dandruff left large, repulsive flakes of dead skin on his shirt and tie. It was extraordinarily difficult for patients to remember any conversation they ever had with the fellow, as the scaly skin that shed like falling snowflakes in a winter storm was rather distracting yet nonetheless mesmerizing to behold.

When Brewster first met Dr. Axelrod, the student was initially intimidated by the fellow's dermatological affliction. In fact, Brewster was afraid to shake the crab picker's hand.

"Hello. My name is Brewster. For the last two weeks of my dermatology clerkship, I've been assigned to the EC unit."

Without making any eye contact, the oncology fellow said, "It's time for you to meet Jackson Schultz. Everybody knows him as the Smurf."

Toward the end of Brewster's career, there would be a whole alphabet soup of effective agents to manage metastatic melanoma, including BRAF inhibitors, MEK inhibitors, immunomodulatory programmable cell-death checkpoint inhibitors, CTLA4-blocking antibodies, adoptive immunotherapies, and the like.

Back in 1981, the choice of treatments for metastatic melanoma were much more limited. There were only a few marginally effective conventional cytotoxic chemotherapy agents available at that time, such as DTIC, microtubule disruptors, and nitrous urea compounds. As far as any available nascent immunotherapy, there was interferon, an agent notorious for causing fatigue, nausea, fever, depression, and lassitude. People who took aggressive interferon therapy felt as if they were always coming off a bad case of the flu.

There had always been a rule of thumb in oncology that the cancer patient population should at least have been aware of. Oftentimes, oncologists had at their disposal a bunch of crappy, marginally effective drugs that could only do a half-ass job of controlling cancer if and when the compounds were utilized in a single-agent modality protocol.

In those situations, you could bet your bottom dollar that some ambitious crab picker was going to come along and throw all of the crappy and marginally effective drugs into a pot of chili. Depending on the circumstances, that pot of chili might have two distinctly different flavors.

In some circumstances, a multi-agent cancer treatment protocol might raise the bar. Patients might end up with a higher response rate, a higher survival rate, and sometimes a higher cure rate.

In other circumstances, a multi-agent cancer treatment protocol could turn out to be an unmitigated disaster. Patients might end up with a much higher degree of toxicity without an increase in clinical benefit. Unfortunately, in the case of metastatic melanoma, the latter would be the case, but that fact was unknown in the early 1980s. Combined chemotherapeutic agents, or chemotherapy combined with interferon, would make patients as sick as broke-dick dogs without an additional improvement in response rates or survivorship.

⸺⸺⸺

"Who's the Smurf?" Brewster asked. "And why did anybody give the poor sumbitch such a dreadful nickname?"

"You'll see soon enough," Axelrod replied.

"Did you know that in Smurfville, or wherever those little blue bastards live, there's only one female Smurf?" Brewster asked.

"Do tell."

"Who do you think gets to doink the Smurfette?" Brewster said. "I'd do her in a New York minute, but since she's so small, I'd probably have to lube up pretty good to do the deed. I think she's hot. I know she wears high-heel pumps, but I think she would look even better if she had fishnet stockings and dressed up like a nun. That is the ticket. With only one Smurfette, do you think those other horny little blue bastards have to take turns in the barrel? Maybe the little Smurfette doesn't have to put out at all. Maybe all the guys who live in Smurfville are bunch of homo-satchels. That's it! That makes the most sense to me."

"Don't be a dumbass," Axelrod said. "The Smurf will be, without doubt, one of the most extraordinary people you will ever encounter during your entire life. He has widely disseminated metastatic melanoma. In fact, his entire integument has been invaded by melanoma to the point where his skin is entirely blue. I can't make this shit up. You'll have to see it to believe it. He has so much malignant melanoma in his body and is spilling so much melanin pigment systemically that his urine is discolored."

"Is his urine black, or is it blue?" Brewster asked.

"It's the color of coffee," Axelrod said. "Check this out: the color of his urine is not from hyperbilirubinemia. It's from melanin! This is a bona fide case of true melanuria. Dude is actually pissing melanin pigment from his cancer. You'll never see a case like this again for the rest of your medical training. In fact, you won't want to see a case like this for the rest of your medical career!"

"I'm just here to learn something," Brewster said.

"Not really," Axelrod replied. "You're just another callow numbskull at this medical school who's being terrorized to the point where you'll eventually become a desensitized and dehumanized psychopath. Tell me, junior—are you there yet?"

"Not yet," Brewster lied. "Just so you know, you just happen to be talkin' to 'Mr. Sensitivity' over here."

"Can't prove it by me from what little I already have heard about you," Axelrod said.

"For shit's sake," Brewster said, "can't we just stay focused on the clinical case at hand?"

"Have it your way," Axelrod said. "Let's talk about the Smurf then. To date, and to everybody's amazement, negative CT scan imaging studies have confirmed that there's no obvious evidence of measurable visceral metastases attacking his internal organs at this time. I'm sure someday his cancer will eventually pop up in his lungs, liver, brain, bones, and anywhere else it damn well pleases, but for now, it is all in his skin."

"Odd, yes?"

"Although his cancer predominantly has a superficial spreading pattern, his body is peppered with multiple black-and-blue nevi, but none of them are any larger than about half a centimeter in diameter. Dr. Stiles and I are going to write this up as a case report and see if we can get the article published in the journal CA."

"Where do I fit in with all of this?" Brewster asked.

"We have him on an in-house experimental protocol utilizing both DTIC and interferon at the same time," Axelrod answered. "It is too soon to tell if this combination treatment will be any better than a single-agent palliative systemic therapy, but we don't have enough patients enrolled in the study as of yet to proceed with a statistical analysis. In any event, he's not tolerating the treatment very well. He's sick all of the time, and he wants to withdraw from the study."

"Well," Brewster asked, "who gives a shit? Let him drop out of the experimental study then."

"That's not how it works," Axelrod replied. "I've been told that you're a real 'people person' and have excellent skills when it comes to talking to patients about their problems."

"That's bullshit!" Brewster said. "To be frank, at this point in my life, I really can't stand being around any of my other fellow human beings. What about you?"

"Personally, I'm not very good at talking to other people," Axelrod confessed. "When I get nervous, I start to fumble my words like I have a dick in my mouth."

"What?!"

"I know my own limitation," Axelrod said. "I want you to go in there and tell the patient that he needs to stay on the experimental protocol."

Once Dr. Axelrod was out of earshot, Brewster said aloud in the safety of his own solitude, "What a crock! If patients don't want to stay on experimental studies, it's their right to withdraw at any time they want." Brewster realized at times, that he was an exceptionally brave man, especially when nobody else was around.

When Brewster met the Smurf, he realized that Dr. Axelrod had not exaggerated one bit. The man was entirely blue in color. When Brewster sat down to have a chat with the patient, he said, "I understand you're disabled now. What did you do for a living before you contracted this skin cancer?"

"Believe it or not, I used to do stand-up at the local bars and dinner theaters about town," the patient replied. "Now that I'm entirely blue, I have this idea that I should move to Las Vegas and open up a comedy routine called the Blue Man. If there are other people out there who look like me, perhaps they can join me in my routine. We can call ourselves the Blue Man Group."

"I'm sorry, but I think that's a stupid idea, and it'll likely never have any commercial value whatsoever," Brewster said. "I'm here because Dr. Axelrod doesn't want you to drop out of the experimental study. Now, what I'm going to talk to you about will be confidential. After all, there was once a time when the United States was allegedly a free country."

"So I've heard."

"If you discontinue aggressive management and want to declare that you have a DNR designation, such a decision is certainly your right," Brewster said. "I'll simply tell Dr. Axelrod that I tried my best to keep you enrolled on the experimental treatment program, but you were adamant about your desire to abandon the clinical trial."

The Smurf had a look of relief on his face once Brewster gave him permission to discontinue treatment. The Smurf pulled a pinkie ring off of his finger. It was gold and had a small quarter-carat diamond mounted on it. He gave it to Brewster and said, "You are the most decent person I've met since I've been getting my cancer treatment here. I want you to keep this as a gift from me to you. I really don't need this anymore. In fact, very soon I won't be needing anything at all. Thank you for stopping by and talking with me tonight."

Brewster smiled as he left the patient's room, realizing he now had an engagement ring he could give to Stella.

⸻

During his consignment to the metastatic melanoma service, Brewster would come to realize he had become a psycho magnet. Marlynne Mato was a former photojournalist for Gulf Coast Monthly Magazine. Two years prior to her current presentation, Marlynne had developed a large black-and-blue exophytic tumor in the midline of her back, right between her shoulder blades.

She immediately recognized that the tumor was a malignant black mole cancer. As she was a photojournalist and also batshit crazy, the patient thought it would be a wonderful thing to monitor the natural history of the cancer up to the point of her own death. In other words, she never had any intention of receiving any treatment for the malignancy, even at the outset of the cancer's initial presentation, when it was all still a theoretically curable disease process.

Wow! Brewster had no idea what to say to Marlynne Mato, but he couldn't rightfully critique her decision, as, after all, the United States was allegedly a free country.

Because she had difficulty photographing her own back, she would come into the Gulf Coast University Hospital to have either the dermatologists or the oncologists on the melanoma service photograph her cancerous skin lesions over time. She would come in at three-month intervals for that purpose, but at no time did she ever accept any type of recommended cancer therapy.

Over the course of a two-year period, she developed multiple lesions on her back that coalesced together. They appeared to aggregate into the perfect pattern of a black-and-blue classic Christmas tree that covered her entire back. As it was approaching the holiday season, Ms. Mato was going to have customized greeting cards made from the photographs taken of the cancerous Christmas tree consuming her body.

She planned to mail out the macabre greeting cards to her friends and family members to celebrate the birth of Jesus. Without a doubt, the members of the Mato family must have been thrilled to receive such priceless treasures delivered to their mailboxes through the courtesy of the United States Postal Service.

After reviewing the patient's chart, Brewster went into the exam room to have a face-to-face encounter with the bona fide stark raving lunatic.

"I'm sorry I got here late for my appointment today," Ms. Mato said, "but my pet goat, Gertrude, committed suicide last night. I knew she was depressed, but she didn't even have the decency to leave behind a suicide note. To make matters worse, my dog got a telephone call this morning from NORAD. No matter how many times I've scolded that scoundrel, he just won't ever hang up the telephone back in the cradle after discussing strategic matters with the United States Air Force. You look like a nice young man. Perhaps if I bring my dog in to see you, you'll be able to give him a stern lecture and straighten him out once and for all."

"Now, Ms. Mato," Brewster said, "it seems to me that your thoughts are a bit jumbled right now. Are you having some issues with confusion?"

"What are you saying?"

"You don't really think the North American Air Defense System actually called your dog on the telephone today, now, do you?" Brewster asked.

"Absolutely!" Marlynne said. "The one we need to be on the lookout for is President Ronald Reagan, I tell you. Reagan. Ray gun. Zap! I can tell you right now that he's trying to get into my brain!"

Brewster stood up from his position at the desk in the examination room and said, "Madam, I have to talk to my boss, Dr. Axelrod. I'll be back momentarily."

Brewster went down the hall to find the physician from the Department of Experimental Chemotherapeutics. "Look, Axe, Ms. Mato is talking loony tunes over here. I'm not sure if she's just a garden-variety paranoid schizophrenic, or perhaps something much more organic is going on between her ears. After all, melanoma is supposed to be able to metastasize anywhere in the human body, right? Maybe her cancer has already spread to her brain, and it's having an adverse effect on her thought processes. I think it would be a good idea for us to get a CT scan of her head—and also on the rest of her body, for that matter."

"To what end?" Axelrod asked. "Does she have any focal findings on exam?"

"No, but let's get some imaging studies as part of a staging workup," Brewster said. "We should take a look at everything from A to Z, including her chest, abdomen, and pelvis, to know exactly what evil entities might be lurking inside her."

"That would be just a waste of time and money, Brew," Axelrod said. "After all, she's refused treatment from the get–go. I don't want to get any CT scans as a simple intellectual exercise. To be frank, at this point, I just couldn't give two shits if her cancer is occupying every cubic centimeter of her body. As she doesn't want cancer treatment, I'd just as soon not know anything about her current clinical status. After all, you can lead a patient to water, but if she doesn't drink, you can't take a lead pipe and bash her fucking brains out as much as you'd like to, now can you?"

Brewster went upstairs to the nurses' lounge on the med-surg service. The medical student opened the refrigerator to search for any tasty delectable that might have been hidden inside. He picked out a peanut butter sandwich that belonged to Missy Brownwood and proceeded to consume it in about three bites. He purposefully kept the sheet of foil that the sandwich had been wrapped in. The medical student took the foil paper back down to the examination room where Ms. Mato was patiently waiting. With utmost care, Brewster gently wrapped the sheet of foil around the head of Ms. Mato.

"This will help keep your thoughts from being stolen by the government," Brewster said. "Would you be so kind as to tell me why you didn't want any cancer treatment when you first discovered you had a black mole in the middle of your back?"

"Well," the patient replied, "after all, I'm coming back as a dolphin."

"Ms. Mato, if you're not dating anybody at this time," Brewster said, "I know a musician who still wears leisure suits who I think would be a perfect match for you. He has a big cancer growing through the middle of his chest, so it would seem the two of you would have something in common. Let me know if you would like to meet him, and I'll set it all up for you."

Before the rotation on the dermatology service was over, Ms. Mato made certain to return the overt act of kindness Brewster had shown to her. She brought him her pet skunk, Pepe, as a parting gift.

"Don't worry, Mr. Brewster. Pepe is very easy to care for," the patient said. "He eats vegetables and a little bit of meat once in a while. He likes to snuggle."

Wow! How thoughtful.

"Now, wait just one minute," Brewster said. "I've been around dogs for most of my life, and I know a thing or two about cats, but I don't know jack shit about taking care of skunks. Is it even legal to own a pet skunk in the state of Texas?"

"Of course not," the woman replied. "Most states don't allow people to own skunks. It's permissible in a backwater, primitive state like New Mexico but not in the Lone Star State. The issue is that there's a high prevalence of rabies among skunks in the wild, and none of the commercial rabies vaccines are known to be completely effective in this type of animal. If you get caught by animal control, Pepe will be confiscated and then destroyed."

"Well, see?" Brewster said. "It might be a bad idea for me to adopt this stinky weasel."

"You'll have to pay a hefty fine, and you might even go to jail if the authorities ever find out that you own a pet skunk, so my simple suggestion to you is that you shouldn't get caught with it. These creatures are very smart, and they're curious critters. You'll need to childproof your home, as Pepe will open up your cabinets and drawers, and he can get into serious trouble."

Brewster pressed on with more questions. "I guess I can just keep it outside like a dog then. Is that correct?"

"Oh, for heaven's sake, you can't do that!" Ms. Mato replied. "Skunks, unlike dogs, have no homing instincts. If Pepe wanders away from your property, he'll get lost. I guess they don't have a good sense of smell. Since Pepe had his scent glands surgically removed, he wouldn't be able to defend himself against any predators. Pepe knows how to use a litter box like a cat, and his projected life expectancy as a pet is around six years or so."

"Is there anything else I need to know about this varmint before I agree to take him on as a new pet?" Brewster asked.

"When you come home from work, he enjoys constant attention," Ms. Mato answered. "You must play with him, pet him, and snuggle with him around the clock. If you don't, he'll get extremely pissed off, and he'll bite the shit out of you. Oh, by the way, he has really long and sharp teeth, if you were at all curious about the status of his incisors. I must warn you that he also has extremely powerful jaws."

"How so?"

"As a case in point, Pepe at one time opened up a drawer in my bathroom vanity and managed to find my favorite hairbrush. He bit the plastic handle in half, and then he took a dump in my bathroom sink. I guess I wasn't paying enough attention to him at the time. I truly think he'd be capable of easily amputating a person's index finger if he really became angry. After all, he's in the weasel family."

"Pepe sounds like just what I need at this time in my life," Brewster said as he sadly accepted the fact that his own frame of mind was becoming as unhinged as that of the patient population he was exposed to at the Gulf Coast College of Medicine.

—⁂—

At the Italian restaurant over in North University Place, Brewster made arrangements with the restaurant manager to bring out a dish of sorbet for dessert after he and Stella finished their romantic dinner together. Brewster entrusted the restaurant manager with the gold-and-diamond pinkie ring the Smurf had given him. The medical student instructed that when dessert was brought out, the gold ring should be set on top of Stella's sorbet. He thought that would be a clever way for him to propose matrimony.

When dessert was brought to Stella that evening, she jumped out of her chair as soon as she recognized that somebody's ring was imbedded atop the goblet of sorbet.

"That's disgusting! It looks like the dessert chef was careless and he must have dropped his cheap-ass pinkie ring on top of my bowl of this fancy-shmancy ice cream. For fuck's sake! This ring is nothing but a fake, sorry looking, pimp-shit piece of costume jewelry to boot!"

Brewster was stunned. He realized that his attempt at being romantic had just taken a torpedo. "Now, just wait a moment, Stella," Brewster said, attempting to explain. "Let me tell you—"

It was too late. Before Brewster could stop her, Stella ran back into the kitchen, carrying the offensive crystal goblet of sorbet. She momentarily returned, and she had an enormous smile upon her face after the line cook had explained to her that the gold ring was supposed to be a surprise gift. Some handsome gentleman who was hoping to become her fiancé had brought in the ring earlier.

Overwhelmed with emotion, Stella threw her arms around Brewster. With tears of joy, she cast him out of his chair and squarely onto the dining room floor as if she were a linebacker who had just flattened the opposing quarterback during an all-out blitz.

If Stella behaved in such a fashion while overcome with joy, Brewster decided he would make it a point to never, ever piss Stella off. It was hard for Brewster to imagine what she was capable of if she ever got angry.

<hr />

Afflicted with acute situational depression over his failed relationship with the tenured pathologist, Dr. Stiles decided to take a week of sick leave during the end of October. His unexpected departure afforded Brewster the opportunity to rejoin the resident physician, Dr. Cole, on the general dermatology service.

"Okay, Brew, we have an inpatient consult to knock out. Do you know what a chloroma is or what it looks like?"

"Is this a game of pimp and pone?" Brewster asked.

"No," Dr. Cole answered. "This is just a straightforward clinical query. Either you know the answer to this question, or you don't. Sometimes patients who may present with acute leukemia can get an infiltration of blast cells into the skin, and it can look like an erythematous abscess. Generally, one of these rare chloroma lesions might not be as fluctuant as an infectious abscess, and it may present with a firmer texture. I think we have a case of this upstairs on the pediatric leukemia service."

"Give me the details," Brewster said.

"The patient's name is Webster Stack," Dr. Cole replied, "and he's only ten years old. He just got admitted today, and the crab pickers are going to drill his marrow in about an hour. I would like to get up there first so we can get a skin biopsy knocked out now. The young boy's white cell count is already blasting off to the moon, and it's now at one hundred thirty-eight thousand. Unfortunately ninety percent of these cells are malignant circulating blasts. He's already at a high risk for complications of leukostasis. His white cell count is high enough that he's going to start clogging up the circulation of his small vessels, and he's at high risk already for end-organ damage. For certain, he's anemic. His platelet count is only eighteen thousand, but I suspect it's high enough for us to get away with a simple punch skin biopsy if we use ferric subsulfate chemical cautery to coagulate the biopsy crater. Let's get to it."

Webster's parents met the dermatology team and quickly agreed to allow a skin-punch biopsy to be performed on the large, erythematous, and painful lesion on the dorsum of the young boy's hand. After the procedure was done, Webster asked the medical student if he was the man named Brewster who was supposedly a historical expert on World War II.

When Brewster answered in the affirmative, the young boy asked, "Did you know that the first military jet was actually introduced by the Nazis in World War II?"

"Yes, it was the Me 262," Brewster answered, "and it was armed with no fewer than four automatic cannons in its nose. It had a rather high service ceiling, and it was a hundred miles per hour faster than America's Mustang P-51 fighter plane. Fortunately for the Allies, this weapon was introduced far too late in the conflict to have any real impact on the outcome of the war."

"Wow, Brewster," Webster said, "you're really smart!"

"Okay, Webster, I'll tell you what I am going to do," Brewster said with a smile. "Since you're going to be stuck here in the hospital for the better part of a month or more, how would you like me to buy you a model airplane of this fighter jet? It'll be a gift from me to you." As Brewster would never have any children of his own, the medical student took great delight in doing something nice for the young boy he'd just met on the leukemia service.

Webster's father and mother agreed to the capital idea, as they thought it would help to cheer up their son, who was facing a potentially lethal illness. Unfortunately for Brewster and for his new little friend Webster, no good deed went unpunished for long.

Brewster knew there was a toy shop located off of Kirby Street, and he went there to buy a model of the military jet plane for the young patient to enjoy. When Brewster returned with the gift, Webster became so excited that he jumped out of his hospital bed to greet the medical student.

As he did so, the young boy's feet slipped out from under him, and Webster fell to his left side and struck the left temporal area of his head against the knob of the in-suite bathroom door. With the low platelet count caused by the leukemia, Webster suffered an immediate intracranial blowout. The young boy never got off the floor.

In horror, Brewster and the boy's parents watched helplessly as Webster assumed a terminal decerebrate posture, a grave, abnormal body position that occurred as a consequence of a severe head injury. It was readily recognized when the arms and legs extended outward, the toes pointed sharply downward, and the head and neck violently arched backward. Webster's body became rigid, and he then experienced what appeared to be a grand mal epileptic event, which occurred right before the young lad's heart quit beating inside his chest.

———ⵉⵉⵉ———

Wracked with guilt, Webster's parents bought a panel in the obituary section of the Houston Post newspaper to commemorate the brief life and tragic death of their only child. They would continue that tradition on every anniversary date of the boy's death for the rest of their lives.

Wracked with guilt, J. D. Brewster refused to render any future medical care to any child for the remainder of his career. Brewster commemorated the brief life and tragic death of Webster Stack by getting drunk. He would continue that tradition on every anniversary date of the boy's death for the rest of his life.

9

WHAT'S WRONG WITH PA?

S tella and Brewster went to the local doughnut shop to pick up a baker's dozen box of jelly doughnuts, when a fellow patron felt compelled to make a comment about the marginal quality of Stella's engagement ring.

"That is, without a doubt, the ugliest engagement ring I've ever seen," the obnoxious slob said rudely. "The diamond is microscopic, and it looks like it's some pimp's cheap-ass pinkie ring! Is that your fiancé standing beside you? He must be a major-league loser."

Brewster was about to give the boor the thrashing he deserved, when Stella said, "Relax, lover boy. I've got this under control."

She turned to the man who'd made the offensive remarks and said, "I'm sorry, but you really should take a better look at my ring. It's really quite beautiful. In fact, it'll knock your socks off."

With that, Stella grabbed the man's shirt with her right hand and bitch-slapped him with her left hand. "How does my ring look now, asshole?"

While Stella was giving the rude man a slap-down, Brewster got up from his chair, picked up the jelly doughnut the man had just purchased, and proceeded to eat it. All the while, he was cheering Stella on.

"You're my champion, Stella! I love you. Teach that bastard a lesson he'll never forget!"

"I love you too, J. D.," Stella said as she continued to drop the hammer on the miscreant. "Why don't you order me a latte and an eight-ounce glass of ice-cold half-and-half while I finish up business over here? Oh, by the way, be a dear and grab me a jumbo blueberry scone with two pats of real butter, not that fake margarine crap. Have the barista 'wave the scone on high for about twenty seconds. I'm starting to work up a big appetite!"

A love so true was a wondrous treasure to behold.

Arby Fuller passed out the automatic shotguns and then whispered instructions to Brewster and Brother Bill. "Each gun has three rounds of bird shot. Pay attention to the safety, and keep it on until we make the jump. The secret to bringing down ducks paddling around in a cattle water tank is to sneak up on them and then pop up to catch them in a triangulation of firepower. Remember, let's not get greedy, and let's not end up shooting each other."

"I'm a bit nervous about all of this," J. D. said.

"Relax," Fuller said. "Lead your target before you pull the trigger. If we get one or two ducks apiece, that would be icing on the cake. I know it'll be a pain in the ass to crawl up to the edge of the tank on our bellies, but if we don't, they'll see us coming, and they'll fly off before we can even crank out a single shot."

"How will we know when to coordinate the time that we jump up and start shooting?" Brother Bill asked. "That tank is easily forty feet across, and the three of us will be out of the line of site with each other."

"Keep your voice down," Fuller said. "You'll just know, okay? Have you ever seen those nature films where a pack of wolves coordinate an attack to bring down a baby moose? They come in from all sides at the same time. What unseen force is there in nature that can possibly drive the wolves to know how and when to do exactly what they do?"

"Mother Nature is a bitch on wheels," Brewster said.

"Precisely," Arby said. "The wolf pack splits up, and they can't see each other in the woods. What trigger gets pulled to make these canines attack like that? Some unseen force no doubt. The very same question should be asked about the nature of human beings. What kind of trigger gets pulled to make human beings instantaneously and simultaneously strike out without saying a word?"

"Maybe there's something dark and primal in us," Bill said. "Maybe that's why human beings have such an affinity to be around dogs and keep them as pets, and vice versa. Maybe when it comes right down to it, humans are not much more than two-legged wolves."

"Maybe when it comes right down to it, God just backed the wrong primate," Brewster said sadly.

J. D. felt that his orange camouflage safety vest he had borrowed from Arby was too small, as it was starting to pinch him in the axillary region bilaterally. While he was in the prone position, he peeled the vest off, and he left it on the ground behind him. There was about a four-foot dirt rise up to the edge of the water tank, which was basically a big hole in the ground, filled with water to allow thirsty cattle to take a drink. When the hunters reached their assigned positions around the edge of the tank, the din from the quacking ducks was deafening.

Arby was correct; the three men instinctively knew when it was the right time to make the jump and try to bring down a duck or two as the birds flew off from the water tank. As the men jumped up and pointed their shotguns skyward, they saw—well, nothing. They looked down into the water tank to see that it was almost empty, with a short span of shallow water only about eight feet or so in diameter and just a few inches deep. However, within the small confines of a space not much bigger than an oversized hot tub, every square inch of water in the tank was occupied by some sort of fowl, duck or otherwise.

If there was some sort of avian expression akin to "Oh shit!" the birds in the water tank probably uttered that expletive in unison. Before any of the birds could take to wing, the three men discharged their entire allotment of three shots apiece.

What kind of damage could a total of nine shotgun blasts do if they were aimed downward at a flock of birds occupying an area of no more than sixty or so square feet? The carnage was unspeakable. The score card was as follows: twenty-six mallard, one teal, three sparrows, one male peacock, and two mockingbirds, which, incidentally, happened to be the designated state bird of Texas.

There was also one crane blown away in the melee. Sadly, the last creature on the killed-in-action roster happened to be on the endangered-species list! Two of the ducks were only wounded and were futilely flapping about in agony on top of the small pond of water. Arby had to climb down the embankment to finish them off by hand.

The three men sat in silence on the bank of the water tank. They had committed a felony crime. If they had been caught by a game warden, they all would have gone to prison. In all likelihood, they would have never been allowed to own a gun or a water craft, or vote for the rest of their lives. Worse yet, they'd committed a sin against God and nature. If everything in the universe was connected somehow, they only perpetrated a sin and a crime against themselves.

Finally, Arby Fuller stood up and said, "For the love of Jesus, I told you guys not to get greedy!"

Brother Bill stood up, dusted himself off, walked over to Officer Fuller, and hit him square in the mouth with a haymaker. Arby fell over from the blow and slid down the embankment toward the small pond of water. Angrily, Brother Bill shouted out, "Go screw yourself, you sanctimonious sack of shit! Tell me—are you now the president of the Audubon Society, or what? Just how many shells are left in your gun, asshole?"

Bill walked over to Fuller's shotgun and confirmed that he had discharged his weapon three times, just as they had all done. Bill jammed the barrel of the shotgun deep down into the dirt. He cast his eyes upon Arby and said, "Fuller, you're just as guilty as the rest of us."

Despite the blow he received, Arby Fuller did not retaliate. He simply stood at the edge of the pond and gazed down at his palms as a crimson cascade from his bloody nose pooled into his cupped hands.

As they both thought they had exceeded their lifetime limit of shooting game, J. D. Brewster and Brother Bill would never go out hunting ever again. Nevertheless, that would not be the last time J. D. Brewster and his friend Arby Fuller had blood on their hands.

⸺⸺⸺

Shiva Jaclyn Grant was a self-ordained community activist. In layman's terms, that meant she was a radical rabble-rouser who had no visible means of supporting herself financially. An incredibly stupid human being, she once had incited a riot to try to close a military base at Guantanamo Bay. It was not so much that she was upset about that military installation, which had been ceded to the United States after the end of the Spanish-American War through the 1903 Treaty of Relations. Her objection was based upon her irrational fear that the military base had placed so much weight upon the southern aspect of the island that it would cause Cuba to tip over. She had always secretly hoped she would run for Congress one day. As stupid as she was, if she ever were elected to Congress, she would raise the IQ of that legislative body significantly.

An instigator of civil unrest, Shiva Jaclyn Grant took up the mantle of justice for a certain bloodthirsty killer named Mumbo

Jamar Apoo. Although 80 percent of the crimes Apoo had committed during his thirteen-year spree were against other black people, the fact that he had murdered a white police officer was a cause for celebration.

After all, it must have been another case of the white-devil slave master trying to keep the black man down. That was the ticket. Yes indeed, it was time to make Apoo a martyr. She had to be careful about the timing of the insurrection she would incite, as the Kwanzaa holiday was just a few weeks away. She didn't want the holiday season or the pending football playoffs to overshadow her efforts, so she decided to wait until after the 1982 Super Bowl was played in January. Otherwise, her race-baiting mantra would not likely gain any traction that particular time around.

———

Brewster was happy to see that in the month of December, he would be reunited with his old friend Ben Fielder on an elective rotation in hematology. As there was no resident or fellow assigned to the subspecialty at that time of year, the two medical students would be working directly with the attending physician, Dr. Jed Teague. Upon their arrival at the outpatient hematology clinic, it was time for round of pimp and pone.

"Brewster, you are up to bat. Here's the first pitch. What's the Philadelphia chromosome, and what disease is it extrinsically associated with?" Teague asked.

Brewster had that one nailed down. "The Philadelphia chromosome is defined by the 9;22 chromosomal translocation, and it is associated with chronic granulocytic leukemia. It has also been observed in rare cases of ALL."

"Very nice," the attending said. "Here's the second pitch. How much iron is generally stored in an adult male?"

Brewster responded, "I think it's about a thousand milligrams of iron, mostly in the form of ferritin and some in the water-insoluble derivative of ferritin called hemosiderin."

"Well, it looks like you have won this round," Dr. Teague said, "but let's see if you can knock out a grand slam. Here is the third pitch. What's the Richter transformation?"

Brewster was stumped on that question, and his friend Ben Fielder was unable to offer any assistance from the bleachers. The attending said, "Well, it looks like there are still a few things for you to learn on this rotation. Let's get to work."

———

The first patient Brewster had an opportunity to evaluate on his new hematology rotation was brought in by the immigration service. The patient was under arrest for sneaking across the Mexican border into Texas. He'd been apprehended in the city of Houston. The patient was defined as an IAOTM, which was an acronym for an illegal alien other than Mexican. The patient was brought in for an evaluation at the outpatient hematology clinic because he was severely anemic, and the laboratory profile confirmed he had an iron deficiency disorder. As the human body had no way to normally excrete a significant amount of iron, the only way a male could become iron deficient was essentially by pathological blood loss.

Further workup would eventually reveal that the patient was infested with nasty bladder fluke worms. As it turned out, the patient had hematuria for years, and he'd thought that passing blood in his urine was normal. Incidentally, a patient couldn't get infected with bladder worms just anywhere. The Middle East was a common location where the nasty worm could latch on to the inner lining of somebody's bladder.

Although the patient appeared to be Hispanic, el hombre no

habla Español. However, there was a different language in which the mysterious patient was fluent: Arabic.

It was time for Brewster to challenge the patient. "Where are you from?"

"I'm from Syria," the patient replied.

"Well, that's quite interesting," Brewster said. "Why did you sneak into this country?"

The patient gave a cryptic response. "I was ordered to do so."

Brewster found the reply somewhat alarming but nonetheless pressed forward. "Well, you made it across the border. Congratulations. What happens next?"

With a menacing glare, the patient leaned over, licked Brewster on the face, and answered, "I'll wait for further orders!"

When Brewster left the exam room, the agent from the immigration service asked about the next clinical course of action they would undertake. "What do we need to do next?"

At that point, the medical student no longer cared about any medical problem that possibly afflicted the patient he had just interviewed. Instead, Brewster gave a more global, geopolitical response: "I'll tell you what we need to do. We need to build a goddamned wall on our border with Mexico to keep assholes like this out of our country!"

—◆—

One of the few things Brewster had inherited from Uncle John was his bright, shiny silver aluminum Christmas tree. The tree looked like an old-fashioned six-foot-tall roof-mounted television antenna. However, it was clearly not designed for electric lightbulbs to be hung among the metallic branches. It was apparently a safety issue because if an accidental electrical short ever occurred with any of the Christmas lights or electrical wires, it could theoretically electrify the entire tree.

If Uncle John had ever known that fact, he certainly hadn't cared, and neither did his nephew, J. D. Brewster, for that matter. John had kept the tree decorated all the time, and at Christmastime, he'd simply bring it out, pull a dust sheet off of the damned thing, plug in the lights, and then have a holly, jolly—well, whatever. At the end the Christmas season, he would simply unplug the tree, stuff it back into the living room entryway closet, and call it a day.

In December, Brewster brought out John's Christmas monstrosity, and he proceeded to plug it into an electrical outlet in the living room of his small apartment in Bellaire. Fortunately, Brewster did not touch the tree once he had plugged it into the wall socket. Unfortunately, the same could not be said for Brewster's new friend Pepe.

The skunk found the aluminum Christmas tree to be irresistible. Pepe tried to climb up onto the aluminum branches, but he was suddenly smacked with 120 volts of alternating current, which caused the hapless mammal to fly across the room and slam into the refrigerator door in Brewster's kitchen. Needless to say, the skunk was not amused by the experience, and it rightfully blamed its new owner, J. D. Brewster, for being an idiot.

Pepe had to clear the cobwebs out of his head after nearly being electrocuted. Then, instinctively, he ran back toward the Christmas tree, balanced on his front legs, arched his back, and tried to blast the offending metallic structure with stinky skunk spray.

Before J. D. Brewster had acquired Pepe, the unfortunate creature had been surgically altered, so the skunk was walking around in life with a holster but no guns or bullets. As his efforts to retaliate against the aluminum Christmas tree were ultimately futile, Pepe would have to make it a point to bite the shit out of J. D. Brewster the first an opportunity had arisen.

There was a patient in the waiting room, sitting in a wheelchair, and he had the most bizarre pose anyone ever remembered seeing. For unclear reasons, the patient's right hip, knee, and ankle were all fixed into one locked position. If the patient was in a standing position and attempted to balance on his left leg, the man's femur extended out at a rigid sixty-degree angle. While he was sitting in a wheelchair, it appeared as if he were giving a Nazi salute from his right lower extremity.

While Fielder was about to enter another exam room to see a different patient, the family members of the individual stuck in the wheelchair intercepted the medical student and said, "Look over here, boy—what's wrong with Pa?"

Fielder took one look at the man's extended right leg and was immediately intrigued. During a futile attempt to force the man's knee and hip into flexure, the medical student straddled the patient's distal right lower extremity just proximal to the ankle, as if the man's leg were a teeter-totter. The patient's leg did not budge one inch. While singing the song "Drop-Kick Me, Jesus, through the Goalposts of Life," Fielder started to bounce up and down on top of the patient's leg, but to no avail.

Finally, one of the family members spoke out. "What in hell are you doing? We didn't bring him in here because of his laig! They ain't wrong with his laig. It's always been that way. Now, this is the blood clinic—am I right? That's why we're here. Some other feller said that Pa has the bad blood. So I'll ask you again: What's wrong with Pa?"

Embarrassed, Fielder gracefully dismounted from the man's leg, and the medical student finally realized that the unfortunate patient was extraordinarily pale. In fact, his skin had the hue of vanilla ice cream. Upon Fielder's review of the labs, it was clear the patient had severe pancytopenia. In layman's terms, that meant the patient's entire line of blood cells produced by the marrow was dramatically decreased. The patient's white cells, red cells, and platelets were at an astonishingly low level, which could only mean the patient had something seriously wrong with his biological hematopoietic factory.

Dr. Teague told Ben Fielder, "Go get Brewster, and drag him along with you. It's time for you boys to learn how to do a diagnostic bone marrow aspiration and biopsy procedure."

The most optimal position for a patient to assume to undergo a diagnostic marrow aspiration and biopsy was a prone orientation with the patient's butt facing straight up toward the ceiling. That provided a stable platform and allowed the physician to render enough physical leverage to be able to pierce the posterior iliac crest with either an Illinois aspirate needle or a big-bore Jamshidi biopsy needle. Unfortunately, as the elderly patient was afflicted with a peculiar anomaly that had rendered his right leg permanently engaged in a "Sieg Heil!" Nazi salute, it would have been impossible for him to assume the prone position.

As that was the case, Dr. Teague elected to perform the diagnostic bone marrow aspiration and biopsy with the patient lying on his right side. At least his stiff right leg would keep his pelvis from rotating when the biopsy procedure was undertaken.

Something bizarre occurred while Dr. Teague was performing the diagnostic bone marrow core biopsy: the blue handle of the disposable Jamshidi biopsy needle snapped off, and a large residual stainless-steel spike was then stuck in the bone of the patient's posterior iliac crest.

Dr. Teague was able to avert disaster when he gave a direct order to Ben Fielder: "Get down to the maintenance department in the basement, and find Harper. He's probably down there eating doughnuts, drinking Kona coffee, and watching the Rectal Roberts Ministry Hour on his tiny black-and-white. Bring back a big-ass pair of his channel locks from his tool kit. Be quick about it."

When Fielder returned from the basement with the large, heavy tool that had been originally designed as an implement utilized in the plumbing of pipe drains, Dr. Teague was able to grab the end of the broken biopsy needle and yank it out of the patient's pelvis.

After Dr. Teague was finished, he had instructions for Brewster "You may be a stud, but today you are going to be my scut puppy. I've made a couple of smears from the bone marrow aspirate, and I want you to take them to the hematology section of the lab and have the med techs run them through the auto-stain machine. Have them do it twice."

"I thought the standard lab technique was to do a hand stain on the slides," Brewster said.

"You'll find that sometimes in life, it's better to be fast than good," the attending said. "What we'll get won't be quite as sharp as an old-fashioned hand stain, but it will be close enough for government work. Bring it back when the med techs are done with it, and we'll slap it under the doubleheader so we can all take a peek-a-boo at it. If we leave it all up to Dr. Murdock to get the marrow processed according to Hoyle, hell itself will have frozen over by the time we get an official answer. I swear to God, those pathologists come in at ten, go home at two, and take a two-hour lunch break in between!"

When Brewster returned from the lab with the slides of the marrow aspirate that had been stained, Dr. Teague put a slide under the two-headed teaching scope to evaluate what was wrong with old Nazi Leg. Under high-power oil immersion, the patient's problem was as clear as day: aplastic anemia.

In layman's terms, the patient had an empty bone marrow. The patient was admitted for further treatment, but management of aplastic anemia was pretty crappy back in the early 1980s. Even many years later, the disease had only marginally efficacious medical interventions short of a stem-cell transplant.

A rare disorder that struck only one in two hundred thousand people, aplastic anemia had an etiology that was myriad. The causative factor was idiopathic in about half of the cases of the disease process. The other half of the cases could be associated with some type of drug or chemical exposure; radiation exposure; infections, such as hepatitis or HIV; or constitutional or genetic reasons.

There had also been rare cases of aplastic anemia associated with the presence of a thymoma or pregnancy, among a few other causes. Unfortunately, the patient in question had no discernible cause for his bizarre bone marrow failure. The first order of business was to offer the patient a packed red cell transfusion, as his hemoglobin and hematocrit, which reflected his red blood cell status, were both only half of the normal range. The patient was symptomatic with shortness of breath, and he had easy fatigability on minimal exertion. Therefore, it appeared that a red blood cell transfusion would be most beneficial. There was a problem, however: the patient was a Jehovah's Witness, and he adamantly refused any blood cell products. Due to the patient's religious convictions, taking a transfusion would be a sin.

People passing by the patient's room in the hallway of the med-surg unit could easily hear the angry, raised voice of Ben Fielder as he chided the anemic man for his theological persuasions. "What in hell do you mean you can't take a transfusion because of religious beliefs? I've never heard of such nonsense. There's an outside chance you might respond to steroid treatment or immunoglobulin infusions, but you have to help us out here, buddy. You're already symptomatic from your severe anemia, and things will only get worse before there's any chance you might get better."

"You don't understand," the patient replied. "If I take blood products, I'll be excommunicated. I'll no longer be a member of the church."

"Is that so?" Fielder responded. "You'll no longer be a member of the church when you're dead either. I am going to bring in my colleague Brewster. Maybe he'll be able to convince you to do what I believe is the right thing for you to do. If not, it's your funeral, pal."

Upon Brewster's arrival, Ben Fielder said, "Okay, Brew, it's time for you to put your renowned people skills to work here. Keep me posted."

When Fielder left the room, Brewster sat in a chair at the end of the bed to have a chat with the patient. "I understand you're refusing to accept a blood cell transfusion because you are a Jehovah's Witness. To be quite frank with you, I know little, if anything, about your religion. Please explain to me why your faith precludes you from receiving a red cell transfusion—or other blood products, for that matter."

Brewster carefully listened while the patient cited chapter and verse as to why he felt that receiving blood products would be some type of sin: "Genesis 9:4 says, 'Only, you shall not eat flesh with its life, that is, its blood.' There is also another reference that can be found in Leviticus 17:10: 'If anyone of the house of Israel or of the aliens who reside among them eats any blood, I will set my face against that person who eats blood, and will cut that person off from the people.' Can't you see, young man? It's in the Bible!"

"That's fine," Brewster said as he challenged the patient's convictions. "Don't become a vampire. Don't dress up like Bela Lugosi. Don't become a flying bat at midnight and attack your next-door neighbors. Don't suck blood out of your neighbors' jugular veins. Don't eat steak tartare, because you could get infected with tapeworms or some type of nasty-ass, brain-rotting prion. I dig all of that. However, the scripture you just recited didn't say jack shit about transfusions, now, did it?"

"Don't be a blasphemer," the patient replied. "I bid you a good day. Please close my door on your way out."

Clinically, the patient didn't do well after that. Within a few days, the patient's hemoglobin had dropped down to a life-threatening low level of 3.2 milligrams per deciliter with a hematocrit at 9.8 percent. Essentially, his blood volume was at only a quarter of the level found in a normal human being. His blood was so thin that it looked like diluted cherry Kool-Aid, and one could have read a newspaper through a purple-topped tube containing a sample of his blood.

The patient's severe anemia resulted in a markedly diminished oxygen-carrying capacity, which put a tremendous strain on his internal organs. In an attempt to compensate, the patient developed tachycardia. He developed a pathologic cardiac arrhythmia that, on an EKG recording, proved to be atrial fibrillation. Unfortunately, with his severe anemia, it was not a controllable problem.

The patient developed high-output congestive heart failure and subsequently died while gasping for his last breath of air. At the funeral home, the mortician had to fracture the patient's right femur in order for the corpse to fit into a standard casket. It was probably the only time the patient's leg had ever been straight, and sadly, it was a postmortem intervention that resulted in just a cosmetic correction of his orthopedic anomaly.

Oddly, the patient's relatives appeared to be joyful at the ultimate outcome. Brewster and Ben Fielder found their unexpected emotional response to the passing of their loved one to be somewhat disturbing.

Perhaps Brewster should have reeled it in just a bit when he told the family members, "You people must have been standing at the back of the line when they were handing out religions. For God's sake, find a new denomination! After all, there's a shit pot full of other faiths out there for you to choose from. Next time, pick one that's not so stupid."

<hr />

Izzy had sickle-cell disease, and if he ever developed an acute sickle crisis during the holiday season, he would invariably insist on getting admitted to a hospital room located next to the clean utility station on the med-surg service. That way, he would have ready access to a cache of supplies he could pilfer and use as stocking stuffers when Santa Claus came down the chimney. They included tiny bars of soap, toothbrushes, miniscule tubes of toothpaste, and disposable single-use razors. From the hospital storage room, he would also steal hair combs that were so cheap-ass and flimsy they were actually sub-Kmart quality. Although Izzy was essentially a dirtbag, he was somewhat of a likable dirtbag nonetheless.

The management of an acute sickle-cell crisis usually entailed a fairly standard clinical course of action. Patients received aggressive hydration, oxygen therapy, pain medication, and judicious blood-product support if they became severely anemic. In Izzy's case, a sickle-cell crisis would usually work itself out over the course of a few days in the hospital. Sadly, the patient was painfully aware that his diagnosis of sickle-cell disease cursed him with a limited projected life expectancy of maybe only about three or four decades at best, and that was if he was extraordinarily lucky. If that would be the case, Izzy was determined to live life to the fullest.

On occasion, Izzy would unfortunately develop priapism during a sickle-cell attack—in other words, a pathological penile erection. In the case of Izzy, when his normal red cells would assume a sickle-cell shape during an acute attack of his underlying hematological disorder, the abnormal stiff red cells would jam up the circulation to important parts of his body. One of those important body parts was his penis. When that would occur, Izzy would have a painful erection that could last for hours or longer. Determined to take advantage of such a situation, Izzy explained to Ben Fielder that he would dress up in drag and troll for slightly built white male johns who might be looking for a little black nookie over on Congress Street.

Fielder couldn't help himself and asked, "What would you charge for a hum job and a back-door tube steak?"

Izzy replied, "For you, sugar, I can give you a happy-hour special discount. I'll even let you do me once I get through working you over."

"No, I'm sorry for the misunderstanding," Fielder replied, "but it's not for me. My friend Brewster has anger-management issues, and I think it would be good for him to take a walk on the wild side."

"If he be a white man," Izzy said, "bring him down here right now! I want to take a look at the merchandise."

Fielder called Brewster over to Izzy's room to allegedly assist in an IV procedure. When Brewster arrived, Izzy grabbed the medical student's crotch and said, "If you have an Andrew Jackson in your wallet, I'll make sure you get the first dance at the sock hop!"

Startled, Brewster pushed the patient away and then proceeded to threaten him. "If you touch my plumbing one more time, I'll yank your pecker off and shove it up your ass!"

"Some of you white men can be so forceful." Izzy smiled. "I like that."

Once Ben Fielder broke out into hysterical laughter, J. D. Brewster suddenly realized he had been set up. "Ben, has anyone ever told you that you're a deluxe asshole?"

"I hear it every day of the week and twice on Sundays," Fielder replied. "Thank you very much!"

Brewster turned back to Izzy with curiosity and asked, "If you are a male prostitute, do you make a pretty good living in that line of work?"

"When I get all gussied up with fishnet stockings and high-heel shoes, I can make a killing," Izzy answered.

"So you go out in drag?" Brewster asked. "Do the guys you pick up realize that you're a man, or do they think you're a beefy black woman?"

"Baby, I could sell ice to an Eskimo," Izzy said. "Once those skinny little white men figure out that I am packing a bodacious beef log, it's way too late. By then, I've got up a full head of steam, and I'm rollin' downhill. Nothin' is about to stop me then!"

"I just don't know about all of that," Brewster said. "It sounds like rape to me."

"Maybe, but so far, I've never heard anybody ever complain about my complimentary set of romantic skills," Izzy said. "You'd be surprised how many regular customers I have in my Rolodex!"

———•———

Dr. Teague fielded an annoying phone call from a patient who was suffering from a complication of constipation from her oral iron supplementation therapy. For a lot of people who took oral iron treatment, constipation was frequently a troublesome side effect. The attending physician covered the mouthpiece on the telephone receiver, turned his head to Brewster, and pleaded for help. "God spare me, but I'm dealing with a tyranny of small minds. No matter how many times I explain things to this moron, she just doesn't get it. On more than one occasion, I've even given her our bowel-protocol printout on how she can manage her stubborn bowels. Here she is now, back on the telephone, bitching to me that we've done nothing to help her with her goddamn constipation! Come over here, Brew, and deal with this cretin."

"Give me the phone," Brewster said. "I've been told that I'm a top-shelf people person. Let me see if I can live up to my billing."

As Dr. Teague handed the telephone receiver to J. D. Brewster, the attending physician said, "I just can't handle any more idiotic shit from anybody right about now. If you don't mind, I'm just going to sit here and listen in on your side of the conversation."

"Fine, Doc. Behold a master people person at work."

Brewster took the telephone from his attending physician and tried to generate a pleasant and cheerful façade. "Hello, madam. My name is Brewster. How may I help you?" After a pause, he said, "I see. Yes, I understand. Yes, I see. Okay, I think I know what the problem is. It's absolutely mandatory from now on that you remove the suppository from its thick tinfoil wrapper before you shove it up your ass … No, I'm not kidding. What I told you is indeed correct. Why? Because otherwise, the mucosal lining of your bunghole won't absorb the suppository, and the medication will likely be much less efficacious—that's why. You'll need to be careful and stay close to the toidy, because once the laxative finally kicks in, you're going to poop your brains out … No, ma'am, that was just a figure of speech … Well, of course I know, because I'm in medical school. I spent an entire afternoon learning how to shove something up the backside of one of my medical student colleagues … Well, not exactly; it was sort of like pulling a train. Some homely sea hag standing behind me with fat, stubby fingers did the same to me … I don't quite remember if I did, but maybe so. After all, I do recall that she offered me a cigarette after she vigorously massaged my prostate … I know, I know. Well, that's funny you should ask, but I'm quite certain she gloved up. In any event, she appeared to be familiar with the proper use of soap and water … Well, to be honest, I certainly would not let her doink me under any circumstances, if that's what you are getting at. Why? Well, I don't want to kiss and tell, but at best, she was a double-bagger, and I'm saving myself for the right girl. Now, I want you to write down this important information and then stick it on your fridge door with a kitchen magnet so you won't forget, okay? … Oh, that's very kind of you to say. I'm glad I could be of help to you. God bless you too!"

As Brewster hung up the telephone, he raised his arms triumphantly in the air and proclaimed, "Yes! I cured somebody!" He turned to Dr. Teague and said smugly, "Well, that wasn't a particularly difficult problem. For shit's sake, Doc, you really need to work on your people skills."

In mid-December, Brewster received a telephone call from Rip Ford to remind him about the promise they had both made to Uncle Hank Holcombe in the dark on the night he had died several months ago. It was getting toward the end of the year, and they had little time left to fulfill their solemn oath that they would free the big primates incarcerated in the lockdown kennel.

"Is Ms. Coffee from infection control going to help us out again this time?" Brewster asked.

"Sadly," Ford said, "she's going to sit on the sidelines this time around."

"I guess I can't blame her," Brewster said, "since she was put through the ringer by administration after our last failed attempt."

Ford and Brewster had made two prior unsuccessful attempts to liberate the big primates earlier in the fall, but they simply had not had the wherewithal to paralyze the video security system. They had to accomplish that task first to have any realistic expectation of success in their endeavor to become simian liberators. Whatever they were going to do, they had to act fast. As of January 1, 1982, the animals would finally be in the queue to get inoculated with infected material in a GRID study being performed by Parker Coxswain and Dr. Bookman.

"Who's in?"

"You, me, Talbot, and Regina Clemmons," Ford answered.

"That's it?" Brewster said. "The four of us will never be able to pull this off. How in hell are we going to load up the great apes and get them off campus?"

"Relax," Ford said to assuage his colleague. "There will be a lot more than just four people involved in this clandestine enterprise. This time, the Animal Liberation League will be sending down an entire squad to do all of the heavy lifting."

As almost every research scientist at the Gulf Coast College of Medicine had previously predicted, the first experimental study undertaken to try to prove that GRID was a lifestyle disease as a consequence of amyl nitrate poppers being inhaled during recreational homosexual activity had proven to be an unmitigated failure. With the pending closure of the Rectal Trauma GRID Research Study Group, Bookman and his crew had to admit that GRID was likely an infectious disease. It would soon be time to try to horizontally transmit the GRID disease into great apes.

Blood, serum, and semen material harvested from human patients afflicted with GRID would soon be injected into the test subjects, and then the big primates would eventually be sacrificed to ascertain whether or not nonhuman biological entities could also contract the dreaded illness.

Although the clock was ticking, Brewster had significant concerns about pulling off such a caper. "Wait just a minute," Brewster said. "After they upgraded the security system to monitor everything in real time, the ceiling-mounted video recorder will be aimed right at us once we enter the lockdown kennel."

"I know."

"Unless we've got some way to kill the security system, we'll never figure out some way to sneak these beasts out of here. We're going to get nailed to the wall, I tell you. We've made two attempts at this already since Uncle Hank passed away. On each occasion, we were almost caught in the act. I just want to remind you exactly what's at stake. If we get pinched, I'll get thrown out of medical school, and all of us will be headed straight to jail. Do not pass Go! Do not collect two hundred dollars! In fact at one time, those were your very own words."

"We've got an idea on how to disable the recording loop when the time is right," Ford said. "Listen, Brew, your old bandmate from DNR, Zip Talbot, and also Dr. Clemmons hammered out most of the blueprints on this. Come down to the lab tonight, and we'll spell it all out for you."

"Is it a solid plan?" Brewster asked.

"The only turd in the punch bowl is that we haven't figured out a way to clear the lab techs out of the main lab when this caper goes down," Ford answered. "Although we're shooting for Christmas Eve, there still will be some researchers down here in the basement throughout the entire holiday."

"As you may or may not know," Brewster said, "the Rabbi will be starting to work on a new and improved rabies vaccine now that he is not going to get any additional funding for the shingles study he's been working on for the last year or so."

"I know all about it," Ford answered. "What's your point?"

"If you know about this matter," Brewster said, "then most likely, all of the other researchers know about it also. Dr. Rabbi wants to come up with a new rabies vaccine formulation that will result in a more abbreviated course of therapy and will be less painful for patients to receive. We'll use all of this to our advantage, I tell you."

"I don't follow you," Ford said. "Is the rabbi going to incorporate the primates in this rabies trial or what?"

"He's not planning on using the primates at all," Brewster answered. "Check this out, Ford: the rabbi will be using the skunk as the animal model to act as a rabies virus reservoir."

"So?"

"I've got it figured out," Brewster answered. "It came to me in a flash. As long as I can get reasonable assurances from you that the kennel's pesky security system will be effectively neutralized, you can leave the lab personnel problem up to me."

"What's going on in that gray matter of yours?"

"Patience, grasshopper," Brewster answered. "Let's meet with Talbot and Regina Clemmons tonight, and I'll lay my diabolical scheme out for all of you to chew on."

—◦◦◦—

In the year 1981, Christmas Eve fell on a Thursday. The animal laboratory was going to shut down on that day at noon, and there would only be a skeleton crew of veterinarian technicians to care for the animals over the long holiday weekend.

Fortunately for Talbot and his three fellow would-be primate rustlers, there would be only one security guard to contend with at that time. It was the job of Dr. Regina Clemmons to disable the security cameras. To accomplish her mission, she was going to have to break out an unsavory fallacious race card.

"Somebody just left an inflammatory, derogatory, and racist memo on my office door, and I'm not very happy about it," Dr. Clemmons told the security guard.

"I'm sorry to hear that, Dr. Clemmons. What did the note say?"

"It said, 'Who done shook the tree?' I find that comment to be most offensive," Regina answered.

"I'm not sure what that means," the hapless security guard responded. "Are you sure it was meant to be an insult directed at you?"

"Yes, as it was meant to be a racial slur," Dr. Clemmons replied. "It was a specific insult suggesting that I'm nothing more than a subhuman, tree-dwelling primate. I want to catch the bastard who would dare say something like that."

"How can I help you regarding this issue?" the guard asked.

"I want you to open up the security-camera control room, where I can review the security tape," Dr. Clemmons replied.

"I'll meet you down there," the guard said, "but I'll need to be there with you while you review the VHS cassette."

"That will be okay," Dr. Clemmons replied, "because I don't know how any of the equipment works in the monitor room. I can meet you down there in five minutes."

Once the security guard had opened up the camera control room and allowed Dr. Clemmons to enter, he said, "Have a seat at the control desk. We have multiple automatic VHS recording machines, one for every floor of the medical school. Your office is on the sixth floor, so all you have to do is rewind the tape loaded on machine number six, and then you can run the playback to find the culprit who left you that nasty note."

No sooner had Dr. Clemmons become familiar with how the security system operated, the security guard got a telephone call from none other than Rip Ford with a request for assistance. Ford explained that he had "accidentally" broken off his key in the lock of the door to his workstation, and he had to get some important papers out of the office before the long holiday weekend.

"I'm sorry, Dr. Clemmons," the security guard said, "but I'm going to have to leave you here on your own, if you're okay with that. That idiot Rip Ford broke his key off in his door lock, and I'm going to have a hell of a time getting the door to his study cubicle opened up for him. This might turn out to be a job for the maintenance man, and I wouldn't be surprised if Harper has already booked out of here for the Christmas holiday weekend."

Regina patted the security guard on the hand and assured him that when she left, she would simply press the lock button on the inner doorknob to make sure everything was secure upon her departure.

As soon as the security guard left to help Rip Ford out of his contrived predicament, Dr. Clemmons hit the button marked "Eject" on the VHS recording machine that monitored the animal laboratory. As soon as the VHS cassette popped out of the recorder, she closed up the security monitor room and then went downstairs to the laboratory to unlock the roll-up door at the loading dock.

Waiting outside of the loading dock area were a total of three small moving trucks, each with a twelve-foot enclosed van box constructed with steel bars. In addition, there were nine people present from the radical Animal Liberation League. They were all dressed in black and had ski masks pulled over the faces, as they were ready to abscond with the great primates being held as prisoners in the lockdown kennel.

It was time for Brewster to unleash his pet skunk in the

animal lab to chase out the few members of the skeleton crew of veterinarian techs who had the misfortune of being consigned to caring for the laboratory animals over the Christmas vacation. As Brewster entered the lab with Monsieur Pepe, the medical student was dressed in a biohazard outfit, including a mask on his face to hide his identity. He set the skunk down on the floor of the entryway into the animal lab and proceeded to cause a commotion.

"Everybody out! Get the hell out of here! One of the Rabbi's skunks got loose in here, and the goddamned thing has been inoculated with rabies! Run! Run for your lives!"

When the half dozen or so veterinarian techs caught a glimpse of playful Pepe bounding around the laboratory floor and looking for places to get into mischief, they all fled in terror at the speed of Mach 2 with their hair on fire. After all, nobody wanted to be exposed to rabies. If one ever contracted that deadly viral infection, it was box city, baby!

As soon as the animal laboratory had cleared out, Zip Talbot opened the door to the lockdown kennel, and the nine members from ALL entered through the loading-dock area. The ultimate plan was to take the great primates away to an undisclosed sanctuary site.

"Hey, Zip!" Brewster called out to Talbot. "Is everything on schedule?"

Talbot, who was also decked out in a full biohazard suit, responded with a thumbs-up. It was time for Brewster to address la ranchera in charge of the operation. While that individual directed orders to the other ALL members, the liberation league ape wranglers deferentially referred to her as Ramrod.

"You're clearly the chief cook and bottle washer of the whole outfit," Brewster said. "I want to thank you for your help regarding this matter. However, I want to let you know that I don't personally approve of who you people are or what you've done in the past."

"Spill it," the woman said. "I swear, I'm sick and tired of getting blamed for everything that's wrong in this world."

"I was told you tried to assassinate a research veterinarian who was working at a biopharmaceutical company in Austin a while back," Brewster said. "I was informed that he was shot by a sniper and almost died from his injuries. What you people did was downright disgusting."

"Hang on, cowboy," Ramrod replied. "That crime was pinned on us, but we had nothing to do with any of it. We don't commit acts of violence against other people. In that particular situation, our organization simply became a scapegoat—nothing more and nothing less. As it turned out, the dude who got smoked was doinking the wife of his boss at the lab. You do the math. The dude deserved it if you ask me."

"By the way, where are you taking these beasts?" Brewster asked. "Some kind of primate sanctuary, I presume?"

"Can't and won't say," Ramrod said.

As the last primate was loaded up onto one of the moving vans, Ramrod pulled off her ski mask.

"I know who you are," she said to Brewster. "Don't ask me where or when, but I met you before, when you were the front man for that 1960s rock-and-roll cover band called DNR. Your nickname at the time was Thumper. Am I not correct?"

"The shoe fits," Brewster answered.

"I see now that you've been dating a fat, old, hippie, dinosaur loser chick who must be ten years older than you are. She even wears plastic flowers in her hair. How lame is that? Oh my God, are you kidding me?" Ramrod asked.

"Stop right there," Brewster said. "Her name is Stella, and she happens to be my fiancée."

"Listen, Brewster," Ramrod said. "If you ever want to take a swing in the trees with me, give me a call sometime. Talbot has my phone number. You can get it from him. I need to bounce, but before

I go, I'm going to make you cry like a little schoolgirl. It would be good for you, no?"

Before the young woman departed, she bit Brewster's earlobe hard enough to draw blood. Although he moaned in pain, J. D. made no overt effort to thwart the advances from the woman known as Ramrod.

After Brewster and Talbot cleaned up the lab, Brewster loaded Monsieur Pepe back into his travel cage. "I can't believe we pulled this off!" Zip Talbot said. Unfortunately, it was far too soon for them to let their guard down.

Rip Ford entered the lab on a dead sprint, and he was clearly terrified. "Get the hell out of here! The security guard got my office door open quicker than I thought, and then he went straightaway to the security camera monitors. I couldn't stall him. Move it, boys! We're about to get steamrolled!"

No sooner had Rip Ford issued his dire warning than they all heard an angry voice over the medical school intercom system: "To all available security personnel: please report to the basement laboratory immediately!"

Ford realized his best chance to escape was to go back to his work space and resume the meaningless shuffling of papers in a nonchalant manner as if nothing had happened. Fortunately, Regina Clemmons was already in the clear, as she had vacated the premises as soon as she had opened the loading-dock bay to allow the members of the Animal Liberation League to enter the medical school kennel. Sadly, the same could not be said for Brewster or Zip Talbot.

"I'm going out the emergency exit," Brewster said.

"No!" Talbot said. "You'll never make it!"

Talbot grabbed Brewster by the arm and led him out into the hallway. The research scientist pulled J. D. into the adjacent utility room, where the incinerator was located, just steps ahead of the security team that had just arrived on the scene.

"Climb into the furnace with me, Brew," Talbot said.

"What in hell is the matter with you?!"

"I turned the pilot off hours ago to shut down the incinerator before the holiday weekend," Talbot said. "It's our only chance to escape from this shit storm."

"No fucking way!" Brewster said. "If some yahoo comes in here and flips the switch, we're going to get cremated while we're still very much alive!"

"It's your funeral one way or the other," Talbot said as he jumped into the incinerator without hesitation. Reluctantly, Brewster followed suit and closed the heavy iron furnace door behind him just as members of the security team entered the utility room to see if any unauthorized personnel were lurking about.

It was well past nine o'clock that night when the soot-covered culprits found that it was finally safe enough to flee the Texas Medical Center.

Brewster and Talbot headed over to the home of Dr. Regina Clemmons, where Rip Ford was already waiting. Dr. Clemmons had already ordered a couple of large pizzas for everybody to share on that eve of December 24. After all, Dr. Clemmons and her coconspirators were going to need a strong alibi, and a hard-copy receipt from Pizza Butt would go a long way in creating the illusion of innocence.

—◦◦◦—

It was a beautiful thing that Talbot and Rip Ford would spend Christmas Eve with Dr. Clemmons. They were all lonely people. At that particular time, they all desperately needed the company of fellow human beings. After putting a few simple decorations on a small Christmas tree, Ford and Talbot made a point to take Dr. Clemmons to a midnight church service that evening. It was the right thing to do.

As for Brewster, he packed a few essentials into Uncle John's crappy Dodge Dart, and he drove the old bucket of bolts back to Waco with his trusty friend Monsieur Pepe the skunk. Brewster was looking forward to spending Christmas with his fiancée and her parents, although he had considerable reservations that Pork Link might inadvertently misidentify Pepe as a Yankee varmint.

After all Brewster had been through that day, the medical student could only hope his new black-and-white-striped pet would not end up in the crosshairs of a large-bore weapon.

10

LAND OF DISENCHANTMENT

Brewster sat with Stella on the front porch swing of her parents' house near Waco on the day after Christmas. Stella noticed that Brewster was starting to appear leaner and was adding additional muscle mass. She also was aware that he was starting to develop some troublesome acne on the anterior aspect of his neck.

"Lover boy, are you starting to work out at the gym?" Stella asked.

Of course, that was not the case. Brewster had been taking a double dose of testosterone on a monthly basis ever since he had lost his remaining testicle back in June after being assaulted. In addition to aggressive behavior, acne was a classic side effect of bodybuilders who juiced up on male anabolic steroids. As Brewster was taking a double dose of replacement anabolic steroids against medical advice, he clearly fell into the category of men who were juiced up.

"No, baby," Brewster replied, "I'm just living better through modern chemistry."

There was one side effect Brewster did not have to worry about while taking replacement male hormones: testicular atrophy. That was another anomaly widely reported in men who abused anabolic steroids, but it was obviously not a problem, as Brewster no longer had any testicles.

"I think it would be a good time for us to talk about our wedding plans," said Brewster.

"We should try to pick a date around early July," Stella replied, "because that's the time when you and I first went out on a date with each other. Also, that was the time of year when you and I patched up our relationship after we had that little spat awhile back."

"That date will only work if I resurrect my PhD program and am able to stay on here at the Gulf Coast College of Medicine for another year," Brewster said. "If not, after I get my MD degree, I'll be starting my residency training at the beginning of July. I have that internal medicine elective externship coming up in January at the St. Francis College of Medicine in Santa Fe. I don't know, but maybe if I do a good job and they like me, they might offer me a residency training slot."

"What makes you think New Mexico would be interested in you?" Stella asked. "After all, you're from Texas. I'm certain you'll rub those people the wrong way."

"No doubt, but I got a letter two days ago from one of the former braniacs who's now working in Santa Fe. His name is Booker Marshall, but I only know him by reputation. He worked with the big O-rings awhile back at the Gulf Coast, studying MAI infections. It's quite clear to me that he faced the same moral dilemma I previously encountered when I was in the PhD program and struggling to find the courage to do experimental studies on the imprisoned primates. In any event, Booker is trying to recruit some students who will soon graduate from the Gulf Coast to join him out west in Santa Fe. He has a clandestine albeit perhaps a bit grandiose idea to establish what he calls the University of Texas at Santa Fe in an effort to add some culture to the high desert."

"Sounds hinky to me," Stella said. "To my way of thinking, if a bunch of Gulf Coast refugees hightail it across the panhandle and end up in New Mexico, it would be akin to a bunch of banditos going out to the badlands to bury their ill-gotten booty."

"So," Brewster said, a bit bemused, "am I now a bandito?"

"If the shoe fits."

"Perhaps you think I was corrupted by my prior interactions with your former boss, Dr. Corka Sorass," Brewster said in his own defense. "Sorass was a bona fide Nazi collaborator. I'm not a Nazi, I'll have you know!"

"Well, you have your moments," Stella answered. "Truth be told, everybody might be capable of acting like a Nazi under certain circumstances."

"You might be right."

"In any event, if they offer you a slot in the residency match this spring, you should take it. New Mexico is beautiful. As you know, sometimes I have premonitions, and I just don't picture myself being here this time next year," Stella said.

"Is that good or bad?"

"I don't know for certain," Stella answered, "but it's as if my own guardian angel is telling me that it's just about time for me to move on, Brew. As for now, I'll stand by any decision you make."

"We'll make it together then."

"No, lover boy," Stella said. "It's your call."

"I promise you this: it has to be a collective decision," Brewster said.

"Although I can't tell you what to do, I don't think you should try to reenter the dual-training program. It's only caused you grief and heartache," Stella said.

"That it has."

"You burned up an entire year of your life, and you were left with having nothing to show for it. I don't either, for that matter."

"The Oracle at Delphi hath spoken!" Brewster exclaimed as he put his arm around his fiancée. Sadly, neither Brewster nor Stella knew just how accurate her premonitions would turn out to be.

Brewster and Stella returned to Houston after the Christmas holiday break, as there was one more week to go in the hematology elective rotation. By the time Brewster returned to the Gulf Coast College of Medicine, all hell had broken loose over the matter of somebody stealing the six great primates from the lockdown kennel area. Obviously, it had been an inside job. The administration and also detectives Watt and Culp and from the Houston Police Department had interviewed everybody who had access to the laboratory.

Regina Clemmons, Ford, and Talbot all had an alibi that they had spent Christmas Eve together. In fact, Dr. Clemmons still had the receipt showing she had ordered out for pizza that was delivered to her home when the apparent theft had occurred.

A person of interest was obviously J. D. Brewster.

"Where were you on Christmas Eve?" Detective Watt asked.

"Waco."

"Any witnesses?" Detective Culp said.

"My fiancée and her entire family," Brewster replied. "I left the Texas Medical Center at about noon and made it up to Waco by late afternoon. What's this all about?"

"I'm sure you know what this is all about," Watt said. "Six big monkeys were stolen from the primate lab. Inside job, I tell you. You wouldn't happen to know anything about that, now, would you?"

Brewster looked down at the floor and shrugged. "How could I be involved? I no longer have access to the restricted kennels."

"Can anybody else confirm your alibi besides your fiancée and her family?" Culp asked.

"Only my polecat, Pepe," Brewster answered.

"Wait—you said 'polecat.' Do you actually own a damned skunk?" Watt asked. "It's illegal to keep a skunk as a pet in the state of Texas."

"You must have misunderstood what I said," Brewster lied. "I said, 'Only my old cat, Pepe.' Sorry for the misunderstanding. I must have been mumbling."

"Sure, sure, sure," Watt said suspiciously.

As the student had been previously dismissed from the dual-training program, the medical school administration and, subsequently, the law enforcement authorities erroneously thought the human lightning rod known as J. D. Brewster no longer had any access to the laboratory area. That, of course, was not the case, as nobody had ever bothered to ask him to return his laboratory entry key. Brewster was sure as hell not about to give back the key on his own accord.

While chaos swirled all around him, Brewster simply went about his business, and if anybody asked, he professed to know nothing at all. It was quite sad that the trail of evidence regarding the disappearance of the six great primates had gone cold so quickly...

—⸺⫘⫘⫘⫘⫘⫘—

During Brewster's last few days on the hematology rotation at the end of December, he was surprised when a patient he knew from the past showed up for visit at the outpatient clinic. It was none other than Dora Garza. When adult protective services had gotten involved in her case after she was found to have a ball of cat hair in her stomach, the patient had been sent to a long-term custodial-care nursing home facility. The patient had been referred to the hematology clinic for a consult by the nursing home because of some unusual laboratory parameters found on a routine complete blood count. The patient was found to have an elevated red blood cell mean corpuscular volume. In layman's terms, that meant the patient had developed red cells that were larger than normal.

Usually, if a patient was anemic and had a low mean corpuscular volume with red cells that were smaller than normal, that indicated an iron deficiency state or perhaps thalassemia, which was a genetically inheritable red blood cell production disorder. Conversely, if a patient had red cells that were larger than normal in the setting of anemia, that indicated a likely problem of vitamin B12 deficiency, folate deficiency, alcohol abuse, liver disease, hypothyroidism, drug-induced macrocytosis, or perhaps a primary bone marrow disorder, such as a myelodysplastic syndrome. Curiously, Dora Garza's blood profile showed that although her red cells were larger than normal, there was no sign of anemia.

Brewster got permission from the attending physician, Dr. Teague, to order an anemia workup nonetheless, and it was a great surprise to see that Dora Garza did indeed have severe vitamin B12 deficiency after all, without evidence of an overt anemia. How strange. That was important because vitamin B12 not only was an integral component of the normal production of red cells but also was a vitamin crucial to the health of the central and peripheral nervous systems.

A patient afflicted with unrecognized B12 deficiency could develop dementia that was clinically indistinguishable from Alzheimer's disease or other forms of an organic brain syndrome. Dora was placed on B12 injections on a monthly basis, and not only did her abnormal red cell index eventually become corrected over time, but she also had a moderate improvement in her mental status to the point that she was able to return to her own home and enjoy independent living once again!

That was remarkable. Brewster wondered how many other patients at large were suffering from dementia that might be a consequence of unrecognized B12 deficiency and not Alzheimer's disease. After all, if a patient was not anemic, a screen for any other abnormalities might not be undertaken if the only unusual laboratory parameter was an elevated red blood cell mean corpuscular volume.

Brewster pondered that issue for the next several months, and he would eventually discuss the matter much later with the dementia specialist, Dr. Sergio Balbona.

"Brewster, you're on to something," the Cuban refugee declared. "Why don't you forego your upcoming residency training for a while? Let's see if we can get you reinstated into the dual-training program. I have ideas for several studies that can evolve out of what you have discovered. Please think about my suggestion. Besides, you and I never sat down to share a cigar and a Cuba Libre together, mi amigo."

Brewster was indeed onto something, and it was substantially more important than trying to figure out why chimpanzees hurled feces at their human captors in anger. In the meantime, Brewster would make certain he and his colleague Ben Fielder offered sincere apologies to Dora Garza for the time they had permitted the elderly woman to groom Stella's cat, Checkers.

Human beings were not black and white. Human beings were not divided into simple categories of good and evil. Although buried up to his neck in a quagmire of moral decay, Brewster occasionally still had the capacity to try to do the right thing.

The prior year, the two miscreant students had encouraged Dora to lick the feline's fur, and in retrospect, that was not funny. As a matter of fact, it was cruel and disrespectful to a fellow human being. What they had done was wrong, plain and simple. There was no excuse for what had happened, as both Brewster and Ben Fielder had known they were doing something perverted and evil at the time it occurred. Atonement was in order.

———

Brewster packed up the old Dodge Dart on New Year's Day, and Pepe got to ride shotgun. Brewster planned to make a two-day trip to Santa Fe with a stopover for the night in Abilene.

"Give me a kiss, lover boy!" Stella exclaimed. "I want you to call me twice a week, on every Tuesday and Saturday night, no matter what. Drive safe. I want you back in one piece."

"You know I will," Brewster said. "I love you, Stella."

"Well, it's about damned time!" Stella Link reiterated what had now become her signature reply.

With that, Brewster started his long road trip to the Land of Enchantment.

On the late evening of Saturday, January 2, 1982, Brewster finally made his way to the apartment complex where he would be staying for his one-month externship. After he got settled into his furnished unit before the rotation started, he took Pepe out of his cage, as the medical student wanted to roughhouse with the pet skunk.

J. D. watched the nightly national news before the syndicated talk show Live! On Alonzo aired. Brewster became unglued when he saw a segment on the show that lionized Mumbo Jamar Apoo. Never in a million years would Brewster have anticipated that the liberal television talk show host would proclaim that Apoo was a heroic freedom fighter against social injustice.

If Apoo were executed for the crimes he had committed, then he would deservedly become a great American martyr, according to Alonzo. If Apoo had murdered Officer Faulkland, it was just another example of the repressed soul brother rising up against the white-devil slave master who kept the black man down.

If Brewster ever met Alonzo in person, he would have to pimp-slap that idiot up one side and down the other. Brewster realized that a social movement was already afoot to try to mitigate the punishment Apoo would eventually receive at the hands of the criminal justice system, if not to try to render complete exoneration for the vicious killer. Wow! What's wrong with the liberals and progressives who champion such wretched human beings? There was no answer at the time, and sadly, there probably never would be.

Brewster's rotation started on Monday, January 4, and his attending physician was an internist named Dr. Seiler. The resident physician, who was a member of the Navajo tribe, was named Dr. Cloud. The population of patients Brewster would be seeing would be an admixture of the vast array of different people who populated the Southwest corner of the United States.

There was one thing Brewster learned early during his externship: many people who lived in New Mexico were not particularly fond of Texans. When the medical student passed by other individuals who whispered derisive nicknames in his direction, such as shit-kicker or rebel redneck, it was apparent that Brewster was not particularly welcome in the high desert.

To Brewster, the nature of the undercurrent of animosity was unclear, but as the student was a historian, he had a theory that it stemmed from the fact that the Republic of Texas had once claimed the vast majority of the territory that became New Mexico, up until the time the Lone Star made the huge and irreversible mistake of joining the Union back in 1845. In any event, Brewster would spend his first two weeks on the elective rotation on the general medical service, and then he would spend two weeks at the VA annex.

—◁▥◊▥▷—

It got cold in New Mexico during that winter—really cold. Brewster had night call, and Dr. Cloud instructed the medical student to go down to the emergency room and introduce himself to Dr. Julian Dove, who was the attending physician working the night shift.

"I hate to say this about a fellow First American, but Dove's a moron!" Cloud said. "He's a bona fide sieve. Any goddamned thing that walks through the emergency room door is going to get admitted. I swear to God that fucker couldn't keep a petrified mammoth from squeezing into the ER. To be honest with you, I really can't say if it's because he's lazy or if it's because he's stupid."

"Why don't you just refuse the hit if an admission is not warranted?" Brewster asked. "I was once told by one of my mentors back in Houston that it's a man's duty to not accept a transfer—or even an admission, for that matter—if it's nothing but a dump."

"No way, Jose," Dr. Cloud replied. "That's not how it works out here in the Wild West. The institution's policy is that the emergency room physician is the final arbiter. I have no say-so in the matter. Nonetheless, I want you to go down there and introduce yourself to him."

"What difference would that make then?"

"Think about it," Cloud said. "If that savage wagon burner takes a shine to you, then perhaps we won't get hit with as many dumps tonight. Oh, heads-up: don't buy any of his bullshit. The man is not Navajo. He's from the Zuni tribe!"

Well, that explained a lot. The Navajo, Zuni, and Hopi people had butted heads for years over tribal land disputes, and as a historian, Brewster was fairly well versed in the subject matter.

"I get the picture," Brewster said. "Your disdain for Dr. Dove wouldn't have anything to do with the fact that he's from a different tribe, now, would it?"

"I am indeed impressed, pale face," Cloud responded. "It would seem you know something about this matter. Sometimes I believe the official state moniker should be changed to the Land of Disenchantment! I understand that you're from Texas. I've never been there, but I would like to at least see San Antonio someday. You Texans are a bunch of crazy-ass sons of bitches! Oh, sorry; I meant no offense."

"None taken," Brewster said. "In fact, we're very proud of that reputation. I'll tell you what: whenever you want to make the trip, I'll be happy to meet you in the Alamo City, and we'll do the town. There is a 1960s go-go-style night club on the Riverwalk called

Guano Dick's where a person can really get down and do a war dance. Oh, sorry; I meant no offense."

"None taken!" Cloud said. "None taken."

―――――

As it was already early January, Brewster was a bit surprised to see that the emergency room hadn't removed the Christmas decorations yet. There was still an artificial fir tree in the emergency room waiting area, along with tinsel that had been draped over the entryway. Brewster found the attending physician, Dr. Dove, and introduced himself.

"I understand that you are doing an externship from the Gulf Coast College of Medicine," the emergency room doctor said. "Well, I just want to say that I'm happy to meet you. In order for you to have an excellent experience here, I want to assure you that I will plan to admit as many patients as I possibly can to your internal medicine service from my emergency room. I want to make sure I keep you as busy as you've ever been in your entire life. If you take a lot of hits, your fund of knowledge will expand exponentially!"

Swell. That was not exactly what Brewster had wanted to hear from Dr. Dove. Trying to become ingratiated to the emergency room attending had clearly backfired. After all, no good deed went unpunished. Brewster was about to learn that the hostility that existed between Dr. Cloud in Dr. Dove was indeed a two-way street.

―――――

Dr. Cloud was a fine-looking fellow. He had a trim, muscular frame, and he generally wore blue jeans, cowboy boots, and a classic Santa Fe–style belt buckle with handcrafted inlaid ebony and a full moon of turquoise in the upper right corner of the buckle. Tips of silver wire buried into the ebony wood made it appear as if one were looking at a starry sky.

Dr. Cloud must have also had an elaborate collection of bolo ties, as Brewster never saw the same one twice during his rotation in New Mexico. Dr. Cloud had thick, coarse hair that he pulled back into a small, tight bun at the nape of his neck. Try as he might, Brewster could never figure out exactly how Cloud pulled his hair back so tightly, as there was never any evidence of a rubber band or barrette to hold the man-bun together.

"Well, how did things go in your meeting with Dove?" Dr. Cloud asked.

"Frankly, we're going to get shit on—big-time," Brewster answered. "Dr. Dove wants to make sure I have an excellent experience, and he plans on making a point of admitting everything he possibly can to our service from the emergency room."

"I'm sorry," Dr. Cloud replied, "but that's no reflection upon you. Dove is just poking the bear with a sharp stick. Somehow, someway, someday, I'll make certain this bear bites back!"

It appeared J. D. Brewster was about to become collateral damage in somebody else's personal war over the matter of ancient intertribal animosity.

⸻⊙⊙⸻

Jody was a homeless hippie who had come to Santa Fe to feel the good vibes. He planted himself in front of the Woolworth store on the plaza and peacefully assumed the lotus position. Without any pants or jacket, the misguided individual, seeking to become one with the universe, froze to death.

Depending on one's particular theological persuasions, perhaps Jody did indeed become one with the universe. His postmortem evaluation revealed that he had a deep incision on the palm of his left hand that appeared to be a self-inflicted wound. When Jody thawed out, he was found clutching a razor-sharp obsidian knife in his right hand. After he had purposefully cut the palm of his left hand, Jody had left a small pool of blood on the ground in front of him. What did it all mean? Who could say?

On the following morning, when the Woolworth store opened, the manager, Blake Barker, found that Jody was in the same lotus position he had assumed on the store's front portico the night before. The manager walked back to his office and pulled out a complimentary one-way bus ticket to Sedona, Arizona. The store had a stack of them to distribute just for those particular circumstances.

Not realizing Jody was already dead, Blake Barker said, "Wake up, you hippie-stoner loser. What's the matter with you? Did you drink too much bong water last night? You need to get your carcass to Sedona, Arizona, and do it pronto. That's the new place to be. All of your hippie, stoner, and loser friends are heading there right now. There's going to be a love-in there, so be sure to wear some flowers in your hair. If you arrive in time, you could experience the orgasmic sensation of lightning bolts shooting out of your ass. Have fun." As Jody had frozen to death, he wasn't about to budge one inch.

What a warm and kind gesture the store manager demonstrated. A casual observer might have believed the uncharitable people from New Mexico disliked their neighbors from Arizona as much as they disliked any visitors from Texas.

In any event, once the emergency medical technicians arrived, they proceeded to load Jody's earthly remains into the ambulance to convey him over to the hospital, where he could officially be pronounced dead. As he was not wearing any pants, Jody's scrotum had frozen to the brick pavers underneath the Woolworth portico. The emergency medical technicians had to forcefully pry the dead man's scrotum free from its icy incarceration, as rigor mortise had already set in. The emergency personnel simply propped Jody's dead, stiff body into the back of the ambulance vehicle as if he were a statue of a blue Buddha.

Although the dearly departed Jody was as dead as a dodo bird and as rigid as a honeymoon pecker, Dr. Dove nonetheless admitted the patient to Cloud's internal medicine service. Brewster and Dr. Cloud waited at the elevator doors for the arrival of their new patient, who allegedly was being admitted to the hospital from the emergency room for problems of hypothermia as a consequence to exposure to the extremely cold night temperatures.

When the doors opened, there was nobody on the elevator, just Jody's dead body, still in the lotus position and propped upright on a wheeled gurney. The dead body had a slightly blue tinge, and it had been draped with the remnant Christmas decorations from the emergency room, including a large boa of tinsel wrapped around the dead patient's neck and a pointy red Santa Claus hat (complete with an attached jingle bell at the tip) upon his head.

A handwritten note affixed to the patient's shirt with a safety pin said, "Dr. Cloud, I'm sorry for this belated Christmas present I've just turfed to you. I hope you enjoy all of the paperwork you'll have to do on this case. Love, Dr. Dove."

Brewster broke out into laughter and said, "Oh my God, this is some of the craziest shit I've ever seen, and I've certainly seen some pretty crazy shit over the last two years!"

Dr. Cloud did not seem amused in the least. "There's no way in hell I am going to put up with this nonsense. Brewster, take this dead body downstairs, wheel it outside, and then abandon the remains of this poor dead bastard beside the trash dumpster at the back of the hospital. Let's make this corpse somebody else's problem."

"You're not joking, are you?" Brewster said in astonishment. "It's not that I give two shits about this stiff, but what in hell is going to happen to me if I get caught?"

"It won't be pretty. You'll get your left nad caught in a ringer," Cloud said.

"Wait—I don't have a left testicle–or a right one, for that matter."

"Well, if you already have an empty ball sack," Cloud said with a wry smile, "I simply suggest that you don't get caught!"

Brewster was filled to the brim with self-loathing when he abandoned the corpse at the back dumpster behind the hospital's loading dock. After he tossed a thin hospital blanket over the dead body, he fled the scene. As he turned back toward the facility's rear maintenance area to rejoin Dr. Cloud in the hospital, Brewster was surprised to see an ill-appearing, spindly black man in a white lab coat waiting for him at the back entry.

"It's about time I met you face-to-face. I'm Dr. Booker Marshall. I used to be at the Gulf Coast, but now I'm a research scientist here in Santa Fe. I must say, Mr. Brewster, it appears your reputation precedes you."

"You pegged me," Brewster said. "I got your letter, and I'd like to thank you for the warm invitation you extended to me for this challenging externship out here in the Land of Disenchantment," the student said as he clinically scrutinized the frail man standing before him. "That goes double, as you already likely know by now that I'm a bona fide southern redneck. Dr. Marshall, you look, well, how should I say—"

"Sickle cell. Battled it all my life. I'm now starting to lose the war."

"Sorry to hear that," Brewster said, "but nonetheless, I would surmise that you're an eyewitness to the shenanigans I just perpetrated. I just shot my own dick off at the hub, didn't I? Sadly, I would guess right about now, the St. Francis College of Medicine would never consider a man like me to come back here for future postgraduate residency training."

"Au contraire, mon ami," Dr. Marshall said with a malicious smile.

"Wow!" Brewster said. "If that's the case, maybe there's hope for my redemption and perhaps even salvation."

Well, perhaps not.

Dr. Marshall uttered a final comment to the student that was damning praise indeed: "When you wrap up the loose ends in your life, I want you to look me up. If the truth be told, you're exactly the type of man who should be collaborating with me in the future."

—⋘⟊⟊⟊⋙—

The following day, Dr. Seiler officially probed why the dead body of a patient admitted to his internal medicine service had ended up beside the trash dumpster at the back of the hospital.

"Well, I received a call from Dr. Dove that we were going to take a hit," Dr. Cloud explained, "but the patient never showed up. I guess the guy wandered out of the emergency room against medical advice and died from exposure out there last night. I suggest you drop the hammer on Dr. Dove's sorry ass, as it would appear he's running a pretty loose ship down there for something like that to happen around here."

—⋘⟊⟊⟊⋙—

Brewster assumed the care of an elderly Navajo gentleman who had been admitted to the hospital for the management of acute pancreatitis as a consequence of an acute binge of hard liquor.

Caucasians had originally been exposed to alcohol thousands of years ago. Unfortunately, the First Americans in the Southwest corner of United States had first been introduced to fire water only about four hundred years ago. That historical and scientific fact certainly had bearing as to why the First Americans had such difficulty in dealing with the consequences of ethanol compared to their counterparts of European origin. Besides European infectious diseases, such as smallpox, ethanol might have been one of the worst things Anglos could have ever bestowed upon the Native Americans.

With gut rest, IV hydration, and the judicious use of pain medication, the elderly Navajo patient was starting to make a good recovery from his serious illness. The patient was a man of few words and knew no English, as he had spent his entire life on the reservation.

How could it be that the United States had failed so miserably as a nation during its voracious westward expansion through the sanctimonious doctrine of Manifest Destiny? Sadly, Anglos were incapable of fully incorporating Native Americans into being part of "us," and conversely, the settlers looked upon those various First American tribes as being part of "them."

As the alleged American melting pot had worked so well in other circumstances, why had it failed so badly in that situation? After all, were the First Americans anything less than fellow living and breathing human beings?

Brewster shared his feelings with Dr. Cloud. "It would appear the patient with pancreatitis is starting to turn the corner, but he's certainly a quiet fellow. Even with a Navajo translator present, he doesn't say very much."

"I know this man because I have taken care of him before in the past," Dr. Cloud said. "He's of the belief that he's been given a certain genetically predetermined number of words he can speak during his lifetime. Once he speaks all of the words he has bottled up inside, his life will then be over. That's why he is, as you say, a man of few words."

"I don't think the patient likes me very much," J. D. Brewster said. "I try to treat him with courtesy and respect, but every time I walk by his room, I believe he's giving me the stink eye."

"What in hell are you talking about?" Dr. Cloud asked.

"I'm serious," Brewster said. "I think he's putting a curse on me. Every time he sees me standing out in the hallway in front of his room, he raises his right hand and says, 'Yá'át'ééh! Yá'át'ééh!'"

Dr. Cloud broke out into laughter and said, "Brewster, you are such a dumbass. The old man is saying, 'Hello! Hello!'"

—⸺⸺—

Shirley Bellows was a thirty-nine-year-old registered nurse who worked for the VA annex in Santa Fe. Prior to Brewster's arrival to New Mexico, back in December, the patient had been previously diagnosed with a poorly differentiated five-centimeter papillary thyroid cancer that involved both lobes of the gland. She had undergone a surgical thyroidectomy to remove the offensive organ several weeks prior to her current admission. However, it was now time for her to receive a dose of adjuvant radioactive iodine to ensure a higher probability of her being cured above and beyond the surgery she had already received.

That specific radioactive iodine treatment was highly recommended, as half of the patients with that type of cancer might already have micrometastatic disease involving the lymph nodes at the time of their original diagnoses. Once a patient received a high dose of radioactive iodine, the individual had to remain in protective isolation for a few days in the hospital to prevent radioactive contamination to friends, family members, and the personnel providing medical care. Brewster went in to see the patient to take a history and physical examination before she received her dose of adjuvant radioactive iodine from the nuclear medicine service. Once treated, she would be placed in a protective and shielded lockdown room for a few days.

"I was always afraid I would come down with cancer someday," Shirley told Brewster, "but I guess with all things considered, I have a high probability of coming out from this situation in pretty good shape."

"Why on earth would you think you would be at risk for coming down with cancer one day?" Brewster asked.

"I'm originally from Las Vegas, Nevada, but I moved to New Mexico after I graduated from nursing school," the patient replied. "You probably don't know anything about what I am going to tell you, but I was only ten years old when my classmates and I were privileged to witness the atomic bomb blast named test-shot Harry. It was part of the Upshot Butthole test series at the Nevada proving grounds back in 1953."

As Brewster was an idiot savant, he knew a lot of things about a lot of things. Excitedly, he got up from his chair in the patient's room and said, "Oh my God! I need to correct you, because the name of the test series was Upshot Knothole, not Butthole, as you said. It was a thirty-two-kiloton bomb that had the code name Harry, and it was the ninth atmospheric atomic blast in the Upshot Knothole test series."

"I'm stunned," the patient said with a slack jaw.

"It was an extraordinarily efficient pure fission bomb designed at the National Laboratory," Brewster said. "The bomb was exploded on top of a three-hundred-foot tower on May 19, 1953, at Yucca Flats, test site number three."

"How in the world would you know such a thing?" Nurse Bellows asked.

"Purely by chance, I assure you," Brewster said. "I actually did a report on the subject matter back when I was at Dick Dowling University. I took a course called Film Appreciation in college, and I remember learning that Howard Hughes filmed a movie called The Conquerors at St. George, Utah, soon after the test blast occurred. Half of the motion picture film crew eventually contracted cancer, and most of them eventually died from it."

"Yes!" the patient said. "The bomb explosion released millions of curies of radioactive isotope fallout. Sadly, St. George, which was downwind from the atomic blast, got shit upon. Big-time. The people who were exposed to that deadly radiation are now known as the 'down-winders.' Sadly, a lot of people in the community are contracting cancer and dying because of that particular test shot."

"That's why the test explosion is now remembered as the Dirty Harry blast," Brewster said. "I can't believe you were there."

The woman jumped out of her hospital bed and gave Brewster a big hug. "Let me tell you more. My classmates and I were put on school buses and taken out to Mercury, Nevada. We got to sit in lawn chairs and wear heavy goggles when the bomb went off. I remember that officials from the Atomic Energy Commission rubbed zinc oxide on our faces to protect us from the atomic blast. In retrospect, I guess the zinc oxide facial cream was not a particularly good deterrent against trillions of electron volts of gamma radiation—or radioactive isotopes, for that matter. We couldn't have been more than a few miles away from the explosion when we saw it. I must admit it was a real hoot! If I was a man, I would have given up both of my testicles to have watched that event."

"Been there, done that, and got the T-shirt for it on my way out the door," Brewster said.

"I'm glad you understand," the patient said.

"I'm not sure if this will be of much help to you," Brewster said, "but I'd be willing to write a letter on your behalf suggesting that your thyroid cancer is a direct consequence of the above-ground atmospheric atomic bomb testing undertaken by the federal government back in the 1950s. Take the letter to a lawyer, and see if there is some way you can receive some type of compensation from Uncle Sam for the troubles you are now going through."

"Mr. Brewster, you are a gem of a human being," the patient said. "Would you mind very much if I let the VA hospital system know you would be willing to be an advocate for the atomic soldiers who acquired illnesses because of our country's development of atomic weapons?"

At the risk of poking a tempestuous old bastard named Uncle Sam in the eye with sharp stick, Brewster replied in the affirmative.

———✦———

Brewster had never gone snow skiing before, and he was going to make it a point to try it at least once while he was on his rotation in Santa Fe. Brewster drove up into the Sangre de Cristo Mountains, to the ski-lift area, to try his hand at some ski lessons. As it would turn out, he was not good at that sport, much less any other, for that matter. Exhausted and with cramps in his lower extremities, Brewster decided to take a break and have some lunch in the lodge. He ordered a bowl of chili but was disappointed to find out that it was just standard Tex-Mex brown chili, not a bowl of New Mexico's famous red or green style, which he incidentally found to be a far superior product.

"I was hoping for New Mexico–style chili. I can always get Tex-Mex style back in Houston, where I'm from," Brewster said to the young woman working behind the counter.

A New Mexican standing behind Brewster in the checkout line overheard what Brewster said and, for some reason, felt compelled to utter a hostile editorial comment. "You should go back to Houston. If God had ever wanted you bastards from Texas to ski, he would have made your bullshit white."

The extra dosages of testosterone Brewster had been receiving against medical advice probably directly contributed to the medical student's inflammatory response. "Oh yeah? If God had ever wanted you bastards from New Mexico to ski, he would have given you money!"

With that direct reference to the perpetually low economic status of the state of New Mexico, the stranger backed down.

———✦———

"It's good to hear from you, Stella!" Brewster said.

"Come home, lover boy," Stella pleaded. "I haven't been feeling well lately."

"What's wrong?" Brewster asked as he pulled on the telephone cord.

"I'm feeling short of breath from time to time, and I'm having indigestion in my chest, even when I'm not eating anything."

"Pop some antacid tablets," Brewster suggested. "If you're still having problems when I get home at the beginning of February, we'll make sure you get a checkup over at the outpatient internal medicine clinic."

"I hope you're right," Stella said.

"I am," Brewster said with confidence.

Distracted by recent news coming out about Mumbo Jamar Apoo, Brewster was more than eager to conclude his telephone conversation with Stella. Whenever he heard any news about Apoo, Brewster became agitated with hatred. Whenever Brewster became agitated with hatred, he felt, well–really good.

"Why don't you turn in early tonight and get some rest?" Brewster suggested. "For now, I'm going to turn on the boob tube to find out what's going on in the world."

Brewster flipped on the evening news in his apartment to see political activist Shiva Jaclyn Grant standing in front of a row of microphones at a podium. She proceeded to proclaim laudatory praise over a freedom fighter and a true champion of the black race. The object of her admiration was none other than Mumbo Jamar Apoo. He was "down with the struggle," she said, as he was a man fighting against social injustice. Yes, he might have accidentally shot and killed a Houston police officer, but Apoo had just been defending himself. After all, it must have been just another example of a white-devil slave master trying to keep the black man down.

As Grant continued to spew her race-baiting tripe, well-paid agitators in the crowd began a series of hostile chants promoting anarchy: "Pigs in a blanket! Fry 'em like bacon! Give us Apoo! Put Apoo on us! Give us Apoo! Put Apoo on us!"

It was all disgusting. Things were just beginning to heat up, when the radical activist reached underneath the podium, found a bullhorn, and added gasoline to an already raging inferno.

"What do we want?"

"Dead cops!" the crowd answered.

"When do we want it?" Shiva shouted.

"Now!" the crowd answered in unison.

Nice. Brewster and his colleagues back in Houston had no idea how bad things were about to get. The political bowel movement to liberate Apoo had already stretched across the pond to Europe. Brewster was shocked to learn that a seaside fishing village named Le Con in southern France, which perpetually emitted a malodorous stench reminiscent of rotting mackerel, apparently saw fit to go as far as to name one of their city's beloved boulevards after Mumbo Jamar Apoo.

As it turned out, the boulevard's name had too many letters to fit on a standard street sign, so the wretched city officials decided to simply name the road Apoo. The abbreviated name that the despicable frogs chose for their precious boulevard appeared to be a much more fitting description of not only a street moniker but also the entire reprehensible community.

⸺⸻⸺

It was late in the month of January. Back in Houston, Stella Link had just finished feeding her cat, Checkers, and she was looking forward to having her fiancé return home from his externship in New Mexico at the end of the month. Earlier during the day, she'd felt a few transient episodes of self-limited chest pain, but after taking a few chewable antacid tablets, she hadn't thought much more about the fleeting sensations. When Stella suddenly experienced a severe pain in the middle of her chest, she intuitively knew that something was dreadfully wrong.

Stella became terrified because she thought she was dying. Sadly, she was right. Acutely short of breath, she felt as if a fat lady wearing a horned Viking hat was sitting on the middle of her chest.

The frightened woman began to feel light-headed as she tried to make her way toward the telephone in the kitchen. She never found her way there. Stella stumbled, collapsed, and died right there on the kitchen floor. Just like that, her life was over.

The premonition she had shared with her fiancé over the Christmas holiday had proven to be true but, obviously, for a different reason. It appeared her metabolic syndrome manifested by obesity, untreated hypertension, and unmanaged adult-onset type II diabetes with hypercholesterolemia was directly responsible for her sudden death event.

Another unrecognized complication was the fact that Stella unfortunately was afflicted with a hypercoaguable state as a consequence of a previously occult circulating lupus procoagulant protein. In layman's terms, Stella had blood that was technically stickier than normal.

She was a walking blood clot just waiting to happen. Sadly, it would be several days before anybody would discover that Stella had died alone at home. If the truth be told, everybody died alone. Her cat, Checkers, had to sustain himself by drinking from the toilet and nibbling upon the decaying flesh of his beloved dead master.

—⟨⟨⟨∘⟩⟩⟩—

On his crossover rotation at the VA annex during a dark and cold night, Brewster encountered two heavily bearded, toothless bushwhackers who suddenly appeared at the life-support room.

They both seemed to be agitated. Wearing heavy work boots and coveralls without shirts, the two ridge runners danced about while proclaiming a calamity was at hand.

"Come help! Paw-Paw—he sick! Come help! Come help quick!"

The attending at the life-support room instructed Brewster to follow the two men out into the parking lot to see what could possibly be the matter with Paw-Paw. When Brewster looked into the back of their truck, he witnessed an old, frail man lying in the bed of the pickup with a horse blanket thrown over him. The elderly bearded man was dressed in the exact same attire as the two men who were presumably his sons.

With his legs crossed and his arms extended out from his torso at ninety degrees, it seemed as if the elderly man was a Thracian gladiator who had just been subjected to the most extreme form of punishment ever witnessed along the Apian Way. Reportedly utilized by the ancient Romans to suppress the Spartacus rebellion circa 73 BC, crucifixion was indeed a terrifying form of punishment.

By the obvious advanced age of the unresponsive individual, Brewster readily assumed Paw-Paw probably had been a firsthand eyewitness to the ancient historical events that had occurred during the Roman Empire. As the old man appeared to be totally unresponsive, Brewster initially thought Paw-Paw had already croaked en route to the hospital.

"What in hell is going on here?" Brewster demanded.

"Paw-Paw—he got the COPD. Got it bad," one of the two hillbillies said. "He up and said, 'Boys, my lungs is a-goin' bad again. Ah cain't be a-breathin' no mo'! You best get me to the VA!' We used to live here in New Mexico, and this is where we always took Paw-Paw when he got the COPD flare-ups and his lungs got all poned up with snot and shit. Well, we up and threw him in the back of the truck, and then my brother up and drove all nonstop-like just to get us here."

Brewster asked, "Well, where in hell did you people come from?"

One of the hillbillies replied, "San Bernardino."

Brewster scratched his head momentarily to collect his thoughts. Brewster believed he knew the various townships of New Mexico fairly well, but he hadn't heard of San Bernardino.

"Is that somewhere near Las Cruces?" Brewster asked.

One of the bushwhackers responded, "No, dumbass! San Bernardino, California!"

Brewster was momentarily stunned before he was able to compose himself to respond. "San Bernardino, California? Are you kidding me? You passed VA facilities in San Bernardino, Phoenix, Tucson, El Paso, and Albuquerque just to get here. You idiots have driven hundreds of miles out of your way! Please answer me this: Do you not realize that there is more than one VA hospital located in the United States?"

The two ridge runners looked at each other in astonishment, looked back to Brewster, and then looked back at each other yet again before they said in unison, "Go on!"

Just then, Paw-Paw cut loose with an ear shattering fart and let out a big sigh. The unexpected expulsion of noxious fumes suggested the old coot was still very much alive. Brewster ran back into the life-support room to grab a wheeled gurney and a couple of other medical personnel to help transport the elderly man into the medical facility for evaluation.

"Does your father have an advanced directive?" Brewster asked. His question was met with blank stares. "Do you know what his wishes would be if he inadvertently suffers a cardiopulmonary arrest right now while he's under our care here at this VA annex?" Brewster said, trying a second time.

"Talk like you was a red-blooded, patriotic Murakin and not one of them damned furiners comin' on over yar to be a stealin' our jobs!" one of the bushwhackers demanded.

"Let me try this again," Brewster said. "Do you think Paw-Paw would wish for a do-not-resuscitate code status, or would he want us to try to revive him if a medical emergency were to occur in which his heart and lungs quit working?"

"He wouldn't want none of that DNR business," the patient's elder son answered. "He got asked that question all the time when Paw-Paw used to come to this hospital. If his heart and lungs quit working, we expect you to bring him back to life. Do you hear me?"

That was indeed a tall order.

Clinically, the patient was profoundly hypothermic, and his heart rate was down to about twenty-eight beats per minute. The old man's blood pressure was not measurable when he first arrived. As it turned out, the patient had an exacerbation of chronic obstructive pulmonary disease, which had led to acute pneumonia and subsequent bacterial sepsis.

His two sons had unwittingly kept their father alive by putting the old codger in what was essentially a refrigerated ice box in the back of the pickup truck. When the two hillbillies ferried their father several hundred miles through the frigid night air, Paw-Paw's body temperature had cooled down to a point where the invasive microbes were left in a near suspended state of animation.

Their act of supreme stupidity had inadvertently slowed bacterial propagation and sepsis until the old man was finally able to get admitted to the hospital for proper medical management!

Amazingly, the patient would fully recover, leave the hospital, and eventually head back to the hill country outside of San Bernardino, California. It appeared God looked out for hillbillies, ridge runners, bushwhackers, and other small and dimwitted creatures that were apparently unable to fend for themselves.

—◦—

Brewster tried to call Stella on several occasions to tell her about the bizarre story concerning the two bushwhackers and their near-frozen father in the back of the pickup truck. For some reason, she wasn't answering the telephone. Where could Stella be? Perhaps, Brewster erroneously thought, she had gone back up to Waco to visit her parents for a few days. If Stella didn't pick up the phone the next time Brewster tried to place a call, he would try to call her parents at their ranch house in Waco. For now, though, Brewster was compelled to turn on the television to see if there was any more news about his nemesis, Mumbo Jamar Apoo.

—◦◦◦—

Horton became inebriated long before he took a stroll south of the railroad district. When he decided to lean back against an adjacent fence to sleep it off, he immediately fell unconscious from acute alcohol intoxication. Therefore, Horton was sadly unaware of what was going on when two cruel hooligans managed to drag his body across the railroad tracks. They left Horton there to suffer the unspeakable fate that awaited him.

When a freight train came rolling through, Horton lost both of his lower extremities, right below the knees. A passerby was quick to respond, and he was able to use the bolo tie he was wearing and a bungee cord from the trunk of his car to stem the flow of blood. The patient was brought by private vehicle to the life-support unit at the VA, but that type of injury far exceeded the limited capabilities of the annex.

While Brewster struggled to apply proper tourniquets to the unfortunate man's lower extremities, the attending called for an ambulance to transport the patient to the St. Francis University Medical Center.

Before the transport ambulance arrived, the attending physician received an emergency phone call. Upon answering the call, the attending looked over to Brewster in stunned silence. The physician had to somehow muster up enough courage to tell Brewster that the phone call was actually for the medical student and not for the attending.

"Brew, you have an emergency phone call," the attending said. "You have to take it right now."

"I'm almost done here," Brewster replied. "I'll be over there in a minute as soon as I'm sure that this guy has been stabilized."

"Take the call now, damn it!" the attending demanded. "I'll finish up with these tourniquets."

When Brewster finally answered the phone, he immediately recognized the voice of his old friend Ben Fielder.

"Ben, you old son of a gun, how in hell are you? Qué pasa, mi amigo?"

Momentarily, all of the color drained from Brewster's face as he became acutely blind in his left eye. After he had vomited, he developed dry heaves and began to retch uncontrollably until the attending physician took Brewster aside and administered a dose of parenteral prochlorperazine.

After the antiemetic medication took effect, Brewster gathered his composure and drove back to his apartment. After gathering his few belongings, including his pet skunk, he began the arduous drive back to Texas.

Instead of Houston, Brewster would be heading directly to Waco. After all, that was where his late fiancée would be interred. This time, his trip home to the Lone Star State would be a nonstop, sleepless journey.

Over the course of hundreds of miles, while driving the old Dodge Dart eastward on Interstate 40, Brewster would alternately pray and then curse at God in heaven. He often did both within the context of the same sentence.

It was unlikely God was offended, as after all, it wasn't as if He hadn't heard it all before. He heard it on a daily basis all over the world and had from the first time He granted Homo sapiens the gift of a soul and free will.

—⦅⦆—

Stella's funeral was well attended. As Brewster gave hugs to the members of the Link family, Stella's mother tried to give the engagement ring back to the medical student. Without a word, Brewster put the ring into the palm of Stella's mother and slowly folded her fingers across the token. He was incapable of speaking, but Brewster felt that Stella's ring belonged with her parents, as they had lost their only daughter. After all, Brewster was a young man, and surely he would learn to love again, would he not? Sadly, he would not.

After everybody else had left the grave-side service, Brewster was stunned when Ben Fielder and Missy Brownwood proceeded to hurl a barrage of devastating insults in his direction.

"You're one selfish son of a bitch," Missy said. "You didn't deserve to have a woman like Stella in your life. Last year, Stella stopped all of her high-blood-pressure, diabetes, and cholesterol medicines because of you. She lost forty pounds, but after you criticized her, she regained all of the weight she had previously lost."

"Stella had high blood pressure and diabetes?" Brewster asked. "I didn't know!"

"You're a moron," Missy said. "You should have been able to figure that out. She said you would only love her if she was fat. Ben wanted to tell you all about it, but he and I both kept our lips zipped because Stella made us keep it a secret. Well, Mr. Brewster, you disgust me."

Ben Fielder said nothing, but he nonetheless looked upon Brewster with contempt.

Brewster was saddled with a guilt he would carry for the rest of his life. He had no idea Stella battled such serious medical problems, but in retrospect, how could he not have known?

There was only one thing to do: stay buried even deeper in his work to try to prevent any emotions except for anger and hatred from penetrating his immortal soul, which was already on the threshold of eternal damnation.

11

TELOMERES AND ONCOGENES

Political oncological degradation reflects the sad decline of a nation, state, or city as a consequence of uncontrolled, pervasive societal malignancies just as the decline of the human body might happen as a consequence of uncontrolled, pervasive biological malignances. One process serves as a direct metaphor for the other.

Malignant disease is a voracious, hungry, angry, dreaded crab beast with an insatiable appetite. That's why it's called cancer. Obvious to anybody misfortunate enough to be afflicted with an invasive neoplastic process in its advanced stages, cancer does everything it possibly can to try to kill the host organism.

Unfortunately, cancer has many weapons at its disposal. It will eat away at a patient's internal organs. It can and will attack a patient's bones, brain, lungs, pancreas, hepatobiliary system, large bowels, small bowels, muscles, skin, nervous system, esophagus, stomach, kidneys, urinary tract, bladder, and male or female plumbing. Direct cancer cell invasion into the myometrium of the heart can also occur on rare occasions.

Cancer will try to starve a patient to death with tumor-induced cachexia. It's not uncommon for cancer patients to appear no bigger around than the circumference of a pencil at the time they take their last breath. That's a consequence of inflammatory cytokines invoked by the malignant process. Cancer will also predispose unfortunate patients to a hypercoagulable state wherein the individuals will be at a high risk of dying from complications of blood clots and pulmonary emboli. This unpleasant detail about the relationship between cancer and coagulation was recognized as far back as the mid-1800s.

Cancer will do everything it can to overwhelm the immune system. First, there's a breakdown in immune surveillance that initially allows cancer cells to move into nice neighborhoods to set up their nefarious crack houses and chop shops. These unhealthy and illegal activities will bring down the value of the local real estate market of the occupied internal organ. Gentrification of the major organ systems will occur soon after. Unfortunately, when cancer cells move into a new neighborhood, the normal organ tissues already residing at that particular address are unable to flee to the suburbs.

The entire neighborhood becomes a haven for hoodlum cancer cells looking to knock over benign visceral parenchymal cells to misappropriate nutritional sustenance. The cancer cells will invariably start stealing hubcaps and car radios and, finally, plunder residential establishments at the next level of local or regional organ invasion.

Malignant graffiti will suddenly appear, crudely spray-painted onto endothelial and lymphatic vascular walls. Cancer cells, once recognized underneath a microscope by immunofluorescent staining or other tumor-marker studies employed by the pathology service, are never to be trifled with.

Cancer cells are not members of some JV team. While disastrous liberal ideations have destroyed any chance of even a modestly favorable future legacy, the previous effete administrative containment and degradation policies employed by homeopaths in the recent past are no longer recognized as viable planks in a political oncology platform that has already miserably failed time and time again.

Conversely, a full-frontal assault and subsequent annihilation of the enemy may achieve a complete remission that might be tantamount to long-term survivability and perhaps even an eventual cure. That could only be accomplished when the tumor burden is still rather small and manageable by the host.

The hoodlum cancer cells can be readily seen loitering about in either large or small gangs, wearing their oversize, baggie genes, which are typically hanging halfway down their ass cracks. When cancer cells are not engaged in locally invasive or metastatic activities, one may readily find them huffing paint or smoking a crack pipe down at the local lymph node parlor.

Cancer cells are poorly educated, with dismal reading and writing skills. They generally come from broken homes without the benefit of a bona fide father figure on the premise. If only there is a responsible, fully functional, normal immune-surveillance system that has not been imprisoned by often overzealous programmed-cell-death-ligand checkpoints, then the neighborhood in question might have a chance.

If the NK subset of the T cells in question actually have decent, high-paying jobs while working for an immune system unencumbered by a corporate tax system that has historically been one of the highest in the industrialized world, all the while facing neck-breaking, ineffectual, and anticapitalistic host regulations, then malignant dedifferentiation and proliferation might not occur in the first place.

If there's an on-site authoritarian figure who can modulate the propensity of the cancer cells to have mitotic cellular divisions out of wedlock, then perhaps the miserable, miscreant juvenile-delinquent cancer cells can be directed away from a life of crime.

A more normalized number of cellular divisions with functional and finite telomeres are clearly necessary in such a dysfunctional cellular community. If that were to occur, autoprogrammable cell death would certainly improve the general welfare of the neighborhood. Perhaps the chain of poverty caused by the well-intentioned but terminally flawed liberal policies of the Great Malignant Society could finally be broken once and for all.

For the time being, the host organism continues to turn a blind eye toward the fundamental issues of cancer, including the oncogenes responsible for malignant cell immortality and the associated utter disregard that cancer cells have for basement membrane integrity. Until the body is willing to set aside that self-destructive, politically correct, liberal immune tolerance for miscreant behavior, cancer will continue to run amok.

Maybe someday cancer cells will stop and look in the mirror. They need to stop blaming institutionalized immuno-oncological tolerance as a cause for their own societal woes. After all, one in three humans is destined to get a malignant process during the course of his or her life. Cancer cells need to quit blaming the man for the issues of opioid intolerance that result in great suffering before a patient dies. The self-inflicted high unemployment rate, in conjunction with a propensity to kill the host organism, is at the root of this misery. President Nixon launched the War on Cancer in 1970. That was ages ago.

When cancer cells go out into the lymphatic and vascular channels and carry placards that say, "Cancer Cells Matter," then their own hypocritical behavior is clearly on display for everyone to see. If cancer cells really matter to other cancer cells, why do they kill each other? They often outstrip their own blood supply, which invariably results in the central autonecrosis of a tumor mass.

The host organism is sick and tired of cancer cells playing the metastases card over and over again. Shut up, stay in school, get a job, don't become dedifferentiated, and recognize the basement membranes that separate you from other well-established and properly functioning organ systems. And for the love of Pete, keep your damn fly zipped up, and quit undergoing cellular mitoses out of wedlock!

Unfortunately, cancer cells are not generally considered to be gainfully employable by the host body at large. Cancer cells collect welfare from the host by secreting angiogenic factors that force the body to bring blood vessels into the growing malignant aggregation just to feed it.

The conservative body does just this, but it's certainly not of its own volition. Once cancer cells take over a neighborhood, a liberal cancer coalition is invariably formed that becomes politically active. More and more of the body's resources, in the form of nutritional supplementation, are diverted to support the cancer cells on welfare. The normal cells of the body, simply trying to get by on an honest day's salary, find they're subjected to backbreaking taxes, through which essential caloric support is inexplicably shunted away from their own previously normally functioning cellular neighborhoods.

The second assault on the immune system occurs by the cancer community's San Francisco–style open-border sanctuary-city status. Once cancer cells set up shop in a neighborhood, they readily allow any illegal alien bacteria (often referred to as undocumented migrants) to invade the host and further parasitize an already strained health-care system.

That happens irrespective of whether any of the illegal-alien bacteria have been guilty of any violent crimes upon other organ systems in the past, including such vibrant and vital neighborhoods as the urinary tract, the lungs, the skin, or any other minor or major host site, for that matter.

That's indeed the case irrespective of whether or not the illegal-alien microbes have previously been involved in heinous crimes against normal, peace-loving cellular citizens of various organs. Such nefarious activities include urosepsis, pneumonia, abscess formations, and cellulitis.

As most of the illegal aliens are third-world prokaryotic organisms more than willing to work for sub-minimum-wage standards, the general economy of the body starts to fail as the temperature starts to rise. Many of the illegal-alien bacteria invade via the true shit-hole parts of the host, such as the intraluminal recesses of the rectum or colon, as is the case for Gram-negative microbial species.

At times, the prokaryotic organisms become radicalized. They have no intention of being integrated into a benign, noninvasive Western-style flora willing to coexist in the same geographical space already occupied by the organ systems of the host body.

The radicalized bacteria have one operative rule and one rule only: submit, convert, or die. The host has no other option, as it can't make peace with these infidels trying to occupy the same area already occupied by more culturally and spiritually advanced eukaryotic cells.

It's lunacy to say that one cell line is equivalent to another cell line. Liberal thinking like that is going to get the host killed. It's a cultural and biological fight to the death. If the prokaryotic organisms can infiltrate their way across the porous southern borders and make their way into the bloodstream, they will cause sepsis, and then there will be a complete collapse of the host. Bacteria will strap on suicide-bomb vests and indiscriminately lyse as many other normal cells as they possibly can.

Infection is also a consequence of a frontal assault on the immune system directly caused by the cancer treatment itself. At the beginning of the twenty-first century, oncologists are only on the threshold of being able to master targeted treatment. Much of the time, warfare against the dreaded crab beast relies on unsophisticated carpet bombing. Cancer specialists often wonder if the methodologies employed by medical oncology are not all that different from the weaponry utilized during the Vietnam War. After all, America had to drop napalm on communist-occupied villages and burn them to the ground in order to free them.

Yes, perhaps Victor Charles can be crushed by this particularly crude methodology, but a lot of innocent organ systems are often damaged through this crude form of warfare. As things stand, it's unlikely the medical oncology community will ever be able to truly win over the hearts and minds of the normal, peaceful, benign cells of the human body until targeted cancer treatment improves.

Political oncology, in a nutshell, is simply a combination of Oncology 101 and Conservatism 101. Class dismissed.

—◦◦◦◦◦—

Past was prologue but not when it came to the matters of the personal life of J. D. Brewster. Although Brewster was a historian, he had somehow largely compartmentalized his own life as if it had never even happened.

"Don't look into the rearview mirror," Brewster said aloud as he inadvertently looked into the rearview mirror of the old Dart while driving from Waco back to Houston. After all, nothing was there. Determined to travel in a straight line, Brewster kept his eyes on the horizon. The medical student realized that the easiest way to deal with a personal tragedy was to simply not deal with a personal tragedy.

Stella was gone. Brewster tried to convince himself that it didn't matter. He would press on and simply get to the finish line of life as fast as possible. Unfortunately, there was a major technical flaw within the boundaries of such an operational blueprint.

"Time to get on with it," Brewster said as he purposefully took down the calendar from the wall in his apartment kitchen. While he systematically pulled off each prior month of the calendar and then jammed each one symbolically into a wastepaper basket, Brewster was essentially isolating the existential matters of life, death, and love within the confines of the penitentiary of his own mind.

There was only one thing he did not isolate: his feelings of hatred.

Sadly for Brewster, his bottled-up memories would eventually come back to haunt him, and they would do so with a vengeance.

—⫷⫸—

At the beginning of February, Brewster was about to spend a month working with the crab pickers. Crab picker was a derisive slang term used to describe a medical oncologist. The medical student would soon meet his new attending physician on the oncology service, Dr. Turban Dykes, and the hematology and oncology fellow, Preston Falls. The rotation was going to be split between both the inpatient and outpatient setting. It would be a solo gig for Brewster, as no other student was going to be doing the elective rotation with him in February 1982. Brewster felt he had to get back to work as soon as possible. He couldn't afford to allow any intrusive memories to creep into his psyche and cause any perceptible vibrations on the tight rope on which he was delicately perched.

During the first week of the rotation, Dr. Falls instructed Brewster to start an initial workup on a patient who had arrived at the clinic. "Brewster, I understand that you have a reputation for being able to deal with crazy people. The next patient you're going to see is a young woman with a diagnosis of breast cancer. She was seen here two years ago when she was first diagnosed, but she refused conventional treatment at that time. She is allegedly looking for somebody she can talk to about fine-tuning her chakra nodes for a deeper penetration of the prana."

"Come again?"

"I don't know what in hell that could possibly mean," Preston said, "but I do know it's right up your alley."

"Tell me, Dr. Falls," Brewster asked. "Are those coital positions found in the Kama Sutra?"

"Get in there, dumbass, and do your job," the fellow said as he became annoyed.

Brewster protested, as he felt he did not have the energy to see any crazy people at that time. "Now, wait a minute. I'm not going in there if this person wants me to sprinkle fairy dust upon her or perhaps administer nutmeg-flavored walnut-shell enemas."

"Get in there, dumbass, and do your job," the fellow said again.

Brewster entered the exam room and introduced himself. "I see now that you're only twenty-six years old, and you were originally diagnosed with cancer involving the upper outer quadrant of your right breast almost two years ago. That's astounding! I'm sorry, but it looks like you were dealt some very bad cards."

"It must be karma," the woman replied. "Perhaps I was something very evil in one of my past lives. Perhaps I was a Nazi, a Tartar, or perhaps even a Mongol. May Shiva forbid, but perhaps I was even a liberal Democrat!"

"Now, let's not go overboard." Brewster tried to calm the woman. "I'm sure you were never that bad in any of your former lives. What have you been doing to try to manage your underlying cancer since, according to the records, you refused conventional treatment?"

"Now, don't start acting like my decision was a bad thing," the patient said. "If you are going to be judgmental like the other doctors and medical students I've met at this institution of Western medicine, then I'm going to walk right out this door. My sister, who was five years older than me, died from breast cancer before she was even thirty years old. She went through surgery, chemotherapy, and radiation therapy, and frankly, nothing worked for her. It was a classic slashing, poisoning, and burn of the rain forest. I refuse to accept that recommended course of action, come hell or high water."

"So it would seem."

"Besides," the young patient said, "I believe you people may already have a cure for my type of cancer. You guys are just keeping it a secret."

Brewster became irate at the patient's idiotic supposition.

"Listen, lady, if you actually believe that, I need to tell you a story. My own uncle died from gastric cancer about fifteen years ago, when I was just a boy."

"What's that supposed to prove? That just means you're able to keep a secret."

"If you think I or anybody else knows a secret cure for cancer," Brewster said, "I'd like to show you an urn that contains the ashes of my former mentor, Dr. Hank Holcombe. He was a research scientist, and I watched him die a horrible death from advanced cancer. If a secret universal cure for cancer is currently in existence, we would've certainly opened up a bottle of the stuff and then administered all of it to Dr. Holcombe before he cashed in his chips. So I'm telling you right now, you can take that conspiracy theory line of bullshit and shove it!"

The patient was stunned by Brewster's response. "Wow, do you talk to all of your patients like that?"

"Every day of the week and twice on Sunday," Brewster answered harshly.

"I think that's very hot!" the patient said. "That's such a turn-on. I'll let you talk dirty to me anytime. Now that I've cured myself of my own cancer, I want you to have your way with me!"

Brewster put up both of his hands in a defensive motion and said, "Let's stay focused on the problem at hand, okay? Please tell me what you're talking about."

"I have a shaman, and he has given me a powerful mantra," the patient replied.

"Well, what is it?" Brewster asked.

"If I tell you, it'll lose its power. I have to keep it a secret. Let me ask you: Are you open-minded?" the patient asked. "If you're willing to accept that your Western medicine is driven purely by capitalism, I will show you the benefits that may occur when you rapidly apply vibrations to excite your chakra to a whole new plane of awareness."

In light of the patient's previous overt sexual advances, Brewster momentarily thought that the chakra was a local or regional colloquial term for the clitoris. However, as with most things, Brewster was wrong about that supposition, also.

The patient reported that her secret mantra, in conjunction with a natural (yet magical) concoction of eleven herbs and spices, had effectively driven the tumor out of her body. The magical potion would soon be known throughout the Gulf Coast College of Medicine, and it would be derisively referred to as the Kentucky Fried Chicken Cancer Treatment Protocol.

Brewster was incredulous. "Frankly, I can't believe something like that would be possible."

Defiantly, the woman opened up her purse, pulled out a ziplock bag, and set it on the counter. "Well, here's the proof," she said. "My father used to play poker, and whenever he had a good hand, he would lay his cards out on the table and exclaim, 'Read 'em and weep!' That's what I now say to you."

Brewster picked up the zip-lock bag and examined it. It was cold to the touch because it had most likely come out of the refrigerator in the kitchen of the patient's apartment. The material was comprised of bloody, fibro-fatty tissue that looked much like the skin one would pull off of a chicken from the supermarket before throwing it into a deep fryer.

At first, Brewster had no idea what kind of tissue he was examining, although it was a hefty amount of material that probably weighed well over a pound. As he manipulated the material through the plastic bag, he suddenly recognized a shocking anatomical structure: a nipple-areolar complex!

The patient had brought Brewster her own necrotic right breast, which had simply fallen off of her body. Brewster set the ziplock bag down on the counter in the examination room and said, "Excuse me, but I am going to bring in the nurse now so we can take a look at your chest wall. I am going to give you this disposable paper gown, and I would like you to remove your top and drape this over yourself. I'll be back momentarily."

After the vision returned to Brewster's left eye and he had freshened up a bit in the men's room, he returned to the patient's examination stall and brought along an assistant nurse to chaperone him while he performed a thorough examination.

"Okay, let's take a look at what's going on here."

As Brewster peeled down the patient's paper examination gown, the nurse who was present was so stunned that she actually had to sit down on the examination stool and turn her head away from what she had seen.

"As you can see," the patient said cheerfully, "my cancer is all gone! It happened this past Tuesday. I was in the kitchen, getting a glass of orange juice, when my breast just fell off my body and landed right upon the kitchen floor. Splat! I scraped it off the linoleum with a spatula, and then I put it into this zip-lock bag so I could show it to you doctors. I had to be quick, I tell you, because Mr. Whiskers almost snagged it, and I have no doubt he would have surely eaten it!"

The patient's right breast had undergone an auto-mastectomy and simply fallen off of her body. As the cancer had grown out in a radial fashion, it had outstripped its central blood supply, causing necrosis of what was remaining of the right breast.

After a polite curtsy to the host, the diseased and rotting malignant breast tissue had sadly bid a fare-thee-well and then permanently parted company from the rest of the body. The area the right breast had previously occupied was now a large, open wound the size of a coffee saucer that involved the anterior chest wall. It was a deep, malignant crater that went all the way down to the rib cage. Her rib bones and intercostal muscles were exposed to the atmosphere.

The open wound was almost a perfect circle, and the outer rim of the wound was a tender, centimeter-thick red rim of fire-breathing, viable cancer. The patient had angry, malignant satellite nodules peppered on her anterior chest wall around the large wound and multiple fixed, hard, painful lymph nodes the size of Ping-Pong balls in her right axillary region.

Although the patient had painful edema involving her right upper extremity, she nonetheless proudly proclaimed, "I'm cured! I did this to myself."

"I'm sorry," Brewster said. "It would appear to me that you're dying. You did this to yourself."

Convinced Brewster was merely a tool for the vast right-wing pharmacological, medical, and industrial complex, she didn't believe a word the medical student had said. She chose to believe that Brewster was lying to her for purposes of monetary gain, although nothing could have been further from the truth.

Brewster went out to find the fellow, Dr. Falls, to confirm the patient's status. Dr. Falls convinced the patient to undergo a staging CT scan of the chest, abdomen, and pelvis, and he also ordered a bone scan. In addition, he cajoled the unfortunate and misguided individual into undergoing a three-millimeter punch biopsy of the angry red rim of tissue that surrounded the hole in her anterior chest wall. As Brewster was well versed in that minor procedure, the fellow afforded the medical student the opportunity to get the job done.

The young woman returned to the outpatient oncology clinic a few days later to discuss the results of her staging workup. As it turned out, the tumor was hormone-receptor negative, and it was indeed an adenocarcinoma that appeared to be consistent with a poorly differentiated breast cancer primary.

The skin-punch biopsy Brewster had performed of the patient's anterior chest wall confirmed the tissue diagnosis. The CT scan revealed multiple pulmonary, liver, and bone metastases. Brewster had been correct after all: the patient was indeed dying. Despite those facts, the patient continued to refuse to consider conventional chemotherapy, even for palliative purposes.

On her follow-up visit, the patient informed Brewster that she was simply going to have to find a new mantra and a quartz power crystal. That was the ticket. Sadly, the patient was dead before the summer of 1982.

In retrospect, the patient probably had familial BRCA 1 or BRCA 2 breast cancer. It would be decades before cancer specialists recognized those oncogenes. Although she was the first cancer patient Brewster had ever seen who had elected to be treated with a magical, natural concoction of eleven herbs and spices found in what he euphemistically referred to as the Kentucky Fried Chicken Cancer Treatment Protocol, she would not be the last patient of that type he encountered in the course of his long and strange career.

—⟨⟨⟨⟨ ⟩⟩⟩⟩—

What was the inciting event that made normal cells become bad actors and turn into cancer? A root cause might have been found among the oncogenes. As they were incorporated into the human genome, an oncogene might not necessarily in and of itself have been considered a pathological genetic happenstance. However, an oncogene might have the potential to incite a cellular malignant transformation if it became mutated or if there were replicative copies that occurred through what was known as gene amplification.

Normally, cellular entities were programmed to have a finite lifespan. If a mutation occurred at a genetic level, it was imperative for a cell to undergo active programmable cell death, which was done to protect the host organism from being attacked by bad actors. If an oncogene was switched into the on position, then it might be possible for a mutated cell to bypass programmable cell death and then proliferate through a malignant transformation.

Complex biological organisms were hardwired to follow a set of blueprints. Humans were meant to be born, live, and eventually die.

Frankly, the cycle of life was a beautiful thing to behold. That was just how things were meant to be.

The lifespan of a cellular entity was contingent on the number of replicative events that occurred during the lifespan of the particular cell in question. At the endcaps of chromosomes were a finite number of structures known as telomeres. With each cellular division, the telomeres would become shortened. Once a cell ran out of telomeres, it reached the end of its biological ability to reproduce itself, and that was when the cell in question would eventually succumb to senescence.

One fundamental difference between cancer cells and normal cellular entities was that the telomeres found in the aberrant chromosomes within cancer cells often replenished themselves indefinitely through the activity of abnormal telomerase enzymes. Barring other extrinsic forces, cancer cells might theoretically undergo cellular replication indefinitely.

If a human secularist was looking to achieve biological immortality, then he or she likely would have to contend with myriad malignant diseases eventually. No matter how hard humans tried, no one could live forever.

—◦◦◦—

Remission induction chemotherapy for the management of acute myelogenous leukemia had centered on what was known as the 7+3 protocol since the early 1980s. There was a main treatment exception for patients afflicted with a specific AFB subclass of AML known as the M3 variant. Courtesy of the sneaky Chicoms who would discover retinoid and arsenical therapeutics for that rare M3 subset of acute leukemia, the 7+3 protocol would otherwise remain the treatment foundation for most other subtypes of AML.

One other small exception would be icing-on-the-cake treatment discovered for patients who manifested the FLIP3 or

NPM1 cytogenetic quirks. The resurrection of Anti-CD33 agents and also newer fledging immunotherapies would be moot, as they would not be stumbled upon until the end of Brewster's career many years later.

Although there were a few variations of the theme, most hematology and oncology specialists were well versed with the use of that dual-drug protocol, which consisted of an anti-mammalian anthracycline antibiotic, such as daunorubicin or, alternatively, epirubicin, in conjunction with, for the most part, an antimetabolite known as cytosine arabinoside. The treatment worked, and for the most part, it worked well.

An effective fund of knowledge regarding cancer management was generally achieved through trial and error, and a definite error was made in the early 1980s, when there was controversy as to whether or not another newer anthracycline, doxorubicin, was superior to the older drug, daunorubicin.

Just because something was newer did not necessarily mean it was better. Unfortunately, the Gulf Coast Tumor Institute had to learn that fact the hard way when it embarked on what would turn out to be a disastrous randomized clinical trial, TROG-AML 80-07.

The study was designed to see if the drug doxorubicin, when utilized as a component of the 7+3 acute myelogenous leukemia protocol, would result in higher remission or survival statistics. Sadly, researchers eventually confirmed that the drug doxorubicin, when utilized in the setting of AML, was inferior to daunorubicin because it resulted in a higher death rate from treatment complications.

Because of those findings and similar confirmatory studies done at other research institutions at the time, the drug doxorubicin is no longer employed in the 7+3 leukemia protocol in modern times. As one might gather, in order for researchers to come to that conclusion, patients afflicted with acute myelogenous leukemia who were exposed to doxorubicin as part of their treatment plan were much more likely to suffer tragic injury or death along the way as a consequence of the therapy. One such patient was a young twenty-five-year-old woman from the Middle East named Raiza.

⟞⟋⟍⟞

When Raiza was diagnosed with acute myelogenous leukemia, her wealthy family flew her to Houston in order for her to be treated at the world-famous Texas Medical Center. Upon her arrival at the airport, the family made arrangements for their daughter to be transported to the Gulf Coast Tumor Institute by a medical helicopter. As there was a heliport landing pad on top of the Tumor Institute, her transfer to the inpatient setting would not be a particularly complex process.

The only political turmoil caused by the ordeal was the fact that the family insisted that a large canvas tarp be placed over the giant word Tumor, which was affixed to the side of the cancer center as part of the facility's signage. The large metallic letters stood more than two stories tall. When illuminated at night, the name of the cancer treatment facility could be easily seen more than a mile away from the Texas Medical Center. Oddly enough, the family did not want their daughter to know she was afflicted with a potentially lethal malignant process.

At first, the Gulf Coast Tumor Institute adamantly refused to participate in such a charade, but of course, with enough money, anything was possible. The family eventually got its way, and a giant brown canvas tarp was utilized to cloak the offending word, Tumor, emblazoned among the other letters that comprised the name of the facility on the side of the giant multistory edifice.

When it was time for the helicopter to land on top of the cancer center, the young woman hopefully would not have any idea what was going on or what exactly was wrong with her, for that matter. After the helicopter touched down on the roof of the cancer center, the young patient asked the pilot a pertinent question.

"While the helicopter was landing, I saw the big sign on the side of the building that said, 'Gulf Coast _____ Institute.' One of the words on the sign is covered up with a big brown sheet of canvas. What's the hidden word underneath the big sheet of tent canvas?"

"Madam, I am not authorized to talk to you about anything," the pilot responded.

Raiza was not stupid, and she was quickly able to put two and two together. Unfortunately, in her particular situation, as it would turn out, two and two was about to equal 7+3.

Upon her arrival to the floor, Dr. Dykes told both Preston Falls and J. D. Brewster that under no circumstances was the patient allowed to know she had cancer.

"I am not going to play this game with you," Preston said in anger to the attending physician. "The patient is of majority age. She's a human being, and she has the right to know what's going on with her. I'm going to march right into her hospital room and tell her that she has a diagnosis of acute leukemia!"

"Go ahead, Preston," Dykes said. "The minute you do that, you'll be suspended without pay. Am I coming in loud and clear?"

"Crystal," Preston replied.

"I know what kind of person you are," Dykes said as he turned to Brewster. "If you try to pull any of your patented bullshit shenanigans, I'll make sure you never graduate from this institution. Am I coming in loud and clear?"

"Crystal," Brewster replied.

"I want you to go down and do a history and physical on Raiza," Dykes said. "Make sure the following signs are posted on the patient's door: strict handwashing, no fresh fruits or vegetables, mask and gloves at all times prior to patient contact, and no fresh flowers."

Brewster was at a loss regarding the reason for a restriction of fresh fruits and vegetables and also fresh flowers.

"It'll reduce the risk for foodborne pathogens, and it also might decrease the risk for patient exposure to pseudomonas organisms and other bugs that could be lurking in a bouquet of flowers," Dr. Dykes said. "Hey, Brewster, I'm sorry I jumped on your ass a moment ago. Step forward. I want to ask you question"

"I refuse to play a damned game of pimp and pone with you," Brewster said.

"Doesn't matter one bit"—Dr. Dykes smirked—"because you're up to bat."

"You've got to be kidding me," Brewster said. "I'm too short for this shit."

"Don't worry," Dr. Dykes said with assurance. "I'm only going to pimp you with one question. If you get this right, you'll make honors on this rotation."

"We'll see about that," Brewster said as he shrugged. "Okay, throw me the pitch."

"Can you tell me the difference between Shea Stadium in New York City and New York's world-famous Sloan Kettering Cancer Center?" Dykes asked.

"Dr. Dykes," Brewster replied, "I have no idea how to answer that question."

The professor chuckled. "Well, son, at the Sloan, the mets always win!"

Brewster shook his head and broke out laughing. "That's a hoot and a holler! I must admit that was some sick shit, but that was really funny."

<hr>

After J. D. Brewster introduced himself to Raiza, the young woman had a request. "I need you to do me a great favor. I've just figured out that I have cancer. When I got off of the elevator, there was a big sign on the wall: Leukemia Unit."

"It looks like you have it all figured out," Brewster said.

"I know I'm in serious trouble, but I just can't let my parents know that I have cancer," Raiza said. "Will you promise me that you'll keep it a secret from them?"

How sad it all seemed. The parents did not want their beloved daughter to know she had cancer. Similarly, the daughter did not want her beloved parents to know she had cancer. From a sociological standpoint, Brewster would never understand the pervasive cultural stigmata associated with the diagnosis of cancer. After all, the disease was part of the human condition, not a sin.

At morning report, Brewster explained to the fellow and the attending that the patient had figured out that she had leukemia and was ready to proceed with recommended chemotherapy.

"I see that she's a candidate for a TROG experimental study," Brewster said. "What does that acronym stand for?"

"We have access to experimental protocols from two different study groups," Dr. Dykes explained. "One is from the TROG, which stands for the Texas Regional Oncology Group. Fortunately, we're not limited to an exclusive clinical study contract with any experimental group of researchers. We also have access to experimental studies from FROG, which stands for the French Oncology Group. My own personal bias is to try to select clinical trials from TROG when we have the opportunity. Through my own experience, I've found that the experimental protocols from FROG are a bit sketchy. In fact, more times than not, the FROG stinks to high heaven."

The patient would undergo a confirmatory diagnostic bone marrow aspiration biopsy, a pre-chemotherapy pulmonary function test, an echocardiogram, and a Panorex film to make sure there were no hidden infections in her gums or teeth, and then she would have an external multilumen subclavian vein catheter placed into her anterior chest wall in an effort to help facilitate the administration of chemotherapy and the blood products she would require to get her through her remission-induction therapy.

As the cat was out of the bag and the patient was well aware she was facing a potentially lethal hematological malignant disease process, it appeared the patient would be an excellent candidate for the randomized TROG experimental study group clinical trial.

The patient was started on a 7+3 protocol variant, and she was randomized to receive doxorubicin treatment instead of the daunorubicin treatment. Fortunately, after the end of the first week, everything seemed to have gone well up until that point.

Afterward, the patient's blood counts started to rapidly fall, and she was quickly approaching her bone marrow nadir as the cancerous myeloblast cells were being effectively exterminated. On one occasion, while Brewster was making rounds, Raiza made a specific point of having a private and personal conversation with the young medical student.

"Missy Brownwood told me that you were previously engaged and that your fiancée, sadly, died last month. I'm very sorry to hear about that. You must be heartbroken."

"Thank you for your condolences," Brewster said, "but I really don't want to talk about it."

"I don't want to appear to be bold, but I need to ask you a very private and personal question. First, I must tell you that I've never danced before. I was wondering about something. Before I get sick from this chemotherapy treatment I just received, could you show me how a lady and gentleman are supposed to dance together? I would be most honored if you could just do a simple move with me called the box step."

"That's it?" Brewster asked. "That's the private and personal question you wanted to ask me? Wow! Nothing to the box step, really."

"I'll tell you a secret: among my possessions, I have a book that teaches young people how to dance together," Raiza said.

"I don't get it," Brewster said. "What's the big, screaming deal?"

"Dancing would be a punishable offense in my country, but now that I'm here in this strange place called Texas, I think it would be a fun and exciting thing to do."

"Now, wait," Brewster said. "I don't want you to get all worked up about something that's actually fairly mundane. For you, this should be a rather unimportant matter in the course of your life's events."

"Who are you to judge what should matter to me in my own life? I tell you now, even if I only danced once in my life before I died, it would certainly be important to me," Raiza said. "Don't be shy. I promise I won't bite you—unless you wanted me to do such a thing. If so, I could make you cry like a little schoolgirl. That would be good for you, no?"

"Why did you pick me to be your dance instructor?" Brewster asked.

"Missy Brownwood said you know how to dance."

"Missy Brownwood and I are no longer on speaking terms," Brewster said. "Besides, Missy Brownwood talks too much. Apparently, you and I come from different backgrounds and different religions. There are people from your part of the world who would consider me to be an infidel. If I danced with you and somebody from your country caught us in the act, I'd likely be subjected to a beheading, and then some crazed imam would perform a violent clitorectomy on you with a pair of needle-nosed pliers. After that, you would likely be stoned to death by your own family in an honor killing."

"Yes," Raiza replied, "that's all quite true, but you shouldn't be afraid of living. I, for one, am not. However, I am not so certain I can say the same about you."

Brewster made a mistake when he made another promise to somebody in the dark. "I'll tell you this: once we get you into remission, I'll dance with you. In fact, if you like, I'll even take you out to dinner. That will be something we can both look forward to."

"It will be our secret!" Raiza squealed with excitement.

Once again, Brewster had blown it. It would have taken only five minutes to find an appropriate song on the radio to teach the young woman how to make a basic box-step motion while engaged in the act of a simple and innocent style of ballroom dancing. Perhaps he could have even given her a shallow dip while he danced with her. That no doubt would have been thrilling, and it would have delighted Raiza immensely. In fact, as things were about to turn out, it would have been something she would have remembered for the rest of what would turn out to be a short, painful, and brutal life. Sadly, Brewster and Raiza shared only a fleeting moment. Because the opportunity was not seized, it was forever lost.

Wednesday, March 24, 1982, marked day fifteen of the remission-induction protocol. Unfortunately, something had clearly gone awry. Raiza had become dreadfully ill with severe abdominal pain and cramps, and she'd started to pass bright red blood per rectum. Although her physical examination at that time was fairly unremarkable, a flat plate and upright abdominal x-ray series revealed that a catastrophic event had occurred: the patient had developed a lethal complication of her leukemia treatment called typhlitis, known more commonly in later times as neutropenic necrotizing enterocolitis.

In layman's terms, it was a medical condition wherein the cecum of the large colon became markedly inflamed, and a bacterial infection started to spread through the inner lining of the bowel wall itself. Without an adequate immune system to fight off the catastrophe, such a diagnosis ensured the patient would eventually get transferred to the celestial eternal care unit sooner rather than later.

Although the chemotherapy had already been administered, it could easily be another seven to ten days before her blood counts started showing signs of recovery. Unfortunately, Raiza did not have seven to ten days of life left to enjoy.

The patient was transferred to the intensive care unit, where she required antibiotic therapy for sepsis management and also pressor and ventilator support. The surgery service believed Raiza was too unstable to undergo surgical resection of her infected ascending colon, which was afflicted with typhlitis. After all, if she died on the table, the team that had wielded the sharp scalpel would get a black mark on the surgical mortality statistical ledger.

In any event, conservative efforts failed, as the patient suffered an intracranial bleed from her low platelet count, despite blood-product support. The neurology service evaluated the patient, and they declared Raiza brain dead on Thursday, March 25.

Unbeknownst to the oncology community at the time, the risk of neutropenic necrotizing enterocolitis was much higher in patients who underwent remission-induction chemotherapy with doxorubicin instead of daunorubicin. For that reason, doxorubicin was later banned from the 7+3 protocol.

Just because the patient was dead, there was no reason to take her off of the experimental protocol. After all, her counts were expected to recover within a week to ten days, and it was highly likely her bone marrow would recover with a complete hematological remission. If the crab pickers could sustain the body long enough on the ventilator to confirm a solid bone marrow remission, then they could add whatever they learned about her case to the protocol data registry.

The hematology and oncology fellow, Preston Falls, was determined to make sure that would be the case, while medical student J. D. Brewster was equally determined to torpedo the entire endeavor.

"What in hell am I missing here? Maybe because I'm just a stupid medical student," Brewster said sarcastically, "Perhaps I don't understand the meaning of the word dead. Why don't you spell it out for me, Dr. Falls? Do you want me to go down to the medical library and grab a damned Stedman's Dictionary? I'll even blow up a bag of microwave popcorn when I get back for us to enjoy, and then you can give me a didactic!"

"Look, asshole," Falls replied, "in the Department of Experimental

Chemotherapeutics, our job is to collect data. That's the only way the ball moves forward on the playing field."

"You make me sick," Brewster said. "Primarily, our job is to provide advanced medical care with compassion, not to fabricate data!"

"Hypocrite!" Falls answered. "You don't even like people."

"True," Brewster responded, "but that does not mean I don't care for them."

Over the course of the next five days, while waiting for the dead woman's bone marrow and peripheral blood counts to recover from the lethal dose of chemotherapy she had received, Brewster continued to make rounds on the slowly decomposing corpse in the intensive care unit. At the end of each SOAP hospital note, Brewster would write a caustic and sarcastic summary: "Assessment: Patient is still dead. Plan: Continue ventilator support until somebody from the hospital admin finally realizes the patient is dead and puts a merciful end to this immoral travesty."

Needless to say, the diddly squat finally hit the oscillating blades of the fan. Dr. Turban Dykes and Preston Falls were called out onto the carpet and severely reprimanded. The hospital ethics committee got involved to help revamp the policies and procedures within the clinical trials program.

Despite the considerable animosity engendered with the fellow and attending physician, Brewster somehow skated past the aforementioned fiasco. Once the young woman's parents learned their daughter was brain dead, they agreed to a DNR code status, and the patient was subsequently taken off of the ventilator. Sadly, Raiza had died without ever having a boyfriend or learning a simple ballroom box-step dance motion. Brewster would have to label that unfortunate and tragic event as another personal failure among an ever-expanding list of unfortunate and tragic events in his life.

Mumbo Jamar Apoo was transferred to the Gulf Coast General Hospital in late February 1982 for management of an atypical pneumonia that had developed as a consequence of the prisoner's underlying affliction with GRID infection. When the patient did not respond to an immediate course of conventional broad-spectrum antibiotic therapy, Apoo underwent a bronchoscopy from the pulmonary service. Upon completion of his workup, it was confirmed that Apoo was infected with an atypical organism known as Pneumocystis carinii.

Although pneumocystis pneumonia later became a well-appreciated infection among that particular patient population, it was a scarcely recognized comorbid risk for GRID patients back at the beginning of the outbreak of the disease in the early 1980s.

When J. D. Brewster and Willy Mammon learned Apoo was in the hospital, they made a point to case the med-surg unit to see if there would be an available opportunity to put the wheels of the clinical justice system into motion. As it turned out, Brewster's friend Arby Fuller was on administrative leave for anger-management issues. A new correctional officer, Reynolds, accompanied the prisoner to the hospital on that particular occasion.

"Officer Reynolds?" Brewster said. "My name is J. D., and this is my colleague Willy Mammon. We've previously provided medical care in the past for Mumbo Jamar Apoo."

"What of it?"

"Well," Wooly said, "we just wanted to come by to wish him a speedy recovery."

"Oh yeah?" Reynolds said. "No visitors. Get the fuck out of here."

It quickly became clear to Brewster and Mammon after their casual and rather pleasant little introductory chat with Officer Reynolds that the new correctional officer would only work strictly by the book. There was no way they would have a crack at getting their hands on the prisoner at that time to eliminate him once and for all as a societal threat.

Politically, things were getting further out of control, as the has-been actress Luzanne Saranrap and community organizer Shiva Jaclyn Grant held rallies outside the front of the hospital in support of Apoo.

"You have the power, people!" Shiva barked through a bullhorn.

"It's time to rise up and free the innocent Mumbo Jamar Apoo. We must do it by force if necessary! Are you people down for the struggle?" the anorectic, proptotic, and washed-up starlet bellowed out to the well-financed agitators.

A gathering of hostile protestors began chanting threats to the members of the Houston Police Department. When a riot broke out, protesters threw bricks at the police officers who were present and commissioned with the responsibility of preventing pandemonium.

As the large plate-glass windows at the hospital entryway were being violently shattered, Russian Bear's wife, Larisa, was assigned to initiate a scheduled antibiotic infusion. When she bent over to start a new IV access site for Mumbo Jamar Apoo, she was somewhat alarmed by the violent riot occurring outside. Finally, fire hoses were turned upon the rioters to disperse the crowd.

"Can you hear all of that?" Larisa asked. "There's a riot going on outside of this hospital because of you. Do you honestly think you deserve all of this attention?"

That was the wrong thing for Larisa to say. Apoo had just been insulted by a woman—a white woman. He sure as hell was not about to stand for that.

Long before the advent of soft, indwelling venous catheters, which became commonplace in later times, stainless-steel butterfly needles were often used in the hospital setting back in the early 1980s. In anger, Mumbo Jamar Apoo pulled the sharp butterfly needle out of his arm and then stabbed Larisa in her left eye with it while she was still bent over the prisoner.

"White bitch, you is a-gonna get da gay cancer now!" Apoo exclaimed as he viciously laughed at the now infected nurse. "I bet that hurt, nursy girl! Sorry 'bout all dat. Jus' bend over and let me kiss you, and I'll make you feel better!"

Officer Reynolds beat back Apoo with his baton, but the damage had already been done. Like Brewster, Larisa had acutely lost the vision in her left eye. Unlike Brewster, however, she would be permanently blind. Sadly for Larisa and her husband, Russian Bear, her sudden unilateral blindness would not be the worst of things yet to come. The lives of the hapless Russian couple were about to take a rapid downward spiral into an all-enveloping, pervasive darkness.

⟶⟨⟩⟵

Without the love of his life, Stella Link, Brewster had lost his moral compass. The student paced back and forth in his apartment while cursing incessantly. Brewster would intermittently smash his forehead against the hollow bedroom door in his unit until he punctured a four-foot-by-four-foot crater into the wood-veneered portal.

Brewster was suddenly not only a ship without a rudder but also a ship about to be cast upon a barrier reef. If that were to occur, there would be no realistic way Brewster would ever be able to readily extricate himself. His immortal soul had become a prisoner entrapped within the confines of despair and personal failure.

Winter would be coming to end in just a matter of a few weeks or so, and Pepe the skunk instinctively noted that the days were starting to lengthen. Pepe needed attention from his owner, and he needed it right away. As Brewster reclined on a bare mattress in his bedroom, the pet skunk began to scratch incessantly at Brewster's bedside to rouse him.

Although it was well past midnight, the skunk suddenly became energetic and needed affection. His owner bent over, picked up the skunk, and then set him on the end of the mattress. As Brewster immediately returned to a reclined position and closed his eyes, the delta waves that an operative EEG machine would have registered as restorative slumber quickly returned to the medical student's brain.

With a furrowed brow, the skunk climbed upon Brewster's chest and got within just a few inches of the face of his companion. After Pepe studied his owner with great interest and even greater affection, the skunk finally decided to nestle into the crook of Brewster's arm before dozing off to sleep.

Brewster soon awoke to learn that his pet skunk snored loudly. In light of his chronic sleep deprivation, which had acutely worsened after his fiancée had died, Brewster found that having a pet skunk that snored at night was definitely an irritant.

The student felt trapped in an unpleasant predicament. Although he longed for the deserved misery of a self-imposed solitude, Brewster was now adjacent to another living being that pined for his attention. A simple mammal that was a member of the weasel family, Monsieur Pepe was a relatively benign and affectionate warm-blooded creature. Despite those attributes, Brewster found little, if any, comfort in Pepe—or in anything else, for that matter.

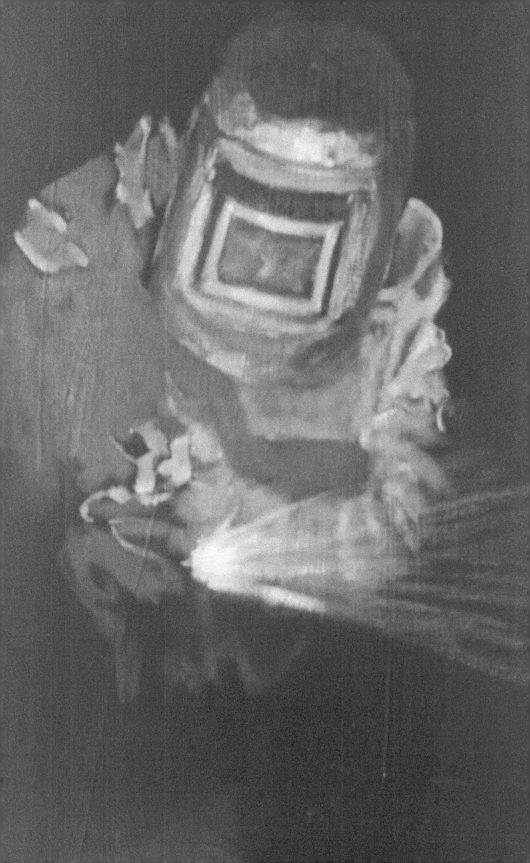

12

SPOT WELDING

I t was March 1, 1982, and J. D. Brewster was ready to start his next elective rotation on the radiation oncology service. Brewster was going to be working with the crab zappers. Unlike the medical oncologists, who were known as the crab pickers, the radiation oncologists were proud of the nickname that had been bestowed upon them. They also had another nickname they were equally proud of. It was not uncommon for members of the medical school house staff to refer to the radiation oncologists as the "free radicals."

As Brewster still had marginal hope about rejoining the PhD research program one day, he had to make a point of seeing Dr. Danny Sassman to talk to him about the idea of investigating vitamin B12 deficiency and its association with clinical dementia before his clerkship ramped up. There were many questions to answer, including its degree of prevalence among nursing home patients and whether or not it might be a disease entity different from the more readily recognized pernicious anemia and B12 deficiency disorder. Perhaps it was all just one disease process, but then again, perhaps not.

After all, the patient Dora Garza had B12 deficiency with associated dementia and a macrocytic RBC index but not with an overt anemia per se. As a case in point, B12 supplementation had dramatically improved her mental status to the point where she had been able to resume independent living. That had been an extraordinary event, and perhaps it was not a one-off anecdotal clinical happenstance.

Maybe there was a lot more to it. Both Brewster and the research scientist who was investigating dementia, Dr. Sergio Balbona, certainly thought the matter should be pursued. It had been many months since Dr. Sassman had unceremoniously suspended Brewster from the PhD arm of the dual-training program, and the medical student was uncertain how well his former mentor would receive him.

Surprisingly, Danny Sassman warmly greeted the medical student when Brewster knocked upon the professor's office door. "Brewster, I was terribly sorry to hear that your fiancée, Stella Link, died from what appeared to have been a cardiac sudden-death event. We were all stunned by the bad news, and I wanted to let you know that our thoughts and prayers were with you. What, might I ask, has brought you back down to the bowels of the research center?"

Brewster explained his ideas to investigate the association of B12 deficiency and dementia in the nursing home setting, and he reported that Dr. Balbona was also recently enthusiastic about the subject matter.

"Well," Dr. Sassman asked, "do you want back in? If so, you'll be starting from scratch. Of course, this would mean that if you finish your clerkship rotations and get your MD degree in June, you'd be stuck here at least until 1984 and maybe even longer. Hell, son, you started here back in 1977. By the time you finish up with a PhD degree, you would have spent one quarter of your life at that point confined within the walls of this institution. Would you be okay with all of that?"

"Maybe."

"I would assume a man like you would still likely go on to do residency and fellowship training somewhere after you get your

PhD degree," Sassman said. "After it was all said and done, you wouldn't be a young man anymore. In fact, it's highly likely that by the time you'd go off to look for a real job, you'd have already passed the one-third point in the projected life expectancy of a Caucasian male living in the Western Hemisphere."

"Well, I didn't look at it exactly that way," Brewster said, "but I'm really not sure what I want to do with my life. As a backup, I've applied for an internal medicine residency training post in Santa Fe. The residency match is coming out this month, but nothing is written in stone until I sign a contract."

"Hematology and neuropsychology are disciplines that are outside of my wheelhouse," Denny Sassman said, "but if you have a blessing from Dr. Balbona, you'll also have my support to rejoin the dual-training program. I'll need a letter from you stating that you're requesting your reinstatement into the PhD research group, and I'll also obviously need your formal research proposal outline."

"I can pull that together for you."

"If Dr. Balbona is going to be your research adviser on this matter, I'll also need the same from him. If you want to move forward with all of this, I'll present it to the board at the time of our next meeting in mid-April. In the meantime, do you want to join me on my annual spring pilgrimage to the forests of East Texas to set up motion-triggered cameras to try to catch a picture of a Sasquatch? I'll be heading out to the Fertile Myrtle wellhead near Dayton in four weeks, and I'd like you to tag along. I believe this is the time of year when the creatures may be migrating through the thicket."

"What about Ford?" Brewster asked. "He's usually your copilot on these misadventures. Besides, I promised that I'd shoot you and bury you out in the swampy woods for pissing on me last year. I assure you, Dr. Sassman, that was no idle threat!"

"Ford is tied up with his GRID research, and he'll not be able to join me this time around. I'm just not comfortable going out there alone anymore for some reason."

Brewster had to respectfully decline the invitation because of his commitment to finish up the last of his clerkships in a timely fashion. The two men shook hands before the medical student went to the radiation oncology unit to begin his new rotation.

Upon Brewster's departure, the research professor walked over to the office of Dr. Bruce Beathard to have a chat. "Say, Bruce, you said a while back you wanted to know the next time I was planning to go out into the forest to look for Sasquatch. As it turns out, I'm going to be heading out into East Texas swamp a month from now. That gives you plenty of time to make plans if you need to, as I definitely would like you to make this field trip with me. I'll give you directions on how to find the place, and you can meet me out at the wellhead where I usually set up my motion-triggered trail cameras around the pump-jack assembly."

Beathard was still seething over the fact that he had been overlooked to be the head of the research program at the Gulf Coast College of Medicine and that Denny Sassman, with his lowly degree awarded from an osteopathic school of medicine, was officially in charge.

Without looking up from his desk to face his political adversary, Dr. Bruce Beathard said, "Well, isn't that interesting? I'll make a point of clearing my calendar for the first weekend in April. Just give me the directions or a map on how to get out there. When I find my way out into the boonies, I promise I'll give you a big surprise!"

J. D. Brewster met his new radiation oncology attending, Dr. Bichon Moan, and her fellow, who was a Canadian with the name Dallas Birdwell. Dr. Moan was originally from a place that she herself uncharitably referred to as "the city of soot." Of course, she was referring to Pittsburgh, Pennsylvania. The radiation oncology attending physician was not married, but she had employed Dr. Birdwell to be her professional sexual consort and to live with her, as she was afflicted with a hyperactive libido.

Although Dr. Birdwell had sired a baby on behalf of Dr. Moan, by contractual arrangement, he was not allowed to have any official interaction with the child per se. As it turned out, Dr. Birdwell would ultimately find the agreement to be onerous, as the baby girl, after all, was also his own flesh and blood. How could a real man not have feelings for his own offspring? Perhaps it would have been proper for him to have an opportunity to at least offer an opinion once in a while as to how the child should be reared. Unfortunately for Dr. Birdwell, it wasn't in the contract.

⸺⧓⸺

By the time Brewster started his radiation oncology clerkship, D' Shea Dalton was already at the one-year milestone from the time she had been diagnosed with what should have been a terminal primary brain malignancy.

"Dallas," Brewster said with sincere admiration for the radiation oncology service, "the fact that this patient is still very much alive and thriving is truly remarkable! You crab zappers deserve a hearty round of applause. I just learned that D' Shea Dalton, who had a glioblastoma, appears to be still in a complete remission at this time. Maybe you cured her!"

For Brewster, it was time for a lesson in humility.

"You need to pay attention to what I'm about to tell you, stud," Dallas Birdwell replied. "Don't ever take credit if a patient ever gets well. Be humble."

"Why?" Brewster asked. "You need to brag about this, Doc!"

"The first time you start to toot your own horn, it will be the first time, and likely the last time, you'll get struck by lightning," Dallas said. "The best we can do is nudge a cancer patient toward what we believe is the right direction regarding therapeutic intervention."

"And when a patient gets well?"

"If a cancer patient gets well, that's between the patient and the Almighty," Dallas Birdwell said.

"I'll try to remember that."

"Also, don't be too quick to judge yourself if a patient doesn't do well and eventually succumbs to an underlying disease process," Dallas added, "be it a malignant illness or some other malady."

"So let me get this straight," Brewster said, looking for clarity as he furrowed his brow. "If I'm an oncologist and a patient does well, then I shouldn't take credit for it. If I'm an oncologist and a patient doesn't do well, then I shouldn't take the blame for it either. Does that about sum it up? If so, then what in hell am I doing here?"

"Nobody gets off this planet alive, Brew. If you come to grips with this righteous philosophy, your future career as a physician will be much more satisfying. You'll also probably live longer."

"To be frank," Brewster said, "I find nothing that's satisfying in my life right about now."

"Are you a spiritual person?"

"Not anymore."

"Find a purpose. Do it now!" Dallas said. "That way, you won't end up with a self-inflated big head when things go well, and you won't likely ever beat yourself up too badly when things go south."

"So far, how are you personally holding up in this particular line of work?" Brewster asked.

"The field of oncology has a very high burnout rate, and oncologists have a shorter projected life expectancy than the general population at large by about ten years," Dallas said. "Try not to carry too much of a burden upon your own shoulders, no matter what specialty or subspecialty you decide to pursue once you graduate from medical school."

Dallas Birdwell had no doubt offered sage advice. There was obviously an overlapping universe between knowledge and wisdom. If wisdom was a consequence of "been there, done that, and learned from it," perhaps the radiation oncology resident had also picked up a T-shirt as he went out the door to commemorate the valuable pearls he'd acquired along the way.

The relationship between Dr. Moan and her sexual consort had always been strained at best. On a previous New Year's Eve, Bichon Moan elected to administer an unsolicited act of fellatio upon Dr. Birdwell while he was driving in savage holiday traffic on the 610 Loop.

Needless to say, many men who've traversed upon the face of the planet with at least a modicum of purposeful intent would likely find that similar robust sexual activity would be at least somewhat distracting. This would be especially true if the recipient of such an intense and intimate encounter was engaged in the potentially dangerous act of driving an automobile on a freeway in Houston during heavy rush-hour traffic at the time.

Dallas Birdwell asked Bichon to cease and desist so he could concentrate on the serious task at hand, but his request was only met with a series of vicious bites inflicted upon Dr. Birdwell's reproductive member. Birdwell pulled Bichon Moan away from his painfully masticated unit by the back of her hair, and then he smashed her forehead against the dashboard. As could be expected, that defensive measure resulted in nothing less than a closed-fisted mano-a-mano donnybrook.

Birdwell pulled the car over to the side of the loop, and both parties got out of the automobile. They began to exchange serious blows to each other's head and neck region in a bare-knuckled, ferocious, fierce, full-out, fisticuff fight.

Finally, as Moan was a large and furry beast, she was able to knock Dr. Birdwell unconscious with a right hook. She stuffed her contracted consort into the trunk of the sedan and then drove the poor bastard back home. As it turned out, the misfortunate Dr. Birdwell remained in the trunk of that car all night long.

Dr. Moan always insisted that Dr. Birdwell needed to be ready to perform at the fullest of his sexual capabilities whenever she required his services. After all, she could readily make such demands anytime and anywhere. After all, it was in the sexual consort contract.

If Dr. Birdwell ever became too fatigued to perform or was unable to fully maintain a complete erection to satisfy the wanton desires of Dr. Moan, she would subsequently manhandle Dallas by subjecting him to a vicious, bare-knuckle beatdown.

In order to supplement her sexual cravings, Dr. Moan relied upon a live-in domestic to service her from time to time. Her new pet project was an achondroplastic dwarf named Igor, and the little man moved into the home shared by Bichon Moan and Dallas Birdwell. The vertically challenged individual was required to wear leather chaps and sleep in a caged area underneath the stairwell of their home. Igor was at a perfect height to offer a muff munch while he was standing erect, affording Dr. Moan the luxury of being able to prop a cold can of beer upon the broad skull of the dwarf at the same time.

It was a win-win situation; however, nobody could have blamed Dr. Birdwell when he initiated a clandestine romantic interlude with Arby Fuller's older sister, who happened to be a greasy, grumpy, purple-haired mechanic, fully equipped with a new set of dentures purchased from a mail order service in the Philippines. Birdwell's secret side snack worked down at the Fuel Stop auto repair shop and gas station over in North University Place.

Sadly, the daughter that Dr. Moan and Birdwell shared, named Judy, was afflicted with a serious pediatric malignant process called retinoblastoma, a rare cancer that afflicted about three children per one million individuals. The average age at the time of disease presentation was about the eighteen-month mark of life. The diagnosis was often suspected when the child developed a white pupil. Occasionally, periorbital inflammation or a visual squint could be associated with the cancer. As for baby Judy, the cancer and complications of its management left the young child completely blind in her left eye. Post enucleation, the toddler had a gaping hole in her socket where her left eyeball had once resided.

Fortunately, the majority of pediatric patients who contracted retinoblastoma were cured. Unfortunately, if the cancer invaded the orbit, the mortality rate could exceed 80 percent. Despite aggressive surgery, radiation treatment, and chemotherapy, the retinoblastoma cancer that attacked Judy invaded the orbit. By the time J. D. Brewster had joined the radiation oncology service, the young child was already terminally ill.

—◁▥◁▥▷▥▷—

The Gulf Coast had just secured a brand-new radiation treatment unit that was a linear accelerator. The new device was a direct replacement for the older, obsolete, and less precise cobalt unit that had been disassembled and subsequently set aside in a spare radiation treatment vault. The older unit was scheduled to be crated up and then shipped off to someplace in South America, where it would hopefully be put back into good use.

A big problem arose, however, when the cobalt unit was scheduled to be decommissioned. The radiation oncology service—and, more specifically, radiation physicist Jonas Adams, PhD—inadvertently ran afoul of the United States nuclear regulatory agency, and the entire radiation oncology program ended up being placed on probation.

What kind of problem could possibly have been so great that it would cause the radiation oncology service at the Gulf Coast College of Medicine to be at risk for losing its all–important accreditation? Well, it was a big problem indeed: the potentially deadly radioactive material from the obsolete cobalt machine had mysteriously disappeared!

What could have happened to the radioactive cobalt core? Had terrorists gotten their hands on the material to make a dirty bomb? Perhaps some idiot had dumped the sealed safety container containing the cobalt into a trash bin. If that were the case, the radioactive material would've ended up in a landfill somewhere to eventually contaminate the regional ground water supply!

In any event, compared to an older cobalt machine, one of the great technical advancements with a linear accelerator was that it did not contain internal radioactive material per se. Instead, the newer linear accelerator radiation therapy machine generated its own high-energy photons to be propelled down the accelerator tube to treat a cancer within a specific target ring.

—◦◦◦—

Radiation physicist Jonas Adams had a productivity clause in his employment contract. He got a percentage of the technical fees generated at the radiation oncology unit, based on the number of cancer patients who required his services to calculate their overall treatment plan. That, of course, was done in conjunction with the radiation oncologist.

Essentially, the radiation physicist was the person who would figure out where to aim the beam and for what length of time the cancer needed to be zapped from any given angle of attack while the patient was underneath the radiation accelerator column.

In an effort to drum up business, Dr. Adams received permission from Dr. Bichon Moan to place a cigarette-dispensing machine in the lobby. The machine was loaded up with rather tasty unfiltered cigarettes to increase the likelihood that any patient who smoked them would experience an untoward terminal malignant outcome.

For existing cancer patients, the cigarettes were gratis. Patients simply had to get free copper tokens at the registration desk, and then they were allotted to receive up to a total of two packs of cigarettes per day if they so desired. The patients were encouraged to smoke as much as they wanted. As for the general population of people just walking in off the street, the cigarettes were sold to them at a significant discount compared to what they had to pay at their local supermarket or nearby convenience store.

Brewster took umbrage with that particular business model, and he felt compelled to challenge Dr. Adams over what seemed to be an immoral and unethical violation of the Hippocratic oath.

"I've seen some evil shit since I've been here at the Gulf Coast, but what's going on here certainly takes the cake. What you're doing here is just plain wrong. We're supposed to be here to foster the health care of our patient population and not to promote cancer, heart disease, and God knows what else."

Dr. Adams simply scoffed at J. D. Brewster's sudden sanctimonious pontifications. "Brewster, don't be a dumbass. I've done the mathematical calculations on all of this. If I can draw up the treatment plan for just another twenty lung cancer patients or so, I'll be able to buy myself a new Ferrari!"

"Doesn't make it right."

"Hypocrite!" Dr. Adams charged. "You smoke cigars, don't you?"

"Touché."

⋘∭∫∭⋙

Brewster would soon learn that there was a huge difference in the mind-sets of the medical oncologists, or the crab pickers, and the radiation oncologists. Although both subspecialists dealt with the management of patients afflicted with malignant disorders, the field of medical oncology had evolved out of the subspecialty of hematology. After all, the first effective cancer treatments that utilized medications instead of surgery or radiation were used on the "liquid cancers", including leukemia and lymphomas. Knowing that, it was understandable how the field of medical oncology had come into existence. It was finally recognized as its own discipline by the medical subspecialty boards in 1972.

The discipline of radiation oncology, however, evolved out of diagnostic radiology, which made sense, as it was radiologists who first started to tinker around with the utilization of x-rays not only in the setting of diagnostic imagery but also as a therapeutic modality. Radiation oncologists, by necessity, were more technically oriented than their medical oncology counterparts.

As with everything, there was give and take. Oftentimes, with increased technical proficiency, there was a diminution in the clinical skills required to utilize medications to intercede with cancer management, pain control, or treatment complications. That was why it was imperative that medical oncologists and radiation oncologists needed to be collegial professionals.

At the medical school, the students and house staff alike would utilize the colloquial expression that any patient in need of radiation therapy warranted a bit of "spot welding," and any patient going down to the radiation unit was about to get "zapped."

A malignant tumor underneath the crosshairs of a subatomic particle linear accelerator tube was about to get "lit up." The clinical objective was, of course, to aggressively "burn out" the cancer from the "foxhole" in which it was entrenched for a beneficial therapeutic outcome.

It was highly likely those inaccurate but commonly employed militaristic expressions were utilized throughout most medical schools and cancer treatment centers throughout the country. Well, then again, maybe not. The above-noted blue-collar expressions were at least the slang terms utilized at the Gulf Coast College of Medicine at the time.

————

Although accustomed to seeing weird things, Brewster was unprepared to see the patient who had been assigned to him by the resident.

"I've heard really good things about you, Brewster," Dr. Dallas Birdwell said. "Your medical student colleagues have told me you're a first-rate people person who's able to defuse uncomfortable situations."

"That's a bald-ass lie," Brewster replied. "If the truth be told, I despise my fellow human beings."

"Swell," the attending, Bichon Moan said. "If that's the case, I have a patient for you to see. You might have heard of him already, as he's a local artist who creates abstract paintings. He's known only by his first name. It's Pedro. He's a contemporary of Pablo Picasso."

"I took art appreciation in college, and I can assure you I've never heard of this guy," Brewster said. "Does he have a last name?"

"Yeah—it's Pedro," Dr. Moan added.

"Oh, for shit sake.

"Even though this guy's pushing ninety years old, he has two younger twins in tow who tag-team the old bastard," Birdwell explained. "They both appear to be in their thirties at most. One of the twins is a nasty, toothless wench who must have done a lot of meth in the past."

"Can't wait to meet the entire clan," Brewster said with apprehension.

"Despite her rather shabby appearance, I'll bet my left nad that the toothless freak could still suck the chromosomes right out of a sperm!"

"Are you talking gamete or cetacean?" Brewster asked.

"Both, dumbass!" Dr. Birdwell said. "The twins have medical power of attorney over this guy, and they make all of the decisions regarding his medical management. I'm sorry about this, but you'll have to deal with them, and frankly, they're batshit crazy."

"Now, wait just one moment," Brewster said. "As I've testified, I'm not a people person. Don't do this to me. Whether or not, as you so claim, I'm able to diffuse uncomfortable situations, I should be at least granted the courtesy of a right of first refusal in regard to this particular patient. From a clinical standpoint, what am I going to be dealing with here?"

"Pedro has widely metastatic prostate cancer with extensive painful bone disease. His acid phosphatase is sky high, and he's been referred to our clinic for recommendations regarding palliative radiation therapy to manage some of his troublesome metastatic foci."

"Does this old fossil have any visceral mets?"

"No. The cancer has only spread to his bones as best we can discern by imaging studies. There's a newer experimental blood test out there to monitor prostate cancer that's called the PSA assay that will likely turn out to be a better test than the acid phosphatase screen, but our laboratory here isn't ramped up to run a PSA test as of yet. Be that as it may, you have a simple enough task, Brewster. Get in there. You can handle this. After all, you're a hunk and a half!" Dr. Bichon Moan answered with a wink and a sly grin.

"Sounds easy, I guess" Brewster said, "but what's the catch?"

"Now, check this out, Brew," Birdwell said, "because this is where things get weird. The patient has never had any type of primary cancer therapy. When he was diagnosed several years ago, he had localized and potentially curable disease, but nothing was ever done. Sadly, he's now going to die from his cancer sooner rather than later. At the time of his original diagnosis, he was given the option of either radiation treatment or a radical surgical prostatectomy for curative intent, but no form of treatment was ever undertaken."

"What happened?" J. D. asked. "Did this guy simply fall through the cracks, or what?"

"No, that was not the situation at all," Bichon Moan replied. "The two twins originally refused to allow Pedro to have any type of treatment whatsoever because they didn't want anything to affect his renowned virility. I guess this guy has a reputation for being some sort of hard chargin' love monkey."

"No way!" Brewster said. "I can tell you right now that this medical center isn't big enough for more than one love monkey, and I happen to be the real McCoy!"

"Nevertheless," Birdwell said, "here's old Pedro now, with his body being eaten alive by his prostate gland, which decided to go south on him. Nice."

"Did you say this guy is in his late eighties?" Brewster asked for clarification.

The radiation oncology resident replied, "He'll be ninety next month."

"Oh, hell no!" Brewster said. "Pedro's already made it to the bonus round in life. I elect not to see this guy or his crazy girlfriends either."

Apparently, refusal was not an option. The free-radical resident replied, "Do you want to get a passing grade on this elective rotation? If so, get in there, and talk to these people."

When Brewster entered the exam room to evaluate the patient, one of the women present in the exam stall was giving Pedro a hum job while the twin was coaching her on the intricate technique of delivering gratification without rendering a painful injury to the recipient. After all, she had to be careful not to rake the dorsal aspect of the old man's penile corona with the high-quality prosthetic incisors embedded in the dental appliances she had obtained through a shady mail-order service in the Philippines.

The lover engaged in the act of fellatio responded, "Don't worry, Sis; I took my dentures out already. I'm just going to gum on Pedro for a while longer."

Brewster, being a polite southern gentleman, said, "Perhaps I should come back later. It would seem you ladies are still trying to choke down the sad news that Pedro's underlying cancer is now spreading through his bones."

The twin functioning as the blow-job arbiter said, "No, wait! If you know anything about giving decent head, maybe you can stay and give my sister some pointers."

As for Pedro, his eyelids were at half-mast as he drooled on his wife-beater tank top peppered with flecks of oil-based paint. Brewster could not help but notice the enormous erection Pedro sported. It was no wonder why the elderly gentleman was in a semi-comatose state; his entire blood volume must have been vacuumed up inside of his prodigious, pulsating pecker.

"In regard to any pointers or pearls of wisdom," Brewster said, "I truly believe your sister must be doing a good job. After all, it looks like she's given Pedro a pointer of his very own—and a monstrous one at that."

At that juncture, the toothless woman began to make a gurgling sound, and when she broke away from her amorous activities, she said, "You are welcome to stay and watch if you like."

"We can give Pedro some radiation treatment for the cancer spreading through his bones," Brewster said as he politely ignored the opportunity to become a voyeur, "but you should know that if Pedro gets anti-hormone treatment or a simple castration, he might possibly live for another year or even longer."

Of course, the twins roundly rejected Brewster's suggestion. One of the women said, "You can't do that!"

"Well, why not?" Brewster asked.

In unison, the women replied, "It's Pedro!"

Brewster was relieved by the succinct response the two women had uttered. Their answer, after all, explained everything.

Once the sisters refused to allow Pedro to get cancer treatment, Brewster slapped a DNR form on the desk in front of the old man's goofy girlfriends. Oddly, the two women refused to sign the document.

When the two women left Pedro alone momentarily to use the ladies' room to gargle with a splash of mouth wash, Brewster took it upon himself to put a pen in the old man's hand. Brewster proceeded to wrap his own hand around Pedro's mitt to make a big X on the DNR form's signature line. Once the clerk at the registration desk cosigned the document as a witness, Pedro was officially designated to have a do-not-resuscitate code status.

When the two women wheeled Pedro out to their car to leave, Brewster waved at them and said, "Goodbye, bitches!"

Years later, Brewster would reflect upon the incident, and he could not specifically recall if he had used his loud, inner, angry and abrasive voice or his his soft and deferential outer voice to bid the trio farewell when Pedro and his concubines departed the clinic. More times than not, Brewster sadly tended to use his loud, inner, angry and abrasive voice when dealing with other human beings.

Dr. Moan became been a victim of medical insurance fraud. Sadly, that did indeed occur from time to time. She treated a patient who needed mantle field radiation for early stage Hodgkin's lymphoma, but as it turned out, the patient was an illegal alien who had utilized somebody else's identification information to ensure he would be able to get his expensive cancer treatment for free. In the early 1980s, if illegal aliens made it across the border and had about $1,200 in their pockets, they could buy false identification papers, including medical insurance cards. The patient with the aforementioned Hodgkin's disease completed his entire course of therapy before a medical insurance company finally called Dr. Moan to inform her that she had just gotten ripped off. In fact, all of the monetary payments the insurance company had made to the Gulf Coast College of Medicine had to be returned.

Bichon Moan called the Immigration and Naturalization Service to formally demand that the federal government apprehend the patient who had committed the act of fraud and then deport him from the country. She received a terse reply from the federal government that instructed Dr. Moan to buy a bus ticket for the perpetrator in order for him to take a trip downtown to the local INS regional office. They promised that if he showed up for a visit, they would interview him.

If it appeared he had been involved in some type of nefarious activity while he was a guest in the country, they would look into the possibility of issuing a strong verbal reprimand to the individual. If it appeared the illegal alien had committed any other serious crimes while he was in the state of Texas, the federal government would be obligated at that point to dispense a critical form letter that included the use of some very harsh words. That, however, would be the extent of the punishment the individual could expect to receive.

Dr. Moan scoffed at this apparent lunacy and decided to write a letter to her congressman, Lumpy McStain, to voice her concerns. Dr. Moan eventually received a return form letter from McStain's office that explained that what she'd experienced was a perfect example of why the United States should have a formal guest worker program for the hardworking people coming into the country from Mexico who would willingly perform the labor that the inept native gringo population was just to goddamned lazy to do anymore.

McStain's dogmatic conviction was espoused irrespective of

the simple economic fact that such an ill-conceived policy imposed upon the United States would eventually drive down the wages for the unskilled native Americans workers who already lived here, toiling away in societal margins of the voiceless shadows.

How did such a formal response have anything to do with the proverbial price of tea in China? It was a non-sequitur response from a non-sequitur politician. Sadly, with her only offspring facing a terminal illness, the additional flippant insult from the federal government made Dr. Moan even more cynical. What she rudely experienced would turn out to be a contributing factor to a disturbing untoward outcome for a new lung cancer patient in the queue for radiation treatment.

⎯⎯⏛⎯⎯

Dolly was only in her late forties when she acquired an unresectable stage-IIIB squamous-cell bronchogenic carcinoma involving her right main-stem bronchus that invaded the hilum and mediastinum. At the time Brewster was completing his medical school training, there was no proven effective systemic chemotherapy for advanced non-small-cell bronchogenic carcinoma, and therefore, the patient subsequently received single-modality palliative radiation treatment. On one fateful day, while the patient was receiving a dose of her scheduled daily radiation therapy, Dolly had a blowout of her right pulmonary artery and began to choke on her own blood. As she gasped for air, she coughed up copious quantities of bright red blood.

Dr. Moan panicked and called the resident and the medical student, Brewster, to lend immediate assistance in the vault room. Brewster rolled the patient onto her side while the free-radical resident, Dr. Birdwell, tried to keep her airway free of blood. Sadly, their efforts would be in vain.

When the patient coughed up a significant amount of blood all over Dr. Birdwell's white jacket, Dr. Moan exclaimed, "Don't touch her, Dallas! You're going to get shit all over you. If you do, you'll have to go home and get cleaned up. We have a busy schedule this afternoon. She's circling the drain already. Just let her go!"

With that, Dolly glared harshly at Dr. Moan before she simply drowned. Her lungs filled up with her own blood, which she was no longer strong enough to expectorate. It was a terrifying death for J. D. Brewster and Dr. Dallas Birdwell to behold, but for Dr. Bichon Moan, it was just another day at the ranch.

"How could you say such a wretched thing, Dr. Moan?" Brewster asked. "We should call a code blue!"

"No, she was made DNR at the time of her original diagnosis," Dr. Moan responded.

A radiation therapist entered the room and said, "Dolly's family wants to know what's going on. They're outside the vault, and they want to come in here."

"Don't let them in here yet," Dr. Birdwell said. "We have to get all of this bloody mess cleaned up first. Brewster, give me a hand. Call housekeeping and let's see if we can mop up this shit before the patient's family is allowed to come in to pay their last respects."

To Brewster, that made sense. It seemed to be the right thing to do, as the blood splattered all over the therapy table and linear accelerator tube made it appear as if Dolly had been violently murdered!

Unfortunately, Dr. Moan didn't see it that way. The attending physician took the offensive an brought the family in while Brewster and Dr. Birdwell were in the process of trying to clean up the bloody scene with towels and bleach.

Upon entering the radiation vault, the patient's husband dropped to his knees when he saw the lifeless, naked bloody body of his wife supine on the treatment table. Meanwhile, Dolly's teenage daughter developed dry heaves while she bitterly wept.

It was no time for a lecture from Dr. Moan about the

self-destructive personal choice of smoking tobacco, but that didn't stop the attending from scolding the family members.

"You did this! This is your fault, I tell ya'!" Moan said. "You let Dolly smoke, and she died from lung cancer. Shame! Shame on all of you! If I was Dolly, I'd come back from the grave to haunt you people. If you'd kept her from smoking, she wouldn't have gotten lung cancer to begin with. You people disgust me..."

Brewster had never witnessed a family being raked over the coals after a loved one had just died. It was totally inappropriate. The medical student threw the bloody towel he held in his hands onto the floor and stormed out of the radiation vault.

Brewster wouldn't be there to see it, but years later a legend percolated through the medical school that the radiation therapy vault at the cancer treatment center was haunted by the spirit of a woman who had died there from complications of lung cancer. If that were indeed the case, it should not have been a surprise to anybody in light of the horrors that had occurred at the time Dolly died on the radiation therapy table.

—————

Bichon Moan wanted to personally thank J. D. Brewster for his calm and collected actions at the time Dolly had sadly passed away. Dr. Moan invited J. D. over for dinner and adult beverages at her house. Although Dr. Moan was creepy beyond measure, Brewster was not about to pass up a free dinner and a cold beer.

Upon his arrival, Brewster realized Dr. Birdwell was nowhere to be seen.

"Is Dallas working tonight?" Brewster asked.

"I don't need him now," Dr. Grunt replied. "I need you. How would you like to have an opportunity to get a grade of the honors on this rotation? You're a smart boy. I think you can figure out what you need to do tonight to make that happen!"

Just then, Brewster noted a small and frightening specter in a makeshift cage underneath the stairwell. Dr.Moan's domesticated dwarf started to growl and shake the bars of his cage. Dr. Moan removed a leather sash she was wearing across her breasts and started to softly slap at the bars that imprisoned the vertically challenged being.

"Igor, you're an impetuous boy!" Moan exclaimed. "It is not time for you to come out and play. Get back! Get back, I say!"

"Dr. Moan, I need to leave right now," Brewster said in terror. "I forgot to feed my pet skunk, Pepe. He needs me much more right now than you do."

With that, Brewster bolted from the home, narrowly escaping his horny attending physician and her horny pet dwarf.

By the time J. D. made it back to his old Dodge Dart, Dr. Moan had released Igor from his bondage. As Brewster put the key into the ignition switch, he looked back in horror to see that Igor was in hot pursuit, hobbling toward his car with his stumpy little lower extremities pumping away as fast as the dwarf could possibly muster.

"Dear God, let my car start," Brewster prayed. "Go, go, go!"

The starter on the old Dart sounded like a fat, asthmatic hamster taking a spin on an exercise wheel. Nonetheless, the old beater finally fired up, and Brewster was able to sputter away to ascetic safety just in the nick of time.

—◦◦◦—

There was a catastrophically obese male patient who had contracted GRID, and his body was layered with violaceous plaques from Kaposi's sarcoma. His name was Richard, but everybody referred to him as Cheese Dick. Brewster never figured out if having a cheese dick was a good thing or a bad thing, but nonetheless, the radiation oncology service initiated a trial of external-beam shallow radiation to try to get the cancer under better control. When the patient was two weeks into his treatment, it was time for him to be evaluated for his response to the spot welding. In addition to multiple cancerous plaques, the patient's body was covered with multiple tattoos of butterflies. Brewster took a careful examination of one of the butterflies, which turned out to be a penis with the wings of a moth.

"Is there some sort of social significance in having your body covered with multiple tattoos of flying peckers?" Brewster asked.

"Why, of course, silly. Everybody knows that the disease GRID is transmitted by moths," the patient replied.

"Of course it is," Brewster said as he was about to step out into the hallway. "Get into this gown, and I'll take a look at you momentarily."

When Brewster walked back into the room to examine the patient, the individual was butt-naked and had an enormous erection. The patient said, "I'm ready!"

As Brewster turned and walked back out of the room, he said, "I'm not!"

⬥

Capri Dolenz was a sixty-four-year-old female who had developed a large primary breast cancer involving the upper outer quadrant of her left breast. Although she had successfully undergone a modified radical mastectomy, multiple lymph nodes were found to be positive for metastatic disease in her axillary region. Therefore, postoperative radiation therapy was warranted to try to improve her chances of long-term disease-free survival.

Capri came in for her radiation treatment one day in mid-March, and that time, she brought her harem with her. Brewster was amazed to see a battery of young women dressed as belly dancers hovering about the matronly patient and attending to her every need.

"Tell me, Capri," Brewster said. "Are these young women your employees?"

"Don't be silly," the patient replied. "They're my love slaves! They refer to me as Captain Cruncher the Carpet Muncher. I'd like to invite you to come over to my mansion to play house with us sometime."

"Would you mind if I brought over a six-pack of beer and a jumbo bag of spicy pork rinds?" Brewster asked.

"Okay, but would you be willing to share?" Capri said in return.

"That's funny," Brewster said. "I was going to ask you the same question!"

<hr/>

"Where in hell have you been?" Dr. Birdwell asked Brewster when the medical student showed up ten minutes late for the afternoon outpatient radiation oncology clinic. "Don't tell me you've been out jerking off in the broom closet once again."

"Perish the thought," Brewster answered as he set a cold Mr. Pibb soda on the counter in radiation oncology suite. "I stopped over at the Vinyl Lounge to score a frozen bean and cheese burrito. ¿Que pasa?"

"You're up to bat."

"Is this a pimp and pone challenge?" Brewster asked.

"We're too damned dignified to play that stupid game over here on the rad-onc service."

"What then?" Brewster queried.

"There's an established patient in examination room number two who's named Javelina Grunt," Birdwell answered. "You need to get in there and get a handle on her situation."

"Give me the set up," Brewster requested.

"The patient is a 68-year-old low-budget prostitute who was diagnosed with a T-3 poorly differentiated adenocarcinoma at the recto-sigmoid junction. The patient was placed on the FROG-RT 80-06 clinical trial program. After the patient received a temporary diverting colostomy to move her fecal stream directly away from the involved malignant field, the patient was subsequently managed with external beam radiation therapy in conjunction with continuous infusion 5-fluorouracil systemic chemotherapy," Dr. Birdwell explained.

"Why 5-FU?"

"Only damned drug on the market in this modern era that's proven to have any efficacy, albeit modest, against colorectal cancer," Birdwell answered.

"Fair enough, I suppose," Brewster asked, "but did it work?"

"Did it ever!" Birdwell and enthusiastically reported. "Worked like a charm. The patient went into complete remission!"

"By what criteria?" Brewster pressed.

"The lady got scoped post treatment and there was no sign of residual cancer. Biopsies were taken of the original tumor bed and the pathology report was negative," Birdwell answered. "The only thing that showed up on the path report was moderately severe radiation therapy induced proctitis."

"No kidding!" Brewster exclaimed. "Strong work, Dr. Birdwell. What happens now?"

"Well, according to the protocol, she's still supposed to get a resection of the previously identified tumor bed to reduce her future risk of local recurrence. Despite the protocol guidelines and our own rather rude and insistent recommendations, the patient refuses to be subjected to definitive surgical management at this juncture," Birdwell explained.

"Well, it's her life," Brewster said. "I'm a libertarian at heart, and if she wants to take a 'watch and wait' approach, so be it. That's her business. I guess we should just send her over to Dr. John 'Wayne' Gray to request from him a consideration to reverse her colostomy with a re-anastamosis procedure. I'll bet she'll be pretty damned happy if she doesn't have to poop into a plastic bag that's taped to her abdominal wall anymore!"

"That is not the case," Birdwell said. "For some reason, she doesn't want to have a reversal of her temporary colostomy."

"What?! That just doesn't make sense," Brewster said. "Maybe she's just afraid of anesthesia. Perhaps there's some other logical excuse. Did she give you any reasons regarding this peculiar decision?"

"Nope," Birdwell answered. "I want you to go in there and sort it out."

When Brewster entered the patient's room, he found an elderly patient who could have easily been twenty years older than her stated age by her grotesque and haggard chronological appearance. "Hello, madam," Brewster said. My name is Brewster and I understand at this point in time that you don't want to have a reversal of your temporary colostomy despite the fact that you've elected not to get any further cancer treatment. That doesn't make any sense at all to me and I wanted to talk to you about your decision regarding this matter."

"My name is Javelina Grunt, and I'm happy to report that since I've had this new poop chute, my income as a prostitute has increased dramatically. I want to keep it as a permanent colostomy now."

"Please explain."

"I can make quite a bit of money 'on the side' now, if you catch my meaning!" The prostitute explained enthusiastically. "I want to keep my new poop portal as a permanent colostomy now."

"I'm indeed sorry, madam," Brewster said, "but I just don't follow your line of reasoning."

"Don't call me madam," the patient said with a scowl. "That makes me feel old."

"Won't happen again," Brewster said apologetically. "Please continue with this sordid elaboration of your current circumstances."

"Nothing sordid about it," the patient said. "Just last night, for example, I made a killing. I got pimped out to give some experienced whore lovin' to four graduate students who're working on their PHD degrees in mathematics at Rice University last night. It was an on-campus encounter at the library, to boot! They were certainly a bunch of nerds, but nice young fellows nonetheless. I felt as if I was their grandmother guiding them into the wonderful world of dirty and illicit sexual satisfaction! Guess what, Mr. Brewster?"

"I couldn't begin to know where any of this is going," Brewster answered.

"I did all four of them at the same time!"

"What?!"

"I took one in the twat while I let another fellow fuck me in the ass at the same time. While all of that was going on, I was giving the third student a blow job. The fourth young man happened to be a very bashful colored kid. As he was rather inexperienced in the art of love making, I actually let him ram it home, straight into the colostomy opening in my left abdominal wall. Wow! Talk about putting an eight ball into the side pocket!" The prostitute cheerfully explained.

"Excuse me momentarily," Brewster sheepishly said.

"Say, where are you going, stud? I was just about to ask you if you wanted to give me a ride. It'd be a freebie! Just think of it—a tasty gift from me to you!"

Oddly enough, Brewster began to slur his words while he covered the palm of his left hand over his left eye. "I'm going out to put a bit of cool water on my face. I'll be sending my attending physician, Dr. Moan, in here directly. I'm certain that she'd be very interested in getting to know you and your clientele quite a bit better in an intimate way right about now."

—◁∭◊∭▷—

Sooner rather than later, Brewster was up to his old tricks. He began rifling through the refrigerator in the employee lounge at the radiation oncology clinic. When he ate an avocado that physicist Dr. Jonas Adams had brought in, there would be hell to pay. Jonas Adams set a trap for Brewster with a new avocado that he brought in to work the following day. He set the avocado on the treatment table in the radiation therapy vault and simply allowed events to naturally unfold. It didn't take long for Brewster to find the avocado in the radiation unit, and the medical student thought to himself that he should eat the delicious and calorie-packed fruit before it went bad.

About an hour or so after Brewster had eaten the avocado, Dr. Adams went into a contrived and well-rehearsed panic mode and started to run about the radiation oncology clinic, asking the staff if they had seen the avocado that had been left in the radiation therapy vault.

When Brewster acted as if he knew nothing about the missing avocado, Dr. Adams said, "Good God, I hope I find it. That avocado was impregnated with the radioactive isotope, strontium 90. We were using it to calibrate our dosimetry equipment. If somebody ate that avocado by mistake, he or she received a lethal internal dose of radiation. Within a few days, the victim's bone marrow will simply fail, and the person's intestinal tract will liquefy. The terminally doomed individual will start to vomit and shit blood until he or she dies in agony. Whoever ate that avocado will likely wish he or she had never been born. It will be a horrible way to go, I tell you. There is no known antidote for radioactive poisoning from strontium 90!"

Although he had become acutely blind in his left eye at that precise moment, Brewster was able to stumble to the men's room, where he jammed his index finger and middle finger down his throat to induce vomiting by triggering his gag reflex.

"God no, God no, God no!" Brewster cried out as he knelt in front of the urinal.

Suddenly, the door to the men's restroom swung wide open, and the entire radiation oncology staff entered the facility to openly jeer at Brewster for being so gullible. Dr. Adams pressed his right foot against Brewster's hip to push him over onto the bathroom floor.

"I swear to God, if any of us ever catches you stealing somebody else's food from the staff refrigerator ever again, I'll truly poison you with a radioactive isotope," Dr. Adams said. "Just to let you know, I'm smart enough to be able to get away with it. You'll just end up being another casualty of the clinical justice system that goes on around here."

Brewster was humiliated, and his resolve to retaliate by inflicting injury on somebody—anybody—was now at wide-open throttle.

As the retinoblastoma cancer involving the face of Dr. Moan's daughter continued to progress, such a desperate circumstance warranted that a Gypsy from Romania named Mother Magnesium was hired to cast magical spells over the doomed child.

Dr. Birdwell protested against such superstitious mumbo jumbo, but Dr. Moan said, "I've watched Mother Magnesium sit by our daughter for hours, concentrating while the powers of the universe are harnessed to focus in on our little Judy. The Gypsy woman will close her eyes, and she can concentrate on the baby all day long without moving a muscle."

"You're an idiot," Dr. Birdwell said. "Mother Magnesium is only sleeping when you walk in on her like that."

"No! You must believe me!"

As the powers of Mother Magnesium waned because of the daunting task she faced, the mysterious woman insisted Dr. Moan hire another Gypsy to get on board the crazy train to help out with additional magical incantations. Surprisingly, the man she asked to assist with the clinical care of the cancer-stricken child happened to be a close friend of Mother Magnesium. His name was Brother Barium.

Dr. Birdwell protested against such superstitious mumbo jumbo, but Dr. Moan said, "I've heard Mother Magnesium and Brother Barium while they're in the room adjacent to our daughter's crib. I can hear them huffing and puffing together for hours, concentrating while the powers of the universe are harnessed to focus in on our little Judy. Sometimes I can actually hear Mother Magnesium utter low and painful cries of passion, while Brother Barium shouts out, 'Yes, yes! Oh, sweet Jesus, yes!'"

"You're an idiot," Dr. Birdwell said. "Mother Magnesium brought Brother Barium into this home for one reason and one reason only: she's fucking his brains out!"

"No! You must believe me!"

<hr/>

One day after work, Dallas Birdwell returned home and found that his kitchen had the unmistakable odor of urine. The free-radical resident found out that Mother Magnesium and Brother Barium actually had a pot of urine on the front burner of the stove, on a fast boil. When Birdwell arrived, it appeared the Gypsies were adding eleven magical herbs and spices to the pungent concoction. As unbelievable as it seemed, the magical Gypsies intended to allow Birdwell's terminally ill daughter, Judy, to consume the putrid potion.

"What in hell is going on in here?" Dr. Birdwell demanded.

"Brother Barium and I are full of magic," Mother Magnesium replied.

"No," Dr. Birdwell replied, "you're full of shit!"

"Silence, you fool," Brother Barium said. "Even our urine is magical! We're going to have your daughter drink our urine in addition to eleven added secret herbs and spices. It'll only cost Dr.

Moan two grand. Trust us. This urine bomb will make Baby Judy well."

"Not on my watch!" Dr. Birdwell picked up the boiling pot from the stove by the handle and threw the scalding urine into the face of Mother Magnesium. As the woman bent over and screamed in agony, Dallas Birdwell conked Brother Barium square on the forehead with the empty pot, hitting the Gypsy as hard as he could with it. Birdwell then grabbed both of the rascals by their hair and dragged them out onto the front lawn of his home.

"I'll kill both of you if you ever come back here!" Dr. Birdwell called out as the two grifters fled in terror.

As no good deed went unpunished, Dr. Birdwell's vigilance was rewarded with a rolling pin forcefully administered to the right side of his head by an angry Dr.Moan. Days later, Dallas Birdwell was found dehydrated and walking about in a fugue state on the open Texas prairie. Dallas Birdwell was wearing only flip-flops and a thread-bare pair of orca-print boxer shorts modified with a large, convenient blowout hole on the backside.

The emergency medical technicians who found the resident physician wandering aimlessly about were able to lasso Dr. Birdwell, hog-tie him, and then bring him to the hospital for management of his acute concussion.

⸺☙⸺

In the last week of March, the residency match was announced, and Brewster was offered a position in the internal medicine program at the St. Francis College of Medicine in Santa Fe. Brewster still had secret hopes that he could one day also be awarded a PhD degree. However, if it eventually turned out he was not going to get reinstated into the dual-training program, he at least had a backup plan in New Mexico.

The medical students in the graduating class of 1982 were going to have a big party to celebrate their future careers, but sadly, J. D. did not receive an invitation to attend the festivities.

"Tell me, big man," Brewster said to his friend Willy. "Have you heard anything about a residency-selection party going on this weekend?"

With the death of his fiancée, Stella Link, and the prevailing belief that he was somehow responsible for her premature demise, Brewster had become a pariah among his classmates.

"Nope," Willy said in passing. "Not a thing."

—⊸⫘⫘⊸—

Terrified that Larisa might have been exposed to a potentially lethal horizontally transmissible agent when Mumbo Jamar Apoo stabbed her in the left eye with a needle, the infectious disease service at the Gulf Coast General Hospital ordered a series of immunoglobulin infusions to be administered to try to bolster the young woman's immune system. Perhaps if the novel treatment was successful, it would prevent Larisa from acquiring the same disease that would likely eventually kill her vicious assailant.

Sadly, the virus that caused Larisa's infection could not be immunologically eradicated. The virus was as evil as it was clever. Genetic drift prevented the entity from becoming a recognizable target for the host immune system.

Except for the permanent loss of vision in her left eye, Larisa actually felt quite well for several weeks. However, one month to the day after she had been assaulted, she began to have symptoms of fevers and chills with a pounding headache. She had progressive symptoms of fatigue in addition to pharyngitis. When she developed a prominent macular cutaneous eruption with associated diffuse and painful lymphadenopathy, it was time to go back to visit the physicians on the infectious disease service for another clinical evaluation.

"What did the infectious disease doctors say to you today?" Russian Bear asked his wife.

"Hold me, Ilya," Larisa told Russian Bear. "I'm so afraid."

Her laboratory profile revealed that Larisa was already starting to drop out her CD4 lymphocytes. With that pathognomonic finding, the infectious disease specialists at the Gulf Coast College of Medicine diagnosed Larisa with the transmissible disease known simply as GRID.

"What did they say?" Bear again pressed for an answer.

"I'm sorry, Ilya. I'm dying."

13

JOHN 11:44

D
r. Sassman made it out to the Fertile Myrtle wellhead as planned at the end of the first week in April, but there was no sign of Dr. Bruce Beathard or anybody else in the vicinity. As absentminded as ever, Dr. Sassman left the keys in the ignition of the old Bronco. More importantly, he also left his shotgun safely zipped up in its carrying case, stashed in the back parcel area in the rear of the vehicle. Sadly, out in the thicket, that was never a wise thing to do.

The professor brought out a duffel bag of equipment in addition to some camping gear that had been stored in the back of the Bronco. He proceeded to mount two of the motion-triggered trail cameras he'd brought in strategic locations at the outer perimeter of the pump-jack assembly.

He decided he would safely secure the other two monitoring devices still in the duffle bag deeper in the woods. He specifically planned to stake out a new area he had found along an inexplicable trail he stumbled upon in the middle of nowhere. As the professor walked toward the sluice, he suddenly heard some rustling in the brush. It was moving rapidly toward him. Denny was in deep trouble, and he knew it.

Whether true or not, reportedly the last transmission a doomed jet fighter pilot would say over the radio before he left a smoking hole in the ground was, "Oh shit!" When Sassman realized there was no way he could make it back to the rear of his Bronco in time to recover the shotgun to defend himself from the assailant, his last words were, "Oh shit!"

Just like that, Professor Denny Sassman, DO, PhD, and research director at the Gulf Coast College of Medicine, simply disappeared. He would never be seen or heard from ever again.

All conversations between a convicted criminal and a free civilian at a prison complex were obviously monitored and subsequently recorded to make certain no illegal business was being planned or executed. Therefore, it was necessary for those conversing to utilize careful code-speak to make certain the correctional officers were not privy to the true meaning of any words exchanged in such circumstances.

Russian Bear and Brewster waited patiently behind a thick, bulletproof pane of glass beside a wall-mounted telephone as they anticipated the arrival of Big Tom to pay a five-minute visit. Neither of the medical students had any idea what to expect, as they never before had had any cause to visit an individual incarcerated within the penal system.

Big Tom sat down in a chair on the other side of the glass barrier and then picked up the telephone to speak with his two visitors. The convict was a ruggedly handsome and bespectacled middle-aged individual with sharp facial features. Russian Bear spoke first in his thick Russian accent.

"I would like to thank you for opportunity to, how do you say, chitchat. First, condolences on the injury that your son Joey the Bull recently sustained. He will recover, no?"

Big Tom was a polite man who spoke in a soft yet deliberate and businesslike manner. "Thank you very much for your kind words. I assure you that your condolences are much appreciated, and I'll pass them on to my son Joey as soon as he recovers. He took a sharpened screwdriver in his flank, and he lost his right kidney over the whole ordeal. He was simply walking down a corridor, minding his own business, when he passed these four monkey mooks who were presumably the bodyguards for our new VIP."

"Joey was minding his own personal business at the time no doubt," Brewster said.

"No doubt," Tom agreed. "I guess my son must have given these animals the stink eye when he got jumped. It was all very sad. He lost so much blood that his heart stopped. Technically, my sweet baby boy died on the scene, but the emergency ambulance technicians who arrived were able to resuscitate him. He was raised from the dead! After what happened, I've subsequently given specific instructions to my other son, Nick, to simply stand down and not get into any trouble over this mess."

Russian Bear proceeded to ask a delicate question. "It's a terrible story. Any way to, how do you say, rectify the situation?"

"You know, prison is a tough place. Sometimes it's a lot tougher than usual," Tom answered. "There are certainly enough politics going on in this prison right now to choke a horse. Sometimes justice don't get served up like it should."

"Big Tom, you appear to be exhausted," Brewster said. "Is there anything we can do to help make things right?"

The prisoner thought for moment before he gave a covert yet ominous suggestion. "You know, even convicted criminals who are facing life without any chance of parole can still occasionally get a breath of fresh air if they're ever in need of medical care that can't be rendered here at the Sharpstown Correctional Center."

"The Gulf Coast has a contract with your prison," Bear confirmed.

"Exactly," Big Tom said. "The screw, Arby Fuller, is actually quite helpful in transporting convicts down to the Texas Medical Center. You gentlemen appear to be respectful of our circumstances here.

Do me a favor: if anybody we're concerned about ever gets sick here in this prison and then needs to go down to the Gulf Coast to get proper treatment, I want you to personally promise me that you'll take care of him. I would be forever in your debt. I assure you that once I get out of here, I'll find you boys someday and square up with you with an appropriate lucrative scholarship, if you catch my meaning."

At that point, Brewster took the phone back from Russian Bear and said, "I promise you we'll do our best. Before my friend and I leave you, I want to let you know that you're nothing like the man I had anticipated meeting."

"So you thought I would be a bent-nosed thug?" Big Tom asked as he broadly smiled. "What do you think of me now?"

Brewster scratched his chin for a moment before he answered. "Well, I believe you're the type of guy who would have made an excellent pharmaceutical representative."

The convict laughed out loud at the joke. "Now, don't go off and insult me like that! I was just starting to like you, kid!"

Brewster and Russian Bear were readily able to decipher what Big Tom had conveyed. Other prisoners were now protecting Apoo as bodyguards. From there on out, Big Nig would be well insulated after Joey the Bull had botched an assassination attempt. After Joey had taken a screwdriver to his right kidney, there was no way Big Tom would be willing to expose his other son, Nick the Shiv, to that degree of danger.

Last but not least, if there would ever be retribution, it would somehow have to be administered through the clinical justice system, not the criminal justice system.

—◀◀◀⟪∭⟫▶▶▶—

Moritz the Mouse was getting discharged from the hospital after a brief inpatient stay for management of acute on chronic congestive heart failure, which, sadly, was a consequence of his history of long-standing drug abuse. Moritz was only thirty-three years old, but he had the cardiac ejection fraction of a man three times his age. Before he left the hospital, he insisted he wanted to see his old friend Ben Fielder one more time.

Ben had just started a month of training on the cardiology service as an elective clinical, rotation when he went down to see the Mexican Marauder motorcycle club member, whom he knew rather well.

"Are you going to use your prescribed oxygen this time," Fielder said, "or are you just going to blow it off like you did every other time you were admitted to this hospital over the past year or so?"

"You know me," Mouse replied, "and therefore, you know what I am going to do. Look, I don't know about this premonition that I've had for a while, but for some reason, I think I'm getting closer to the finish line of my life. I am leaving my colors here with you. I'm going down to Mexico, and I'm going to try to square things up with those Vampiros who murdered my kin."

"You can't do that, Mouse," Ben Fielder said with alarm. "That's a fight you just can't win."

"I know, but I plan to go down swinging at the plate," the Marauder replied. "Don't worry about me, because the other boys in my crew, El Jefe and Tuco, will be coming down with me. It would appear that all of the members of the Three Mouseketeers have some kind of score to settle."

"Godspeed."

"Listen, I think of you as much a brother as the other members of my club. I have a secret I want to tell you: I've come to love my old lady, Carlita. I feel terrible that I beat her in the past and knocked out all of her teeth. I need redemption and perhaps even salvation for what I did. After I'm gone, I want you to take care of her and get her out of the life she's now living. Help me make this right, brother, and I'll put in a good word for you when I meet the Man upstairs, which is likely going to happen much sooner rather than later."

"Wait," Fielder said. "How can I possibly find your old lady?"

"Her phone number and apartment address are written on the condom packet in my jacket," Mouse replied.

With that, Moritz gave Ben Fielder a firm punch in the sternum as a final act of male bonding. Mouse would leave the hospital and head down to Mexico with El Jefe and Tuco on a one-way trip to hell. Although the three men reportedly were able to extract at least a pound of flesh from their adversaries, the Three Mouseketeers were never to be seen or heard from again. One might surmise that the Calle Vampiro drug cartel would be none too pleased about anybody coming down from Texas to shit in their cat box.

The biker's girlfriend, Carlita, could only hope the ultimate demise of Moritz the Mouse and his two associates would not be a prolonged and tortuous ordeal. Sadly, that would not turn out to be the case.

Fielder and his girlfriend, Missy Brownwood, contacted Carlita, who had been the former property of Moritz the Mouse. The couple invited Carlita over to the apartment where Missy was living. Fielder and Missy scraped up about fifty dollars and subsequently bought Carlita a secondhand wardrobe from the Salvation Army.

Fielder and Missy also made sure Carlita had at least a somewhat functional and moderately well-fitting used set of dentures that Ben illicitly appropriated from a nursing home patient who had recently expired. After everything was buttoned up, Ben and Missy purchased a bus ticket for Carlita to return to her hometown of Amarillo.

As she stepped onto the bus that was about to ferry her away from a life of crime and drugs, Carlita asked, "Why are you doing all of this for me?"

"I made a promise to Mouse that I would help take care of you,"

Fielder answered. "I'm sorry, but this is the best that Missy and I can do for you. Nonetheless, I certainly hope it's enough to give you a new leg up on life. Missy and I pray you'll find redemption and perhaps even salvation."

Carlita turned back to give Ben Fielder and Missy Brownwood a hug. "You know, I heard it once said that no good deed goes—"

"Stop right there!" Fielder exclaimed as he cut her off at the pass. "That sounds like a jaded load of manure that some idiot named J. D. Brewster would likely say."

"I don't know the man," Carlita replied. "Friend of yours?"

"Hardly," Fielder answered. "That cynical son of a bitch is dead wrong about good deeds. In fact, as best as I can tell, he's never been right about anything he's ever said or done as long as I've ever known him."

"From my own experience, no good deed goes unrewarded," Missy Brownwood said. "Goodbye, Carlita. I hope those are words you can live by in the future."

Carlita was so overwhelmed with emotion that she broke down crying as the doors to the bus closed.

"I will never be able to repay you for what you have done for me. I'm reborn! I feel as if I've been raised from the dead."

———

Police detectives were diligently interviewing the scientists from Gulf Coast College of Medicine in addition to the students who were enrolled in the dual-training program to see if they had any clues as to what might have happened to the director of the research program. When J. D. Brewster heard that Dr. Sassman had simply disappeared, he feared the worst. He called the Houston Police Department to tell them he would like to speak with one of the detectives on the case about some ideas he had as to what might have happened to his former mentor. The police assured Brewster that the authorities would eventually make a point of speaking to him sooner rather than later.

When the police detectives interviewed Dr. Bruce Beathard about Denny's disappearance, he reportedly said that he had no idea what might have happened to the research scientist. Beathard failed to mention to the authorities the specific information many weeks ago that Dr. Sassman had mentioned a plan to go into the woods to look for Sasquatch.

Perhaps Dr. Beathard simply forgot that particular detail. That must have been it—a simple lapse of memory. After all, physicians were busy people, and sometimes things fell through the cracks. After all, Dr. Denny Sassman had apparently fallen through the cracks.

Baby Judy, the daughter of Dr. Moan and Dallas Birdwell, developed a black residue involving her left eye socket. Unfortunately, all concerned parties realized that this new complication was finally the end of the road. The young child had developed an invasive fungal infection with a black-mold organism called mucormycosis.

Although opinions varied among infectious-disease specialists, mucormycosis might have been the nastiest fungus that could ever infect a human being. Short of surgically resecting the infected field, it was nearly impossible to eradicate the mold. Even if doctors attempted surgical extirpation to provide clean and disease-free margins, the godamned fungus might still come back and kill the patient eventually.

If the nasal passages or eye sockets got invaded, the organism would soon invade the brain, and the infected patient would end up dying from squash rot. No matter how nasty a person thought an infection like that could be, it was actually much worse than that.

When Dr. Birdwell told Brewster that Baby Judy was terminal, he asked the medical student if he would be so kind as to go by the patient's room to pay his respects. The free-radical resident said that a visit from J. D. Brewster would mean a lot to Dr. Birdwell and also to Dr. Moan.

Sadly, Brewster could not bring himself to exhibit that simple act of compassion. After all, the medical student had never emotionally recovered from the last pediatric patient he'd provided care for, who'd passed away from acute leukemia, much less from the recent death of his own fiancée, Stella Link.

Sadly, Baby Judy died on Friday, April 9, 1982. It was Good Friday when she expired. Dr. Bichon Moan had always been a bit, well–sideways. After her only child died a horrible death from being eaten alive by an infectious black mold, Dr. Moan went from being sideways to a bit, well–upside down.

In the end, there was a strong disagreement between Dr. Birdwell and Dr. Moan as to whether or not their daughter, Judy, should be consigned a full-court-press resuscitative status or a DNR. The ensuing fistfight, this time won by Dr. Birdwell, ensured the baby girl had a do-not-resuscitate code status at the time she finally died.

After Dr. Birdwell momentarily blinded Bichon Moan after throwing spicy chili powder into her eyes at the onset of the fistfight, he coldcocked her. While he loomed over his fallen adversary, Dallas started to sing the national anthem of his beloved homeland: "O Canada! O Canada!" One should have tipped a hat to those Canucks; they seemed to be pretty resourceful people when they got into a pinch.

——

As Brewster felt a strong kinship with the servicemen who fought valiantly for his country, he elected to sign up for another rotation at the VA annex in Bellaire. The VFW had provided funding for a longitudinal study to evaluate the fallout that the atomic soldiers had experienced during the era of above-ground atmospheric atomic weapon tests between 1945 and 1961.

The federal government was certainly not ready to declare that any of the misfortunate human guinea pigs involved with those activities were facing any increased lifetime health risks compared to any other person among the general population. Brewster considered the potentially dangerous consequences for the American servicemen who were exposed to that peculiar situation: atomic bomb plus human subject. What could possibly go wrong with that particular mathematical equation?

—⊪∩⊪—

Martin was an ordnance engineer who'd worked under Deke Parsons on the original bomb project. Martin had been on the team that had loaded the grapefruit-sized eleven-pound plutonium core into the spherical array of implosive Composition B at the McDonald ranch house, about seventeen miles south of what was known as the Mustang Gate near San Antonio, New Mexico.

A massive block-and-tackle system was able to hoist the device onto the top of a hundred-foot steel tower, and at precisely 5:29:45 a.m. (Mountain War Time) on July 16, 1945, the relay switches on the test shot known as the Trinity were flipped on.

The atomic genie suddenly escaped from the bottle. Sadly, mankind would never be able to stuff the nasty bastard back inside the bottle from which it came, because it was something man simply couldn't unlearn. Humans would always know how to make atomic weapons. They'd always know how to exterminate life from the face of planet Earth.

Some historians, Brewster included, believed it was appropriate to mark July 16, 1945, as the starting point for a new epoch in the history of mankind: day 1, year 1 ABA (anno bomba atomicus).

From each fractured nucleus of a fissile, man-made, Pu 239

atom (or the rare but naturally occurring U 235 isotope), 170 million electron volts of energy were released. It was rather astonishing to think that this was enough energy to cause a visible flash of light while propelling a grain of salt across the floor. That was just the consequence of the energy released from one atom undergoing nuclear fission!

Martin was allegedly safe inside the steel-and-concrete-reinforced bunker thousands of feet downrange from the blast as the hundred-foot steel tower was vaporized down to its footings from an epicenter temperature of a million degrees Celsius. After the smoke had cleared, Martin was permitted to walk up to the test site, where the sand had been fused into a green-colored glass.

Although Martin only strolled up to the edge of the blast site for a few seconds, he foolishly picked up some of the fused glass on the ground and put it in the pocket of his trousers to take home as a souvenir.

"I guess I was an idiot," the old ordnance engineer said.

"How so?" Brewster asked.

"I picked up a chunk of fused radioactive glass and put it in my pocket. It was beautiful to behold, as it had a milky dark green color," Martin answered. "It reminded me of the volcanic material called obsidian that the ancient Mesoamericans fashioned into extraordinarily sharp bladed weapons."

"Is it still in your possession?" Brewster asked.

"Why, most certainly," Martin answered.

"May I have it?"

"Why, most certainly not," Martin answered. "The boys on the Manhattan Project named the fused green glass Trinitite. For all these years, I kept that radioactive chunk of fused sand in an empty mayonnaise jar on top of my office desk."

"Tell me, Martin," Brewster asked. "Is it still radioactive?"

"You might not believe this, but after all of these years, that chunk of glass is still warm to the touch to this very day," Martin replied. "I'd often take it out of the jar and roll it around in my hand for good luck. In all likelihood, after all of this time, it's hopefully only cranking out low energy radioactive alpha particles, but I'm not really sure about all of that."

"Oops," Brewster said.

"I guess now, in retrospect, that was not one of the smartest things I ever did, but it was all very exciting."

The neutron flux from the Trinity blast transmuted the surrounding earth, making it highly radioactive. After the explosion, the background radiation was astonishing, at 0.3 to 0.4 centigray per hour, or three hundred to four hundred rad per hour. It should be noted that 0.5 centigray, or five hundred rad, in a single fraction, was the recognized LD50 (Lethal Dose of radiation in 50 percent of exposed human subjects).

Martin survived the test blast without any apparent overt harm, but thirty-five years after the event, Martin was dying from bone marrow failure. The data concerning his life and death would be submitted to the federal government for its thoughtful consideration regarding this delicate matter.

—⊷∙⊶—

Another patient Brewster was assigned to evaluate was a man named Larry, who also was involved with above-ground atmospheric atomic bomb testing. Unfortunately, his military record had been mysteriously purged. The only things in his service file were his date of entry into the United States military and the date of his honorable discharge. Everything else had been redacted. Brewster thought, Our government wouldn't possibly do anything like that on purpose, now, would it? Nah, it must have been a clerical error.

Brewster had never met a patient with four different synchronous cancers before, but Larry did indeed have four different problematic malignant disorders at the same time: primary lung cancer, primary bladder cancer, lymphoma, and multiple recurrent basal cell and squamous cell carcinomas that, curiously, appeared on non-sun-exposed areas of his integument.

"Well, what's your story?" Brewster asked.

"I was involved in the Sandstone Project's test shot Yoke at Enewetak Atoll on April 30, 1948," Larry answered. "It was a forty-nine-kiloton fission-bomb tower shot. I was on a B-29 bomber, and our job was to guide an obsolete, unmanned B-17 that had been turned into a radio-controlled drone to fly directly through the atomic cloud. As we commandeered the B-17 through the middle of the cloud, my B-29 flew at an accelerated rate circumferentially around the mushroom cap to intercept the B-17 when it popped through the atomic cloud on the other side. Filters had been welded onto the wings of the drone plane to capture radioactive fallout in order for the Los Alamos boys to determine the yield of the blast in kilotons just by the daughter elements and isotopes that were created and subsequently captured in the filters. It was all very exciting."

"Well, how far was your B-29 plane away from the mushroom cloud?" Brewster asked.

"For our role in the test shot, we were given strict instructions that we should stay at least four hundred yards away from the atomic cloud at all times," the patient answered.

"Four hundred yards?" Brewster was stunned. "Are you kidding me? Holy shit, Batman! How about four hundred miles? That sounds better. Yeah, that's the ticket!"

Larry would die from cancer. What a surprise. What cancer did he die from? In the infamous words uttered by a future ruthless secretary of state and eventual Democratic Party presidential nominee during the immediate aftermath of a terrorist attack upon an American compound in Libya, "What difference does it make?"

The data concerning Larry's life and death would be submitted to the federal government for its thoughtful consideration regarding this delicate matter.

———◁◠▷———

Bob was dying from stage-four metastatic non-small-cell bronchogenic carcinoma, and it was an adenocarcinoma subtype. Of interest, Bob was a nonsmoker. Brewster asked Bob to explain what he had been through.

"I served on the USS Laffy, and I was a participant in the Operation Crossroads project at Bikini Atoll. I was privileged to witness the Able shot on July 1, 1946, and also the Baker shot at the end of the month. The Able shot was a twenty-three-kiloton fission device dropped from a B-29 named Dave's Dream, which was flown out from the 509th atomic bomb group in Roswell. The target ring was a test fleet of obsolete warships leftover from World War II. The bomb missed the target by half a mile, not that it made any difference. The effect on the test fleet of ghost ships was devastating. As for my own life, I should have known something would have gone wrong along the way."

"Why would you say that?" Brewster asked.

"The name of the atomic bomb test project was a bad omen that I should have recognized right off the bat," the patient said.

"The Crossroads Project?" Brewster queried as he pulled at his beard. "I don't get it."

"Don't you see?" the patient asked. "After all, you can always find the Devil at the crossroads."

"You mentioned that you saw two atomic explosions during that test series," Brewster said.

"The second test shot, Baker, was an underwater explosion," the patient said. "An atomic bomb was placed on a barge and submerged one hundred feet underwater, when they lit the fuse.

Hundreds of millions of tons of radioactive water blew up into the atmosphere. It was something spectacular to witness. It was all very exciting."

"What was your job besides being a witness?" Brewster asked.

"Our ship was commissioned on both test shots to follow the atomic clouds until they had completely dispersed," the patient said. "We were ordered to pick up any dead and dying sea critters we came upon along the way. There were scientists and biologists onboard to try to determine if the sea creatures had died as a consequence of either the shock wave from the blast or the high-energy radiation, or perhaps it was just one big-ass fish fry! When we returned to port in San Francisco in September 1946, the superstructure of the Laffy was so radioactive that the ship had to be decommissioned. I'm not certain, but perhaps some of the steel of the ship had been converted into radioactive cobalt by neutron bombardment. We were that close to the detonation. Does that sound scary? As I understand it, they had to completely strip off the superstructure and rebuild the entire ship from the hull up."

The medical student was curious, and he pressed on for more information. "Please don't tell me they just dumped all of that radioactive steel into the San Francisco Bay."

"What I'm going to tell you is still classified, but at this point in my life, I just don't give a shit any longer. Believe it or not, parts of the Hunters Point shipyard in Frisco are still hot enough to cook a hot dog without a camp fire! Although I do indeed believe that the city of San Francisco likely deserved such an egregious insult, I heard an unsubstantiated rumor that the radioactive and contaminated material was sold as scrap metal to the auto industry to be recycled into new cars," the patient said.

"What?!"

"If that was the case," Bob mused, "going down to your local car dealership to buy a new 'hot rod' would certainly have an entirely different meaning, now would it not?"

"I can't believe I'm hearing this," Brewster said as he vigorously rubbed at his left eye.

"A sad thing to think about regarding this whole ordeal is what we did to the Bikini islanders. Do you know when the people from Bikini will be allowed to move back to their beloved island?"

"Tell me!"

"Never," Bob answered. "Does never work for you? Never works for me! I guess we really messed things, didn't we? Well, I was a young man then, and it was all very exciting."

Bob eventually died from his lung cancer. The data concerning his life and death would be submitted to the federal government for their thoughtful consideration regarding this delicate matter.

After Brewster graduated from medical school, he would write a letter on behalf of Bob and his family concerning his honest medical opinion that the patient's death from lung cancer was a direct consequence of his participation in the Operation Crossroads project. After all, the patient was a nonsmoker. Bob's surviving family members finally got a settlement from the federal government; however, they had to sign a nondisclosure clause that they would never speak about the subject to the other living participants who had been involved with any of the atmospheric atomic bomb testing.

Uncle Sam would catch up to J. D. Brewster a few years after he graduated from medical school, and he was also asked to sign a nondisclosure clause that he would never discuss anything about his knowledge regarding what had happened when the Devil showed up at the Crossroads.

Brewster returned the letter to the federal government and politely asked them to stick it where the sun didn't shine. By then, the covert deep-state government was well entrenched in the United States, as the Internal Revenue Service had been weaponized long before against the average American citizen.

It seemed after all that corrupt career bureaucrats in the DOJ and the IRS were indeed the low-life, swamp-dwelling demonic entities that really controlled the country anyhow. Perhaps that was one of the reasons J. D. Brewster would be audited time and again over his federal income tax returns on a yearly basis for the better part of the next thirty-five years.

Following the death of baby Judy, Dr. Moan directly blamed her hired sexual consort, Dr. Birdwell, for the child's demise. After all, if Birdwell had not interrupted the plans of Mother Magnesium and Brother Barium, Baby Judy would have been allowed to drink the magical urine bomb fortified with no fewer than eleven magical herbs and spices.

Bichon was certain that the two magical Gypsies had magical powers, and they'd prepared a magical treatment for the critically ill little girl. However, because Birdwell had thrown a wrench in the monkey works, the child never had received the urine-based magical potion.

After throwing Dallas Birdwell out of the house, Dr. Moan contacted the two Gypsies and asked them to harvest the powers of the universe one last time and focus them upon the corpse of the dead child.

In the third week of April, Mother Magnesium proclaimed something astounding: "Brother Barium and I have been concentrating so hard on the little girl that we've brought her back to life. I promise you; she's been raised from the dead! You don't have much time. You'll need to get a court order and have the body exhumed before she runs out of air in the coffin!"

Bichon Moan went to see a judge to get an emergency court order to have the body of the child exhumed legally. Of course, the judge immediately realized the woman was a stark raving maniac.

The judge eventually acquiesced to the bizarre request and signed the court order to allow the body of Baby Judy to be retrieved from the grave for a proper forensic reexamination.

Dr. Moan insisted that medical student J. D. Brewster be present as a witness. When the lid to the coffin was opened, the baby was still dead. What a shocking surprise. With a furrowed brow, Bichon Moan looked over to Mother Magnesium and Brother Barium in dismay and furious anger.

"What the fuck?!" Bichon Moan asked with overwhelming disappointment before the two Gypsies departed from the cemetery in shame. Obviously, the bereaved mother was looking for an explanation.

The Gypsy woman shrugged as she slowly retreated from the grave site in an attempt to escape a pending prosecution for fraud. "Guess I was wrong!"

Brother Barium was also now starting to back away from Dr. Moan, much like a frightened snail avoiding a generous application of table salt dispensed by a miscreant adolescent.

"Not so fast," Brewster said. "If you bragged that you were going to raise this baby from the dead, which one of you is now proclaiming to be the way, the truth, and the light? I must know right now so I may pay you the reverential homage you so rightly deserve."

Sadly, word got out at the medical school and also throughout the Gulf Coast University Hospital that an attending physician had suffered a psychotic break from reality. Dr. Moan was forced into retirement after the fiasco. As she was legally declared non compos mentis, Bichon Moan was never allowed to practice medicine ever again.

———

On a bright, moonlit night a week later, Mother Magnesium

tried to flee the mysterious vigilante who was in pursuit, but by then, it was too late. The Gypsy woman collapsed in the alleyway, crying out in agony. Although not unconscious, she was stunned with a severe concussion. She certainly would not be able to get up and run away anytime soon.

After his lover sustained a blow to her cranium, Brother Barium decided to face the angry assailant with a modicum of bravery—but perhaps without discernable dignity. "Look, pal, you're just getting way too worked up over all of this. This was just another business opportunity for us—that's all. Nothing more and nothing less. It wasn't personal. After all, this is just what we do. Our mission is to dispense a little bit of hope when people are struggling with darkness and depression."

"You call that hope?" the vigilante assailant asked with incredulity.

"It's our belief that we're actually trying to do something good for people," Barium said. "Without hope, what do any of us truly have? Honestly, is what we do actually any worse than what the cancer doctors do when they treat somebody who has a terminal malignant disease? It's hypocritical to think otherwise. You don't have to do this. Please! I'm asking that you just let me go. I'm begging you."

"You both claimed that Baby Judy would arise from the dead," the vigilante assailant said. "You weren't selling hope; you were just selling bullshit!"

Momentarily, the attacker smashed a lead pipe against the skull of Brother Barium, and he too crumpled to the pavement, where he would twitch and growl for several hours in a semiconscious state.

The throbbing headache and photophobia that Mother Magnesium and Brother Barium would experience would last for weeks. After the beating they had received, Mother Magnesium and Brother Barium thought that the better part of valor would be for both of them to give up the grift and try to seek out gainful employment. There was no doubt that the two Gypsies had been subjected to a most highly deserved retribution that was administered through the underground clinical justice system!

———◆———

Larisa was running a high fever and had developed the sudden-onset symptoms of a blood-tinged productive cough with shortness of breath when she showed up in the hospital lobby.

"Larisa!" Brewster said. "How did you get up here to the hospital?"

"I drove."

"Not a good idea if you're blind in your left eye," Brewster said. "Where's Bear?"

"I don't know. I called the ward several times, but my messages weren't getting through."

"Next time, call me," Brewster said.

"The way I'm feeling now, I'm afraid there won't be a next time," Larisa said weakly.

Brewster grabbed a lobby wheelchair and took Larisa straightaway to the emergency room. After she was registered to be seen, the medical student plowed upstairs to find Russian Bear and pull him away to attend to Larisa.

The chest x-ray revealed bilateral pneumonia, and as she was on the threshold of overt pulmonary failure, she was intubated and placed on a ventilator. The pulmonary service performed bronchial washings and confirmed that the patient was infected with the troublesome Pneumocystis carinii bug associated with GRID. The appropriate antibiotic regimen was initiated, but antibiotics could only do so much. For patients to survive such an ordeal, they needed a functional immune system. Infected with the mysterious GRID disease, Larisa no longer had a functional immune system.

"Larisa," Bear softly said, "you must pull through. I'll be lost without you."

Sadly, his wife was too weak to even open her eyes at that point.

Her husband and friends initiated an around-the-clock vigil, although it was generally a direct violation of the hospital's rules and regulations to allow visitors to stay overnight in the intensive care unit. Russian Bear found solace in prayer. Although he beseeched God in heaven to allow the only love he'd ever had to survive the calamity, he always added a specific modifier at the end of every request for a miracle: "Thy will be done."

Apparently, it was not God's will for Larisa to survive the tribulation, and she died on April 29, 1982. Russian Bear declared that Larisa had a DNR status just before she passed away. When Brewster and his friend Arby Fuller went by the intensive care unit to pay their respects to Russian Bear immediately after Larisa passed away, Feral Cheryl and Willy Mammon were already at the bedside.

If the truth be told, the die had been cast long before Larisa actually expired from an acute, fulminant case of GRID. The five people standing around the bedside who were viewing the tragic scene were no longer merely friends and colleagues. They were much more than that; collectively, they were now five clandestine coconspirators bound for vengeance.

———

Once Dr. Sassman had been reported missing, it took a full three weeks for the state police to discover that his old Bronco was at the Fertile Myrtle wellhead. Although the authorities had already been out there to scour the site as a first order of business, they originally hadn't seen his vehicle and other equipment because it had all been purposefully dumped into the sluice of gradeaux. Once they finally found the Bronco and towed it out of the swampy sluice, the authorities noted that the key to the vehicle was still in the ignition switch. In addition, they recovered the professor's shotgun from the back of the vehicle.

Once the galvanized sheet-metal waterway dam was slipped into the sluice cradle, it was then possible for the authorities to drain the swamp with gas-powered pumps and hoses. Upon further investigation, they found camping equipment and other various and sundry valuable items that also appeared to have been purposefully thrown into the sluice.

What the authorities found during their investigations made no sense whatsoever. If Sassman had been a victim of foul play, why hadn't the perpetrator simply stolen the Bronco, shotgun, and other expensive equipment? Instead, many expensive items had simply been destroyed when they were pushed or thrown into the waterway. It was inexplicable.

In addition, when they towed the Bronco out of the swamp, they found something extraordinarily odd: the parking brake was on. Although the car had a manual transmission and the gear had been left in neutral, either somebody with enormous strength had pushed the car into the waterway with the parking brake engaged, or somebody had driven the car into the body of water and then pulled the parking-brake hand lever once the car was submerged underwater. Both possibilities seemed to be improbabilities.

The authorities had already interviewed everybody in the lab and the students who had been actively involved in the dual-training program. It was time to fan out and talk to other persons of interest. It was finally time for the detectives to have a visit with medical student J. D. Brewster.

—————

On his last clerkship in May 1982, Brewster decided to accept the path of least resistance, and he signed up for a rotation on the pathology service. He expressed little, if any, interest in the technical end of the path lab, including the automated machinery that could generate a complete blood count or chemistry reports. However, Brewster did have interest in honing his skills in evaluating biopsy specimens underneath the microscope. As his rotation was scheduled to begin at 10:00 a.m., the medical student still had two hours to kill until the pathologists showed up at the lab. Brewster decided to hang out in the Vinyl Lounge to catch up on the news.

The television show Live! On Alonzo came on the air, and Brewster was aghast to see the talk show host interviewing famous civil rights attorney Johnny Koch Succor, who had accepted the offer to be the defense attorney for Mumbo Jamar Apoo.

Succor would represent his high-profile client pro bono. Succor explained to Alonzo, "This is an open-and-shut case of white-on-black racism. This is just another example of the blue-eyed white-devil slave master keeping the black man down. We're going to prove in a court of law beyond a shadow of a doubt that Officer Faulkland committed suicide because he could no longer stand the burden of the white man's guilt or the white man's privilege. The previous confessions my client made to the police were coerced, and he now retracts his previous attestations of any wrongdoing. When he was arrested, the two weapons found near my client were planted there by the police, I tell you."

As if he were a black preacher at a tent revival, Johnny Koch Succor stood up, walked to the edge of the television studio stage to face the crowded audience, and started to chant. "The gun was planted, I tell you. If the gun don't fit, you mus' acquit! If the gun don't fit, you mus' acquit!"

The crowded started to shout out the same chant. It was clear Succor was already trying the case in the court of urban opinion.

Brewster came to the likely but infuriating conclusion that there was no way in hell Big Nig would ever be convicted at that point.

After the television show concluded, Brewster decided to listen to a 1960s oldies station on the radio in the Vinyl Lounge for a while to pass the time. He was unaware that his colleague Victoria Campos was in the kitchenette area in the back of the lounge, heating up a frozen bean burrito in the microwave.

The song "Seventh Son," originally written by Willie Dixon and recorded by Johnny Rivers during a live performance at the Whisky a Go-Go in Hollywood, suddenly blared out over the airways. Although the song had been released in May 1965, Brewster remembered the tune by heart.

J. D. grabbed an empty can of Mr. Pibb soda as if it were a microphone, and he began to belt out the lyrics: "I can talk these words that will sound so sweet, they will even make your little heart skip a beat. Heal the sick! Raise the dead! Make the little girls talk out of their heads. I'm the one. Oh yeah, I'm the one. I'm the one. I'm the one, the one they call the seventh son."

When Brewster dropped to his knees during his solo performance, Victoria Campos emerged from the kitchenette area and started to dance the pony around her colleague. At the conclusion of the song, Victoria put her arms around Brewster's neck and gave him a hug.

"I'm terribly sorry to hear that your fiancée, Stella, passed away a few months ago. I found out that you were accepted for an internal medicine residency training program in New Mexico. Congratulations! As for me, I am jumping over to the University of Texas Medical Branch in Galveston."

"I'm happy for you, Vick!"

"Guess what?" Victoria added. "I'm going to be doing a residency training program in internal medicine also."

"They'll be lucky to have you on the island."

"I hope that in the future," Victoria said, "I'll have a chance to see you again, and we can pick up where we left off. Maybe if you move out into the badlands, you can officially become Hispanic."

"Yo hablo the lingo, little girl."

"I know you do," Victoria said. "I've always thought you were just a bad-ass Mexican bandito hiding behind the clothing of either a sheep or a gringo."

"Maybe both," Brewster said. "Depends on the day of the week, I suppose. I'll be the first to admit that I've not even faced my own life with either bravery or even a sense of purpose."

"You've always sold yourself short, amigo," Victoria said. "In any event, my sister owns a Sonoran-style restaurant in Casa Grande, Arizona."

"What's the name of the place?" Brewster asked.

"La Placenta!"

"Yummy in my tummy," Brewster replied.

"I plan to take a road trip out there someday. If I do, I'd love to see you when I swing through New Mexico. I happen to like Casa Grande!"

"What in the world are you talking about?" Brewster asked. "Years ago, I went on a road trip to California, and I remember passing through Casa Grande, Arizona. As I recall, it was little more than a dried-up dog turd infested with filthy flies engaged in horrific acts of coprophagic dining."

"Well, it's indeed hot and grimy there," Victoria said, "and it has lots of dust storms. However, I'm happy to report that Casa Grande probably has the highest quality of filth in the entire world! It's as fine as talcum powder. I bet just a dash of it would keep my muff dry for a week! You can actually taste the grit when the wind blows."

"I'm sure there's still a boatload of that nasty filth lodged deep in the alveoli of my lungs from my previous solitary visit to that nasty little berg."

"I must admit," Victoria said, "if anybody lived down there for any length of time, he or she would probably end up with pulmonary failure as a consequence of silicosis, pulmonary fibrosis, or valley fever. Every damned dog my sister has owned since she's lived out in Arizona has died from valley fever!"

"Sounds lovely," Brewster said sarcastically. "Why in hell would any sane being elect to live out there?"

"Well," Victoria answered, "the same reason any idiot would live anywhere in Arizona."

"The reason being?"

"People only end up there when the family station wagon breaks down on the way to California," Victoria said. "People just get stuck out there. There could be no other explanation. I'm straight up with you!"

"Well, maybe so." Brewster laughed. "I've always liked you, Victoria. I can't deny that I've always felt there was a certain spark between us."

After Victoria kissed Brewster and gently cupped his crotch briefly with her left hand, she slipped out of the Vinyl Lounge and disappeared. Her colleague, who at that time was lost at sea and far from the safety of terra firma, belatedly sighed.

"Just maybe, if I ever pull myself together," Brewster said, "I'll have a chance to look you up someday."

Would Brewster ever pull himself together? Upon graduation from medical school, Victoria Campos would be long gone. Again, another opportunity in his life would be forever lost. Yet again, Brewster missed the big picture.

Once Victoria left the Vinyl Lounge, Brewster still had an hour to kill until his new rotation was scheduled to start. The lounge telephone rang just as the voice of televangelist Rectal Roberts blared out over the television screen. Brewster was mesmerized by what he saw: the huckster claimed that one of his parishioners was about to be raised from the dead, and it was all going to be broadcast live from Hope, Arkansas!

"Wow! If this guy can raise somebody from the dead," Brewster said aloud in the otherwise empty lounge, "I need to pay him a visit. Maybe if I donate a couple of Ben Bens, this dude can scrape up a new pair of testicles for me!"

At first, Brewster was not inclined to answer the ringing telephone because the likelihood that it was a call for him was extraordinarily low. The phone continued to ring off the wall, and it became annoying.

Finally, Brewster picked up the receiver and said, "Holmes Road County Dump—Rufus speaking. How may I help you?"

The person on the other end of the line was none other than Ben Fielder. "Brew, it's me. What took you so long to answer the damned phone?"

"Why are you bothering me, string bean?" Brewster asked. "We're no longer on speaking terms, as I recall."

"Listen up, asshole," Fielder replied. "Mammoth is down in the ER. He's in status!"

Terrified, Brewster dropped the telephone receiver upon the floor and promptly ran next door to the emergency room to see if he could lend any assistance in the medical management of the big man.

Willy Mammon had developed a complication called status epilepticus, a medical emergency wherein a patient suffering from epilepsy developed a nonstop seizure that couldn't readily be broken. If a seizure couldn't be medically interrupted, a patient suffering from such an event would surely develop brain damage or perhaps not survive the event at all and end up dying.

When Brewster arrived at the emergency room, Cheryl and Ben Fielder were waiting outside of Willy's emergency room stall. Although Fielder and Brewster did not say anything to each other, they attempted to behave in a civil manner. They at least begrudgingly shook each other's hand.

Cheryl grabbed Brewster by the arm and asked, "Do you think Willy is going to be all right?"

"I just don't know, Cheryl," Brewster honestly replied. "I just don't know."

Momentarily, Brewster and Fielder both felt a great sense of relief when they heard harsh snoring sounds emanating from Willy Mammon's stall. The sonorous cacophony could mean only one thing: Willy was now in a postictal state, and the seizure had finally broken.

As the emergency room physician pulled back the curtain to the stall, Dr. Bryan looked frazzled. "Jesus, I swear we must have used up all of the Valium in the pharmacy to finally break this goddamned thing. We're getting swamped down here. Can you boys help out? I need somebody to knock out Willy's H and P so we can get him upstairs. I don't know where in the hell the neurons are, but they've obviously gophered out on us."

Brewster and Fielder looked at each other, and without a word, they played a round of paper, rock, and scissors. The medical students were tied after the first two rounds, as each had thrown out rocks on both of the prior challenges. Fielder won the third round when he threw out a paper to Brewster's third rock in a row.

As Ben Fielder and Cheryl remained by the patient's bedside, Brewster wandered over to the dictation area to complete the extensive paperwork necessary for Willy to be shipped out of the ER and into a hospital bed on the med-surg unit.

The paperwork would be tedious but not a particularly daunting task for Brewster, as the medical student already knew all of the details about the big man's social circumstances, and Brewster was also well versed in Willy's medical conditions.

Besides, as Willy was uncommunicative in a postictal state, Brewster would not have to complete the review-of-systems section on the H and P. This omission alone would speed up the paperwork process dramatically.

In a room adjacent to where Brewster started the admission paperwork was none other than Dr. Frank Barber. When the emergency room attending physician heard Brewster's voice, he stuck his head into the cubicle where the medical student was working.

"Hey, Brew, I heard you were doing a rotation on the path service. Please tell me you're not trying to buff with fluff, are you?"

"I believe I may very well resemble that remark," Brewster answered.

"Well, if that's the case," Barber exclaimed, "batter up!"

"You've got to be kidding me," Brewster replied. "I'm too short for this shit. Mammon just had an episode of status epilepticus, and you're doing this to me? What's wrong with you, Dr. Barber?"

"I'll tell you what's wrong with me: I'm already dead. I died a long time ago. I'm just going through the motions of being alive. Now, I'm only going to pimp you once. Answer the damned question," Frank Barber said.

"Okay, throw me the first pitch," Brewster said as he shrugged and tried to maintain an image that he was still somehow, well, normal.

"Can you tell me the difference between an internist, a surgeon, and a clinical pathologist?" Barber asked.

"Dr. Barber," Brewster replied, "I have no idea how to answer that question."

The professor chuckled when he answered the riddle. "Well, son, the internist knows everything but does nothing. A surgeon knows nothing but does everything. The pathologist knows everything and does everything, but it's always just one day too late!"

"That was really funny!" Brewster said as he shook his head and broke out laughing. "I must admit, that was some sick shit, but that was really funny."

"Say, do you remember that DiSPOSe named Moxie Hightower?" Dr. Barber asked on a more somber note.

"I think so," Brewster replied. "Wasn't he the poor bastard addicted to heroin whom I met down here in the ER last July?"

"One and the same," Barber answered. "Well, guess what? He's underneath a sheet on this gurney beside me. I just gave him two doses of Narcan a few moments ago, but the medication has done nothing to raise him from the dead. It would appear he's finally gone bye-bye once and for all. He's about to take the big dirt nap, and I'm just about to sign the formal declaration."

"Bound to happen sooner or later, I suppose," Brewster said, "especially with his long-standing history of drug abuse."

"For your information," Barber said, "Moxie had what is generally recognized to be one of the worst prognostic indicators a doctor is ever likely to encounter during a face-to-face patient evaluation."

"Could it be any worse than Colima's famous Dr. Blow Sign that I became acquainted with about two years ago?" Brewster asked.

"By far!" Dr. Barber exclaimed. "Check this out: Moxie had a tag on his right great toe that declared he was already DOA. Now, if I may say so, that is a fairly undignified way for a soul to make an exit from this plane of existence."

"Why did you even bother to give him any Narcan at all if that was the case?" Brewster asked. "As I recall from last year, Moxie already had a documented DNR code status, did he not?"

"I don't know," Dr. Barber answered. "Perhaps you're right. Maybe from now on I should learn to let dead dogs simply lie in peace. To be honest with you, I sort of envy Moxie Hightower. For him, it is finished. As for me, it'll be decades before anybody figures out that I have already exceeded my expiration date. Maybe then, and only then, my earthly remains will finally get cremated."

"That's some seriously morbid shit you're spewing out of your pie hole over there, Dr. Barber," Brewster said. "I suggest you snap out of it. Is life not supposed to be a blessing?"

Dr. Barber was pensive momentarily before he answered. "Just listen to what you're saying to me! You're a hypocrite. I know you all too well, Brew. Listen to me, sport; perhaps you should wander off and take a long look at yourself in a mirror. Here you are, sitting in front of me as you righteously proclaim that life's a blessing. Are you sure about that?"

"No, I guess I actually don't believe so after all."

"That's what I thought. Hypocrite! Spare me your existential pontifications," Dr. Barber said. "I suggest that if you really want to say adios to Moxie, do it now. After I complete this death summary, his corpse is going to be dumped into big vat of formalin. Last year, he bequeathed his earthly remains to the medical school effective at the time of his demise, and now it seems he'll be in the queue for the freshman human anatomy dissection class that will be starting up this coming July."

As Brewster couldn't deflect the accusations of hypocrisy levied upon him by Dr. Barber, the medical student had to accept the critique at face value. Nonetheless, he was curious about the details of Moxie Hightower's untimely egress from the realm of the living.

"At what time do you estimate Moxie bought the farm?"

"A Gypsy named Mother Magnesium and her boyfriend, Brother Barium, found him in an alleyway," Barber answered. "I can't believe it, but those two jokers tried to do the right thing. They loaded his body up into their own personal vehicle and brought Moxie here. They told me they were just trying to be Good Samaritans."

"You've got to be kidding me!" Brewster exclaimed. "I happen to know Mother Magnesium and Brother Barium, and they're both scoundrels."

"Well, at the very least, they're both frequent fliers here in the emergency room," Dr. Barber said, "but they seem to have fundamentally changed in one way or another. Perhaps even for the better..."

"How so?" Brewster asked.

"If I had to guess," Dr. Barber said, "it was as if they had the very devil beaten out of them. Nevertheless, what they did was, sadly, just a day late and a dollar short. According to the two Gypsies, they witnessed Moxie sitting in the lotus position out in the alleyway for three full days. At first, they merely believed he was engaged in some sort of a prolonged, extracorporeal astral projection or some other sort of mumbo-jumbo bullshit. In retrospect, it's likely he was dead that entire time."

"Perhaps if Moxie was useless while he was alive," Brewster said, "he'll at least serve some higher purpose as a cadaver subject in the freshman anatomy class now that he's dead."

"I suppose you're correct," Dr. Barber said.

Sister Buena suddenly arrived at the emergency room. Brewster didn't look up, nor did he recognize who was speaking to him when she said, "Excuse me. I'm looking for Brother Moxie Hightower."

While Brewster kept his eyes focused on Willy Mammon's demographic page, he pointed over to the room where Dr. Barber and the body of Moxie Hightower were located. "He's in the room next door, but you're too late, madam," Brewster said. "You don't want to go in there, as he's already been dead for three days now. His body is about to be wheeled down to the morgue."

Sister Buena proceeded to slip into the room where Dr. Barber and the dead body were located.

"Would you mind if I said a few prayers for Moxie Hightower?" the floating nurse from the temp pool asked.

"Go ahead, for what it's worth," Dr. Barber replied. "Knock yourself out, lady. Be mindful, though: if you're going to bother to say a few prayers for the dead bodies in this room, please feel free to punch one out for me. After all, I've certainly been dead a whole lot longer than our dearly and recently departed friend named Moxie Hightower. This humble request for Divine intervention is only submitted, of course, if God in heaven is not too damned busy working on some other more important part of the universe right about now."

Sister Buena raised her face and extended the palms of her hands toward the ceiling in prayer at the foot of the gurney that held

Moxie's lifeless body. After only a few moments, Moxie Hightower became reanimated and threw the sheet that covered him onto the floor!

"No, I'm sorry!" Moxie exclaimed. "Don't ever send me back there! Please! It was horrible! Save me!"

It appeared Moxie had just returned from a bad trip.

"Welcome back, Moxie!" Sister Buena said. "It's time for you to go to work. Follow me."

With that, Sister Buena and Moxie Hightower quietly walked down the hallway to leave the hospital while Frank Barber looked on in stunned silence.

Moxie left the hospital with the DOA-designation tag still affixed to his right great toe with a thin twist-tie wire. Before Sister Buena left through the emergency room exit doors, she turned back to look at Dr. Frank Barber over her shoulder with a broad smile to ask the emergency room physician one last pertinent question.

"Well, aren't you coming? After all, Frank, how many miracles do you need to see?"

Frank Barber suddenly had another out-of-body experience. As he sat down beside Brewster, who was still completing the admission paperwork on Willy Mammon, the emergency room physician briefly felt as if he were standing sideways on the back office wall while looking down upon himself.

The physician was still trembling when he said, "Brewster, check this out: Moxie Hightower just jumped off the gurney and ran out the front door!"

"Thank God!" Brewster replied. "It looks like the Narcan you gave him must have finally kicked in. Strong work, Dr. Barber! Moxie was probably just hypothermic and needed to get warmed up a bit. Nothing more and nothing less."

The medical student's casual reply made Frank Barber jump up in anger. The attending grabbed Brewster by the collar of his short consulting jacket and forcefully pushed him up against the back tiled wall.

"No, damn it, you're not listening to me!" Dr. Barber screamed only inches away from Brewster's face. "I'm telling you right here and right now that I've just witnessed an intersession of Divine providence!"

Although startled, Brewster pulled himself away from the grasp of Dr. Frank Barber and replied, "Miracles do happen, but you never know who's been chosen to be the witness. I guess I just wasn't supposed to see this one."

Dr. Frank Barber sprinted out of the emergency room to catch up to Moxie Hightower and Sister Buena. Dr. Barber would never return to work at the hospital from that point on. He simply abandoned his post.

As for Moxie Hightower, he was able to maintain sobriety for the rest of his life. Moxie eventually became an ordained street preacher, as he had been assigned the specific mission of keeping other young people from making the same terrible mistakes in life that Moxie had previously inflicted upon himself.

Although he had squandered a great deal of his youth as a consequence of heroin abuse and the physical and psychological degradation it had induced, Moxie Hightower finally found redemption and perhaps even salvation.

How could he not? After all, he'd been raised from the dead...

As for Frank Barber, he received specific instructions that his new mission in life would be the creation of a free community clinic in downtown Houston. Once he had accomplished that task, Dr. Barber ended up providing care for the destitute and the homeless. As was often recited, blessed were the poor.

The board-certified emergency medicine physician soon found he was able to completely sustain himself in his noble endeavor through the generous donations of the righteous citizens and altruistic denizens who resided in the fair city of Houston.

In addition, gracious corporate block grants turned out to be unexpected blessings.

It appeared despite the tragedy the emotionally traumatized doctor had experienced when he and his wife, Nancy, were viciously kidnapped and tortured by members of the Calle Vampiro drug cartel, Dr. Frank Barber finally found redemption and perhaps even salvation.

How could he not? After all, he'd been raised from the dead...

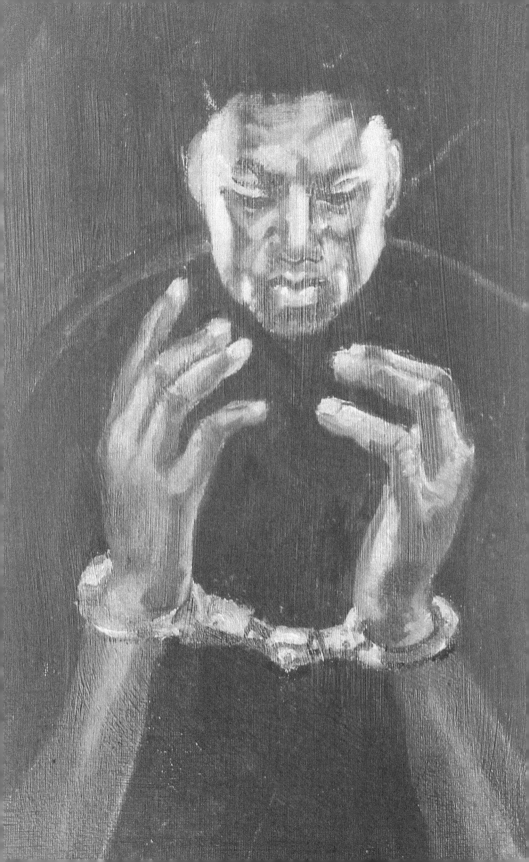

14

LIGHTNING ROD

Although the authorities already had towed away Dr. Sassman's abandoned Bronco found in the swamp, a team of forensic investigators were still at the site of the Fertile Myrtle wellhead to try to find any possible clues as to what had happened to the missing medical research scientist.

The police laboratory had already analyzed the film in the motion-triggered trail cameras they'd found, but they'd discovered no incriminating evidence on any of the devices. Although not under arrest, J. D. Brewster was finally a person of interest to the two homicide detectives, Culp and Watt.

When the unmarked squad car arrived at the wellhead, county sheriffs and a Texas Ranger greeted the detectives. Culp opened the back door of the squad car to allow Brewster to step out, where the medical student would be more vulnerable.

"Why don't you just show us where you buried your professor, and we'll put in a good word to the DA on your behalf?" Watt said sharply. "If this all works out for you, maybe you won't get the big needle at the end of the day."

"I have nothing to confess," Brewster said, "and therefore, I have nothing to fear."

"It's such a pleasant day," Detective Culp sarcastically said, "that I'd like to take a stroll around the parade grounds. Would you care to accompany me, Mr. Brewster? Maybe we can stop over by the midway and pick up a bag of peanuts and a deep-fried Hostess Twinkie. Have you ever had one? They're almost as good as doughnuts, and God knows I love doughnuts. I like the ones that are jelly filled. How 'bout you, J. D.?"

"Jelly doughnuts are indeed near and dear to my heart."

"So let me get this straightened out," Watt said. "If you say you've got nothing to confess, that means you believe you're innocent. Why don't you tell me what you think happened to Professor Sassman? After all, people don't just disappear into thin air."

"There are indeed a myriad of possibilities," Brewster answered. "There are all kinds of ways people could get shit on if they come out here. There are copperheads, corals, and cottonmouths. Dr. Sassman once showed me a plaster-of-paris casting he had taken of a jaguar paw print he found out here. Now, I know for a fact that the last jaguar shooting in the state of Texas happened out in Brownwood around the year 1950, but that doesn't mean they aren't trying to make a comeback."

"A wild animal was the culprit?" Culp asked. "Where are the professor's remains if that's the case?"

"Beats me," Brewster said. "Perhaps even the black bear is starting to make a comeback. Who knows? There is a sluice of gradeaux just north of the pump head where a person could fall in and drown. In addition, Dr. Sassman had two alligators in the sluice, and both were about eight or ten feet long. One was named Popeye, and the other was named Bluto. He used to hand-feed those damned things raw chicken."

"There aren't any big alligators out here now," Watt said.

"I'll swear on a stack!" Brewster said.

"Of Bibles?" Culp asked.

"No, sir!" Brewster replied. "Pancakes! Maybe one day when he was out here performing maintenance work on his wellhead, the gators grabbed him, dragged him off, and ate him."

"We believe it's much more likely that Dr. Sassman has fallen victim to foul play at the hands of one or more fellow human beings rather than falling victim to predation," Culp said.

"Well," Brewster said, "you might be onto something. I know that on more than one occasion, Dr. Sassman encountered some bad hombres who were trying to steal oil from his tank battery. At one time, he even had a shoot-out with a couple of those yahoos. Maybe something else. Perhaps somebody at the medical center had some kind of a beef with him over one matter or another. Maybe there are even other things out here that could've attacked Denny Sassman."

"Come over to this sluice with us, and let's take a look at what we might find," Detective Watt said.

Brewster followed the detectives over to the edge of the sluice, and much to the surprise of the medical student, a galvanized sheet-metal waterway dam had been dropped into the sluice cradle at the east end of what had been a foul and slimy body of water. Subsequently, the authorities had drained the swamp.

"Look what we've done," Watt said.

"I am indeed impressed," Brewster said. "If you boys pulled this off out here in East Texas, I assure you there's a job waiting for you in Washington, DC. After all, there's a big-ass swamp up there that needs to get drained also."

"Very funny," Watt said. "This is where we found Sassman's Bronco, camping equipment, and motion-triggered trail cameras. We found nothing in the sluice except for six baby alligators. None of them were longer than about a foot or so. We didn't find any of the alleged giant alligators you previously mentioned."

"Can't you see?" Brewster said. "If there were baby alligators, there must have also been bigger alligators that sired them. Doesn't that make sense to you guys? What about the quicksand pit? I see you've staked off that area with a big plastic yellow ribbon. You need to take a look inside that pit. A man could get completely buried in there if he accidentally fell into it."

"Not according to the two hydrological engineers we brought in from Squat and Poot," Culp replied. "According to their calculations, the quicksand is only about nine feet deep, and a chunky man the size of Dr. Sassman would've had enough natural buoyancy to get trapped only up to about the level of his waist or chest. There's no way he could have been completely buried in the stuff if he fell in naturally as an accident or even as an overt act of foul play."

"Of course, he could have gotten trapped and then died from exposure or dehydration," Brewster said.

"If that's the case, where's the body, Brewster?" Detective Watt asked.

"Look, Brewster, I don't want to be out here all day," Culp said. "Why don't you just tell us what happened to Dr. Sassman?"

"I just figured it all out, Culp!" Watt said sarcastically. "The good professor got stuck in the quicksand, and the invisible giant alligators came out of the sluice and ate him up after he was trapped. That's the ticket!"

"Go ahead," Brewster said. "Laugh about it, why don't you?"

"We have a more logical explanation," Culp said. "We believe you killed Dr. Sassman, threw him into the quicksand pit, and then used a two-by-four or perhaps a long piece of pipe to shove his body all the way down to the bottom of the pit after tying his corpse to a heavy ballast, such as a scrap piece of heavy drilling equipment that you might have found lying around this pump-jack assembly."

"Bullshit!" Brewster said. "Bring in a backhoe. Let's see what's in that pit."

"Funny you should say that," Watt said. "I think that's an excellent suggestion."

No sooner had the detective made that comment than a semi rolled up to the site. It was towing a flatbed trailer toting a backhoe. Within an hour, the entire quicksand pit had been evacuated, and its contents had been spread out on the ground adjacent to the pump jack. They found no evidence of a dead body—or anything else, for that matter—in the thick, wet, concrete-like muck.

"Are we about done here?" Brewster asked. "Just to show you boys that there are no hard feelings, let's stop in Dayton on our way back to H-Town. I'm talking burgers, fries, and chocolate malts with extra malt powder. I'm buying! Let's get out of here before it gets dark. This place gets creepy when the sun goes down."

"You said something curious back at the wellhead site," Culp said as the two detectives and Brewster headed back toward Interstate 10. "You mentioned that perhaps there were other things out in the woods that could possibly attack a human being. We've learned that Dr. Sassman had some pretty peculiar ideas about the existence of the giant skunk ape that allegedly lives out here in the swamps of East Texas. You weren't making some kind of reference to a Big Foot, now, were you?"

"What do you mean?" Brewster asked.

"Simple," Watt said. "Do you know more than you're telling us?"

"I'm sorry," Brewster replied as he looked down at the thick, rubberized black flooring of the squad car, "but I don't know what you boys are talking about."

⊸⊸⊸

With the disappearance of Dr. Denny Sassman, Dr. Bruce Beathard suddenly became the titular head of the MD/PhD dual-training program. Wow, what a surprise. If one hadn't known better, it might have appeared as if the disappearance of Dr. Sassman and the promotion of Dr. Beathard were somehow intricately linked.

With a new jefe in charge of the dual-training program, it was time for Brewster to pay a visit to administration. Perhaps if he went cap in hand to Dr. Beathard, he could resurrect his suspended quest to earn a PhD degree. It was a long shot, but maybe it was one worth taking. After knocking on Dr. Beathard's door, the medical student was invited in.

"Hello, Brewster," Beathard said. "To be honest, I'm quite surprised to see you. What brings you here?"

"Earlier this past year," Brewster replied, "I did a rotation on the hematology service. I had an opportunity to evaluate a patient who had the signs and symptoms of Alzheimer's disease, but her workup showed she had severe B12 deficiency. Although she was not anemic, her mean corpuscular volume was above the upper limit of the normal range. She was treated with B12 injections, and her mental status dramatically improved within the span of just a few months. It was a miraculous clinical event to behold."

"What of it?"

"I have a multipronged clinical trial in mind that could answer the following questions: How many patients are in nursing homes with a diagnosis of Alzheimer's disease but actually have subclinical B12 deficiency? Although parenteral B12 injections are the standard of care in patients afflicted with B12 deficiency, can we overwhelm patients with oral B12 and replete them in that fashion as opposed to the current injection therapy as a standard of care? Is subclinical B12 deficiency with associated dementia a different animal than classic pernicious macrocytic anemia? Maybe there's some other issue besides a decrease in the gastric intrinsic factor that leads to B12 deficiency," Brewster said. "Well, what do you think?"

"I like where you are going with this," Dr. Beathard replied. "I've made some notes about your suggestions, and I really think we need to offer it up for a feasibility evaluation. I'll be happy to pass this on to the new round of braniacs coming on board here at the beginning of July. Thank you, Brewster. I bid you a good day and wish you good fortune after you graduate from here in the next few weeks."

"Now, wait just a minute here," Brewster said. "This is my idea, and I believe I should be offered an opportunity to see it to the finish line. I want back in on the PhD program. I talked to Dr. Sassman about this idea just before he disappeared. I need to tell you that he seemed to be very enthusiastic about it. He went as far as to tell me he would submit his recommendation to the board that I get reinstated into the dual-training program in order for me to get my PhD degree."

"Well, Dr. Sassman is no longer in charge around here, now is he?" Dr. Beathard asked Brewster with a malevolent smile. "On Denny's posthumous behalf, I would at least reluctantly honor such a request for your reinstatement into the PhD program; however, after rummaging through Dr. Sassman's rather untidy professional documents, I assure you I've not come across any requisition regarding a change in your status within our dual training program."

Brewster had failed to realize up until that moment that the administration considered the student to be nothing more than damaged goods that warranted liquidation through a blue-light special found in the discount bargain bin at Kmart.

Dr. Beathard was about to lay all of his cards out on the table, and in doing so, he was going to torpedo any residual dreams Brewster still had about getting a dual degree at the Gulf Coast College of Medicine.

Dr. Beathard went to a large file cabinet and pulled out a thick metallic binder that had Brewster's name written on it in large block letters across the front.

"However, I must let you know," Beathard said, "that what I did find out about you when I was poking around in Denny's office was rather illuminating."

"What do you mean?" Brewster asked. "You boys have a file on me?"

"Well, where there's smoke, there's fire," Beathard said as he pulled out the heavy metal binder and set it on the desk. "It's all right here in this steel dossier. To be frank, I tried to put the squeeze on your colleagues I thought maybe they'd cough up the dope about you. I thought you'd been in collusion with the Russian over high crimes and misdemeanors, bur nothing impeachable panned out. Nonetheless, there's been a shitload of unsubstantiated allegations about the troublesome mischief you might have been involved with over the last two years. Although we've never been able to nail you down on anything, your name keeps popping up time and again. At some point, the laws of probability ensure that the commonality of peculiar circumstances will eventually cross the threshold from being a coincidence into being, well–a certainty!"

"I have been an exemplary student since I have been here at the Gulf Coast," Brewster said.

Dr. Beathard laughed and wagged his finger at the medical student. "Let me cite chapter and verse. There was a house-staff physician who had an upper gastrointestinal bleed from a Mallory-Weiss tear. It was a consequence to some asshole who apparently placed a novelty rubber cockroach in his meal. You were directly adjacent to that event when it occurred."

"I don't know what you are talking about."

"There was a riot that occurred down in the cafeteria concerning something that had to do with an apparent foreign terrorist cell," Beathard said, "and you were directly adjacent to that event when it occurred."

"I don't know what you are talking about."

"Did you go on a field trip to Hermann Hospital last year to scrub in on an emergency laminectomy on a patient named Joe Diddly?" Beathard asked. "I believe Dr. Wolfgang von Scheiß Kopf was the neurosurgeon from the University Texas who performed the operation."

"What of it?"

"One of the insurance reps from the Gulf Coast HMO levied serious accusations against you. She filed a report that you actually threatened to slap her to death. What would you have done next–turn her into a goddamned lampshade?"

"That's a load," Brewster said. "It was that Nazi, Dr. Scheiß

Kopf, who uttered that specific threat against this particular stupid woman. As a matter of full and honest disclosure however, I would have paid good money to be a ring-side ticket holder to that specific, full-contact sporting event if it was ever commercially available for blood-thirsty public consumption."

"There was a ward clerk in the ICU who was fired for gross insubordination, and you were directly adjacent to that event when it occurred."

"I wasn't there."

"There was an elderly and demented patient who apparently was enticed into grooming a cat by licking it. You were directly adjacent to that event when it occurred," Beathard said. "Are things starting to add up yet?"

"I don't know what you are talking about."

"Although we're certain Dr. Hank Holcombe died from advanced cancer, the administration has become aware that there were some very strange and disturbing activities going on at the time of his demise. You were directly adjacent to that event when it occurred," Beathard said.

"I don't know what—"

"Silence!" Beathard demanded. "I'm not even going to broach the subject of the six primates that mysteriously disappeared from the lockdown kennel, nor am I going to make any implications about the recent peculiar disappearance of Dr. Denny Sassman. Shall I continue?"

"I don't—"

"Spare my life!" Beathard said, interrupting the medical student yet again. "You know damned well what I am talking about. Frankly, Brewster, you're a lightning rod. It's the belief of this administration that upon your graduation with your MD degree, it will be time for you to go away. In fact, it will be time for you to go far away."

Crestfallen, Brewster nonetheless extended his right arm to shake the hand of Dr. Beathard, but Beathard didn't return the common courtesy in kind. So be it. If Brewster was considered persona non grata, there was only one item left on the agenda before he graduated. Time was running out, but it was imperative for Brewster have to a little private chitchat with Mumbo Jamal Apoo.

"Close the door on your way out," Beathard said.

—◁◁◁∩∩▷▷▷—

"This happens to be the nicest restaurant I've ever been in," Brewster said.

"Whenever I come to Houston, I always try to make a point of dining here. I must admit that as the chief scientist in charge of new product development at the Leben Kur, AG pharmaceutical company, my position certainly has its perks."

"So it would seem," Brewster said.

"I hope you don't have any qualms about selling out your medical school this way," the visiting scientist said. "I want you to look upon this transaction as a reimbursement for consultation services you've provided my firm."

"Cut the crap," Brewster said. "At this point in my life, I'm not inclined to sugarcoat something that's an act of pure and simple industrial espionage. I know your pharmaceutical company collaborated with the Nazis during World War II, and frankly, I don't give two shits about that either. To be honest, I don't owe my medical school the sweat from my empty ball sack."

"It sounds to me as if you've got an axe to grind against your alma mater," the scientist said.

"I most certainly do," Brewster said as he passed a small briefcase to the stranger who had invited the medical school student out to dinner. "If the truth be told, I have an axe to grind about everything. Here's the binder on all of the information regarding the technical procedures Yeshua Rabbi and I devised to neutralize any viral contamination one might encounter in human blood and serum during our previous work on the hepatitis B vaccine project. Now, if you would be so kind, I believe you have something for me also."

"Here's a cashier's check that should be more than enough to help you pay off your remaining medical school tuition debt," the West German pharmaceutical representative said with a smile as he handed Brewster a plain white envelope.

He then uttered a final comment to the student that was damning praise indeed. "When you wrap up the loose ends in your life, I want you to look me up," the research scientist said. "If the truth be told, you're exactly the type of man who should be collaborating with me in the future."

The Dalton twins were graduating from the University of Houston, and of course, they'd invited Brewster to the ceremony. After they received their diplomas, the young ladies found Brewster in the crowd. They ran up to J. D., and each gave him a hug and a kiss on the cheek.

As D' Shea was still completely bald from her previous radiation treatment, her sister, D' Nae, had continued her own tradition of shaving her head so the twins could still match each other in their appearance. Brewster was ready to give his graduation present to the Dalton sisters.

During the Juneteenth celebration in 1981, Brewster had made a solemn oath to D' Shea that he would give her the exact gift she previously had asked for if she lived long enough to graduate from college. Well, D' Shea had done her part, and it was now time for the medical student to uphold his end of the bargain.

J. D. Brewster was a man of his word. He pulled off the Houston Astros baseball hat he was wearing to reveal that he had shaved his head. Brewster was now also completely bald.

D' Nae was pleasantly surprised, as she had not been privy

to the original promise J. D. had whispered into her sister's ear at Hermann Park on that fateful night when Brewster was traumatically sterilized. In regard to Brewster's new self-inflicted alopecia, D' Shea had expected nothing less.

"Come sit over here," D' Shea said. "I want to give you a special treat."

When Brewster sat down in one of the empty auditorium chairs, D' Shea pulled out a canister of carnauba car wax and began to apply a thick layer of the creamy material on top of the medical student's head before she buffed it to a bright shine with a small terrycloth towel she had brought with her.

"You look beautiful," the young woman said. "Let's take a picture right now! We've got a cue ball and two eight balls sitting right here."

Brewster winced a bit when D' Nae exclaimed, "Rack 'em up, Baby Girl!"

The sisters apologized that they would not be able to come to J. D. Brewster's pending graduation from medical school, as they were going on a road trip to Northern California at that time. They planned to go camping in the redwood forest. They looked forward to hiking on the Roosevelt Trail at Prairie Creek, and they thought that if they were lucky enough, perhaps they would run into a Sasquatch!

"Be careful what you wish for," Brewster cautioned.

The sisters promised Brewster they would send him postcards along the way.

Brewster said he understood and expected them to go on the important milestone trip together. D' Shea was happy to report something astounding to the man who was presumably her half-brother.

"Check this out, Brew: I just had my restaging scans, and I'm still in complete remission. How could this be? I should have been dead by now. I tell you, it's a miracle! What do you think of that?"

Brewster softly expressed his affirmation about the remarkable phenomenon. "Miracles do happen, but you never know who has been chosen to be the witness. I guess I was finally blessed in that I was supposed to see this one."

⟿⟾

The pathology resident tapped J. D. Brewster on the shoulder and handed him two permanently fixed microscopic slides. "Brew, I want you to take these two slides over to the double-headed scope. The slide on the left is an example of invasive transitional cell carcinoma of the bladder. This bladder biopsy was taken from a particular patient who has already been told the results. He's coming in today to the oncology clinic to discuss treatment options. The other slide is an example of a hypernephroma taken from a different patient who has been diagnosed with primary renal cell carcinoma."

"What of it?"

"Now, these are both examples of malignancies that may arise out of the genitourinary tract, but they're frankly quite different in their appearance and biological behavior," the resident said. "I want to make certain you're able to discern the variance between these two particular urinary tract malignant diseases."

Brewster took a look at the patient's name on the label affixed to the glass microscopic slide designated as an example of transitional cell carcinoma of the bladder. The medical student immediately recognized the name of an elderly Catholic priest, Father Filbert Flynn.

"Look, before we review these slides together at the teaching scope," Brewster said, "I have to go see this patient. I have to see him right now. I know this guy; he was a substitute teacher at my high school here in Houston. According to the pathology log, this patient's path report needs to be sent over right now to the outpatient oncology clinic, where the patient is scheduled for a follow-up visit to discuss these unfavorable results with the crab pickers. Please give me a few moments to pay my respects."

The pathology resident gave Brewster permission to take a twenty-minute break to visit his old high school teacher.

Before Father Flynn had received the call to join the priesthood, he'd been an iron worker who'd helped construct many of Houston's high-rise buildings after the war. Although long removed from construction work, Father Flynn was a man of enormous proportions, despite the fact that he was now in his sixth decade of life. He was physically capable of cracking a macadamia nut in the crook of his right arm. As no standard commercially made cassock would fit over his enormous frame, his clothes were custom tailored out of strips of canvas harvested from circus-tent remnants.

A mathematics teacher early in his career as an educator, Father Flynn eventually had been relegated to the task of working as a substitute teacher. He also had functioned as the school's primary disciplinarian after he suffered premature hearing loss as a consequence of long-term, unprotected exposure to the high-decibel and high-frequency staccato cacophony emitted from the pneumatic riveters he'd utilized as an iron worker.

As it was his primary duty to render corporal punishment at an all-boys high school, Father Flynn had fashioned a disciplinarian tool out of a custom-crafted titanium cricket bat with multiple holes cross-drilled through the blade of the weapon. He'd mechanically accomplished that particular feat of aerodynamic engineering in a NASA-affiliated jet-propulsion wind tunnel laboratory at the Houston Space Center in an effort to reduce wind resistance and increase top-end speed of the mythical butt beater.

The name of the bat was the Atom Smasher. As the device was capable of achieving supersonic speeds on the downswing, it could reportedly blister the backside of a rhino with one swat.

If a second swat from the Mach-1-rated cricket bat was deemed necessary to quell a riot or dissuade other miscreant behavior, the bat was fully capable of welding shut the anal aperture of the misfortunate, humongous, horned mammalian herbivore in question. Needless to say, no student alive ever wanted to cross paths with Father Flynn's supersonic titanium butt blaster.

When Brewster entered the stall on the first-floor outpatient oncology unit occupied by Father Flynn, the elderly educator immediately recognized his former pupil.

"Tell me, Mr. Brewster—did my disciplinarian methodology render you physically impaired, or have you recovered to the point where you are now able to sit down upon that shriveled and atrophied keister of yours?"

"I am sorry to see that you are about to face some tough times with this bladder cancer you've acquired, Father Flynn," Brewster replied. "Is there anything I can do for you?"

"I'm truly frightened, lad." The elderly priest had one specific request. "Would you please bow your head and say the Lord's Prayer with me?"

Brewster was about to oblige his old teacher, but some commotion in the hallway caught his eye and ear. He saw a patient being wheeled into the hospital. The person appeared to be a black man in his mid to late thirties and was wearing an orange prison jumpsuit. It was none other than Brewster's mortal enemy, Mumbo Jamar Apoo.

As the elderly priest afflicted with dramatically reduced auditory acuity closed his eyes and began to pray, Brewster looked with lust at the lunch tray propped on top of the Mayo table beside Father Flynn's examination table.

Brewster pulled off the metal food-warmer cover from Father Flynn's lunch plate and snatched the sandwich from the platter. The meal was intended to be a complimentary lunch provided as a courtesy by the outpatient cancer clinic.

Brewster stuffed the sandwich into his mouth and slipped out of the priest's room before the prayer session had been completed. J.

D. Brewster disappeared down the hallway to follow Mumbo Jamar Apoo, and he was long gone by the time Father Flynn reopened his eyes.

As much as Brewster would have liked to stay and visit with the old priest, the medical student concluded that he had no time to try to talk to God. What was the point? Brewster was convinced God would not be listening anyhow. At that juncture, Brewster was stewing in a cauldron of perpetual anger, simmering upon the crimson flames of chronic hatred.

For now, he had an egregious and evil endeavor to enjoin. By the design of his own malicious premeditation and that of his contributing clandestine coconspirators, Brewster planned a scheduled task that, by its sinister nature, warranted execution well outside the realm of Divine providence. In fact, Brewster was about to orchestrate a conspiracy to be executed within the realm of the clinical justice system.

—·——

Because Mumbo Jamar Apoo had become a cause célèbre, it now took two correctional officers to provide security when he was brought back into the hospital to be readmitted for recurrent pneumonia. Officer Fuller and his assistant, Reynolds, were standing by the elevator, waiting to take Big Nig up to the med-surg unit, when the career criminal pulled off his bioguard face mask and purposefully coughed directly upon the correctional officers.

"If you don't put that goddamned mask back on your face right now," Fuller said, "I'm gonna shove it up your ass with my baton!"

Apoo chuckled while he threw the mask down onto the ground and proceeded to spit a thick wad of yellowish-green phlegm peppered with flecks of blood squarely upon the floor.

"If you make another threat like that against me," the prisoner said, "it'll be all over the news. I'll call up Shiva Jaclyn Grant, the ACLU, Alonzo's television show, and even that frog-eyed white Hollywood bitch ho named Luzanne Saranrap. The shit gonna hit da whirligig when I tell them that you be abusin' me again!"

After Apoo was pushed onto the lift, as the elevator door was just about to close, someone thrust a hand into the elevator box to stop the door from closing completely, and a voice rang out: "Hold the door!" It was Russian Bear.

After Bear entered the elevator, the entire process repeated itself. Just as the door to the lift was about to close, someone thrust a hand into the elevator box to stop the door from closing completely, and a voice rang out: "Hold the door!" This time, Willy Mammon and Feral Cheryl got onto the elevator.

On the third occasion the event repeated itself, J. D. Brewster squeezed onto the lift. Apoo was oblivious as to who any of the people were, but he was clearly irritated in the delay they caused in allowing him to get up to his hospital room in a timely fashion.

"No more, I tell you," Apoo said. "This elevator is full!"

As Apoo was pushed into stall 316, the four colleagues strolled on past the hospital room as if they each had serious business to attend to. Little did Big Nig know, the serious business the four medical personnel had to attend to was a pending dastardly and deadly executive intervention. It was scheduled to take place that day, all within the auspices of the occult clinical justice system.

Cheryl probably had the toughest job assignment. Her mission was to distract Officer Reynolds and keep him sequestered away from the hospital room while her coconspirators arranged for Mumbo Jamar Apoo's big dirt nap.

She batted her eyelashes when she stuck her head into Apoo's room. "Excuse me, Mr. Reynolds, but I'm certain I've met you before."

"Well, I don't recall," the correctional officer said, "but maybe I'll come out there and have a cup of coffee with you, and you can help refresh my memory. Arby, I need you to hold the fort for a while. I'll be back in five or ten."

Once Officer Reynolds had vacated stall 316, Brewster and his two colleagues furtively slipped into the hospital room. When Arby Fuller saw that the full complement of coconspirators had arrived, they had one residual detail to address.

"Did you make him DNR?" Arby asked.

"No," Brewster said, "so we'll have to go with plan B. Is he prepped?"

"I have all of his arms and legs shackled out," Arby answered. "He won't be able to put up a fight. I'll man the door. Let's get this done."

Big Nig suddenly realized he was about to be assassinated. "Hold on, here. I was expecting Sister Buena to pay me a visit. She was gonna have a prayer service with me. I haven't been a church visitor since I killed my—well, since my father died. She said it's time I got right. She said there's still time for me to find redemption and perhaps even salvation."

"If it's the last thing I do," Brewster said, "I'll make sure you won't be saying any prayers tonight. So, are you hoping to be forgiven? I'll do my level best to make sure that'll never happen."

"It looks like it's going to take four of you cocksuckers to take me down," Big calmly said. "You pussies should be ashamed of yourselves."

"Actually," Willy said, "we're rather proud of ourselves for figuring out a way to pull this off."

"You look familiar to me, but I don't remember where I've seen you before," Apoo said as he looked at Brewster. "Look, man, if you and I had some sort of misunderstanding or if I ripped you off in the past, let me make it up to you. You don't have to do this."

"In the famed words of Diogenes the Cynic, who lived back during the times of Alexander the Great, 'What you have taken away, you can never give back.' It's far too late for you to make any deals, you bastard," Brewster said.

Big Nig defensively looked over to Willy Mammon for support. "I clearly understand why these three slices of white bread in here might want to take me out, but you're a soul brother. We need to stay united. After all, I never did anything to you. If you kill me, I'll come back from the grave to seek revenge on you someday, you big monkey son of a bitch. Mark my words!"

"Shut up, asshole," Willy said. "So you think you're going to come back from the grave? Go ahead. If you do, I'll just send you straight back down to the Devil, where you belong. The only regret I'll have after we kill you is that you'll only die once."

"What did I ever do to you?"

"It cracks me that there are people in this country who think you're some kind of a hero or martyr or that you're down with the struggle or some other line of racist bullshit," Willy said as he applied a strip of duct tape across Apoo's face. "I can assure you, nobody will ever remember you once you're gone."

Before Willy applied the pillow across the face of Apoo to muffle any noise, he finally answered Apoo's last question. "I guess I shouldn't be too surprised that you don't remember who I am. Just to fill you in, you ruined my life, and you ruined the life of my fiancée. God only knows how many other people have suffered at your hands. It's people like you who give black folks a bad name. When I see you in hell, I'm going to kick your ass all over again when I get down there and pay a visit to the Devil. Adios, muchacho!"

Apoo tried to scream for help, but to no avail. The duct tape across his mouth stifled any protests. Once Willy Mammon thrust his torso over the head of the shackled prisoner, Big Nig was effectively neutralized. Brewster handed the empty sixty-cubic-centimeter syringe to Russian Bear.

"You have the honor, Ilya," Brewster said. "You've lost more than any of us. Do it!"

Brewster turned off the IV drip and clamped off the tube line in anticipation that Russian Bear was going to give Apoo a lethal, acute air embolism. The Russian suddenly had misgivings regarding what he was about to do and found he couldn't pull the trigger on committing an act of cold-blooded murder.

Even though the vicious animal shackled in front of him had brutally killed Bear's beloved wife, the Russian could only stare at the empty syringe in his hand.

"No," Bear said, "I just don't think I can do this."

"God damn it, Bear, do it!" Brewster said.

Willy Mammon, who was still straddled across the face of Apoo, demanded action. "Somebody had better do something! There's no coming back from this. I don't have all day here, ladies!"

With no further response from his colleague, Brewster yanked the syringe out of Bear's hand and said, "Get out of the way, Bear! It's my turn to step up to the plate."

Time was running out. Brewster rapidly injected one large syringe tube full of air after another into the IV line in Apoo's left arm until the prisoner's body became completely limp.

"It is finished," Willy said as he pulled the pillow off of Apoo's face and peeled away the duct tape that covered his mouth. "Time to bail!"

"No, I'm not done yet!" Brewster said. "I want to cut off his balls, and then I want to ram them up his ass with an IV pole."

"Snap out of it!" Bear pleaded. "You're an animal."

"I am indeed," Brewster admitted. "I want to hack his pecker off with a pair of bandage scissors, and then I'm going to jam that goddamned syphilitic elephant trunk of his into one of his ear canals."

"Knock it off, Brew!" Arby demanded. "Have you lost your mind?"

"After that, I want to use a scalpel to cut his face off just so the nasty, skanky, two-dollar monkey whore who claims to be his mother will be forced to have her son buried in a closed-casket funeral!" Brewster exclaimed. "Yeah, that's it. That's the ticket!"

"No, goddamn you! We need to get out of here now!" Woolly Mammoth said as he grabbed Brewster by his necktie and pulled him out of the patient's room. "It's over, Brew. It is finished."

As the three medical students slipped back out into the hallway of the med-surg unit, Willy turned to Officer Fuller and said, "You know what to do. This dead bastard needs to go down with a full-court press to at least make it look as if somebody actually gave two shits about him. Give us ten seconds to book out of here, and then you need to come out of the room and call for the code-blue team to hit the ground running as soon as Reynolds gets back from flirting with Cheryl at the nurses' station. You have to be able to sell this, Arby, or else we'll all be hung out to dry!"

"It will be my very own personal Academy Award performance," Fuller proudly said. "Just make sure I get an Oscar for this."

Arby knew the drill. He just had to wait a few moments until the medical students had fled the scene. Russian Bear quickly disappeared down the service elevator at the end of the north wing of the med-surg unit, while Willy Mammon pulled a reluctant J. D. Brewster by his necktie down the hallway as if his colleague were a stubborn dog on a leash. The big man was finally successful in dragging Brewster into the stairwell shaft.

"Don't be a fool," Willy said. "Don't go back up there! What's the matter with you?"

"Get your hands off of me, Willy!" Brewster snarled. "Don't tell me what to do."

"You need to get your shit together right now!" Willy said. "Stick to the plan, Brew. I'm busting out of here on the second floor, and you need to work your way out somewhere else. Go to the first floor, go to the basement, or go straight to hell as far as I'm concerned. After all, in light of what we've done here tonight, I'll probably see you there sooner rather than later. Whatever you do, you just need to keep your crazy ass away from me. Am I clear? We shouldn't be talking to each other anymore. Get your head bolts tightened down, and take care of yourself. Goodbye, Brewster."

Much more than a friend or colleague, Willy Mammon had become an integral component to what little sanity and emotional stability Brewster had left. Upon Willy's sudden departure, Brewster felt truly vulnerable.

Once Willy made his exit out of the stairwell on the second floor, the big man quickly vanished like a fleeting summer dust storm that simply dissipated on the wide-open Texas prairie.

"We need help over here!" Arby Fuller yelled out after the coast was clear. "It looks like this patient has quit breathing for some reason!"

Officer Reynolds immediately returned from his coffee break with Cheryl and asked, "What in hell happened in here?"

Arby Fuller professed ignorance. "The patient just started to cough, and then he quit breathing all together! I'm no doctor, but I think he's dead!"

Needless to say, after a great deal of commotion, the code-blue resuscitative efforts proved to be unsuccessful. As the patient was known to be infected with the mysterious GRID syndrome, no postmortem examination was ever requested.

The political activists and Hollywood agitators who had carefully followed the case of Mumbo Jamar Apoo would soon move on to some other meaningless cause célèbre, embroiled in the psychobabble bullshit drivel of social injustice.

Sadly, there still appeared to be a boulevard named after Mumbo Jamar Apoo in the stinky seaside fishing village of Le Con, France. If that's indeed the case, Brewster thought, perhaps the United States should not bail out the goddamned frogs the next time the Hun decide to blitz across the Maginot Line to stir up a little trouble.

⚜

Brewster and his coconspirators were about to go their separate ways both literally and figuratively. At the bottom of the stairwell, Sister Buena was waiting to confront Brewster over his vigilante act of clinical justice.

"What have you done?" Sister Buena asked. "This was not your call!"

J. D. lost vision in his left eye but only for a few seconds. It was the last time in his life he would ever experience that peculiar visual anomaly; it would never recur after the day he and his coconspirators murdered Big Nig.

Brewster brushed aside the mysterious floating nurse from the temp pool without even looking at her. He went straightaway to a concrete bench at Hermann Park, where he lit up a big Churchill to help him collect his thoughts about not only what he had done but also what he would have to live with.

⚜

Was there celestial retribution for the commission of sin? One could only hope. After all, the concept of a day of judgment might have been a driving force in order, morality, and ethical behavior. Perhaps nobody put those existential questions more into focus than when the Russian author and philosopher Dostoevsky once said, "If there is no God, then everything is permitted."

Perhaps the punishment for one's sins might happen when somebody was still alive. After all, within a year of the great sin, Arby Fuller would eat a bullet from his own gun. Years later, Russian Bear would disappear at the hands of the Calle Vampiro drug cartel.

DON W. HILL, M.D.

Willy Mammon would one day have a seizure while driving a car, and the ensuing crash would cost him his life. Feral Cheryl would die a horrible death one day from metastatic breast cancer, while J. D. Brewster would become a prisoner within the confines of his own mind.

Perhaps Brewster and his colleagues should have remembered that one should only render unto Caesar what was Caesar's...

—

After Brewster was handed his diploma, he looked out into the crowd to see if he could find Brother Bill, his cousins, or his mother among the multitude who had attended the graduation ceremony. Sadly, he could not find their faces in the vast darkness that enveloped him.

At the postgraduation reception, Brewster encountered his coconspirators, but they exchanged no words among themselves. They had all suddenly become strangers to each other. After Ben Fielder had previously accused Brewster of being complacent about Stella's failing health, which had led directly to her premature demise, it appeared that friendship was also irreparably fractured.

By the end of the week, J. D. had packed up Uncle John's crappy Dodge Dart to the hilt, and he drove the old bucket of bolts back to the Land of Disenchantment with his trusty friend Monsieur Pepe the skunk.

Dr. J. D. Brewster would start his residency training in internal medicine at the St. Francis College of Medicine in Santa Fe in July 1982. Brewster would find that he would never have the courage to revisit the Texas Medical Center or even Hermann Park, for that matter. After all, it would be unwise for a man who'd committed an act of murder to ever return to the scene of the crime.

Brewster's subsequent decision to pursue additional fellowship training in hematology and oncology at that same facility in New

Mexico would ensure that his extensive postgraduate education would be drawn out for many more years.

Brewster would not return to Bellaire, Texas, until the late 1980s, where he would proceed to toil away at his craft in relative obscurity. Sadly, he would never come to terms with a life destined to be lived in total solitude.

15

ROMANS 3:23

When Dr. J. D. Brewster woke up in the mausoleum, he opened the top drawer of his nightstand to yet again grasp a loaded .45-caliber automatic pistol in his right hand, chamber a live round, and then vigorously suck on the end of the barrel of the weapon until the silver dental fillings imbedded in his molars began to tingle. It was the dawn of another mediocre day in a cursed life of mediocrity, and he would again have to shove a litany of ancient and unforgiven sins back into what the spiritually broken man referred to as his own personal bottle of moral decay. Rote behavior had established a particular ritual, and he had to do it all before the sun rose over the Gulf Coast.

The thirty-fifth anniversary of the year Dr. Brewster's immortal soul had made an irrevocable plunge into darkness was close at hand. The doctor was painfully aware that he had not only violated the Hippocratic oath but also committed a crime so heinous that the grist mill of justice would surely grind him into dust if he were ever arrested and convicted of the foul deed. Unrelenting guilt had driven him to the brink of suicide, and his perpetual loneliness only whetted his resolve to commit the act.

Once he'd accomplished his bizarre perpetual morning ritual of self-flagellation, Brewster would finally be able to at least briefly look at himself in a mirror. After all, for the time being at least, the mortal sin he'd committed had been temporarily shoved back into a bottle already brimming with moral decay.

Brewster ejected the live round from his handgun and carefully replaced the weapon back in the top drawer of his nightstand. Perhaps someday Dr. Brewster would be brave enough to press his index finger against the trigger with enough pressure to discharge the weapon and end his own life. Perhaps after a cup of coffee, that particular morning would be the one, unlike all of the others that had preceded it for the last thirty-five years.

It was only a day after Feral Cheryl had passed away from widely metastatic breast cancer, and the late-March storm had blown over. The weather was crisp and clear. The lonely physician threw on an old pair of boxer shorts festooned with the images of orca whales frolicking in the ocean. He elected to simply remain clad in the old wife-beater T-shirt he'd worn to bed the night before, replete with the crusty drool and dried-up mucoid secretions that had emanated from the posterior pharynx of a man who was a heavy mouth breather.

After gargling with a splash of mouthwash and ingesting his oral regimen of various antihypertensive agents du jour, he went downstairs to make a half pot of Kona coffee. After all, it was supposed to be the best coffee in the world. While the hot water was still being piped through the drip system, the aroma was already intoxicating.

When the doorbell rang, Brewster wondered who could be paying him a visit on that Sunday morning. The doctor opened the door and could only stare in awe as he found Sister Buena holding a vase of a dozen yellow roses.

"Are you going to invite me in, or am I just going to have to stand out here all day long, holding these flowers?"

As Brewster stepped aside to allow the floating nurse from the temp pool to enter his home, he said, "Nobody has ever sent me flowers before. There's no card with this bouquet, Sister Buena. Who sent these to me?"

While the visitor placed the vase of flowers on Brewster's kitchen counter, she said, "If you can't figure that out, I'm not about to tell you. Don't be rude, Dr. Brewster. Are you not going to offer your guest a cup of Kona coffee?"

Brewster went to his cabinet, pulled out a coffee mug, and poured Sister Buena a cup of the brew.

"How do you take it?" J. D. asked.

"To be honest," Sister Buena replied, "I don't know sometimes how I'm able to take it. I'm here to serve and to deliver messages. I, unlike you, lack the gift of a free will. I just follow orders."

"No, I meant how do you take your coffee?" Brewster said as he furrowed his brow and scrutinized his unexpected visitor.

"I'm sorry," Sister Buena said with a hearty laugh. "I just didn't understand your question. I take it with lots of cream and lots of sugar."

"Free will is not what it's cracked up to be," Brewster said. "This thing called free will allows for a lot of mistakes to be made throughout the course of one's life, and it's precisely the very flaw that makes us come short of the glory of God. Be that as it may, is there an upside trade-off for you?"

"Of sorts," the visitor replied. "A fund of knowledge and wisdom has been bestowed upon me that you could scarcely comprehend."

"How did you know I was making Kona coffee?" Brewster asked.

"Were you not paying attention to what I just said about the wisdom and fund of knowledge I possess?" Sister Buena replied.

"I just thought you were speaking in abstract or metaphorical terms," Brewster said. "Who are you?"

"I think you already know the answer to that question."

Brewster said, "Better yet, what are you?"

"I think you already know the answer to that question," she replied again.

"Why are you here?" If nothing else, Brewster was at least persistent.

"I think you already know the answer to that question," she replied for the last time. "I've always had my doubts about you, but let's just see if the long-held supposition you've professed throughout your entire life has been wrong all along. Perhaps it's time for you to come to the realization that God backed the right primate after all. It's time for your atonement. Are you going to do the right thing this time?"

Without a word, Brewster went to his office, opened his wall safe, and pulled out the manuscript he had completed in the darkness only a few hours before dawn. He brought it to the kitchen table and handed it to Sister Buena as he resigned himself to the fact that he indeed had committed grave sins, and retribution was imminent. However, if retribution for Dr. Brewster was pending, it would once and for all be Divinely proscribed. For certain, at the least, it would not be an unsanctioned subclass of penance administered through the auspices of the vigilante clinical justice system.

In a soft monotone, while looking down at the feet of Sister Buena, he humbly muttered an epiphany that was thirty-five years late in its revelation. "Sometimes a man must come full circle before he can face the Truth."

"So it would seem," his visitor said. "Although I've watched your life slowly unravel over the years, you've indeed come full circle at this time. I've come to believe you're now facing in the right direction. Don't prove me wrong."

"What should I do now?"

"Why don't you give the Bellaire Police Department a call?" Sister Buena said. "I think it would be good for you to have a chat with your old friend Detective Aaron Parsons. Brother Bill will be coming down to button up your house, so don't worry about any of that. He needs to get here soon, though, as I'm on a tight schedule.

Mobile Mike Fuller is on his way over with a new battery for your Mustang. After he gets here, when he gets your car running, have him give you a ride over to the police substation. Don't forget to take your written confession with you. After all, it's a confession, is it not?"

"What's going to happen to me?" Brewster asked.

"It's not my call," his ethereal visitor replied. "I don't know. Frankly, the answer to that question is above my pay grade. For what it's worth, I'll put in a good word for you. It's the best I can do."

"What about Arby Fuller and my other friends?" Brewster asked in an effort to find resolution for his dearly departed coconspirators. No, it was more than that. Brewster was pressing for the intercession of Divine providence through a plea for their redemption and perhaps even salvation. "Will my colleagues or I ever be forgiven for what we did?"

Sister Buena shrugged and replied as best as she could. "Asked and answered."

After Mobile Mike Fuller installed the new battery in Brewster's Mustang, the car fired right up.

"Tell your brother, Bobby, it's time for him to tend to my lawn," Brewster said. "Please do me a favor: I need you to give me a lift down to the police station."

As Brewster climbed into the passenger seat of the Mustang, he turned on the radio station to the oldies channel. As he had somehow expected, he heard the song "My Back Pages" by Roger McGuinn and the Byrds. Brewster immediately remembered the time when he'd been the front man for the 1960s cover band DNR.

Brewster was certain God was talking directly to him, but this time, he didn't break down and cry, as he had all of the other times he had heard or sung that song in the past. J. D. had long considered that he was a failure, but for that one shining moment in his life, he was about to do the right thing.

"Mike, I want you to take care of my Mustang for me," Brewster said. "Have fun with it, but stay safe. I don't want you to wrap it around a telephone pole!"

As the mechanic pulled the Mustang out of the driveway, he glanced over at the doctor sitting placidly in the passenger seat beside him. "What's going on, Doc?" he asked. "Are you going on a vacation or something?"

While the jangly sound of the Byrds, featuring Roger McGuinn's atomic twelve-string guitar blared through the car's radio speakers, J. D. Brewster circled his head in a peculiar counterclockwise motion before he finally offered a wry smile and a resolute response of resignation. "Well, it looks like I'll be going away for a while."

GLOSSARY OF TERMS
(MEDICAL OR OTHERWISE)
DNR VOLUMES 1, 2, AND 3

acid phosphatase test: A relatively archaic tumor-marker serum test for prostate cancer that has largely been supplanted by the more appropriate prostatic specific antigen test in modern times.

aerobic organism: An organism that cannot live or grow in the absence of air.

aerophilic organism: An aerobic organism that thrives best in an environment with a high oxygen concentration.

achondroplastic dwarfism: A pathological condition manifested by short, stubby extremities but a relatively normal-sized trunk and head. This clinical condition is a consequence of abnormalities between the epiphyseal plate and bone interface of the long bones of the human body. This clinical presentation is usually an autosomal-dominant inheritance disorder.

Almasty: The Russian equivalent of a Sasquatch. These creatures reportedly live around the Caucus Mountains, and they allegedly emanate a musk that is almost as foul as the often-encountered putrid smegma breath now widely recognized as the baseline attribute of an average liberal's putrid halitosis.

alopecia totalis: Complete pathological baldness. This may be a consequence of prior radiation therapy to the head or an autoimmune disease wherein a patient develops abnormal antibodies against his or her own hair follicles.

alpha-fetoprotein: A serum tumor marker often elevated in some types of testicular cancer and also primary hepatocellular carcinoma.

alveoli: The small air sacks in the deep recesses of the lungs where gas exchange occurs.

Ambu bag: A compressible hand-operated air-pump device about the size of a football. It is often utilized to temporarily ventilate a patient who has suffered from a cardiopulmonary arrest.

AMFYOYO: This is an abbreviation for "Adios, motherfucker. You're on your own." This is a derisive term used to say goodbye to particularly nasty dispose patients being discharged from an emergency room setting or even from a hospital inpatient status. This expression is often preceded by the additional insult "OTD, OTB," which is an abbreviation for "Out the door, on the bus."

anaerobic organism: An organism that is able to live or grow in the absence of air.

anoscope: A transparent plastic tube utilized to visually inspect the rectal vault.

anterolateral thorax: From an anatomical standpoint, this is the front and side of a person's chest wall.

antigen: A foreign material that may be able to insight an immunological response.

atheromatous plaque: A fatty deposit within the interior lining of a vessel that can cause vascular narrowing.

atrial fibrillation: A cardiac arrhythmia manifested by an irregular contraction of the upper chambers of the heart.

Bartholin cyst: A benign vulvar lesion caused by an obstructed Bartholin gland.

benign prostatic hypertrophy: A noncancerous enlargement of the male prostate gland.

Bevo: A specific example of the mammal scientifically known as the Bos taurus, this creature is little more than a common cow with useless, annoying, hypertrophic skull horns. Bevo is the name of the long-horned steer that is the animal mascot for the University of Texas. This misfortunate beast is savagely subjected to an ear-shattering report from a Civil War–era muzzle-loaded cannon (presumably a Napoleonic smooth-bore six-pounder) whenever the University of Texas football team miraculously scores against an opponent during a game. Happily, as that is an extraordinarily rare event during the course of any given college football season, it is highly unlikely the sullen burnt-orange bovine mascot ever experiences any diminution in its auditory acuity from the abuse to which it is subjected. According to Brother Bill (who happens to be a Texas Aggie), this disengaged, docile, cud-chewing, domesticated, inert, flatulent, vegetarian quadruped ungulate is confirmed to be intellectually inferior to a variety of canids. This is especially true if this particular cow is compared to an uberbreed of the Canis lupus familiaris: a widely renowned, loyal, brave, and patriotic dog recognized by the American Kennel Association as a rough collie. For further information, the reader should investigate information about a particular dog named Reveille. I humbly suggest that the University of Texas at Austin should relegate custodial management of **Bevo** to Texas A&M University, where many experts in animal husbandry (and also in the culinary art of crafting slow, mesquite-smoked barbecue brisket) reside within the borders of God's country.

big dirt nap: Dead and buried.

bilateral mastectomy: Surgical removal of both breasts.

bilirubin: Waste material found in bile. It is formed from the biological breakdown of hemoglobin.

biopsy: The surgical sampling of tissue for diagnostic purposes.

bougie: A flexible, cylindrical medical instrument utilized to widen an abnormal stricture.

Bovie: An electrically powered surgical instrument that can be utilized intraoperatively for both dissection and hemostasis.

bowel perforation: A puncture in the bowel wall. If it occurs, it is a medical emergency.

brady down: A slang term that means the slowing of a patient's heart rate.

BRAF: An oncogene that, when mutated, may drive cancer cells' initiation and proliferation.

braniac: A derisive term used to characterize a medical student enrolled in an MD and PhD dual-training program.

BRCA1: An inheritable oncogene that may predispose a patient to acquire breast cancer.

BRCA2: Another recognized inheritable oncogene that may predispose a patient to acquire breast cancer.

bronchus: A major airway pipe that divides off of the trachea to ventilate either lung.

buff with fluff: An attempt by a student to enhance his or her grade point average by taking an elective course that is supposedly not a particularly great intellectual challenge.

cannabinoids: A class of chemical compounds generally found in marijuana that are able to interact with the CBD1 and CBD2 receptors of the human body and perhaps modulate pain perception, appetite, and a sense of well-being.

cardiopulmonary arrest: The cessation of a patient's heartbeat and respiration.

carpal bone: A bone found in the wrist.

CD4+ T cell subset: Components of the immune system, these are also known as the T helper cells. The normal count of these cells is in the range of 500 to 1,200 cells per cubic millimeter of blood. An infection with the AIDS virus will result in a diminution of these important cells over time, resulting in a seriously immunocompromised condition.

cerebral edema: An abnormal swelling in the brain, which may be a consequence of cancer, stroke, or injury.

cerebral hemorrhagic event: A stroke caused by bleeding in the brain.

cervicitis: An inflammatory disease process involving the cervix of the uterus, usually caused by a microbial infection.

cetacean: A cetacean is a member of the whale family. As an example, a sperm whale is a cetacean, and we certainly can't have enough sperm, now, can we?

CGL: Chronic granulocytic leukemia (also known as chronic myelogenous leukemia). This is a serious hematological malignancy that is a consequence of the BCR-ABL oncogene associated with an acquired 9;22 (Philadelphia) chromosomal anomaly.

cGy: Centigray. The international system designation for the unit of absorbed ionizing radiation measured in joules per milligram of matter (cGy = 1m2/s2/1,000). Please don't ask this author complex questions about radiation physics. Years ago, I managed to turn an old Kenmore electric clothes dryer into a cyclotron in an attempt to harvest radioisotopes for a Fourth of July celebration. As I had inadequate lead shielding, I might have inadvertently caused a few chromosomal oncogenic aberrations to occur along the way. Oops. A memo should be sent to the nuclear regulatory authorities; the aforementioned comment was a joke. Please don't send me to Gitmo!

chloroma: A solid or semisolid tumor mass caused by the infiltration of acute leukemia cells into adjacent tissues.

CHOP: A four-drug combination used in the treatment of lymphoma cancer.

choriocarcinoma: A subtype of cancer that may involve the testes.

cirrhosis: A disease of the liver characterized by scarring and fibrosis as a consequence of chronic inflammation caused by a variety of diseases, including viral infections and alcohol abuse.

cholecystectomy: The surgical removal of the gallbladder.

clitorectomy: The surgical mutilation of the female clitoris, usually performed in modern times by adherents to a particular violent, brutal, primitive, anti-Western, sixth-century religious subset. If any readers out there take umbrage with this overt critique, and you damned well know who you are, I would kindly like to refer you to review the glossary of Russian terms at the end of this section.

cholecystitis: Inflammation of the gallbladder, usually as a consequence of gallstones.

clonic phase: The rapid alternation of muscular flexion and contraction that may occur during a major motor seizure event.

coccidioidomycosis: A fairly common pulmonary infection that occurs in the Southwest region of United States and has been confirmed to be caused by a specific fungal organism.

code blue: This is an announced hospital emergency requesting a full-court press to try to resuscitate a patient who has suffered a cardiopulmonary arrest.

code gray: This is an announced hospital emergency requesting security intervention to assist an individual who is being physically assaulted.

code silver: An unauthorized patient elopement event.

communist: A disciple of an economic system wherein the collective welfare supersedes individual merit. Although it is an immoral wealth-redistribution ploy that has failed every single time it has ever been tried anywhere in the world, it is still the cornerstone of flawed liberal and progressive ideology.

COPD: Chronic obstructive pulmonary disease, which is a pathological condition of the lungs caused by an admixture of chronic bronchitis and emphysema.

coprophagy: The oral ingestion of feces, which happens to be the preferred steady diet of flies, certain arthropods, and liberals.

Cowden's syndrome: An autosomal-dominant inherited disorder characterized by an increased risk of certain forms of cancer.

creatinine: A component of nitrogenous waste. Levels of this material found in the blood reflect kidney function.

cretin: A clinical condition manifested by intellectual deficiency as a consequence of congenital hypothyroidism.

CXR: An abbreviation for "chest x-ray."

decerebrate: An abnormal body posture characterized by extension of the extremities that occurs after serious head injury.

dermatode: A derisive slang word used to describe a dermatologist.

dermatome: As it pertains to the field of dermatology and plastic surgery, an electric-powered surgical device that is able to shave off a thin, rectangular section of skin to be utilized during a skin-grafting procedure.

dendritic cell: A component of the immune system that presents processed antigens to T-cell lymphocytes in an effort to ramp up an immunological response to a biological entity that may be a hazard to the host organism.

DiSPOSe: A derisive patient designation that stands for a "drug-seeking piece of shit."

DNR: Do not resuscitate. This is a designated declaration indicating that a patient declines to receive any heroic revitalization attempts in the event of a pending cardiopulmonary arrest.

DOA: A medical designation that a patient is dead on arrival.

doink: The act of engaging in a casual sexual encounter. Sadly, as readily confirmed through my own personal experience, the frequency of getting doinked appears to be inversely proportional not only to a man's chronological and physiological age but also to a man's fasting glucose, cholesterol, and serum hemoglobin A1-C levels. Please note that there is an intellectually inferior term utilized in certain parts of the country that are still afflicted with such extensive problems as hookworm and inbreeding (including Eau Claire, Wisconsin, as one recognized specific location). The phonetically similar word *boink* has been erroneously uttered aloud from time to time. I can sadly confirm that this particular archaic malapropism has been mistakenly utilized by the unwashed and the unenlightened even within the context of our current modern era of running water and flush toilets.

ECOG: Eastern Cooperative Oncology Group.

ECOG performance status: A standardized measurement of a patient's symptoms and ability to participate in life activities. An ECOG 4 indicates that a patient is bedridden and no longer capable of independent living.

EDTA: An abbreviation for ethylenediaminetetraacetic acid, generally referring to a specialized blood-collecting tube.

embolism: A vascular obstruction caused by a clot that has migrated downstream via blood flow from its site of origin.

endometrium: The inner layer of the female uterus.

endorphins: Naturally occurring, self-generated analgesics.

epinephrine: Adrenaline. The primary acute stress hormone released during fight-or-flight situations. It is produced in the adrenal glands.

epispadia: Also known as the pee-in-your-own-face syndrome. This is a disorder wherein urinary flow exits from the dorsal (topside) aspect of the penis as opposed to the normal urethral exit at the tip of the corona.

erythema annulare: A palpable migratory red cutaneous eruption presenting as a target ring.

erythematous: An overt red discoloration.

erythropoietin: A sialic acid protein produced in the kidney that regulates red cell production in the bone marrow.

eschar: A thick, fibrous scab that forms over the site of a severe cutaneous burn injury.

excoriation: A linear cutaneous scratch mark.

estrogen: The primary biological female hormone.

eternal care unit: Heaven.

eukaryotic organism: A more advanced cellular structure that has a defined nucleus.

exophytic mass: A lesion demonstrating externalized, outward proliferation.

fibula: The lesser bone of the lower extremity, found between the knee and the ankle.

frequent flier: A derisive term used to describe a patient who makes frequent and oftentimes inappropriate visits to a hospital's emergency room.

gamete: Either a male (sperm) or female (ovum) haploid cellular entity that is able to engage in conjugation with an opposite sex gamete to form a zygote in the act of biological reproduction.

gastrotomy: A surgical opening into the stomach, generally done for the purpose of exploration.

Genesis 6:5–6 (King James Version): "And God saw that the wickedness of man was great in the earth, and that every imagination of the thoughts of his heart was only evil continually. The Lord regretted that he had made human beings on the earth, and his heart was deeply troubled." Cross reference to *Dr. Blow's Honeybun Diet* 6:5–6: "It looks like God backed the wrong primate."

Genesis 9:4 (King James Version): This passage of scripture is a basis as to why members of the Jehovah's Witnesses faith do not believe in any type of blood-product transfusions: "Only, you shall not eat flesh with its life, that is, its blood."

geographic rash: A generally large, flat cutaneous lesion that is much bigger than a macular eruption.

glioblastoma multiforme: An evil and generally lethal primary brain cancer.

gophered out: To go underground; to disappear.

gradeaux: A nasty, slimy, malodorous sludge that is a wetter version of grunge.

GRID: Gay-related immunodeficiency syndrome. In the early 1980s, this was the name of the disease now known as AIDS.

grunge: A drier version of gradeaux.

gynecomastia: An abnormal enlargement of male breast tissue. Gynecomastia is not an uncommon problem among men being treated with antihormone therapy for metastatic prostate cancer.

gyri: Convolutional contours of the brain.

halitosis: Butt breath. It's bad breath that is even worse than the ass-end of a dead hippopotamus.

hematocrit: A measurement of the percentage of whole blood that is comprised of red cells.

hematoma: An extravascular bleed into tissues or organs. In layman's terms, a hematoma is a badass bruise.

hemoglobin: The oxygen-carrying respiratory protein found in red cells.

hepatitis B: A subset of an inflammatory infection of the liver caused by a specific DNA-type virus.

hepatocytes: Parenchymal cells of the liver.

hepatology: The discipline that involves the study of the liver.

hepatorenal syndrome: A potentially life-threatening illness that results in the degradation of both the liver and the kidneys.

HER2/neu oncogene: An oncogene responsible for a tyrosine-protein kinase component of an epidermal growth factor receptor. Amplification of this oncogene may result in the development and progression of an aggressive form of breast cancer.

Hickman: A large lumen, implantable central intravenous access device.

hilum: In regard to pulmonary structures, the hilum is the area of the lung closest to the mediastinum, where pulmonary vessels and the major bronchial tubes enter the lungs.

HIPAA: The 1996 Health Care Insurance Portability and Accountability Act.

Hodgkin's disease: A specific subclass of lymphoma that biologically has a greater predilection to disseminate through the lymphatic channels in a relatively orderly fashion as compared to disorderly metastases that may occur if dissemination is a happenstance through the vascular system, which is much more likely recognized in other forms of lymphoma. The malignant cell that is the causative factor in the development of Hodgkin's disease is known as the Reed-Sternberg cell.

homo-satchel: The Trans-Pecos dialect's pronunciation of the word homosexual.

hydrocephalus: An abnormal condition of the brain wherein an excessive amount of cerebral spinal fluid accumulates within the ventricles. This abnormality may or may not cause an increase in intracranial pressure.

hyperacusis syndrome: An abnormal condition manifested by excessive sensitivity to noise.

hypercholesterolemia: Elevated cholesterol level.

hypercoagulable state: A clinical condition wherein a patient has an overactive coagulation system that results in a high risk for pathological blood clots that may occur in either the venous or the arterial circulatory system.

hyperpigmented lesion: A skin abnormality manifested by enhanced coloration compared to the normal surrounding tissue.

hypersomnolence: A medical disorder manifested by excessive sleepiness.

hypocapnia: A low systemic carbon dioxide level, which may result in an alkalotic condition manifested by an elevated pH.

hypopigmented lesion: A skin abnormality manifested by diminished coloration compared to the normal surrounding tissue.

hypospadia: Also known as the pee-on-your-shoe syndrome. This is a disorder wherein urinary flow exits from the ventral (back-side) aspect of the penis as opposed to the normal urethral exit at the tip of the corona.

hypotensive state: Low blood pressure.

hypothyroidism: A clinical condition manifested by an underactive thyroid gland with a resultant slowing of metabolism and slowing of mental function, among other anomalies.

hysterectomy: Surgical removal of the female plumbing.

idiot: A moron. See *liberal.*

immunological seroconversion: A clinical situation that is tantamount to the recognition of an antigen by the immune system, with the possible conveyance of immunity.

inflammatory breast cancer: An aggressive form of breast cancer that presents with inflamed and erythematous skin overlying the malignant breast.

integument: Skin.

in vitro: A clinical or scientific event or experiment that takes place beyond the constraints of a normal biological environment. A colloquial or slang equivalent would be a test tube or petri dish experiment.

in vivo: A clinical or scientific event or experiment that takes place within the constraints of a normal biological environment.

John 8:7 (King James Version): "He that is without sin among you, let him cast the first stone."

John 11:44 (King James Version): "And yet he that was dead came forth from the tomb, bound hand and foot with grave clothes."

John 19:34 (King James Version): "One of the soldiers with a spear pierced His side, and forthwith came there out blood and water."

Kaposi sarcoma: A cutaneous malignancy that generally appears as a violaceous plaque associated with AIDS. This is a cancer caused by herpes virus 8.

keloid: A firm, nodular, hyperplastic scar.

Keynesian theory: An idiotic, liberal, lame-ass, unsubstantiated religious conviction that the federal government can tax and spend its way out of any economic depression.

laparotomy: A surgical procedure defined as a long, linear incision made in the abdominal wall to gain access into the peritoneal cavity.

Leviticus 17:10 (King James Version): This passage of scripture is a basis as to why members of the Jehovah's Witnesses faith do not believe in any type of blood-product transfusions: "If anyone of the house of Israel or of the aliens who reside among them eats any blood, I will set my face against that person who eats blood, and will cut that person off from the people."

liberal: A lower life-form that appears to believe in the misguided concept of wealth redistribution. The end result is that a person defined as a liberal has a compulsion to give away free stuff to other people, as long as the commodities being dispensed among others were previously owned by conservative individuals and, specifically, not previously owned by liberals. See idiot. See also Communist and prokaryotic microbe.

libido: Normal sex drive. For an abnormal sex drive, please see the forty-second president of the United States.

lithotomy position: With legs mounted in stirrups, this is the physical position a patient assumes during a normal pelvic examination.

Luke 10:30–32 (King James Version): "A certain man went down from Jerusalem to Jericho, and fell among thieves, which stripped him of his raiment, and wounded him, and departed, leaving him half dead. And by chance there came down a certain priest that way: and when he saw him, he passed by on the other side. And likewise a Levite, when he was at the place, came and looked on him, and passed by on the other side."

Luke 18:16 (King James Version): "Suffer little children to come unto me."

lymphadenopathy: Pathologic lymph nodes affected by some type of disease process, including cancer and infections.

lymphoma: A cancer involving the lymphatic component of the immune system.

lyophilization: Cryodesiccation. A preservation technique utilizing freeze-drying methodology.

macrocytosis: Red blood cells that are morphologically larger than normal. This may be a consequence of a variety of different clinical conditions.

macrophages: The garbage-disposal cells of the reticuloendothelial system. Macrophages are large extravascular cells derived out of monocytes that purposefully leave the circulatory system and enter into tissue spaces. The job of the macrophage is to eat bacteria, foreign material, and cellular debris. The monocytes and macrophages are good guys to have around.

macular eruption: An abnormally pigmented, flat cutaneous eruption.

MAI: Mycobacterium avium intracellulare bacterium.

Mallory-Weiss tear: A pathological rent that may occur at the gastroesophageal junction as a result of violent episodes of vomiting.

Mark 8:18 (King James Version): "Do you have eyes but fail to see, and ears but fail to hear? And don't you remember?"

Matthew 5:29 (King James Version): "And if thy right eye offends thee, pluck it out and cast it from thee."

mediastinum: The anatomic middle of the chest, between the two lungs. The heart dwells within the mediastinum.

MEK: Mitogen-activated protein kinase. MEK1 and MEK2 are extracellular signal pathways that may often drive cancer initiation and proliferation if enzymatic dysregulation occurs.

melanin: Pigmented indole polymers that provide coloration to the integument and hair.

melanocytes: The pigment-producing cells found in the integument.

melanuria: A rare clinical condition manifested by the passage of melanin pigment in the urine. This finding has been reported in cases of disseminated malignant melanoma cancer.

mesenteric lymph nodes: Lymph nodes found within the intra-abdominal area.

metastases: The appearance of cancer that has spread far from its primary site of origin to other body areas via the lymphatic system or blood vessels.

mets: An abbreviation for foci of metastatic cancer.

microangiopathic hemolysis: A small-vessel disease process manifested by protean features that may include the abnormal rupture of red cells, fever, a low platelet count as a consequence of blood-product consumption, and maybe even kidney and brain damage.

microcephalic: The pathological affliction of having a tiny brain. See *liberal*.

monoclonal immunoglobulin: An abnormal concentration of a repetitively produced immunoprotein that may be a harbinger for a variety of different diseases, including **Waldenström's** disease, multiple myeloma cancer, and lymphomas.

mushroom: A lower-life-form fungal reference utilized as a derisive nickname to describe an inexperienced medical student.

mycobacteria: A Gram-positive, aerobic, acid-fast bacteria. Tuberculosis and MAI are two examples of infectious diseases caused by microorganisms designated as mycobacteria.

myeloblast: The bone-marrow-residing parent or precursor of white cells consigned to myelogenous lineage. An overabundance of abnormal myeloblasts is the classic hallmark feature of acute myelogenous leukemia.

myelodysplastic syndrome: One of a half dozen or so disorders that may afflict the bone marrow and result in the inadequate production of red cells, white cells, or platelets. An archaic term once utilized to describe these disorders was preleukemic state.

NCCN: National Comprehensive Cancer Network.

necrotic: An adjective that describes biological material as dead and in state of active decay.

nephrotoxic: A substance that is potentially injurious to the liver.

neurocutaneous syndrome: A constellation of neoplasms that involve both the nervous system and the skin.

neurofibroma: A tumor involving the peripheral nervous system as a consequence of the disorderly, abnormal proliferation of Schwann cells. The Schwann cells provide the insulator matrix of the nerve sheath.

neurons: Nerves cells or a slang term used to describe specialists in the field of neurology or neurosurgery.

neutropenic necrotizing enterocolitis: See *typhlitis*.

nevus: An often pigmented cutaneous lesion that is an aggregation of melanocytes. Atypical nevi are often precursors to melanoma cancer.

non-A, non-B hepatitis: An infectious entity that is now recognized as hepatitis C.

norepinephrine: A secondary acute stress hormone.

omentum: A rubbery, membranous tissue found in the abdomen that acts as a shock absorber for the internal organs.

oncogene: A gene that, when often mutated or amplified, has the potential for cancer initiation and proliferation.

orchidopexy: The surgical fixation of a mal-positioned testicle to its proper location and orientation within the scrotum.

orchiectomy: Surgical removal of the testicles.

osteomyelitis: A bone infection.

pallor: A pale discoloration of the skin.

papular eruption: An outbreak of cutaneous lesions that are well defined, solid nodules but are considerably smaller than a dermatological plaque.

paracentesis: The removal of an abnormal accumulation of fluid within the abdomen.

paraplegic: Paralysis of the lower extremities.

parasite: A life-form that can only survive by drawing its nutritional support from another living entity.

parenchyma: The cellular matrix of a specific gland or organ.

peligro: Spanish word for danger.

peritoneal cavity: The potential intraabdominal space.

pessary: A medical stent utilized to prevent vaginal, uterine, or rectal prolapse, which may occur in patients afflicted with a markedly weakened pelvic floor. Please see the forty-second president of the United States and what he did with Churchill cigars. If any readers out there take umbrage with these factual historical references, I would kindly like to refer them to review the glossary of Russian terms at the end of this section.

petechiae: Punctate red hemorrhagic spots that may appear on the skin, conjunctiva, and mucous membranes.

placenta: The vascular organic interface between the endometrial lining of the uterus and a developing baby that provides nutrition and thermoregulation during the nine months of fetal gestation.

plaque: In regard to a dermatological condition, a relatively large, abnormal, raised, and palpable cutaneous lesion.

plasmacytoid lymphocyte: A relatively mature and differentiated B-cell white blood cell subtype that is a precursor to the plasma cell. The cancer cells associated with Waldenström's disease are an abnormal clonal aggregation of plasmacytoid lymphocytes.

polycystic ovarian syndrome: A well-recognized disorder wherein numerous noncancerous cystic growths may appear on the ovaries. The growths are often associated with hormonal irregularities and fertility problems.

port-a-cath: A central venous access device that is surgically placed in the body to facilitate the administration of intravenous medications, including chemotherapy for the treatment of cancer.

postictal phase: A somnolent state that may occur after a major motor seizure event.

postpartum: The clinical status defined as after maternity.

prion: An infectious biological agent considered to be even more primitive than a virus. Composed of proteins and lacking complex nucleic acids, prions are believed to cause transmissible spongiform encephalopathies, such as mad cow disease and tropical kuru. If humans are infected with these protein entities, a rapid, progressive, irreversible dementia from squash rot of the noodle can and will occur. Sadly, these protein entities may be heat resistant, and they might not be degraded at the temperatures at which meat is cooked for human consumption. As I'm a Texan, I've vowed to continue the consumption of flesh harvested from quadrupeds and other lower life-forms, such as tasty free-range avian biological entities and nonmammalian sea creatures. Prior to the ingestion of said food items, the aforementioned proteinaceous nutritional material should either be grilled or smoked with the tasty carbon residue from the carcinogenic smoke of burning mesquite wood. If any readers out there take umbrage with these comments, I would kindly like to refer them to review the glossary of Russian terms at the end of this section.

proctoscope: A longer version of the anoscope.

progesterone: The secondary biological female hormone.

prokaryotic microbe: A primitive form of bacteria that lacks a defined nucleus.

proprioreception: Spatial orientation.

proptotic: Bug-eyed. As an example, go to Google, and look up a picture of the late English comedian Marty Feldman.

prostatectomy: The surgical removal of the male prostate gland.

proteinuria: The abnormal presence of protein in the urine.

pruritus: An itchy sensation.

psychogenic blindness: A stress-induced, psychiatric dissociative disorder manifested by self-limited unilateral or bilateral loss of visual acuity.

PTEN gene: An oncogene that drives the production of dephosphorylate proteins. Mutation and amplification of this gene can cause human cancers.

pulmonary fibrosis: Scarring of the lung, usually as a consequence of chronic inflammation.

pyelonephritis: A kidney infection.

r: Rad. This is a relatively archaic term describing an absorbed radiation dose (1 r = 0.01 Gy, or 0.01 joules/kg of biological matter).

radical nephrectomy: The surgical removal of a kidney, often done for cancer treatment.

rales: An abnormal auscultatory finding in the lung that has the sound of a sharp crackle. This is often a consequence of either congestion of the alveoli or fibrotic scarring involving the lungs.

respiratory alkalosis: An elevation of systemic pH as a consequence of tachypnea and hypocapnia.

Richter transformation: The biological conversion of a previous low-grade, slowly progressive chronic lymphocytic leukemia into an aggressive, fast-growing, high-grade, and potentially lethal lymphoma.

rigor mortis: A transient postmortem event wherein a corpse becomes rigid. This is why the crude slang word stiff has come to be synonymous with a dead body.

Romans 3:23 (King James Version): "For all have sinned and come short of the glory of God."

rubor: The presence of a red discoloration of the skin.

scut puppy: A midlevel medical school rank. A student with this designation has at least a modest amount of clinical skills and intellectual prowess.

seborrheic keratosis: Scaly, superficial cutaneous lesions that appear as a consequence of dermal senescence.

seminoma: A subtype of cancer that may involve the testes.

sepsis: The presence of toxic, pathogenic microbial organisms within the bloodstream.

serosanguinous: A bodily fluid that is an admixture of blood and watery serum. See reference noted at John 19:34.

silicosis: A fibrotic, inflammatory lung disease that is usually a consequence of the chronic inhalation of silica dust.

SOAP note: The basic written or dictated progress note concerning a patient's clinical course. This term is an acronym for "subjective, observation, assessment, and plan."

solar keratosis: A scaly precancerous skin lesion.

spot weld: A colloquial expression for radiation treatment.

strontium 90: A highly radioactive and dangerous isotope. At the time of this writing, I cannot exactly remember if it is a byproduct of atomic fission or if one could find it in the back of a refrigerator, in some nasty old container of sour cream left undisturbed for an entire year. In any event, if you are exposed to this material, it will mess you up all the way back to last October.

stud: The highest rank a medical student can achieve prior to graduating. The word stud in and of itself is a neutral word and has no gender or sexual orientation, insinuation, or connotation of any sort. If any readers think otherwise, I would kindly like to refer them to the glossary of Russian terms at the end of this section.

sulci: The normal grooves and fissures found on the surface of the brain.

tachycardia: Rapid heart rate.

tachypnea: Rapid breathing.

testosterone: The primary biological male hormone.

thromboembolic cerebral vascular accident: A stroke caused by a clot occurring in the blood supply to the brain.

thromboembolic veno-occlusive event: A blood clot occurring in the venous system.

thymoma: A tumor involving the thymus organ, which is a component organ of the immune system.

thyroidectomy: The surgical removal of the thyroid gland, which is often done for the management of thyroid cancer or a benign but giant thyroid goiter.

tibia: The greater bone of the lower extremity, found between the knee and the ankle.

tonic phase: A state of continuous muscle contraction that may occur during a major motor seizure event.

transient ischemic attack: A completely reversible ministroke event.

Trendelenburg position: A supine body position in which the pelvis is at a higher elevation than the head, usually achieved with a forty-five-degree decline of the head and thorax. This position is often utilized to increase blood flow to the brain during an episode of symptomatic hypotension.

trichobezoar: A hair ball.

triple-negative breast cancer: An aggressive and poor-prognosis form of breast cancer. The cancer cells in this particular subset of breast cancer lack estrogen receptors and progesterone receptors, and there is no amplification of the HER2/neu oncogene.

TURP: Transurethral resection of the prostate. This urosurgical procedure is undertaken to manage benign prostatic hypertrophy. A slang term for a TURP procedure is Roto-Rooter job.

typhlitis: A catastrophic, life-threatening transmural infection involving the ascending colon of the large bowel, usually occurring at or near the cecum. This disorder usually occurs during a profound and prolonged leukopenic condition as a consequence of aggressive systemic cytotoxic chemotherapy employed for the management of aggressive cancers, such as acute leukemia. If the clinical condition of typhlitis occurs, it generally appears during the time of severe bone marrow suppression and resultant deep white-blood-cell-count nadir.

urosepsis: A septic event originating in the urinary tract.

vasoconstriction: A reduction in the caliber of a blood vessel.

ventriculoperitoneal shunt: A long, surgically placed internal drain that is able to diverge an abnormal accumulation of fluid in the brain into the free space of the abdomen. It's a recognized treatment utilized by neurosurgeons in an attempt to manage hydrocephalus.

vesicular eruption: A cutaneous eruption manifested by an outbreak of fluid-filled, blister-like lesions.

VIP: A crude slang acronym for "ventilated, intubated patient."

vitreous intraocular material: The gelatinous material found in the posterior chamber of an eyeball.

vivisection: The dissection of biological entities, including human beings (as was brutally performed upon prisoners of war by the evil doctors who collaborated with the World War II biological warfare Japanese Army 731 Unit), done while the unanesthetized experimental subjects were still alive and in agony. Nice. Perhaps this is another example indicating that God might have backed the wrong primate.

XRT: X-ray therapy or an all-inclusive term for some type of radiation therapy.

yolk sack (tumor): A subtype of cancer that may involve the testes.

Z-track: The introduction into a body cavity of a needle that purposefully follows an irregular path to prevent a postprocedure fluid leak.

zygomatic arch: Part of the skull that protects the eyeball.

GLOSSARY OF RUSSIAN TERMS

захлопни ебальник и иди на хуй! Сейчас въебу тебе в жопу так, что ты поперхнешься моим сапогом, ебаный ублюдок: There are two possible translations for this Russian expression:
1.) Shut up, and go fuck yourself! I'm going to stick my foot so far up your ass that you will be able to taste the leather from my shoe, you nasty bastard.
2.) Have a nice day!

иди на хуй!: There are two possible translations for this Russian expression:
1.) Fuck off!
2.) It was a pleasure to have made your acquaintance!

About the Author

A native of Houston, Donald W. Hill, MD, FACP, graduated from Trinity University in San Antonio, Texas, in 1978. After completing his medical school training at the University of Texas Medical School at Houston in 1982, Dr. Hill completed his postgraduate training in internal medicine, hematology, and oncology at the University of New Mexico in Albuquerque in 1987. At the time he composed this novel, Dr. Hill had completed thirty years of medical practice. He has worked in multispecialty clinics, solo practice, and everything in between, including academia and clinical research. A fellow of the American College of Physicians, Dr. Hill is a published scholar, but this is his first attempt at a work of fiction. Although he was approaching the end of his medical career, Dr. Hill was still in practice in Hawaii when he crafted this novel. A self-described angry man safely nestled behind a superficial, amiable facade of banality, Dr. Hill felt compelled to write this novel in an attempt to make peace with God, the universe, and the practice of medicine. Only time will tell whether he has achieved these lofty objectives.

What Others Are Saying

Sadly, I was the historical eyewitness to much of what was written. Frankly, I was uncertain if I ever wanted to take another unpleasant trip down memory lane. After all, some things, like the dead, should remain forever buried. However, with the interjection of dark humor, I found myself laughing and crying at the same time.

—S. Carol Maple, LPN, Casa Grande, Arizona

A darker twenty-first-century version of *The House of God* on steroids. It will be a big fix to any junkie addicted to the genre of medical drama.

—Kelli Terrell, Tucson, Arizona

Thoroughly disturbing, thoroughly captivating, and, in the end, thoroughly satisfying. If Fyodor Dostoyevsky had penned *Crime and Punishment* in the twenty-first century, it would be this novel.

—Vicky Atkinson, RN, Kona, Hawaii

A fascinating glimpse into the dark underbelly of the medical profession. A must for anyone looking for intrigue, mystery, and a compelling read. It would appear that the more unsavory elements of our society should have much more to worry about from the underground clinical justice system than from our own official criminal justice system.

—J. C. Sullivan, Tucson, Arizona

Kudos, Dr. Hill. A complex modern masterpiece that probes not only the roots of good and evil in the heart and soul of human beings but also humankind's perpetual quest for spiritual redemption and, ultimately, perhaps even salvation.

—C. Darter, Tucson, Arizona

Be prepared for a trip into a dark realm where the demons of humankind's lesser nature may dwell.

—Wynn Madden, Tucson, Arizona

Dr. Hill accurately captures the dehumanization of students during the medical education process during the last half of the twentieth century. The American public should hope its next generation of physicians will arrive with less pathology.

—James F. Fielder, MD, San Antonio, Texas

In the introduction, the author suggests that if any readers become disturbed by the time they have digested this novel, a hot shower and bright sunshine may prove to be an effective antidote. If that were only true.

—Judy Kahler, RN, Kona, Hawaii

DNR is brilliantly disturbing—a throat-grabbing retribution ride with witty, hard-hitting social commentary. Realistic fiction cleverly elevated by a healthy dose of sarcasm!

—Big Tom Cavaretta, Phoenix, Arizona

CPSIA information can be obtained
at www.ICGtesting.com
Printed in the USA
FFHW020540140319
51078762-56485FF

9 781480 867307